HUNTING ANGELS

THE STORY OF UGANDA'S STOLEN GENERATION

I0600969

NOLEEN SANDERSON

DISCLAIMER

While the character names and accounts in this book are fictional, this story is loosely based on real-life experiences reported by children in Northern Uganda and Southern Sudan from 2004 to 2008. Any fictional character names or events that correspond with actual persons are entirely coincidental.

 A catalogue record for this book is available from the National Library of Australia

Hunting Angels
Copyright 2022 ©Noleen Sanderson

Published by Star Label Publishing
P.O. Box 1511, Buderim, QLD, Australia
publishing@starlabel.com.au

Editing: Mandy Chandler
Cover, editing and interior design: Rebecca Moore

1st Edition December, 2022

ISBN: 978-0-6453697-5-5

Endorsements for
Hunting Angels

This story captured my heart and remained with me long after I finished reading. I found myself drawn in emotionally to the plight of the children, scarcely able to believe the dark times these children were forced to endure and then rejoicing in their ultimate triumph.

Rebecca Emery

I was taken on a journey with *Hunting Angels* to a point that I could not put this book down! My eyes were opened to so much I thought I already knew. Noleen took me to a place where I thought I would never go, with my eyes opened and my heart so touched. Through this amazing story I've been awakened to what these children go through in Northern Uganda. This is definitely a book worth reading!

Donna Spence

A compelling, eye-opening and heartbreaking story about the realities many vulnerable children around the world face. Noleen's incredible story-telling ability and her eloquent use of the written word, draws you right into the heart of this story of tragedy, resilience and restoration. If you want a book that leaves you challenged and changed, this is it.

Laura Rowan

This book is dedicated to
the children of Northern Uganda.

To their courage, strength and dignity.

Contents

CHAPTER ONE

SILVIA'S WALK

Where are all the children?
Where has childhood gone?
Has it run away with the garden fairies,
Or been shot down by a gun?

Where are all the children's smiles?
Where are the childhood songs?
Are they hiding behind the blanket of war?
Just waiting until the bullets are gone?

Are they fed up with all this fighting
Are they tired of all these games?
Not allowed to talk to other children,
Unless they look and sound the same.

Have they given up on believing
That one-day they will be free?
Have they lost faith in what we call justice
And thrown away our humanity?

Tell me, where do all the children hide?
Where do they go to be free?
And how can I go there with them
Far away from our absurd reality?

ilvia awoke in the darkness to a sweet rhythmic hum. The sound of hundreds of children breathing, consumed the spaces of night air around her. The drone of it chorused off the bare, stone walls – soft, yet somehow defiantly loud. Mouths gulped the cold, sucking inward. Soft breaths harmonised to become one.

One beat.

One child.

One gasp at freedom.

Dark limbs entwined and encircled one another, each searching desperately for space and comfort. Despite the lack of both, sheer exhaustion led most of them into slumber. As if thrown like ragdolls onto the floor, these young lives lay, quietly waiting for the day. On and on into the night, the waves of breathing continued to beat, like a peaceful protest against the horrors of war.

The children.

Their breath.

The drums of Africa.

Silvia listened for a time, entranced. Most of these children were strangers to her, and yet they were also her family. United in their struggle, their sorrow and their will to survive.

Thousands of children walked into the town of Gulu every night from the surrounding villages and countryside. They came for one reason only – to find a safe place to sleep. In warehouses, under bus shelters, in the marketplace or just on the side of the road – all of these night shelters were safer than their own rural homes. For out in the bush, danger lurked like a bloodthirsty lion ready to pounce. An unseen but ever-present evil that robbed parents of their children, and children of their childhoods.

So, as the sun set every night over the African bush, the children came relentlessly. In doing so, and unbeknownst to them, they were perhaps saving their nation's future. A nation gripped by one of the worst civil wars the world had ever seen. A war fought not by armies, but scandalously, by children.

Silvia was not educated on the specifics of the war that dictated her daily routine. Indeed, she did not even call it war. To her, it was just life. The only life she had ever known. And it hung as it always had, precariously, as if on the knife-edge of a deep divide. At any moment, her whole world could turn into a grisly nightmare. That was just the way it was, although, as a child, she had no real comprehension of the gravity of the situation. She did not realise that the war had raged on for so long, or that so many children had been taken, never to return. She could not have possibly begun to comprehend the complex and bloody political history that tarnished the very ground she walked upon. She was a child after all, and one who lived simply, placing one foot in front of the other each day. She was thankful for the small things that gave her a sense of security.

Silvia was beautiful in her innocent naivety. Her hair cropped short against her ebony skin, thin arms and legs that were lean and stronger than they appeared. Her face was delicate, with pointed chin and high cheekbones that framed her dark eyes. There was nothing remarkable about Silvia's features, except for the broad smile that was an almost permanent feature on her face. Although many of the children around her seemed to have had their smiles suppressed, Silvia could not hide her own. She had tried on occasion to match those who daily walked and slept alongside her, pointing the corners of her mouth down and creasing the small space between her eyebrows, but somehow her smile always reappeared, as if it had a life of its own.

Even here in the dark, she smiled.

It had been an unusually cold night, but on the cement floor it was not hard to find warmth next to another body. Somewhere outside the warehouse, a dog began to howl in a melancholy drone. Was this what had wakened her? Silvia stiffened and stretched her limbs upwards, reaching out to the only available space. She readjusted her hips and involuntarily groaned as her protruding bones rubbed along the hard cement floor. Her eyes pointlessly searched in the darkness for a recognisable form.

It was pitch black around her. And quiet, apart from the drum of breathing. Little Raymond her five-year-old brother stirred beside her, and she groped for a thin blanket that she pulled over his shoulders. Raymond always slept in a foetal position, arms and legs scrunched, and his body curled into a little ball. Still, that worn out blanket somehow always ended up in a ball at his feet.

Suddenly, through a crack high in the roof, a silvery stream of moonlight sent a shaft of light into the darkness of the warehouse. Silvia breathed in deeply and gazed at the path that looked like a stairway into another world. Tiny dust fragments danced and spun in its presence. For a moment, Silvia had an overwhelming sense that this was a heavenly gift sent just for her. She smiled wide and let joy and a bubbling warmth fill her chest. She allowed her thoughts to drift like the dust that had no fixed place to rest.

She thought of her father and pregnant mother at home in the village and whispered their names into the light like a prayer. It was always difficult leaving them to walk into town every evening. The knowledge that they might not be alive in the morning sat like a heavy lump in her chest and weighed her down. Others in her village had lost their parents. Both children and parents seemed in short supply these days, and so she considered her own family's cohesion somewhat of a miracle. It was a risk staying in the village, and many people had fearfully moved into the refugee camps, but Silvia's father was stubborn and resistant to this pressure. He believed that in the camps he would be dependent upon food hand-outs and possibly never be able to return to his own land.

Outside a cockerel crowed, as if suggesting hopefully that morning was drawing close. However, Silvia knew that the old cockerels around here were a little too enthusiastic for the new day, and sunrise was still several hours away. Perhaps, they did not like the night either? Perhaps, even the animals considered the darkness dangerous?

She lay on her back and stared at the shaft of moonlight streaming in towards her. There was such stillness and peace within its confines. She was sure that she had never before seen anything quite so beautiful. It almost seemed angelic, and she wanted to reach up into it and hold onto something bigger than herself. Something strong and safe that would bring her no harm. It spoke of things she had never known, but always hoped for. Things she could not even put into words. Even though she had not experienced life without war, something told her it didn't have to be this way. She secretly longed for more. For freedom from the stresses of mere survival.

As the moon drifted on in its effortless migration across the sky, the warehouse was once again plunged into darkness. Silvia involuntarily shivered and tossed about restlessly before putting her hand on Raymond's side. She let the soft rise and fall of his breathing settle her, and sheer exhaustion eventually led her back into the darkness of her dreams.

When she woke again, a grey light had settled over everything.

She peered through one eye under the pit of her arm and watched dark limbs stirring. Children were beginning to pick up their belongings and preparing to head towards home. Silvia was often one of the first on the road, eager to get back to her village and her mother's embrace, but this morning she lay still and did not immediately wake Raymond. She reasoned that a few more minutes would not matter.

It was a surprisingly silent exodus when she considered the sheer number of children on the move. There was very little speaking as legs and feet slowly made their way towards the light of the open doorway. Soon the warehouse would be empty, and the roads outside would be filled with migratory streams of children.

Raymond stirred beside her, and his back pressed up against her legs. Silvia looked him over. He was such a sweet little boy with a round cheeky face and big almond-shaped eyes. At only five years old, he was full of life and spirit. His arms and legs were thin and his belly round and slightly swollen, but he was as healthy a child as you could find in this place. His short stocky frame carried him well. Silvia smiled as she watched him and marvelled at his peace. She loved him so incredibly much and felt like a second mother to him, even though she was only twelve years old herself. She was the person he looked to for protection every night in town. She tucked him in and made sure he was as comfortable as possible, often giving up her own food so that he would not go to bed hungry.

As she watched him, eyes closed, soft breaths landing on his small chest, it occurred to her again that Raymond would soon become a target. Silvia had heard her mother mention this recently, and the thought troubled her. Rebel soldiers had begun taking children at younger ages than in previous years. It was a terrifying twist in an already horrible war. Uncontrollable images of Raymond being marched through the bush filled Silvia's mind, and she gulped back aching anxiety as she tried to brush the vivid imaginations away. She vowed to herself that she would do all she could to ensure that her little brother, so innocent and beautiful, would never become one of the rebels. She would rather die than let that happen – of this, she was sure.

It was time to move.

"Come on Ray," she nudged him gently. "Wake up, sleepy."

He slowly sat up and rubbed his eyes, watching his big sister as she carefully folded the thin blanket. Out of a small tin, she pulled two pieces of cooked sweet potato and handed him one piece of the food. Raymond hungrily swallowed the sweet red vegetable, almost chocking on it as it went down. Silvia waited for him to finish, and then broke the remaining piece in half, giving him the bigger of the two and eating the other herself. She knew their Mama would prepare food for them later in the day and could wait, but Raymond would struggle during the walk home if his belly was too empty.

"What's the matter?" he asked, looking up at her serious expression.

Silvia smiled gently down at him. "Nothing Ray, all is fine," she reassured. "But let's go quickly and greet Mama and Papa with *double hands*. Perhaps today is the day for Mama to have her baby, what do you think?"

Raymond smiled at this suggestion and the enthusiasm in her tone of voice. He jumped quickly to his feet and looped his hand through her arm to pull her up. Silvia stood and pulled him into a quick embrace before taking his hand. Without another word, they carefully began weaving around still sleepy children as they navigated a path towards the door. Outside in the dawn light, the cool freshness of the morning air hit their faces and sent goose bumps like tiny comets shooting all over their bare skin.

A steady stream of people, mainly children, were already on the move. Some carried bamboo mats under their arms or balanced on their heads. Some were alone while others stuck close together, but few spoke. It was still relatively quiet apart from the distant barking of dogs. There were not even any cars on the roads at this time of day.

Silvia felt Raymond slow down as they passed a lady selling fresh bread. Not wanting to be tormented by its delicious smell, she pulled him along quickly. There was no point lingering over something they could not have.

They walked in a straight line out of town, the crowds thinning as they moved away from the centre. Dry red dust stuck to the soles of their feet. It was still cool from the night air and somehow comforting. Silvia had always enjoyed the feel of her bare feet upon the solid earth. She breathed in deeply, seeking its familiar scent and the way it refreshed her soul.

Silvia enjoyed the morning walk so much more than the walk into town in the evenings. In the morning, the world looked cleaner. The sun lit the trees with golden rays that made the leaves dance and glisten like a million tiny mirrors. It was a peaceful time of day and relatively safe. There was also the anticipation of their mother and home. She liked the thought that they travelled to her embrace, rather than away from her. In a big-sisterly way, Silvia smiled down at Raymond and squeezed his little hand.

Suddenly, she heard her name being called from behind, "Silvia. Silvia, wait for us." Turning, she saw her friend Amos and his three young sisters were hurrying to greet them. She smiled shyly and patiently waited for them to catch up, glad he had found her.

Amos was from the neighbouring village, only a few hundred yards from her own. They had known each other for a long time. He was a good friend, and she cared for him dearly, but she knew he had a past. A past that seemed to hold him in some kind of bondage.

Although he had never spoken openly to her about what had happened to him, Silvia had heard the vague story from eavesdropping on conversations her mother sometimes had with other neighbours. It was a small community. Everybody knew everyone else's business.

According to the neighbours, Amos had been abducted at age ten and had lived with the rebel militia for three years before escaping and finding his way home. He had appeared out of the blue one day, long after everyone had given him up for dead. When he first walked into the village, rail thin and covered in dirt with his eyes bulging out of his head, his mother thought she had seen a ghost.

He was fifteen now, and his eyes still told stories that his lips would never utter. Sometimes, Silvia spied on him from a distance as he sat and stared at nothing, lost completely in his own thoughts. She was never confident enough to ask what he was thinking about and knew that he probably wouldn't tell her anyway. He did not smile much and often seemed to disapprove of Silvia's zest for life, but somehow, despite their striking differences they remained good friends.

"Silvia, we didn't see you last night. We thought your Mama might have had the baby," Amos stammered as they caught up to her and Raymond.

"Not yet, but soon," she responded. "We were just late leaving the village because Father needed some help in the field. The maize is finally ready."

"Do you have any food, Silvia?" asked Alinta the youngest of the three girls.

"Sorry, no," she responded, wishing now that she had saved her share of the sweet potato.

"Maybe we can stop and get some mangos from the big tree on the way home," Raymond piped up. He was referring to a tree located about 100 yards from the track that he and Silvia had been to many times before. At this time of year, it was always dripping with fruit and hard to resist.

Alinta started to agree before Amos cut her off. "No. We should never go off the track. That mango tree is not safe Ray – even in the daylight. You should know that." He gave Silvia a disapproving glance as if blaming her for the fact that Raymond even knew about the mango tree.

Silvia grimaced and looked away. The truth was that if Raymond was struggling with the walk home, Silvia often gave in to his desire to pick mangos. They never stayed long. Just long enough to fill their bellies and pick a few to take home for Mama. She never complained or questioned where they came from, so why should Amos? His scolding sometimes annoyed Silvia.

"It's no big deal Amos," she retaliated. "We've only been a few times. Anyway, you should taste them. They really are the nicest I've ever had."

"Silvia! Do you have no idea about the danger? Sometimes, you surprise me. Please, promise that you will not go to pick mangos again."

She heard the fear in his voice and felt bad for baiting him. After all, he knew what he was talking about. He knew first-hand the terror that lurked behind the trees. "Ok," she replied half-heartedly. Raymond began to protest, but she squeezed his hand to silence him.

"Ok," said Amos emphatically, "Let's go home. Alinta, Mama will have prepared some food for you."

The walk home through the bush was a relatively quiet one. Few words were spoken, partly because they knew they had to keep silent and move with caution, and partly because Silvia was still pouting. She did not like being told what to do.

After a time, the track narrowed, forcing them to walk in single file. It was here that Silvia usually became nervous. The trees and bushes scraped her legs and the roots that jutted upwards dug into her feet. Sometimes, she would run in an attempt to shut down her imagination. She told herself repeatedly that there was no-one behind the trees, and no-one was waiting to catch them. Still, the miles of narrow bush track seemed to go on forever.

Finally, they neared their village, and Raymond broke into a run, eager to throw his arms around his Mama. She was there, as always, waiting to greet them. And, as always, Silvia let out a sigh of relief when she saw her Mama's smiling face. She ran after Ray and, at the last moment, turned and waved at Amos. Now, finally, he smiled at her and for a moment she glimpsed her old carefree friend. She sighed as he waved and headed in the direction of his own home.

"My precious children," sang Jossy as she wrapped Silvia and Raymond up into her embrace. For a long moment, they held each other in silence. Silvia put her head down on her mother's swollen belly and breathed in deeply. It was always so good to be home.

CHAPTER TWO

RESURRECTED

War is a slaughterhouse of pain.
A cycle of senseless hate.
No one can count the sons who have died
By the lies, that sealed their fate.

Reality is – war is no movie script;
Its deep wounds leave a heavy toll.
It's never so easy to pick up the pieces
When forgiveness is not our goal.

We want the other to give in
And let us have our way.
Like children who fight over toys.
War's toys are the people who will die today.

But we ALL fight

We ALL kill

And justify life's fading like it's a throw-away thing.

So how will we answer, when we are asked in the end,
About the peace that WE failed to bring?

Amos sat on the step outside his family's hut. He sat in silence, his chin resting on one knee with his other leg bent awkwardly beneath him. In his hand he held a stick that his fingers twirled around and around in the dirt creating a small hole. He stared at the stick, but did not really see it; his mind's eye instead, lost deep in thought.

Amos often sat in the late afternoon sun before the commute into Gulu began. No one ever bothered him for which he was thankful. Sometimes, his mother would put a hand on his back and look at him sadly. It was as if she read his thoughts, but she never said a word. Her presence was enough to give him some comfort.

Amos's thoughts often carried him back to earlier years when he had lived through the horrors of abduction and rebel combat. Out there, he had felt like he was already dead. It was as if he had been sucked into a dark hole with quicksand on either side. What was the point of anything when you were in a hole like that? If he screamed, no one would hear him. If he ran, he would just slide right back down again. He had felt so utterly alone, and quickly learnt that in order to survive he had to hide behind a stony exterior. If his face betrayed his fear, his life could have quickly been erased. Any form of weakness lead to a terrible reckoning.

Rebel soldiers had come in the night and taken him when he was only ten years old. For three years, the constant fear he lived with was like a lurking beast hunting him down. It did not sleep or rest, but was incessantly on his trail, waiting to pounce, licking its lips at the prospect of devouring his scrawny bones. As a ten-year-old, Amos had been too young and too afraid to question anything he had been told by his abductors. He believed the lies.

Very early on in his captivity, he was told that his family had all been killed. All of them! Not one had been left. The story they told him was explicit. The details of how his mother had died were so gruesome that Amos had experienced recurring nightmares about it throughout his entire captivity. In convincing him he had nothing to return to, his abductors made it clear that his only choice was to live solely for the resistance movement. He had believed them. He had believed every word they said.

He had also been told that the oil they smeared on his body would make him bulletproof. Again, he believed. But the twist to the lie was that he was also told that, if he ever tried to escape, they would use the same oil to track him down. Like all of the abducted children, Amos was too afraid to doubt. Blind belief was safer. It kept you alive for longer.

He had believed the bombardment of propaganda about the rebel commanders being the *true* leaders of Uganda. That, in due course, they would assume control and leadership of the country. He was told everyone who was part of the resistance movement – even hopeless boys like himself – would end up driving nice cars and live in big houses in the capital city. He believed it all, not because it made any kind of sense, but because he was too afraid to question. As a child, he became one of them. In order to stay alive, he could find no alternative.

They had lived like animals. Always starving and thirsty, always cut, bruised, and in some way broken. The irony of their physical weakness was that they were the most feared predators in the jungle. They could mow down a group of children on their way to the night commuter camps and then move on as if they had done nothing more than stub a toe. The sting of it would soon cease.

Their movement was constant. An endless stream of days and nights camped under trees, fighting government soldiers, raiding villages, abducting children, and walking, walking, walking. His feet were often so swollen that the skin on his soles became a bloody ballooned mass of infection. But it didn't matter. Nothing mattered. And even if it had mattered, there was nothing he could do about it anyway. He had to just lift his head and go on, ignoring the pain.

But slowly and despite his best efforts, he had grown tired. Tired of the war. Tired of life. Tired of the constant aching in his body and his soul. Tired of the endless days and nights of hunger. Tired of the brutality. Tired of the weight that pushed down upon him with every waking step. Tired of the nightmares that wouldn't even let him escape during sleep.

In a way, this fatigue had saved him, and in a way, it was still killing him. For it had allowed him the courage to escape without counting the cost, but two years later, Amos still felt bone weary. He felt old.

Amos wondered constantly when the war would end. He wished for it like he wished for the sweet taste of honey on his tongue. Would it end with a ceasefire or perhaps with the death of Kony? What would happen to the children still out there? Would they all be killed? Could life ever be normal after such a war? Indeed, in a place such as Northern Uganda, where the entire population had been ripped apart and ravaged, displaced into refugee camps, abducted by the rebel forces, or killed, could this war ever really end? Was it even possible? While there were survivors like him with haunting memories of the horror of this war, could its end really bring a return of normal life?

Would he ever be able to stop looking over his shoulder?

Amos dared himself to hope, but hope was frightening and a concept he struggled to get his head around. Hope in such circumstances felt like insanity, and yet, if he could not hope, what was the point of anything? Perhaps one day, the people would be able to return to their homes, plant their crops, celebrate the different seasons, and watch their children grow in safety. It sounded so simple and yet at the same time felt so unrealistic.

As the sun set on another beautiful African afternoon, Amos sat on the step of his home enjoying its light, all the while knowing that he would soon have to take his three sisters into town for the night. Still, he found himself allowing his mind to wander again over the events that led to his escape. To him, it was proof that miracles were possible, and that hope had a tangible purpose. It was proof that even for the walking dead, life could be resurrected.

It had started out as many days did in the bush with the militia. Amos and three other rebels were on their way further north, taking their plundered supplies back to the rest of their group whom they would meet at a base camp. They were all starving. Because of their constant moving, there was no opportunity to grow crops, so they had to rely on what they stole or killed in order to survive. Stealing from the outskirts of the refugee camps was very dangerous as government soldiers were everywhere. Besides that, the refugee camps were sparse when it came to food. The people in the camps were prevented from growing crops because the army reasoned that it might mean they were supporting the rebels. So, Amos and the other rebels mostly relied on farmers who had been foolish enough to stay on their land.

Ironically, Amos's own parents were still such farmers. He

knew they were risking their lives to stay in the village. Indeed, he also risked his own life by staying. He could have gone to the city to look for work, but something kept him here. Perhaps it was the simple fact that he was with his family again. He had found what he thought was lost forever, and he could not let it go.

In the early hours of that final day with the rebels, before the sun had even risen, Amos and his group had come across a village that had a ready crop of cassava. It was like stumbling into a mineshaft with gold dripping from the walls. Their starving bellies flipped in excited anticipation of food. At the signal of Lwensha their commander, the three boys all silently began to dig up the crop with their hands. Lwensha just watched and seemed happy to have them grab the food and go without waking anyone in the village. If it hadn't been for the crazy farmer sitting watch over his crop, they would have achieved their goal. If he had only known that his bravery would cost him his life. Amos cringed at the memory of what happened next.

The man had been crouching behind a bush and suddenly appeared shouting and waving his arms in the air. He had run at them causing sudden chaos, and Lwensha, who was the only one holding a rifle, fired without hesitation. In the darkness, his usually precise aim missed its mark, and the man was merely wounded, slumping to the ground in pain. Lwensha, while only a few years older than Amos, had been born into the resistance movement and was a merciless, bloodthirsty rebel who was feared by all. He seemed to get a genuine thrill out of killing and often went to great lengths to make his slaughters as grotesquely dehumanising as possible. Amos could not stop his body shaking in the darkness as he watched Lwensha approach the fallen man.

"Get up," he had hissed, but the man couldn't. The bullet had lodged in his thigh. Lwensha kicked him hard and spat into his face. He waved his gun and barked, "Tie him up. Tie him to that tree."

Amos and the other boys moved fast. They used prepared vines to bind the man's arms and legs tightly around the tree trunk. Helplessly pinned against the tree, he pathetically begged for mercy. His voice was so broken by sobs that Amos could barely discern what he was trying to say. Even if he could, Amos knew it would benefit no one to heed his cries as this man was as good as dead. There was no mercy to hand around.

"Use your machetes," Lwensha ordered. "Kill him quickly, and then let's go."

Amos almost sighed in relief. Yes, they would have to kill the man, but it would be fast and not some drawn out horror that would haunt him for months. He took the first swing and felt the chilled blade of his knife sink into the man's soft skin, ripping through muscle and flesh. The boys pounded his body into the trunk of the tree to which he was tied. It did not take long until the man cried his last, and his head slumped over onto his chest. He was left for someone else to find in the morning, or perhaps a wild animal would get to him first. There were enough hungry vultures in these parts to ensure that his body would not be left to rot.

They gathered up all the cassava they could carry and hurried away. Lwensha seemed pleased with himself, and Amos knew he would exaggerate the gory details of the story when they finally reached base camp. As if it somehow needed exaggerating.

They walked for several hours until the first light of dawn began to flicker through the trees. Sunrise always made Amos think of his family, although he tried desperately to block out all memories of their faces and was glad that he could no longer clearly remember what they looked like. What was the point when he would never see them again? But in his former life, his mother had always risen at sunrise and gone out into the fields to work before the heat of the day became too intense. The only vivid image of her that lingered was seeing her striding off into the field with an empty basket on her head and sunlight dancing off the back of her long skirt.

Many villagers worked at sunrise, so Lwensha ordered the boys to hide in the long grass that grew among the trees. Amos knew this would probably be his only chance to rest. They would stay here until people retreated to their homes to escape the heat of the day. Lwensha allowed them to eat a raw cassava each as they sat and waited. The boys took turns to keep watch while Lwensha slept.

Amos took slow bites of the biggest cassava he could find. He knew the hard, raw flesh would play havoc with his stomach later, but he didn't care. It had been days since he last ate, and his body was beginning to shut down. His swollen belly was hard and full of painful gas.

It was during his third watch that Amos saw the women. Lwensha had instructed them to wake him if anyone should pass by, and Amos was about to speak up when something made him bite his tongue. His breath caught in the back of his throat as a wave of recognition hit him. His body involuntarily shook with a strange kind of excitement and dread. Could it be? One of the women in the group looked like – he sucked in his breath and held it – his mother?

She was thinner than he remembered and slightly older looking, but he was certain it was her. And in that instant, Amos knew the difference between at least one lie and the truth. His mother was *not* dead! She was alive! She was alive, and she was his. His mother! It was almost too good to be true.

Nervously and hardly daring to breathe, Amos looked around at Lwensha and the other boys to make sure they really were asleep. Yes, they were exhausted, but he also knew they were used to sleeping lightly and could be armed and on their feet in an instant. Amos didn't know what to do. His heart sunk as he thought about what Lwensha would do to the women if he woke and saw them.

The women had passed by, not suspecting that they were being watched. Acting on instinct, without giving further thought to the consequences, and with no real plan in mind, Amos began to move. He rose slowly to his feet, held his breath and crept as quietly as he could through the grass away from the sleeping rebel soldiers. Amos's hands trembled as he gripped his machete.

This was crazy. It was certain death if Lwensha woke. In defiance of any rational thought, Amos followed them. Some deep longing drove him on. Something he could not explain.

But as he walked there was something else. Questions began to arise and bombard his mind. Questions he never thought he'd have to ask himself, but that now he was suddenly faced with.

Should he try to catch up with them and speak to his mother? What would he say? Would she run away in fear at the sight of him? Would she even know who he was?

Amos did not have a chance to discover the answer to these questions just then, as a few minutes later he heard Lwensha's angry shouting.

He froze. What had he done? Lwensha was attacking the other boys with his angry words, demanding that they tell him where Amos was, as if they had somehow been party to his disappearance. Of course, Lwensha needed someone to blame.

The women up ahead of Amos heard the shouting too. Amos turned just in time to see their startled backward glances. He thought his mother hesitated for a split second when she saw him, a look of shock and disbelief on her face, but then she turned and ran.

The day suddenly became very quiet, and Amos stood as if caught in a trap, frozen and unable to move. His eyes turned skyward, and he looked out at the endless blue above. Not a cloud in sight. Everything around him came into sharp focus as if someone had turned a light on. His mind was suddenly clear for the first time in years. All the lies he'd been told, all the tragedy he'd witnessed, all the blood he had on his hands. It was enough. He had had enough. Inside his own head, he screamed in a voice so loud he was sure it echoed through the forest.

"No more. No more. No more!"

His feet began to move. Amos sprinted through the trees at a ninety-degree angle that led away from the women's tracks. If Lwensha found him, so be it, but he would not be responsible for his mother's death. Then he stopped again, suddenly dead still, listening for the footsteps behind him. This was wrong. He reasoned that Lwensha would logically follow the same track the women had been on as it was the only clear path through the jungle. What if Lwensha found his mother while he was fleeing like a scared chicken that had slipped through the butcher's hands? What if Amos was later to learn that Lwensha had slaughtered her, robbing him of the chance to meet her again? A thousand 'what ifs' jostled in his head as he fought the ugly demons of fear and terror.

His heart pounded in his chest as he made his way cautiously back to the track. Yes, there they were. Amos crouched and watched. Lwensha was in the lead, and Amos could tell by the way he was marching forward that there was a murderous hate on his mind. Again, Amos hesitated. He knew Lwensha's main aim today was to get back to base camp, but if he happened to find Amos on the way, he would kill him. If he didn't, he would write him off as a traitor. Amos waited for them to move perhaps fifty yards away from him before he began to follow, stalking them from tree to tree, off to the side of the track. As they rounded each bend in the thick bush Amos held his breath. He expected them to stumble upon a village or find his mother and the other women, but it didn't happen. After some time, it became clear to Amos that the women must have also left the track, probably shortly after they heard the shouting and turned to see him. How would he ever find his mother now? After an hour, Amos made the decision to stop walking. He let the rebels disappear from sight and prayed he would never see them again.

He sat down in some tall grasses, hugging his knees tight into his chest. Freedom was something he had thought about so often over the past three years, but he had not expected it to come like this. Plans of escape had played over and over in his mind like twisted fantasies that he did not equate in any way with his own reality. He had seen what happened to children who did attempt it and were recaptured. Their slaughter was unbearable, and they were used as examples to the others. But *was* he free now? Could it really be so simple? Amos wasn't sure of anything and sat in the same spot for a very long time, gently rocking back and forth. He felt so very small, and he wasn't even sure that he liked the feeling of freedom. What would he do?

He looked at his hands. They had done things that his mind

could barely think about without the sick taste of vomit rising into his mouth. Nothing he could do now would ever rid his hands of the blood that stained his skin deep within. He imagined blood dripping from them onto the ground, forming puddles of deep red around his feet that refused to disappear into the earth. It made him want to purge out all of the poison inside him, but he couldn't. There was no way of getting rid of the guilt that filled him. If he ever did find his mother, he was sure she would know. She would look at him, see the blood and know what he had done.

Shame crept up Amos's spine. What had he been thinking? He should have just been happy to let his mother pass by, finally knowing the truth that she was alive. He should have watched her walk away and then thought nothing more of her. He couldn't go back to her now. How could she even look at him like he was her child? Not after what he had done. He had seen the look of shock on her face before she turned to run away. Now he imagined that it was also a look of contempt and disgust.

Amos began sobbing as the full gravity of his situation hit him. He may as well be dead. He had run from his commander and to return now would be suicide, but he could not go to his mother either. She would never take him back. He felt incredibly lost and alone as he sat in the grass, immobilised by the sickening dread of loneliness. One small boy, lost in the middle of a country at war.

His life was worthless, and he knew it.

At some point in the afternoon, Amos fell into a deep sleep and did not wake until darkness had fallen. The moon was high in the sky and the night was clear. Only one thought came to his mind when he woke. He had to find his mother. He tried to push the compulsion away, but an inner voice kept nagging and would not let up. "Find her, find her," it said over and over again, until finally he stood to his feet in submissive frustration and muttered agreement under his breath. He would search for her until he found her or until he was dead – whichever came first. If she rejected him, so be it, but he knew he had to know for sure one way or the other and not spend the rest of his days wondering.

Over the next few days and nights, Amos walked when his strength allowed, and rested and slept whenever he could no longer go on. The luxury of choice was so new to him that he would push himself more than necessary until he remembered he could stop whenever he wanted. He found some wild sweet potato and groundnuts that he ate along the way, but they did little to subdue the constant pains of hunger that clawed at his insides like a snarling animal. He had forgotten what it felt like to feel satisfied, but that did not make the hunger any more tolerable.

Amos wandered in an aimless, almost dream-like state. He lost his sense of direction and often felt like he was going in circles, which lead to certain frustration. Had he not learnt to navigate better in all his years wandering around in the bush?

He was hounded by questions almost constantly. Had he really seen his mother or was the woman he saw merely an illusion? Was his tired mind playing tricks on him? He was sure of nothing and afraid of everything. At first, he thought every shadow was a rebel soldier hunting him down. He became startled at every movement in the bushes, jumping out of his skin with fright. However even that faded with time as he reasoned that it didn't matter anyway. Let them come. Let them catch him if they had nothing better to do. What did it matter anyway? A sense of utter hopelessness descended upon him as he wandered, lost and increasingly unsure about his ability to draw a clear distinction between reality and illusion.

But death did not come as he had thought it might. Instead, in the midst of his dysthymic wandering, he stumbled upon a village. He was past the point of caring what would happen to him, but in that moment, as he squatted on wobbly legs and stared through the undergrowth, he actually saw her again.

Amos sat just outside her village and watched for a long time. He was hidden behind a clump of compacted bamboo shoots, and he saw her come and go into the hut, preparing food, sweeping the dirt away, and collecting water. He saw her smile and cuddle his younger sisters, chatting with them as she worked. The girls were all so much bigger than he remembered, and it was amazing that they were all still alive. His father was absent from the village in the hours Amos watched from his vantage point. He had reasoned that he was most likely dead.

When Amos finally made his move, it was at the conclusion of a long mental battle about whether or not to reveal himself. In the end, he reasoned that he had nothing to lose. If his mother rejected him as he suspected she would, he would simply leave and perhaps head for Gulu where he would try to make it on his own.

His heart was in his mouth as he stood and walked slowly into the village. Neighbours stopped dead in their tracks, disbelief and fear personified across their faces. He put his hands up in surrender to show them that he meant no harm and at that precise moment his mother emerged from her hut. She hesitated at the odd silence and looked questioningly in the direction of the villagers' stares. Then she saw him and in shock dropped her pot of water. It soaked her skirt and the hard earth beneath her bare feet, but she did not look down. Her eyes remained fixed upon him as if she couldn't quite believe what she was seeing.

Amos did not move. He did not know what to do or say. He

waited, expecting anger. Expecting rejection and hatred because of what he had become. But rejection never came. Instead, she began to cry and ran to him, shaking him and touching his face, exclaiming her joy in a tangle of emotion and words that danced out of her mouth like a song.

In that miracle of a moment, something in Amos's heart came back to life. As he felt his mother's unconditional love sweep over him, despite what he was and despite the unspoken assumptions of all he had done, he knew he was exactly where he was meant to be. She loved him. He was still her son. His eyes had brimmed with thick heavy tears, and a lump stuck fast in his throat. They cried and cried as they held each other tight, neither wanting to let the other go. Other village woman, realising what was happening, sang and danced around them with joy, patting him on the back and clapping their hands above their heads. Children gazed on in wonder, his sisters among them. The son they had all thought was lost had been found. He had come home. And perhaps in his coming, there was a seed of hope planted for the other sons and daughters who were yet to return to their mother's embrace.

Amos rose from his spot on the step and stretched his arms above his head. He sucked the sweet air deep into his lungs and let it out slowly. It was time to begin the journey into Gulu with his sisters. Tiredness lingered in his bones, but he smiled despite himself for in his heart was a flame of hope that shone brighter every time he remembered his day of redemption.

Through his mother's love, he had come to understand the true meaning of grace. He was not the sum of his sins. Though he had confessed much to her, purging his soul of its hidden guilt, she did not condemn him for his past. He was her son, and there was nothing that could ever change that.

CHAPTER THREE

AT THE CORE

Who sees you child of Africa?
Does no one know your name?
Your sad eyes tell a story that makes others feel ashamed.
For while you are being abused,
no one seems to hear your cry.
And when your wounds lie open
they turn away and sigh.
Perhaps they've been taught to reason
that your problems are too big?
That they cannot change your future
and have nothing real to give?
But your eyes reach out and touch the soul,
as one tear gently falls.
You long for love and dignity
and your voice will clearly call.

"Will you see this child of Africa?
Will you get to know my name?
Will you trust me with your friendship?
Will you let love cover pain?
Please offer no excuse for the past,
for no justifying will ever do.
But if you let go of your apathy,
perhaps love will pierce on through.
See me!

I'm a child of Africa.
I'm a person just like you.
Don't just speak to me of freedom.
Show me freedom, by what you do."

Out in the bush, far from the reach of civilisation, Grace sheltered in a small hut. This time, she sought shelter from the ominous sky.

Just a small woman. A young woman. Young, but worn down by life, for life had not been kind. Grace was unsure of her real age as she had been abducted by the resistance movement years earlier, and time had become a meaningless blur. There were no calendars to mark the days and the years. Just a growing older and a growing up and a growing hard. Only her children ensured that a softness to her edges remained. For them alone, she lived.

Thunderclouds rolled in over the horizon and ominously sped towards her square patch of dirt. They turned the dimming afternoon sky into a hazy darkness, sucking up all remaining light into the heavy mass above. The towering squall line was like an unstoppable army marching over the landscape as cumulonimbus roared fiercely in a turbulent mass of black. The ground alone seemed grateful. It was slowly transformed from brown to black as heavy drops of rain began to spatter onto its swollen and crusted belly. Animals took refuge in hiding places along the forest floor and in the weighty splendour of sagging branches, as the threat loomed louder. Every aspect of the landscape was instantly changed by the fury being unleashed from above. There was nowhere to run and nowhere to hide, so she sat, and she waited, thankful for the unusual luxury of a tiny, thatched hut.

Clinging to her on either side were her two small children. Her firstborn son Sante huddled close for warmth and slept peacefully despite the chaos above. His thin body moulded to hers; his arms bunched up at his chest. On her other side lay her daughter Judy, small and weak, and still fighting hard against the effects of malaria. She shivered violently from time to time and moaned aloud as her mind slipped in and out of the fog of semi-consciousness. Grace held her daughter tightly and tears welled up in her eyes. There was nothing she could do. Out here in this vast wilderness they were far beyond the reach of medical help. Even fresh water was a precious commodity.

Malaria was a common disease, but this fact did not redeem it from fear. It was a killer that claimed many lives. The young were most vulnerable and prone to repeated bouts. Judy had never before experienced it so badly. This bout had lingered well beyond the normal five-day period and sapped her of all energy and spirit. Her eyes had become glazed and her face expressionless. Only days before, when her body had heaved continually in the midst of persistent vomiting, Judy had been so frail that she did not even have the strength to whimper. At least now, she was making some noise of protest as the malaria toyed with her sleeping mind, warping her dreams.

Grace's fear of losing her child reached into the very depths of her soul. It strangled her heart like an evil black slime that would not stop squeezing and sent icy cold shivers up her spine. The normal numbness of her emotions that had been a life-saving mask of disguise over the years, was now becoming impossible to wear. Even though Grace had survived so many atrocities in times past, nothing compared to the anguish of watching her own child slip so near the clutches of death. She could not lose Judy. Her two children were her only reason to live.

Grace sat and prayed to an unseen God, begging for some kind of mercy. She sat in a place of sorrow and struggle, passion and grief, heartache and pain. In the midst of this war, and in her prison of raw emotional turmoil, she could not help but wonder if her feeble prayers were in vain. The surrounding bush heaved as the oppressive rain met the hot earth, suffocating Grace all the more.

Was there a God who cared? Was there anyone who cared? Was there even such a thing as mercy? She was an unknown woman, considered dispensable even by her own people.

The thunder reached a climax overhead and rain pounded on the thin grass roof, penetrating in places and pooling in puddles on the dirt floor. She fought to keep her tears and panic at bay, but inside she was screaming. "Why doesn't anyone care? Oh God, why don't You help her?" The more her heart cried the more the tears flowed, but no help came. Nothing. She had waited and begged and pounded on God's heavily bolted door and waited some more, but hopelessness washed over her in tumbling waves. Finally, she lifted her face to the heavens and let her tears turn into a downpour as she sobbed in angry desperation. If her life did not matter to other people, why should it matter to God?

It was a relief to let go and cry. As the rain poured down and the earth soaked up her own tears, she allowed her grief to run, knowing that the thunder above kept any of the rebels from hearing her. Her tears ran and ran in unrelenting streams. It was a cathartic outpouring that did not solve her problems or cure Judy's illness but somehow purged her own soul clean.

When the tears ran dry, Grace stopped praying for a moment and held her breath. Should she stop praying completely? A part of her wanted to. She wanted to be done with this uncaring God but didn't know if she had the courage to fully let go. Hope was the most powerful force she had ever known. Even in her lowest moments, it had always kept her coming back to this place of beseeching and begging for mercy. Although there was no redemption yet, her mind would not let go of the possibility of it coming … soon. She reasoned in silent desperation that she just needed to keep herself and her children alive long enough to see it.

Finally, in silence, her anger and anguish washed away, Grace hung her head. She mustered up all the courage she could find and again began to simply pray. It was all she had.

CHAPTER FOUR

JUST THE WAY IT IS

A boy with darkened eyes
Who lives among the trees,
Searching endlessly for meaning
In a chaotic reality.
A boy with darkened limbs
Who gulps desperately at life,
Drowning in tsunamis
As endless days become endless nights.
A boy with broken skin
Who is forced to grow up strange
In a land filled with monsters
Playing wild and endless war games.
But in amongst it all,
Can you still be just a boy?
Will life take that from you as well?
Will you surrender to the enemy's ploy?

ante woke startled from a vivid nightmare, his heart beating wildly in his chest. In the darkness of the night, the images that had toyed with him in sleep still danced in the shadows of his mind, refusing for a time to be relegated back to the realm of subconscious. It was a recurring dream. One that plagued him regularly.

He saw the images again. They intruded on his thoughts as if he didn't have a choice but to sit back and witness the dream all over again. A machete swinging in an arc through the air. The force of it bringing death. But whose death? He could never tell as panic always woke him before the dream could come to a natural end.

"It's ok Sante," his mother Grace soothed as she stroked his head. "Just a dream my son. It's ok. I'm here. You're safe." Her voice was soft and comforting.

As Sante emerged from sleep and the nightmare receded, he became aware that he was clinging to his mother's side. Had he been holding onto her in his sleep as well? He felt somewhat embarrassed by the thought but, for the moment, decided not to allow pride to push him away. She was his bedrock, and there were moments of vulnerability in life when he wasn't afraid to admit it.

The rain was pouring heavily on the thatched roof. His clothes felt damp, and he shivered, suddenly realising how cold it was. Grace hugged him closer. As Sante wrapped his arm around his mother, he felt little Judy's body lying on the other side of her. Suddenly, he was wide awake.

Judy was asleep but groaning. Sante knew she wasn't well. However it had taken him some time to recognise exactly how sick she was. He was only a young boy after all. His world was small and insular, despite the hugeness off the devastation that whirled around him daily. Children have a way of keeping even the most complicated issues of life surprisingly simple.

"Was it the same dream again?" came Grace's voice.

"Yes," he whispered, not wanting to elaborate. He knew she would not make him.

"I'm sorry Sante." He could hear that her voice was raw, as if she'd been crying, and it made him think about her rather than himself for a moment. She was his strength and he loved her relentlessly. So much so that it sometimes frightened him. What would he ever do if anything happened to his mother?

Sante had been born on a hot and windy day, deep in the Ugandan bush. Grace was just a young girl when Sante was born. Young and terrified, yet so incredibly brave.

Like so many other children in Northern Uganda, Grace had been abducted from a small village by a faction of the Lord's Resistance Army (LRA) who were searching for recruits and brides for their commanders. Her whole world had been lost and turned completely upside down. She didn't share the details of the horror with Sante for she knew he would never understand. After all, he had never known any life other than the one they now lived with the LRA. When he had been born to her, delivered by some miracle into her arms, Sante had given Grace a reason to live.

Although Grace had never told Sante the details of her abduction, she had said enough to let him know that she had no one to go back to. When she was taken, she had been forced to kill those who were not being recruited by the rebels. It was not an uncommon story. Sante knew other children were also forced to kill. Kill their parents. Kill their siblings. Kill so that they were immediately turned into rebels with nowhere else to go and no one left to turn to. From one moment to the next, the rebels ensured that they would be outcast from their communities. Branded killers for the rest of their lives. The rebels gambled on it, and it was a bet they often won.

Grace was 'married' to a rebel commander, and a year after her abduction, little Sante was born into a world of war. Born to a mother who loved him fiercely, but silently agonised over the life of her beautiful son.

When she looked into his eyes, she did not see the eyes of her rapist as she had fearfully imagined she might while her baby was growing inside her. She saw the eyes of a precious innocent child. Her child. One who had not asked to be born into a world of violence. One whose adorable trusting eyes spoke of innocence that, at least for a time, would remain untouchable.

As a baby, Sante knew only his mother's embrace. Grace found that his unquestioning need for her love offered her tentative hope for humanity. She saw that at the core of a person, there was only love. Her baby did not know what it was to hate. This was something that life would teach, but it wasn't a necessary part of being human. However, with a deep sadness, she knew that over time Sante's innocence would disappear. It would be destroyed by their world, just like any other casualty of the war. The love that reached out for embrace and comfort could so easily be turned into hatred that reached out to harm. How her heart ached at the thought. A tragic loss that would take place in silence. A loss of joy that only a mother would see.

So, while he was young, Grace had cherished his deep trusting eyes. She had sung whispered lullabies to him and cradled him close. She gently nursed him at her breast and would then wrap him in a cloth and tie him onto her back. It was here that he lived the first years of his life. From breast to his mother's back, he was hardly put down because of her fear that his father would harm him or worse.

As Sante grew up, he thought about life and death a lot. Although he was still a boy, he wondered what it would be like to close his eyes and not open them again. Death was common in the bush. It was everywhere. Sometimes, it was a twisted horrible violence. Sometimes, it was as silent as an underwater scream. Sante was fascinated by it, and every time someone was killed by the rebel soldiers, he had to force himself to look away as his mother had told him to. But he always found himself glancing back at those last moments as life slipped out of a person's eyes. After the horror, he was captivated by the strange sense of calm and peace that fell across even the most mutilated face. It was a peace that he did not understand, and a peace he only ever sensed in those few moments after death had occurred.

In the secret place of Sante's mind where no one could see, his thoughts were often awash with many unanswered questions.

What happens to us when we die?

Where do we go?

Do we just disappear back into the earth?

If we are just flesh and blood and nothing else, why do men care so much about things that are not?

Why do they care about possession of land or possession of others?

Why do men kill each other?

Why does it matter?

Sante's mind burned with such questions. Questions that he could never articulate because if the asking did not make sense, the answers would probably be even stranger. They just spun around in his head like hot lumps of coal.

But like any boy, other things also intrigued him. Like the automatic rifles and machetes that the soldiers carried. In Sante's young mind, these weapons made them men. They symbolised absolute power and security and he fanaticised about the day he too would carry one. He also marvelled whenever he caught a glimpse of a car or truck on odd occasions when they passed near a road. Once his group had hijacked a truck, killed the occupants, and driven it until it ran out of petrol. He had been thrilled by the feeling of the wind rushing past him as he stood holding onto the back of the truck.

Together with some of the other young boys, he would craft small trucks out of wire or sticks. They were crude toys that they drove around in the dirt playing pretend war games. The toys never lasted long, but that was life. Nothing ever seemed to last very long. Everything was disposable.

In a sense, Sante had grown up feeling torn. He knew nothing else but war, and yet his mother Grace had told him from before he could remember that there was a life outside of this forest. He wanted desperately to believe her, but struggled to imagine what another form of life would look like? His entire existence had been a constant bid to survive as they moved around the bush searching for food and new hostages. Sometimes, they would camp for a time in one place. It was rare and usually over as suddenly as it had begun, but it was always a welcome relief from the grind of constant movement.

Sometimes, they would join other groups of rebels and exchange arms or children. At such gatherings, Sante was aware that his mother was always very nervous and attempted to keep an extremely low profile. Although she never said it, it dawned on him one day that they could all become commodities for trade. After that, Sante made sure he and Judy both cooperated with Grace and kept out of sight as much as possible during these encounters. They would spend many hours with the women, hunting, gathering or preparing food away from the men.

Occasionally, when rebel platoons gathered together for

more formal meetings, everyone was required to be present. Sante hated these times because of the strange things that would happen. There were terrifying witch doctors with ugly masks that frightened him so much they later invaded his dreams. They would call upon the spirit world in their witchcraft ceremonies, make grotesque sacrifices to appease the ancestor gods, and force everyone to take strange potions in a bid to aid their success in war. Although these meetings only happened a few times a year, they would often go on for several days. Bloody and gruesome sacrificial examples were made of children who had tried to escape, which were enough to convince most hostages that they had no option but to stay and make the rapid transition from child to rebel soldier.

Every hour of their existence was purposed to support the building, fuelling and political agendas of the resistance movement. Joseph Kony, the notorious witchdoctor who led the rebel militia was mentioned often at the big group meetings, but Sante had only seen him once in person. The impression he left on Sante was one of a strangely quiet man who exuded an air of simmering evil, mystery and normality, all at the same time. He was hard to pin down, and Sante could barely understand what he said. But when he spoke, everyone else listened intently, so Sante assumed that his inability to understand Kony was a sign that he Sante was not as intelligent as the others. What he did grasp were the witchdoctor's orders to win without counting the cost. Cost would be irrelevant when they finally claimed their victory. The resistance movement would one day assume control of their country, and Kony would be their president.

The melting pot of experiences that comprised Sante's first ten years of life, left him with more questions than answers.

Nevertheless, the majority of his life was a monotonous grind of exhaustion, hunger, thirst, trekking, hunting, and moving towards their elusive end – to win *their* war. And when the hunger and thirst got too much, as it often did, all of his questions would cease. When the internal battle over hunger raged fierce, he would simply aim to exist.

In the darkness of the hut, Sante held onto his mother tightly and silently wished they could stay this way forever. Just the three of them.

CHAPTER FIVE

NEW LIFE

Today
I saw a symbol of hope
for the children.
One single flower growing up
between the cracks in the pavement.
Fragile
yet boldly defying the conventions
placed upon it by circumstance.

The sound of her hot breath filled the air as dawn broke over the African landscape. Her mind was in overdrive. Was she running into a trap that she couldn't avoid? Were unseen eyes watching her every move? Her heart raced out of control, more from fear than exertion.

As the sun rose higher, the lingering cool spots under the high treetops began to vanish. It was increasingly difficult to focus her attention on moving between them like they were shadows she could hide in. She was exposed and vulnerable and she knew it. But propelled on by the urgency of her purpose, she continued galloping breathlessly through the trees.

Silvia was not usually out at this time of day. On a normal day she would be just waking up in the night shelter, stretching her stiff limbs and contemplating the walk home with Raymond. Today, she was heading in the opposite direction. She was running towards town and the house of a well-known healer. The previous night had been the first she and Raymond had spent in the village in years. Their mother was having her baby, and Aunty had needed Silvia on hand. It had been two days now, and the baby would not be born.

A knot tightened around Silvia's heart as she thought of the dread etched into her aunt's moonlit face. "Your mother needs you now Silvia," she had said. "I'm sorry to ask you this. I know it's dangerous, but you must run to Gulu and fetch Mama Carol. Tell her, we will pay whatever we can. She must come quickly."

"I will go," Silvia had replied without hesitation, leaving Raymond still sleeping under the tree they had camped beneath all night. Mama Jossy had wanted her to go to the night shelter as usual, but Silvia had uncharacteristically disobeyed, instead bedding down in silent protest under the tree. She was terrified by the thought that if she left, she may never see her mother alive again.

Her father had come from the neighbour's hut every few hours to check on Jossy's progress. His face did not hide his concern as he stood with one foot on a stone and his hands on his hips. His attempts to reassure the children that she would be ok sounded hollow to Silvia. On his breath and skin, Silvia could smell the alcohol that he had used in a vain attempt to wash his fear away. It was as if they were all paralysed in the vortex of a great unknown.

Now, she ran on determined, like the sun, to get to her intended destination. Nothing could stop Silvia now, for her mother's life was at stake. She was not angry with her father for getting drunk and leaving her to take this trip alone. She understood his concern. Without Jossy, he would struggle to fit the pieces of life back together in a way that made any kind of sense.

The healer was renowned in Silvia's village, as she had once saved a man who was bitten by a black mamba, otherwise known as the 'two-step mamba'. Two steps were as far as most victims got before they fell down and did not get up again. Some said she was a witch doctor. Others claimed she was charmed, and others, that she was chosen by God and given special powers to help people. Silvia didn't know what she believed, but she hoped with all her heart that the healer was able to conjure up her powers now and help her mother.

Silvia ran out of the bush and into the open. The smell of town hit her nostrils, the rotting rubbish and overcrowding giving off a particular stench that was somehow comforting. Silvia at once felt safer. She ran past the early morning commuters, marketers and children still sleeping on the side of the road. There was an odd quietness to the scenes that made them seem surreal, as if what she saw was a dream sequence her mind had somehow conjured into reality. The healer's house was at the end of a dirty, dusty street.

Silvia banged on the door set into the heavy iron gate at the end of the garden. It was common for houses to be surrounded by high fences in Gulu, but they were usually noisy enough when banged upon to rouse some attention from inside.

After a few minutes and a little more banging on Silvia's part, an old woman opened the gate. She looked bleary eyed and still half asleep, but she smiled as she saw Silvia's face and began to speak. "My child, you look terrible," she said with blunt motherly concern. "What is your name? What is the problem?"

Silvia explained the situation with her mother and was amazed when Carol immediately leapt into action.

"We will leave right away." She ordered a young girl who hovered in the background to prepare food and water and then called her driver to get the car ready.

Silvia looked on in awe at this small woman. Her stature and appearance seemed a contradiction to the authority with which she spoke.

She turned her attention to Silvia and, while giving her a reassuring smile, began to ask questions about her mother. Had she had a good pregnancy? Was she well before the labour began? Had she remained conscious throughout the labour? Had she had any fits? Had she taken any water?

Silvia did not know the answer to all of the questions, but Carol just smiled kindly. She patted the young girl on her shoulder and said she would pray that God would save her mother and little sister or brother. Silvia wanted to cry, but instead stood in silence and waited.

Soon enough they were directed into a small brown car. All the windows were down, and rust congregated around the doors. The back seat on which Silvia sat was made of a thick black plastic with thread pulling out in various places leaving sharp frayed edges. The journey passed in a blur as she stared out the window at streets she had run along not fifteen minutes before. In a flash, they had reached the end of the road.

"We must walk from here," Silvia motioned in the direction of her village. "It's about one mile into the bush."

Silvia felt her own exhaustion set in as they began to walk. She had found the healer as Aunty requested, but would they make it in time? Would she even be able to do anything to help her mother? Worry over the situation made Silvia's legs feel as heavy as lead.

"We need to hurry Silvia," Carol said every time the girl slowed. These were the only words spoken until the village was within sight. It was a silent acknowledgment of the danger that lurked behind the trees, and every time Silvia heard Carol's prompting to hurry, her legs somehow sped up.

"We are here," Silvia said before breaking into a run in the direction of her family's hut. "Aunty we're here," she called.

Aunty emerged from behind the door with a look on her face so grave that Silvia stopped dead in her tracks. Could it be that they were too late? Had she not moved fast enough? Silvia's heart felt like it stopped beating and her mouth dried up. No words would come.

"Thank you, God," Aunty murmured aloud as they approached. "I knew you would come. I am very worried. The situation is very bad."

Silvia let out a sigh. At least there was time left. She collapsed in the middle of the clearing – a hard lump stuck fast in her throat. The fear of her mother dying was paralysing. What would she do without her? It was too dreadful and frightening to think about, so instead, she distracted herself by getting up and looking for Raymond. He was no longer under the mango tree.

"Ray," she called. "Raymond, where are you?"

No reply. She was about to cross to the neighbour's village to look for him when she heard her mother cry out in agony. Silvia stood still, not sure which way to turn. Finally, she walked hesitantly back to the hut. She opened the door a crack and slid inside hoping no one would notice, but as her eyes adjusted to the dim light, she wished she had stayed out in the fresh air. She involuntarily gasped at the sight before her. Her mother lay helpless and groaning while Carol reached up between her legs. Aunty noticed Silvia standing stiffly in the corner and quickly came to her side.

"Silvia, it's ok. Carol is trying to turn the baby. The position is wrong, and the baby needs to be moved so it can be born."

"Will Mama be ok?" she whispered.

"Pray that she will be. She is very weak, and the baby may be in distress." There was an unspoken anxiety in her voice that Silvia couldn't read, but it made her wonder if the baby was also going to die. She hadn't even considered that possibility before. She had been too preoccupied with worry over her mother.

With her heart breaking, Silvia slumped to her knees sobbing.

"No, no," came a silent scream from deep within her. "This can't be happening. Please God, save them. Please, I'll do anything. Please save them."

Aunty bent to stroke Silvia's back before moving away to assist Carol as her mother groaned again and began writhing in pain.

"I need you to hold her still," Carol ordered. "I can feel the head."

"Help me," begged her mother. "Please …" Her voice was not much more than a whisper. Silvia could not look up. She could not bear to see her mother's pain and wanted to block her ears from the sound of her agony.

"Oh God," she cried again, "if I never ask for another thing, please save her. Please."

"Yes," Carol cried. "The baby's head is down. Now listen to

me Jossy. You have to summon all your strength and courage and push this baby out. You can do it now."

Jossy cried out in pain. "No. Please no, I can't. Please don't make me," came her irrational cry. "I can't. I can't do it."

Silvia suddenly jumped to her feet and in two paces was at her mother's side. "Mama, please try," she begged. "Please, you can do it and it will all be over. It will be ok."

Jossy looked at her beautiful daughter in the lull between contractions and cupped her cheek with her hand. How she loved this girl with her shiny black skin, round face and big innocent eyes. Somehow, she found strength in her daughter's desperate plea.

As the next contraction hit, a groan came from deep within as Jossy pushed with such force that her upper body rose off the bed and the veins stood out in her neck. She gripped Silvia's hand so hard that the girl had to stifle a scream.

"Good, good," Carol said calmly. "I have the head. And once more now. You can do this."

The next contraction came almost immediately, and Jossy gripped Silvia's hand as she pushed. Carol's next shout was one of joy. "It's a boy. It's a beautiful little boy."

Jossy collapsed back in exhaustion and closed her eyes. Silvia only heard her mother's next words because she was looking intently at her face while Aunty and Carol focused on the baby. Her eyes still closed, she whispered, "Is he alive?"

Silvia looked up just as the baby let out a weak little cry. An overwhelming emotion enveloped her, and she began sobbing, big tears rolling uncontrollably down her face as she laughed and cried at the same time. "Yes Mama, yes. He is alive!"

Silvia looked on in awe. A little baby boy. Still breathing. Still alive. The women wrapped him gently in a new traditional cloth that Jossy had saved for this very moment and handed him to Jossy. Silvia watched in awe as her mother looked lovingly into the tiny screwed up little face. Suddenly, it was as if the air in the room brightened, and everyone seemed to breathe in a deep, unified sigh of relief. It was over.

As the women began to attend to her, Jossy handed the little bundle gently to Silvia. Silvia took the baby from her mother's arms with great care and sat on a stool by the wall. She could do nothing else, but stare in wonder at the miracle. He was beautiful. Beautifully formed with chubby cheeks and sweet little features that seemed marvellously and intricately perfect. Silvia was oblivious to everything around her as she held her baby brother, silently thanking God for the miracle that had unfolded before her.

The rest of the day passed in a blur as both mother and baby were attended to and cared for. Jossy had lost a lot of blood and was exhausted. So, as she and the baby slept, Silvia helped to prepare food, clean up the hut and wash all of her mother's clothes and bedding. It was no small task with water collected from a well in two small buckets.

Later in the afternoon, when all the chores were done, Silvia and Amos escorted Carol back to her car. The old woman had refused all forms of payment that had been offered to her, including one of the family's few chickens. She had insisted that to take anything would cause her insult, and so Aunty and Silvia had gratefully accepted her help free of charge. Carol's only condition was that Silvia come and visit her in a week or two and tell her how her mother and the baby were doing.

"Carol," Silvia asked hesitantly as they arrived back at her car. "Will my mother really be ok? She looks so weak."

"She is weak my dear, but she should be fine. Just take care of her as best you can. Do not allow her to do anything but rest and feed her baby for the next few days. Perhaps you can even stay with her during the nights. I know it is dangerous in the village, but your mother is not fit to travel, and she should not be left alone."

"I will stay too," Amos volunteered, and Silvia looked at him in surprise. "I will help the family. It will be safer if I stay and guard them," he explained.

"Thank you, Amos. This is a good thing that you do." As she turned to leave, Carol looked back and smiled. "Take care you two. Look after each other."

Silvia waved as the car rolled away.

She knew now that Carol was no witchdoctor. There were no potions, incantations or tree roots used to drive away evil spirits. Instead, Silvia had overheard Carol praying to God in much the same way she had. Simple prayers that were full of faith and little else.

Silvia could not help smiling as she reflected on the day, again silently whispering her thanks. She felt more confident now than ever before, that her small voice was somehow being heard by a God who cared.

CHAPTER SIX

GRACE REMEMBERS

A timeless and forgotten light shines from within your core.
It could illuminate every dark place if you would turn it on.
Perhaps it's not so simple.
Perhaps it is naïve.
But in the madness of the modern day, it is overlooked.
Hidden.
Seems so out of reach.
Still, it can never be destroyed.
Look closely
O Africa,
And search your soul.
It is there that you will find yourself again.
Not in war, destruction, elimination or greed.
But by navigating soul deep with the compass of your own
heartbeat.
Search
O Africa
Let the journey begin.

race trembled as Manwena walked into the hut and ordered her to follow him. It was not a question, but a demand. One that she dared not disobey. She quickly busied Sante and Judy with cleaning up the pots and then retreated inside behind the man who forced her to bare the title 'wife'. She told herself that Sante and Judy remained unaware of what was happening, but in her heart, she suspected that at least Sante knew something was amiss. For when Manwena disappeared with her, Grace observed that Sante always managed to keep Judy busy and entertained until she reappeared. He did this without being asked.

Grace had been raped by Manwena almost every day for as long as she could remember. If they were on the move and not resting at a base camp as they were now, he would drag her off into the forest and push her up against a tree. In the early years after her abduction, she had lived in a constant agonising terror of his brutality. He was not a kind or gentle man and took her like he took everything else in life – with force and violence. The more scared she became, the more he seemed to enjoy himself, and over time, Grace began to realise that it was her fear that fed his lust. So, for her own survival she had learnt to go through the motions in an unthinking robotic way. Her face portrayed no emotion, and her lips uttered not a sound. Sometimes, she felt like she was able to totally disconnect from what was happening to her body. She would find herself watching objectively from a distance as Manwena stood over her like a wild animal that was about to devour its helpless prey. Sometimes, Grace found that she did not have to watch at all. Her mind was able to completely abandon her current moment and transport her to another time and place when life had been sweeter. A time she had experienced many moons ago.

As Grace entered the hut on this night, she saw that Manwena had picked up his favourite weapon – a large stick – and she involuntary cowered in fear. He held the stick in one hand and used the other to caress its worn edges, bringing it to his lips and kissing the end before turning to her with an evil grin.

"Undress," he demanded, waving the stick at her. The power he wielded was the most frightening part of this whole ordeal. Grace knew that if Manwena was in any way offended by her, he could easily take her life without blinking twice. Only her children would mourn. The rest of the group would pretend not to notice or care as another disposable woman fell.

Grace shuddered as she removed her skirt and worn t-shirt and placed them on the floor. She stood naked before him, and although she felt ashamed, she held her shoulders back and fixed her eyes on the mud wall in front of her. Her stare was blank and expressionless. Outside, she could hear Judy singing in her sweet voice. Manwena placed one end of the stick on her chest and walked around her in a circle, never letting the stick leave her thin body. He snickered aloud, mocking her vulnerability as if he was disgusted by what he saw. Grace could feel her body tensing and let her mind slip away.

As the first blow came hard across the back of her thighs, Grace fell to the floor onto all fours and did not move. Her body reacted like a manipulated puppet, but in her mind, she had already departed and was far away.

She was a young girl again, playing in her family's village.

Manwena placed the stick under her stomach and used it to pull her up so that her arms were dangling down towards the ground, and she was left helpless and unable to move. Grace was a small woman, and Manwena had no trouble picking her up and manipulating her in any way he chose. His muscles were as hard as steel, and his black shiny skin tightly bound over them like ribbons of elastic.

Grace let her thoughts wander to her past life and the family she had once known. As Manwena panted like a dog behind her, she looked beyond the dirt floor and pictured her own mother's face smiling at her. She saw herself as a young girl, running carefree in the village, laughing and singing with the other children. She saw her older sister humming lullabies to her baby as the sun set low over the grasslands and cast endless shadows on the ground. Grace's mind took her away and did not allow her to feel the pain of rape. She was a survivor.

When it was over, Manwena quickly put his clothes back on, and without glancing down at her crumpled body, he walked quickly out of the door and past Sante and Judy. He still held the stick in one hand and casually picked up his machete with the other.

Sante watched him go.

Grace's legs were shaking as she slowly dressed herself. She detested the smell that lingered after Manwena had raped her. It seemed to sit in her nostrils and made her feel like she was part of some disgusting disease. The backs of her legs were bruised from the beating, and Grace hobbled slowly towards the door feeling suddenly like a very old woman. When she emerged, she noticed that Sante did not look up, but instead turned his head away from her. For a moment, she could not hide the acknowledgment that he knew and felt shame wash over her. That her son had to bear witness to her abuse was a heart-breaking reality.

Grace felt suddenly dizzy, so she sat tentatively on the step. "He has gone," Sante said without making eye contact.

"Gone where?" she asked quietly.

"On a raid, I think. He left quickly with the other men. When he walked over, they all gathered together and went that way." Sante pointed in a direction that looked like every other direction. They were totally surrounded by the forest's walls.

Grace sighed in relief and forced herself to smile at him. "Fill the bucket with water please son. Soon we will sleep."

Sante rose, took the old tin bucket from its resting place and began walking to a nearby creek to fill it up. He had still not looked at her, and Grace could not shake off her shame.

"Come, Judy," she reached out to her daughter and whispered in her ear. "Shall we have special stories tonight?"

"Oh yes, Mama," the little girl responded, placing her head on her mother's chest. Grace wept silently, knowing that if circumstances did not change, one day Judy would have to face the same abuse at the hands of another man, or maybe even the same one. Judy was still very weak, so Grace carried her inside and gently put her down on the floor. They had one thin blanket and would share it between the three of them during the night. If Manwena had been there, he would have had the blanket for himself.

When Sante returned, the chores were finished, and Grace used a little of the water to wash the smell of Manwena away from her body as best she could. Sante sat with his back to the wall inside the hut while Judy huddled in close, and Grace began telling them tales from her childhood.

"When I was a small child," Grace began, "Life was so simple. I would play and sing and dance with my friends while my mother and father worked in the fields. Often, I would go and help them, and we would gather the food together. Everything in nature taught me something about life. The way flowers folded their petals in at night to protect themselves from the cool air. The way insects only appeared when there were crops to eat. The way the dry earth cracked open beneath our feet to beg the sky for rain. The way the spider immediately set to work rebuilding its web after I had run it through with a stick. The spider never seemed to question why or feel sorry for itself, for it seemed to realise how fragile its home was and accept its destruction as part of life. But I never believed that we were like the spider. I always thought that life would never change, and that it would simply stay that way forever.

"When I was a little girl, my village life revolved in predictable patterns. For every season and occasion there was a song. A song for the birth of a new child. A song to encourage the rain to come and another to welcome the first few drops. A song to celebrate the passing from childhood into adulthood. A song to mark every significant day."

"Sing us a song, Mama," Judy interrupted as she shivered and cuddled into her mother. She was still fighting the lingering effects of malaria.

Grace smiled and began singing a simple little tune in a soft voice that carried a depth of feeling her children could not understand.

"When you are born
Sweet child, sweet child
Turn your face up to the sun.
Let the dawn break
And bring you a smile
For we will all love you

Sweet child sweet child.
We will all love you
Until the day is done."

"I love that song Mama," Judy laughed.

"Shall I keep going with my stories?" Grace asked.

"Yes, Mama," Sante replied moving closer so that he now sat beside her. Grace knew he had heard her stories a hundred times before, but he listened as if she was telling him for the first time, and she smiled warmly at him.

"You know, it was the songs sung in the village that helped us children keep track of time. The song for market day meant that it had been ten days since the last one. The song for harvest time meant that our tummies would soon be full of lots of foods. Posho, matoka, sweet potato, pumpkin leaves, toasted maize, and okra would fill our bellies in the season of plenty. My mother and I spent what seemed like hours each day bent over small charcoal fires preparing food. This happened regardless of how much food there was to eat, and somehow the routine gave us comfort – even when our hunger remained."

"What was your favourite food?" Sante asked. Food was one of his favourite subjects, and he wanted to hear more despite grumbles of protest from his own hungry belly.

"I loved okra and maize," Grace replied. "They were my favourites by far. My village was cut off from the world by the surrounding forest. There were no roads or cars, no machines and no material wants other than food and shelter. But what we did have were the birds in the trees to wake us each morning, and the sun and moon to dictate the working day. Rains came and rains went, and the earth breathed in rhythm with it all."

"Sounds a lot like the way we live," said Judy innocently.

Grace sighed. "I wish it were. When I was small, I did not know that there was trouble in our country like you children know it. We had more freedom then. We weren't afraid of things. There didn't seem any need to be afraid."

"What about your family? Did they know there was trouble coming?" Sante asked.

Grace was anxious to share only her positive memories with the children, so she took a different approach. "I don't think so," she lied. "My big sister Evelyn was three years older than me and was married at the age of fourteen. Soon afterwards, she gave birth to her own baby, a beautiful little girl, whose big brown eyes melted my heart. At night, when I lay in bed in my family's single room hut with my two little brothers cuddled up to me for warmth, I'd picture the baby girl's face in my mind. She always made me smile. Nswento and Jacob used to cuddle me just like you cuddle me now. They were beautiful brothers and so full of energy and adventure. They had big wide smiles and would always come up and jump on my back for a ride. They were adored by the entire community, and every night we would sit around the fire after supper and listen as my father told stories, and Nswento and Jacob entertained us with songs and dancing."

"What were your parent's like?" asked Sante.

"Both of my parents were strong people. They were tough and resourceful, working every day in the fields, planting, harvesting, and tending to the crops. They did not have a big plot of land but living in community meant that we shared with our neighbours, and everyone usually managed to have enough. If we were hungry, it simply meant that our neighbours were also hungry. Although we were not well off, we never knew what true starvation or desperation was. My parents taught me what it means to love unconditionally. To love until it hurts." Grace stopped speaking, and a lump formed in her throat. She could not talk about her parents for long without feeling an overwhelming sense of sadness that tainted her memory of them. Such loss. Such senseless waste. Such hurt that had buried itself deep within her soul.

"How about I just sing you some more songs as you go to sleep?"

"Ok," said Judy. "Sing the songs your Mama used to sing you."

Grace smiled at the thought of her own mother's sweet voice and sang as the children drifted off to sleep. She then sat for a time in silence and thought back over her early life. Her memories gave her present circumstances a perspective that her children did not have, but Grace constantly wondered whether the events that seemed so vivid in her mind's eye had actually been warped and changed by the passage of time. Perhaps, her memory was not based on reality at all but was some childish version of the truth. She wondered if her childhood could really have been so happy and untroubled. It hardly seemed possible. Was life really as simple and idyllic as she recalled?

It was not a question she could answer, and perhaps would never answer, so she decided again to hold onto believing that her memories were real, and that, for a brief moment in time, she had been privileged to live a life of peace and freedom.

In the village where she had lived, family had been everything. Family was her lifeblood. Her purpose. Their lives were interconnected by cords so strong, Grace never imagined they could be broken. Only now, when she reflected on the past, could she see how delicate those cords actually were. They were like the fine strands of a spider's web that, once gone, were never the same.

Grace was only eleven years old when the simplicity and loveliness of the life she had known was brought to an abrupt halt. Looking back, she could see the signs that should have told her something was very wrong, but as a naïve young girl, she simply didn't notice.

She was on the cusp between childhood and the traditional transition into the beginning of womanhood. Her head was full of ideas of betrothal and marriage. Preparations for her future marriage had already begun with drawn out negotiations between the respective parties for a dowry. Her husband-to-be had been a family friend for many years. He was older than Grace and in the traditional way, his cousin had come to her parents on his behalf to negotiate. It was not Grace's place to know the details of the discussions; only that, after many months of on-going talks, they had accepted his offer. So, by the time she was thirteen she would be preparing for life as a wife, away from her parents and in the village of her husband's family. Grace had been both excited and nervous, not really knowing what to expect from this new chapter. But it consumed her thoughts and her time, and she failed to notice the signs of disturbance that began to rock her parent's world.

Had she been watching more closely, she would have seen the way her mother Amane, glanced nervously at her father whenever there was mention at village meetings of the emergence of a new rebel group. Amane had searched her husband's face for a reassurance. She had never been good at hiding her feelings. Grace's father was much more stoic and reserved. He was difficult to read. Or perhaps, he simply did not want to worry his children and wife. Either way, he did not openly express any misgivings.

No one really knew who this rebel group were, although they were similar in nature to the former 'Holy Spirit' rebel group, led by Kony's cousin Alice. After remnants of the defeated 'Holy Spirit Army' had fled into Sudan and Kenya, there had been many months of optimism in Northern Uganda, as people clung on to the hope of lasting peace. However, that faded fast as the new group began to wreak havoc and cause chaos. It began slowly at first – like a cancer. Small and unnoticed, until it had gained enough power to be a force that would require a reckoning. But at the time, exactly who they were, why they were causing problems, and what it was all about, utterly escaped Grace.

Had she been listening, she would have paid more attention to the instructions the village elders gave her and the other children about what to do if the rebels ever came. They were to run away from the village into the forest and stay there for at least three days – or was it four? Grace had never really believed they would come to her village. What could they want from their village anyway? They were not rich and could give them nothing but some food and chickens. She had been sure the rebels wouldn't bother them.

Had she been more sensitive to the undercurrents of change that were sweeping into their lives, she would have recognised the forewarning that came the night a man ran into their village begging for help. She had been afraid of him at first, as he looked so wild and afraid. His clothes, or what was left of them, were torn to shreds. He had deep cuts on his feet from running over thorns and rocks for many miles, and scratches on his arms and legs from tree branches. His eyes darted to-and-fro as if waiting for a lion to pounce. To Grace's initial horror, her parents immediately went out to help him. Her mother Amane took him inside and immediately began making a warm stew while another village woman tended to his wounds. Her father and the village chief waived normal protocol and began asking the man a thousand questions right there as the women tried to patch him up. He had been a sorry sight, but what had frightened Grace most were his eyes. He had wild crazy eyes that kept darting to-and-fro as if he was being hunted. She had peered through the cracks in the mud bricks and watched as he spoke. He initially struggled to string a sentence together, but with the infusion of food and water, he revived enough to share his story. Grace and some of the other village children had overhead it all.

His name was Moses, and he came from a village to the West, a three-day walk from her own. He said the rebels had come in the night and destroyed everything, burned the houses and taken some of the people away, tied by their hands and feet. Others had been killed. After days of hiding in the forest, Moses finally found the courage to venture back to his home only to discover the smouldering burnt remains of mud bricks and old cooking pots. Nothing was left standing, and not a sound could be heard. Not even the animals remained. He saw some bodies that had been dumped under a tree. Friends he had once known and shared meals with. His own family, his wife and four children, were nowhere to be found. He had lost them in the chaos of the night, and now he feared for their lives. There was no point staying in the village, so he left, heading northeast, in search of the refugee camps he had heard were being established. He hoped his family had also headed in that direction in an attempt to reach safety. He did not ask whether anyone had seen them. Their silence was answer enough.

Had Grace taken more notice of these warnings, she would

have realised what shaky ground they all stood on, but such incidents came and went from her thoughts without raising too much concern. Within a few weeks she had virtually forgotten about Moses. It was only afterwards that she was able to truly recognise the unspoken fear in the glances her mother had given her father. Only afterwards did she wish she'd paid more attention to the elder's instructions about where to hide in the forest that would be safe.

If only, if only, if only …

Although Grace now knew her own abduction was not unusual, oh how she wished it were. If she were the only one to suffer such loss – perhaps then the pain that strangled her heart would be easier to bear. In reality, hundreds or perhaps even thousands of children had been abducted by the resistance movement and kept for use as slaves, soldiers, wives and pawns in a war that continued to ravage their homes and destroy their families. In Grace's mind, the rebels had systematically killed the spirit and will of their victims the Acholi people, ensuring that they had no voice in a world that seemed to have no ears. She barely dared consider what it would look like if life returned to normal, and yet she found herself clinging to that one tiny thread of hope – like the last few strands of the spider's web that refuse to break.

CHAPTER SEVEN

MERCY'S RAIN

A mother's love goes on forever,
Past the pages of memory.
Beyond conditions or agendas
Into the sweet realms of divinity.
Swept up into the arms of comfort
She offers protection and security.
A mother's love would die to save you,
But she has the wisdom to set you free.
The only way to protect you child
From what this cruel world brings,
Is to plant deep roots in fertile soil
And then to give you wings.
Let this love lift you soaring upwards,
Past every trial that you face;
For you will always land so softly
On her unconditional grace.

His mother's love was like a storm. It began as any storm does with those first few drops of gentle rain. A sweet promise and a slow unravelling of potential. A hope offering that continues to fall, until suddenly you're dancing in the deluge. Soaked from head to toe in cool, refreshing life-giving water.

The love and mercy Amos received from his mother, was to him like a downpour. It started gently at first. When he initially escaped the rebels and landed back in her arms, he hardly allowed himself to believe that it was real. But as it lingered and as his hope grew, the hard stone that was his heart slowly began to soften. His mother's unconditional love taught him not only what love was, but also that it was powerful. That even in the middle of a bloody war, love was a force that could effect change and bring life back to a thirsty and dying soul.

He was sure that without her love, even though he had escaped the clutches of the resistance movement, he would have ended up in a place of total self-destruction. The forces of hate that had surrounded him for years had come to reside within him. He had forgotten how to relate to people as people, for his indoctrination had taught him that people were either commanders to be feared or victims who were dispensable. There were only these two categories, and in this way, the rebels kept things very simple. Fear or despise. Bow down to or inflict pain upon.

Amos's mother saw his heart. She had not judged him for it, but she had slowly and deliberately taught him that there was a way to live that did not involve hatred. She did not give hatred room to fester, and instead at every turn, she gently combated it with the power of her own love. The unconditional love she held for her son.

At first, she had given him permission to grieve. Grieve for the years he had lost and the people he had lost. Grieve for the horrors he had experienced and the pain he had inflicted. His own victims haunted him most. Those he had been forced to kill. For them, he grieved.

She would sit beside him, and simply let him cry. She did not lecture him or tell him that he had cried enough. She simply gave him space and understanding. She also gave him permission to be angry. She made it clear that what had happened to him was not right. Furthermore, she let him know that he was not to blame. For Amos, this was a key in his recovery.

This freedom came when he began voicing to her the questions that ran around in his mind, tormenting him at every opportunity.

"Why?"

"Why has this happened to me?"

"Was I somehow at fault?"

"Was I a bad child in some way? Did I used to disobey you?"

"Why did God allow me to be punished?"

Amos's mother made sure he knew that he was *not* to blame. But, while it was ok to be angry over the injustice, she did not allow him to stay angry. She simply explained that if he chose to hold on to his anger, it would grow inside him like a weed that would eventually choke everything good in his heart and in his life. She taught him that the way he treated others, was like a mirror being held up to his own heart. His actions and words revealed the condition it was in.

As his mother loved and taught him, he slowly began to accept himself again. This in turn allowed him to care once more for others in a genuine way.

There was one more key for Amos. One more lesson she knew he had to learn and apply to his life. But as his mother, she knew it would be his greatest challenge. Could he forgive? Could he possibly forgive those who had abducted him and those who had forced him to commit atrocities? Furthermore, could he contemplate the hardest task of all, that of forgiving himself? She began to introduce this concept to him a couple of years after he returned home.

Local flooding in the area had cut off roads and access to the town, so he and his sisters had not ventured to the night shelters for a few days. On the third night in the village, he had woken in the darkness, startled from another terrifying dream, sweat running down his face. Had he been crying out in his dream? He couldn't be sure, but he found his mother sitting beside him, gently wiping the sweat from his sticky forehead.

"Hush," she had whispered, "Amos, you're safe. It's ok. It's ok. I'm here." He had reached over and attempted to wrap his body in a foetal position around her forearm that rested beside him.

"Amos …" she hesitated. "Amos, there is something I want to tell you." Suddenly he was wide-awake and curious, but he waited for her to continue. "I have wanted to tell you this for a long time, but I have resisted because I know it may be hard for you to hear."

"What is it?" he could feel his muscles tightening.

"Well, it's really about what happened to me after you were taken."

"What happened to you?" His emotions were in turmoil as he suddenly began imagining the worst.

"Hush, it's nothing bad … I mean … Let me explain …" Amos thought he could hear a tremble in her voice, which was so soft that it was barely above a whisper.

"Oh, my dear son, when you were taken, I felt like my whole world came crashing down." She paused. Not for effect, but because speaking her memories aloud was still painful. "I found it hard to breathe. Life stopped making sense." Another pause, and she looked down at her hands. "I couldn't see a way forward. I didn't know how to go on. Every day I would wonder where you were and what had happened to you and if you were even still … alive. I felt like I didn't know how to live anymore. Your abduction was so far beyond my control. I wanted you back so desperately, and yet, I felt like there was nothing I could do.

"After my tears began to dry, I became very angry. I was so full of hate and anger for those who had taken you, and I wanted revenge. I even spoke about forming some kind of people's militia to go and take back our children, but no one would join me. The people here are too afraid. Even the men don't want to stand up against the rebel soldiers. They believe that the evil spirits that assist the rebels make them somehow unstoppable. But I was determined to do something, even if it was going to be on my own. The problem was, I couldn't go and leave your sisters. They were vulnerable enough, even with me here."

"So, what did you do?" Amos was stunned. He had never heard his mother speak like this before. In fact, he had never allowed himself to think too deeply about what she might have gone through after his abduction.

"Well," her voice was strong now, "I hated Kony, and I hated the men who took you, and I wanted to see them killed. I needed action. I couldn't just go on with life pretending that what was happening all around us was ok."

"So, what did you do?" Amos repeated, sitting up now to

face his mother. Though he couldn't quite make out her striking features in the darkness, he could see her silhouette and sensed the deep lines that were creasing her brow as she spoke.

"Well, what happened next was a little surprising. You see, I went to a friend whom I felt would surely get behind me as she has lost both her husband and two children to this war. You know her. Aunty Freeda. She had nothing left to lose. She lives alone now in a nearby camp, and she struggles to survive.

"I explained to her how I felt. I told her that I needed to find you or at least find justice before I died. I had this idea that if we gathered enough people, some could act as caretakers for the remaining children while the others went out to fight the rebels. Looking back, I can see that I wasn't really thinking rationally. I had no weapons, and no access to weapons other than our small gardening tools, but I felt like I had no other option."

"And Aunty agreed with you?"

"Well, not exactly, but let me assure you that she understood how I felt, and she made that clear. After I had told her about my vague plans, she put her arms around me and held me close, and I don't know why, but I just started crying again. Perhaps it was because it was the first time anyone had ever seemed to care about my pain."

"And then did you manage to make a militia?" Amos was already gearing himself up to be recruited into the ranks of his mother's mysterious band of soldiers.

"Actually no. Not exactly. You see, she showed me another way." At this point his mother lit a candle that illuminated a small sphere of space between them in a beautiful yellow glow. Then from under the folds of the fabric wrapped around her, she produced a thin tattered red book. Amos looked at it curiously for a moment, wondering what his mother was trying to tell him. She turned the thin book over, and he saw a picture of two hands clasped together in a strong grip of friendship.

"This is called *Empower*. It is a program that Aunty Freeda participated in, and it is sweeping through the camps. Aunty explained to me how she had also experienced not only anger after her family had been taken, but also such terrible trauma, nightmares, and depression that she failed to function. She could not eat, and she was afraid to sleep. She had felt like she was just waiting to die. Her sister dragged her to a meeting where they were conducting this program, and she said that there she had begun to learn about many things that helped her. For one thing, she said she realised for the first time that the things she was experiencing were actually normal. The sadness, nightmares, lack of appetite, feelings of panic and wanting to die, were things she had not wanted to talk about to anyone for fear that people would think she was crazy or cursed. But she realised that many people had similar things happening to them as well, and they were able to talk honestly about them together. She also told me that she was taught how to control the feelings she had. Then most importantly, she was taught about the power of forgiveness."

When his mother hesitated again, Amos leapt in, "What do you mean forgiveness? Forgiveness for who?"

"Well, she learnt to forgive those who had taken away her family."

"Why would she want to do that?" Amos could feel himself getting defensive.

"I didn't understand either at first. I was so full of anger and hate that I couldn't see straight. But Aunty encouraged me to participate in the program myself. You see, she made a bargain with me. She said that if I joined the group and still felt the same way about seeking revenge, she wouldn't stand in my way. She said she would even look after the children for me if I went away. I couldn't say no to that offer as it was the best I had, so I decided to endure the meetings for two weeks and then reformulate my plan with Freeda's support."

"And what happened?" Amos was still half expecting to be recruited.

"Amos, I learnt some very important things in that program. I am not saying that it is the only answer to our troubles, but it has helped me to begin a journey that is positive. I learnt that I needed to forgive, not just those who took you away from me, but I also needed to forgive myself."

"Why yourself? You did nothing wrong!"

"I didn't do my job as a mother. I didn't protect you. I couldn't protect you, and I hated myself for that. But as I began to let go of my hurt, pain and bitterness, I was able to love again. I was able to actually pity those rebels rather than hate them."

"Pity them?" Amos was beginning to think his mother was delusional. The idea of pitying those blood-hungry violent rebels was insane.

"Yes, pity them. The reason why I pity them is because they have touched and damaged the children that God loves most. His children are the jewel in His crown. And I pity them because like you, most of them were abducted when they were still children. They have been forced to fight in a war that is not theirs. They have been forced to kill and do terrible things that they will carry for the rest of their lives. There are no winners in this war. Most of the rebels suffer just as we Acholi suffer."

Amos was silent and lost for words.

"My darling boy, I never gave up hope of finding you. But I did give up on my agenda for revenge because I began to see so clearly the cycle of violence that we as a people are locked into. One crime brings another and another and another, and people hate so deeply that there will be no victory in the end. Even if the fighting stopped tomorrow, how would we pick up the pieces and move on if everyone continues to hate each other? The Uganda I long for is one of freedom and peace. But freedom and peace *cannot* exist hand in hand with hate, violence and war. One must die in order for the other to live. We must put away our hatred and our weapons."

"What about Kony?" Amos stated defiantly. "He is not some innocent child abducted into this war. He is the one who orchestrates it. He is evil! What about his commanders? The men who force the abducted children to commit horrible crimes?" Amos's eyes began to well with tears.

"Amos you must very clearly understand what I am saying. I am not excusing the behaviour of anyone who lifts a finger against someone else. I am not saying that what is happening to our children is in any way right. We will all be held to account for the part we have played in this war. And I do pray that justice is done and that the perpetrators of this war will one day be brought to account. But God, not me, is the ultimate judge. When Kony dies, I believe he will stand before God and have to give an account. Thankfully, I am not God, and you are not God, and we can leave the verdict up to Him. But for your own sanity and your own freedom, choose forgiveness for it will bring you liberty like nothing else can."

"I can't really begin to know how … I don't understand what you are saying."

"It is like this, when you do not forgive, the hate and bitterness enter your bloodstream like the poison from a snake bite. If you let it continue to invade your system, it will ultimately destroy you. They used this example in the program. Forgiveness is not so much about the one who hurt you as it is about you. Forgiveness sets you free for when you forgive, you halt the flow of poison and the power it has over you."

"I still don't understand, Mama. It doesn't make sense to me."

"Just do one thing for me. Don't make any decisions about such big matters until you feel that you fully understand. Please take this book and join one of the programs when they begin again. Right now, they are in Anaka camp, but I have heard that next month the leaders will be back in our region again. You can wait for them to come, or perhaps you can go through the program together with Aunty Freeda. What do you think?"

Amos felt pushed into a corner. One part of him was curious, while the other tried to suppress the sudden anger that rose within him. His mother sat quietly waiting for an answer. He looked at her hands that were grasped tightly together, her thumbs rolling over and over one another like she was trying to make a fire with them. He felt her anguish and realised that he couldn't say no. That was when the full force of the downpour hit him. Her love and mercy were so unconditional, and he realised that she had even forgiven him for the crimes he may have committed that she never even asked about. He *was* that solider that some other parent and some other child would have to forgive. He was as guilty as everyone else.

"Ok Mama. I'll do it for you." She leapt up instantly and threw her arms around him and the downpour of mercy drenched them both.

"When the program returns, ok? Not with Aunty, but when it returns." Amos didn't want to have to divulge any secrets to anyone he knew.

"Yes, Amos. Of course."

Amos never did get the opportunity to take part in the program his mother had spoken to him about. Although he had been willing, by the time the program returned, it was too late.

Life had taken another tragic turn.

CHAPTER EIGHT

TAKEN

I loved you for a moment
Before your soul passed on its way.
And though I could not say it.
My heart begged for you to stay.

You were a glimpse of love
With all its possibility,
Then you were gone forever
And I drown in this reality.

Sometimes I do wonder
Whether I slept and dreamt of you
But I remember your face so well
That I know your love was true.

Your laughter and your smile,
Your gentle warm embrace,
Where are you now my mother?
Please save me from this place.

The night was clear and beautiful. Clouds sporadically covered the moon as they journeyed across the sky. Silent stories told with their changing shapes. Silvia had spent the last half hour before bed sitting with Raymond on the step of their hut. They sang songs and listened to their quiet voices drift upwards into the treetops. It was such a peaceful time of day. She simply did not want it to end.

As her mother still needed her help around the village, Silvia had not returned to the night shelter since baby Kalunga had been born almost a week earlier. Kalunga was doing well and already seemed to be getting chubbier – his soft little folds of dark skin creasing his legs and arms in ways that made Silvia smile.

After a time, Jossy beckoned her two older children inside. Silvia's family's hut was not spacious, but she had always loved the cosiness of their little home. Still, when the baby cried in the night everyone woke. Jossy tried hard to hush Kalunga quickly for fear of drawing any rebel soldiers to the village. Staying in the village was a calculated gamble that they reasoned was made safer by living relatively close to Gulu. However, her father had spoken recently about travelling as a family to the night shelters in Gulu from now on. As soon as Jossy was fit enough to make the journey they were to begin. Perhaps, he had some deep sense of foreboding. He had never before wanted to leave his village. Silvia wondered, but did not ask, just happy that it meant they would always stay together as a family.

This particular evening, Silvia fell asleep on a bamboo bed with a torn blanket pulled up over her shoulders. Little Raymond lay cuddled into her side for warmth. The night was quiet apart from the sounds of nocturnal animals that busied themselves about the forest floor. As the evening wore on, clouds became thick in the sky above. They hid the moon behind their silvery edges, only occasionally relenting to let it peer through at the earth below. Everything was peaceful.

In the early hours of morning, sometime after midnight, Silvia woke with a sudden fright. It was late. She knew that because even her father, who often stayed up long after everyone else was in bed, was fast asleep. She sat bolt upright, her heart pounding in fear, sure that she had heard something outside. Something was out of place. Was it a noise or the odd silence that echoed in her ears? She wondered where the usual nocturnal sounds had gone.

A strange foreboding rose in the pit of her stomach. Her breathing was fast and chaotic as her mind raced away in dark imaginings. The rest of her family was asleep, but her eyes and ears strained in the darkness and tried to pick up on anything unusual. She hugged the blanket up to her chest and shivered, trying to control her breathing. It was a futile attempt.

Suddenly the door was flung open, and men began barging into the hut. They were shouting. "Everyone out. Get up. Get out." Silvia sat frozen, completely paralysed in fear and panic. Bile rose, and she gulped it back down into her stomach. Her body shook uncontrollably.

The rest of her family woke at once, and chaos broke out. Raymond and the baby began crying. Silvia heard her father tell them to run, then a rebel clubbed him over the back of the head. Miraculously, he stayed standing and staggered outside clutching his wife's arm. Jossy held Kalunga close to her chest. He was screaming. Heavy hands pulled Silvia to her feet, and she managed to grab Raymond at the last second before she was pushed outside. All she could see were dark silhouetted figures moving everywhere. She was being pushed along in the darkness. A hand held her neck and roughly manoeuvred her into a group of other children. She heard her father still trying to shout at them to run, but it was a vain hope. There was nowhere to run to.

Raymond was clinging tightly to her, and Silvia fought hard to keep tears from blurring her eyes. There was a voice in her head that kept telling her to stay calm and not to cry. She needed to see what was happening and try to look for a way to escape into the forest. Raymond had buried his little face into her shoulder and wrapped his arms around her neck so tightly she thought he might strangle her, but she let him cling on.

Silvia saw that the other villagers were being herded into groups. Grass roofs were set on fire and the brilliant orange flames lit up the night sky. She could see the terror on people's faces and the silent ache in their eyes that said so much. The delicate structure of their lives and families was being shattered into a million pieces. Some were running, being chased down and killed right there in front of them. So much noise, shouting, and chaos paralysed Silvia, and she did not know which way to turn.

To her horror, Raymond was suddenly ripped out of her grasp. Utter panic gripped her as she screamed his name and tried to hold on. She heard him crying, but he somehow just disappeared from sight. Silvia wasn't even sure whether it was a villager or rebel who had pulled him from her. Perhaps it was a villager and they had escaped into the forest, but then why was she left behind? She knew that he would never be able to find his way to the refugee camp on his own.

There was no time to think rationally. Silvia searched wildly for his face, but she was being shoved into a tighter group of children and surrounded by shouting men and arms that waved machetes far too close for comfort. In those moments, everything seemed so surreal – like she was struggling to wake up from a terrifying nightmare. Only the nightmare refused to release her from its grip.

Then came the moment they took her parents away.

Unspeakable pain ripped and clawed at Silvia's heart as she watched two men drag her mother, father and baby Kalunga to the edge of the forest. She wanted to gouge out her eyes so that she wouldn't have to face the horror anymore. Already, so many people lost in one single night, and now her family was disappearing right in front of her. No final words were spoken. She could not say goodbye and only watched silently as her parents held each other. Her mother sobbed uncontrollably. Baby Kalunga cried.

Silvia looked away, but her ears could not block out their screams.

Her heart ached as if it had literally been sliced into raw and jagged pieces of pulsating flesh and stomped into the dirt. She did not know how she would take another breath. Her parents were her protection and security in a world of unpredictability. They were her everything. It didn't seem to make sense that she could even remain in existence without them.

Someone grabbed her hands and tied them tightly together with a piece of rope. She realised she was being tied into a line of children. Why didn't they just kill her as well? She felt desperate and panicked. She wanted to run to where she had last seen her parents, but she was being pulled in the opposite direction.

Her mind began to do strange things, imagining that perhaps she'd see them around the next tree, standing in the shadows waiting for her, but no, they were never there. After a time, some small sense of reason inside told her that her parents would not be coming to rescue her. Perhaps they would have if they could.

Perhaps they were watching from the other side of life, wanting to reach out and take her with them, but she was moving too fast.

So fast. Crashing along through the trees. Silvia in a line of children. Hands all roped together. They were being pushed and pulled along in the darkness too quickly for her feet to keep up. She could feel her bare soles being punctured by sharp rocks, while thick, jagged tree branches scraped her arms and legs. Every few meters, someone fell creating mild chaos as the rebels shouted aggressively for everyone to hurry up. It was pitch dark as they moved away from the fires of the village, and Silvia couldn't see anything except the black silhouette of a small child's head bobbing in front of her. Apart from the rebel's constant pressure to move, there was an eerie silence in the forest. Her insides felt like they were liquefying from the pain of it all, and she was sure that her body might eventually melt and become part of the forest floor.

The shadows of the rebels constantly moved alongside the captured children. Minutes felt like hours as they walked and walked – in endless motion. Silvia tried to count how many rebels there were, but the movement and the blackness made it almost impossible. One voice from somewhere out in front gave orders. They were told to be very quiet, and occasionally, the rebels pulled them to a standstill and they would stop with a jerk as the rope was yanked from behind. No one breathed as the rebels stood up against trees and strained their ears for unusual noises. Silvia didn't know what it was that alerted them to the possible presence of unwanted danger, but in the stillness of those moments all she could sense was fear. The cold, raw fear of the children around her whose world had just been turned upside down made her feel even more terrified. Flashbacks of the horrible carnage they had left behind stole into her mind. She tried to stop the images, but there was no controlling the compulsive thoughts.

Where was Raymond? Was he in the line as well?

She saw eyes. Faces. Hands begging. Blood. And her parents disappearing right before her eyes. She wanted so desperately to curl up in the branches of a tree and escape it all, but instead her mind replayed the whole dreadful scene over and over and over again as they marched endlessly through the night.

Time became irrelevant as the children staggered through the forest surrounded by rebels. They walked on into the morning – without food, without water, without ceasing. Silvia had never been so glad to see the sun rise above the trees, as part of her did not really believe they would live to see another day. She had imagined the rebels marching them towards a big pit that they would simply walk into before being buried alive. Now that the sun was up, surely some kind of hope would come with it.

Just as the sun was appearing, the small girl in front of Silvia fell and did not get up. Silvia looked closely at her for the first time and recognised Alinta – Amos' youngest sister. Silvia wondered again if her Raymond was also there. It had been such a terrifying night, and she had felt so utterly alone that, apart from her brother, she had not stopped to consider the other children. A rebel boy with a machete, kicked Alinta hard and shouted at her to move. She did not. Instead, hanging her head, she started to sob. Silvia could see the sweat trickling down the back of her neck. It was then she noticed the blood on Alinta's right side that had caked thick and dark on her torn shirt. The cruel raw wound from a knife or machete was evident despite the mess of blood, as if she'd been violently sliced open by the jaws of an angry beast.

"Move or I'll kill you," came the terrible warning from one of the men.

She did not move.

Silvia shook with fear and wondered if they really would carry out such a threat there in broad daylight. Then her mind flashed back again to the night before, and she knew it was possible. Perhaps even probable. Once more, she saw her parents' eyes and heard her mother's cries. It wasn't a bad dream, and none of them were going to wake up. Silvia's legs began to give way, but she was so afraid of falling too that she managed them. Alinta's hands were untied from the rope, and she was hauled roughly to the side where they again threatened her with death, this time holding a machete to her neck.

"Wait," said a voice behind Silvia, "I'll carry her." She turned her head and saw Amos looking at the rebels.

Silvia was shocked that she had not realised he was right behind her.

The large terrifying-looking man who was giving orders paused momentarily as if surprised by this offer. Then he began to snicker. "You?" He scoffed looking over Amos's slender frame. Then he laughed in a menacing way. "If you can carry her, then do it, but if you slow us down or if you drop her, you will have to kill her yourself. Do you understand?"

Amos looked down at his hands. Silvia thought she saw him hesitate for a second, before he simply nodded. The rope was untied from his hands and retied around his waist instead, so that he was still part of the line.

"Pick her up boy," the commander ordered.

Amos obeyed. As gently as he could, he lifted his little sister and placed her on his back with her arms around his neck. He held her arms tight and bent down almost double so that she was virtually lying on top of his back. Alinta did not make a sound.

Many of the rebels seemed to find this amusing – like they were anticipating an entertaining show when his endurance failed. They joked with one another and began taking bets as to how many paces he might make before falling.

"We go," the commander announced, grinding their sadistic humour to an abrupt halt.

Although Alinta was only small, Silvia reasoned that carrying her must have been utterly exhausting, as she was not fully coherent and therefore like a dead weight. Amos had to pick her up and put her on his back without assistance. He refused to show any weakness. Silvia's heart swelled with love for her friend, and his bravery astounded her. Still, she was concerned over his current predicament and tried to walk as carefully as possible without yanking the rope between them. Whenever another child fell, Amos was able to stop and rest a moment, but he never put Alinta down, and he never faltered.

For the next several hours until the sun was getting high overhead, he walked behind Silvia, his footsteps as methodical as his breathing. It gave Silvia something to focus on other than the lingering terror in her gut. She imagined that those deep slow breaths of his were actually conducting the entire forest's rhythm.

When they finally reached what appeared to be a destination, Silvia was surprised to see other people there. In fact, she was somewhat surprised to come upon a destination at all, as the enforced march had felt so endless. The clearing that they stumbled into was a village of sorts, with small huts surrounding a central area. Women and children seemed busy, and many did not even look up as the hostages entered, as if the sight of a captive line of children was an everyday occurrence.

Silvia tried to keep her eyes low but glanced up and noticed that some were cooking, while others swept dirt floors, prepared food and stirred big vats of foul-smelling liquid. For all intents and purposes, it looked almost like a normal village, but Silvia was immediately aware of the silence. There was no singing, no sounds of laughter, no children's games, no distant conversations. The women and children went about their tasks in relative silence.

The hostage children were ordered to sit in the centre of camp. Two boys sat nearby holding machetes while the rest of the rebels retreated back into the forest. They sat like a row of chickens lined up for slaughter. It was a moment when time seemed to stand still.

They sat.

No one spoke.

No one acknowledged their presence.

It left Silvia feeling both invisible and strangely self-conscious.

The idleness of sitting gave their feet a rest, but as the afternoon progressed, Silvia's mind seemed to play tricks on her, dancing between reality and illusion to the point where she was not sure what was real and what was not. Not having slept, eaten or had anything to drink since the previous day, her body longed to curl up in the dust and rest, but she was too afraid of the possible consequences to allow herself such luxury. Instead, lucid delusions, some comforting, some terrifying, plagued her mind every time she closed her eyes.

She saw herself sitting at a lavish feast. Food of every description was laid out before her in a beautiful, colourful display. She floated above the food, smelling all of its succulence, and feeling satisfied with its sight alone. Birds landed on her shoulders, and she fed them morsels from the table.

Then, in a whirl, reality would hit again, and she'd find

herself shivering despite the hot sun that beat down upon her head. She closed her eyes and attempted to find that dream again, but this time it was replaced by monsters lurking out of the shadows trying to grab her arms and legs, their faces twisted and grotesque as she tried to mentally undo their hold. She heard children screaming and saw her parents being pulled away from her. She tried to reach out to them and run to save them, but her feet simply would not move. She was stuck to the ground then pushed face first into the dirt.

Silvia cried aloud, waking herself from the nightmarish delusion and returning to reality – sitting in the camp in the line of children. Amos was on her right, still holding Alinta who appeared to be barely breathing. Silvia wanted so badly to speak to him, but no words would come, and her mind kept slipping away.

At some point in the afternoon, Silvia watched as a young boy approached them to offer bananas and water. She grabbed at the food and water and was instantly revived as the warmth of it slid down her throat and hit her empty stomach.

Silvia watched the boy as he handed the food around and noticed there was an unusual intensity in his eyes. Perhaps even a kindness too. In the midst of her nightmare, this boy had broken in and offered her something so much more important than food – a faint glimmer of hope. Silvia could not help staring at him, but quickly looked down when from over his shoulder, she saw a woman approach. She was frantic and pleading with the boy to leave them, but before she could finish, a man launched with a lion-like fury onto the scene. The commander!

Murderous hatred filled his eyes as he grabbed the boy and started shouting. A woman ran over, trying to shield the boy with her own body, but she was no match for the commander. He directed his vengeance towards her for a few moments before beating her to the ground. Without looking back, he then pushed the boy out of sight behind the wall of trees at the edge of the clearing.

And just like that, it was over.

Silvia's heart sunk as she guessed more killing was about to follow. She did not want the boy to die. The only hope she had seen since being abducted was the light in his face.

She could not take the pain any longer and forced herself to sink into a fitful sleep. She imagined her mother's arms around her. Too exhausted now to care whether or not she would wake, she began to hope that she would not. The possibility of death felt like sweet relief.

CHAPTER NINE

BORN TO FIGHT

By chance you were born into battle,
With a string of bullets
Around your neck.
Forced to fight as a child soldier;
This is no life.
There is no rest.

But you breathe, you breathe,
You silently cry.
Hoping and praying for reprieve,
You breathe.

Circumstance made you a dispensable pawn
In somebody else's war.
Pushed along by undercurrents
Of cruelty and hatred.
This is no life.
Your wounds lie raw.

In the end a sword will claim you
And finally lay you to rest.
Down deep in the dirt on a blood-soaked hill

With no one to mourn your passing.
This was no life.
But you did your best.

You breathe, you breathe,
You silently cry.
Hoping and praying for reprieve,
You breathe.

S ante was sitting outside on a small flat stone, drawing figures in the dirt when the hostages were brought into camp. It was early in the afternoon, the sun just beginning to dip down through the trees. He looked up suddenly, surprised by their appearance even though such a raggedy bunch of children being hauled into their midst was nothing new. There were both boys and girls and at a guess they ranged in age from about eight to fifteen years old. Every time a new group of hostage children were recruited, Sante saw the same haunted look in their eyes. They were roped together and walked in single file – their faces downcast. Sante tried, as he always did, to catch their eyes, but they never looked his way.

They appeared like ghosts who had seen the devil face to face.

As he watched the sad procession, he overheard two older rebel boys talking about the raid. It made his stomach turn to hear the gruesome details of how they had slaughtered most of the villagers and taken these forlorn children hostage. No wonder they looked so strange. Like they had seen things which humans should never see and now struggled to know how to be human again.

And this was just the beginning.

Sante knew that the path ahead of them was a dangerous one that many would not survive. Of those who did, many would wish they hadn't.

That afternoon when the hostages were brought into camp, the rebels did not start eating and drinking as they normally did after a raid. They left two boys with Manwena to keep watch and then returned like shadows into the forest. As soon as they were gone, Manwena disappeared into his hut to sleep, and the two boys guarding the hostages relaxed noticeably. Sante did not move. He sat like a statue on a rock reasoning that if he was still enough he might not be noticed.

Both boys who had been left to guard the hostages were abducted when they were young and immediately groomed as soldiers. Sante knew them well and had watched them change over the years. Evans, the older of the two, had been captured at the age of seven and taught to kill anyone at a moment's notice if that was what the commander ordered. He did not even flinch anymore. Sante had once watched Evans kill a big man who was brought into camp. The man had been used to carry stolen weapons and food, but once they arrived, he was dispensable and would have been a problem had he remained alive. Death was the easiest way to solve such a problem, and Evans was the solution that day. On the commander's word, he had walked calmly over to the man and beaten his head with a makeshift axe until the contents escaped from his collapsed skull. Had Evans looked into the man's eyes as Sante had, he would have seen him begging for mercy. He was so big and powerfully built, and yet in the end, found himself helpless at the hands of a young child. But Evans never saw the man's unspoken plea. He never noticed his shaking hands and the sweat that poured from his face. He had learnt through years of violence that in order to survive this life, he must obey in an unquestioning, unthinking, unmerciful way. Anything else would only result in his own death.

The other boy was Alfred. He was younger than Evans by a few years and had not yet managed to build up such a hard exterior. Sante watched him as he occasionally allowed his eyes to dart over the hostages, almost as if he was searching for someone he knew. What would he do if he saw a brother or sister among the children? For his own sake, Sante hoped he didn't find any familiar faces.

"Bring us brew," Evans suddenly shouted to no one in particular. A woman hurried to meet his demand. With drinks in hand, the two boys relaxed further. They tossed crude jokes back and forth about the young captives that made the girls squirm in fear and discomfort.

Around Sante, other people had returned to their chores. Although Sante knew he should be helping his mother, he remained where he was, cautiously staring at the children. He did not want to watch them so blatantly, but they were like a magnet from which he could not drag his gaze away. He knew they held secrets of a life far removed from his own, and he longed to break the wall of silence and discover something about where they had come from.

It wasn't long before Evans and Alfred lay in drunken stupors as the fermented brew hit their tired and hungry bodies. It was doubtful whether they could even lift a machete in their state. Manwena also remained inside the hut. Sante reasoned that he was most likely asleep and would not emerge again for several hours.

Suddenly an idea hit him that initially appeared ludicrous,

and he quickly dismissed it as dangerous folly. But as he sat watching the children, the idea returned, and he allowed himself to at least contemplate the notion. His contemplation finally led him to action.

He would attempt to break that wall.

Taking a pot of water in one hand and some precious bananas in the other, Sante tentatively stood and walked slowly over to the group of hostages. The women around camp initially did not notice, although the shackled children glanced up in nervous apprehension as he neared them. There were eleven children in all – four boys and seven girls. Sante tried to offer them some reassurance.

"Don't be scared," he whispered. "I just want to give you some food and water."

Their hands were tied, so Sante had to lift the pot to each child's lips in order to let them drink. He tried to give them equal portions and not waste any by spilling. The children seemed to realise this and took only a few sips each time he offered the pot. When the water was gone, Sante peeled five bananas and shared them among the group. It was a slow process, but he became absorbed in the task, smiling at each child and offering a few kind words. He didn't even notice the women around camp stopping to watch.

"Sante, Sante!" one Aunty suddenly came running over to him, her shrill voice breaking through his focus. She attempted to pull the banana in his hand away from a little girl's open mouth, but Sante resisted and managed to give her the food. "Sante," came her cry, "if the men come and find you or if someone tells Manwena what you're doing …" Her voice faded for a moment. "You must stop now before you get into trouble."

Sante could hear the distress in her voice but was planning to ignore it until he heard another voice from behind her.

"How dare you!" Manwena shouted.

Sante's body froze – petrified in fear and a terrible sinking feeling engulfed him.

Manwena grabbed Sante by the shoulders and shook him violently before throwing him to the ground. "You will pay for this," he seethed – his evil intentions clear in every word.

Grace, who had only just noticed the commotion, ran over and stood between her son and Manwena, trying to protect him from the man's fury. He pushed her angrily out of the way. "This is your fault," Manwena shouted as he turned his look of hatred towards her. "You have protected him like he is some kind of prince, but I've had enough. He is old enough to fight now. He will be initiated and join the soldiers. You will no longer call him your son."

Grace was desperately frightened. "No, no," she wept. Manwena's frustration was quickly reaching a peak and with clenched fist he punched her in the face, sending her flying backwards into the dirt. Grace covered her head and sobbed, consumed by terror at being unable to protect her son.

"Quiet. I have had enough of you." He turned and grabbed Sante by the arm, half carrying and half dragging him into the forest. Sante's legs scrambled to keep up. His heart thumped a thousand miles a minute, and he did not dare look back at his mother and the hostage children who all sat staring after him in terrified silence.

Grace was more afraid in that moment than she had ever been before. Would she ever see her son again?

It was late in the afternoon, and the sun cast an orange glow through the trees. Shadows danced and flickered on the ground. Sante stood with two other boys in the darkening forest while Manwena, along with another commander, prepared the boys for their final initiation. The hours of beatings, endurance tests and witchcraft rituals had been long and slow. All three boys had been born and raised in the resistance movement and were now considered old enough to join the raiding parties.

Had this initiation ritual been long in the planning? Or was it simply an angry reaction to his feeding of the children? Sante did not know. The presence of the other boys both confused and unnerved him.

Sante's eyes gleamed in the final rays of sunlight, even as his features darkened with the dusk. His chocolate-coloured skin was smooth and soft, not yet weathered by the passage of time. His lips were pursed tightly together, and his black eyes stared intently at the cracked and leathery skin on his father's feet. He did not want to lift his eyes. Sante held his hands tightly behind his back, his bony limbs protruding oddly out of his bloated malnourished torso.

Shea nut oil was roughly smeared onto each boy's small body, creating a greasy white film. Manwena was chanting as he used his oil-smothered index finger to draw a crude looking cross on Sante's forehead, chest, back, hands and feet.

"These markings are more than just decoration," he suddenly began. "This is a vital part of who we are – like our blood. You have seen it used before on new recruits. It gives us our power from the spirit world. This oil will make you bulletproof and will protect you in battle. You will be able to fight for the LRA, and if you are a true soldier with no treason in you, you will not be harmed." He almost smirked at Sante as he said the words. "No need to hide behind rocks and trees when you are a *true* rebel fighter. You can walk right up to the enemy and the bullets they fire at you will bounce right off your skin. Nothing can harm you."

Sante had heard it all before, but he stood entranced by the thought of such power. Was this really the reason his father always returned from raids alive while others did not? Was he a true soldier, pure and untainted by thoughts of treason? Was he indestructible?

Manwena continued, his voice now darkening and his glare boring holes into the top of Sante's skull as he spoke. The boy kept his head down and his eyes squarely fixed on the dirty feet in front of him. "I warn you now," he seethed "that you should never let anyone deceive you, for you will not live to be fooled a second time. You will never rise to be above the rank of solider. You will never leave the militia. This is your true purpose. This is why you were born. There is nowhere else for you to go, and you must forget everything else but fighting for the cause of the LRA. If you ever try to escape, even if you make it a certain distance, the oil will never let you go. It will allow us to track you down no matter where you are, and once we find you, we will kill you. All traitors must be killed."

Stony silence followed Manwena's lecture. With his head still down, Sante glanced sideways at the other young boys beside him, and fear crept up his spine. He wondered where he would possibly go if he ever did try to leave. Being born into this life meant he had no point of reference with which to question it other than his mother's stories. The other boys also stood looking down, but unlike Sante, their backs were straight, and they showed no obvious fear. Sante knew that they were looking forward to finally getting their chance to hold a gun or machete. They had been told all about the glory of killing, had witnessed numerous slaughters, as Sante had, and there was no reason for them to think that this was anything but normal. The gun was the ultimate symbol of power, force and strength – all that encompassed what it meant to be a man.

Sante felt differently to the others, but he was desperately trying not to let it show. He couldn't help but wonder about the world that existed beyond the forest's walls. In his heart, he had stored up all the stories his mother whispered to him about how life was meant to be. He had seen the sadness in her eyes when she spoke about her past, as if everything in her soul longed for it. He had seen horror in the eyes of the people the rebels brutalised and left for dead. He had seen the helpless grief in the eyes of the people who were used as pack mules to carry weapons and supplies to camp before being slaughtered. A deep canyon of pain was etched into every victim's face that left him with questions he could never seem to get beyond.

Lewis, the other commander who stood beside Manwena, was chanting and callously slapping small handfuls of water over the boys' bodies. He then threw the remains onto the burning embers of the fire. Sante's eyes and nostrils were filled with smoke and steam as Lewis waved it in their direction, still chanting in a melancholic drone.

Suddenly, Manwena's sharp voice snapped Sante back to attention, and he involuntarily jerked and looked up into his father's eyes.

"You are ready," Manwena shouted as he looked to the sky and held his fist in the air. "You are now a part of our movement's fighting army. Together, we will assist Kony to win the war and lead Uganda to victory. We will take control and possess the rightful places of leadership owed to us. We will serve Kony as our true president, and we will fight for his honour."

Nothing more was said. The commanders dismissed the boys abruptly and wandered back to their huts as casually as if they had just returned from an afternoon stroll through the forest. The two other boys followed, but Sante did not move. He watched as the distance between them increased, and little by little, he allowed his body to relax against a tree trunk. A deep sigh escaped his lungs as if it had been held in for hours. Sante's eyes remained fixed on Manwena for a time, like a forest creature watching its enemy – fearful yet oddly fascinated.

Manwena was not a man to be trusted. His eyes glazed with a burning glare that could set damp wood on fire when he looked someone square in the face. A scar that ran along his left cheekbone from his ear to the corner of his lips twisted his face in a frightening way when he smiled – like he was made up of pieces that hadn't been put together properly. As far back as Sante could remember Manwena had been a cruel, calculating man who did not seem to know the meaning of mercy or remorse. Sante's earliest memory of his father was receiving a blow from his fist to the top of his head. Pain and brutality were like second nature to him, and over the years, it had freely rained down upon Sante, Grace and Judy alike. An all-consuming loathing for this man strangled Sante's heart and held him captive within the confines of his own hatred.

Manwena's pattern of abuse had always been so erratic that the family lived in constant fear. Only one thing was constant and that was the heavy drinking that followed his shouting and violence. When he finally slumped down in a drunken stupor, no one dared go near him for fear of waking him and incurring his wrath. Grace would wake Sante and Judy early in the morning to help her with the chores so that Manwena's anger might be pacified when he woke. If there was food for him, he was more likely to be calm and subdued.

Sante's mind again shifted back to the present, and he wondered why he struggled so much to concentrate on any one thing. Why did his mind drift to things that he ultimately didn't like thinking about? It was as if he couldn't escape his pain, even within the confines of his own head. Silent tears welled up in his eyes and toppled over, forging furrows down his cheeks and chin, as he contemplated the raids and fighting to come. All his life he had somehow believed that he would escape having to fight. The thought of it made him sick to his stomach. He knew the brutality of these men and did not want to become one of them.

As he stood at the edge of the village, he looked up into the tree branches above and caught a scent of something he did not recognise or understand. He couldn't put his finger on it, but it was as if something was beckoning him, so he remained still and silent for a very long time. The tears dried on his cheeks as a bird fluttered from branch to branch and sung in a sweet voice. A butterfly danced past, carried on the soft breeze. Clouds rolled over the darkening skyline in a lazy way as if they had not a care in the world. The leaves swayed gently and seemed to be trying to tilt themselves in the direction of the setting sun. Another bird joined the first, and they danced around each other as if playing a game of tag. What was it that held his attention? Sante waited and listened, and then suddenly he understood.

He was witnessing freedom.

For the first time in his short life, he noticed the freedom with which the natural world moved. There was an unforced rhythm to it that his soul craved. The animals embodied it, and even the trees exuded it. So, he told himself it must be real. His mother must be right, and it must be possible for human beings to have it too.

He took a deep, slow breath and pushed air into his lungs until they were bursting.

Freedom!

He wanted it!

He could hardly comprehend it, and yet, he desired it. He longed for it. He felt an urgent desperation to find it and to know what it tasted and felt like. More importantly, he wanted to know where freedom might lead.

CHAPTER TEN

NO RHYME OR REASON

What is there left to say
When all words fail,
And no justifications will do?
When the bell that tolls for humanity
Is broken sheer in two.
When conviction dries up
In the face of a gun,
And our "great" leaders destroy
Before understanding has even begun.

What is there left to shout about
When our voices can't be heard?
For deaf ears resound with emptiness
And justifications continue
To sound absurd.
When children forget how to play,
And terror won't leave their eyes.
When they realise for themselves
That war makes a mockery of their lives.
What is there left to care about

When all you love is swept away?
The future held to ransom
As peace disappears
In a smoke-filled haze?
I beg to know the answers
But no answers ever come,
For war has held up truth
And shot it down with a gun.

Grace was astonished by her son's actions. He had never dared be so foolish before, and she did not understand why he had approached the hostages. No amount of going over the sequence of events in her mind added any more insight, and anguish filled her soul. That afternoon Sante had been dragged into the forest by his father, and as evening approached, Manwena, Lewis and two other boys returned, but Sante did not. Grace ached to know what had happened to him, but she dared not ask. It felt like her precious child had slipped out of her grasp into a pit of evil, and there was nothing at all she could do about it.

Was he even still alive?

Adding to Grace's turmoil was Judy's sudden turn for the worst. She had been recovering steadily from her last bout of malaria, but now the symptoms appeared to be returning and were gripping her body for the second time in a week. Grace sat by her young daughter who huddled on the floor, her head in Grace's lap and her body shivering in a sweaty fever. Grace stroked her head and wanted to sing softly to bring Judy some comfort, but her voice was cracked and broken.

Sound simply refused to escape her lips.

It was dark in the mud brick hut; only a small window allowed a single column of dim evening light to filter in. A cloth hung over the doorframe that Manwena pushed aside every time he prowled in or out. He was in a rage, but there was also a smug evil look about him that made Grace's skin crawl. It was more terrifying than his anger. She feared that at any moment his anger would be turned in her direction, and for the sake of Judy, she held her tongue.

She often felt like a small child in Manwena's presence. Like the young girl who was taken all those years ago and kept hostage by this strange and brutal man. But she wasn't a girl anymore, and she wasn't alone. She was a mother and had her children to care for. Judy needed her more than ever. So, she turned her attention away from Manwena, attempted to put her worry about Sante aside and again focused on her daughter.

Judy's forehead was moist with sweat, and yet, she huddled in a ball and shivered as if she was freezing. Grace knew her pain. Malaria hit everyone at one point or another. Most people suffered at least one bout a year. The fever, headaches, diarrhoea and stomach-aches were so common they were spoken of like one would casually mention having a sore tooth. A normal bout of malaria was usually over in five days. Grace knew how deadly malaria could be, and Judy was only a small girl. Two strikes in a row from the parasite could be the end. Grace felt physically sick at the thought of losing Judy. Anxious worry consumed her and filled the room with a thick heavy cloud of depression.

What would she do if she lost Judy?

What would she do if Sante never came back?

Could she really go on?

As evening drew closer, Manwena entered the hut and ordered Grace outside to make him some food. "But Judy is very ill," Grace protested weakly. "I should not leave her."

"I need food woman," he seethed, annoyed that she would dare insult him in such a manner.

Grace rose quietly and gently laid Judy's head on a rolled-up piece of cloth. She hurried outside and quickly gathered a few green bananas to begin making matoke. Manwena remained inside the hut with Judy, which made Grace terribly agitated and uncomfortable. She looked around and noticed her neighbour already dishing out food to her children. Without thinking twice, Grace dropped the bananas and hurried over to her.

"Excuse me, Sarah," she whispered, "but Judy's malaria has returned with force, and she is very ill again. I must be with her, but Manwena also needs food. Can I have some of your food and give some vegetables to you in exchange?"

Sarah did not hesitate and quickly handed Grace the bowl from which she was about to eat. "God, bless you," she whispered. "I will pray for Judy."

Grace took the rusty tin bowl in both hands and silently bent her head in thanks, backing away from Sarah to show her respect. Like Grace, Sarah was also abducted as a young girl and was now the mother of several children. Unlike Grace, she had come from a well-to-do family and had been educated at a good school before she was taken. The rebels had come and stolen her along with many other girls from the school dormitories as they all slept one night. Some had escaped, but Sarah remained. The road she walked was a hard one, but Grace admired her strength. She stood straight and tall, and although her face was often expressionless, Grace sensed a deep undercurrent of dignity. She had always wanted to ask Sarah about this but had never found the opportunity.

Returning to the hut, Grace swung the cloth aside and knelt before Manwena with her head down and the bowl presented to him. She hoped it met with his approval and that he did not question why it had appeared so quickly. Manwena grabbed it and had devoured half of the bowl's contents before she rose to her feet. He did not utter a word, so she returned to Judy who was still shivering on the floor. Grace sat with her feet tucked up under her and gently placed Judy's head back into her lap. She used the cloth to wipe her forehead.

Slowly, the sounds from outside began to fade as the night drew on. Grace did not sleep. She sat quietly rocking on her legs that were now so numb they felt no pain. Manwena had fallen fast asleep in the corner shortly after he had finished eating. Outside in the forest, the bush rats came out of their hiding places and scurried around in a frantic night-time frenzy of activity. Grace's thoughts swung from Judy to Sante. She hoped that he was close.

She prayed he was alive.

It was late in the night when Judy's body suddenly convulsed. An instant terror filled Grace, and she watched on helplessly while her daughter violently writhed on the floor. Grace did not know how to help her, so she cried out in horror, begging her daughter to stop. The first seizure lasted minutes and left Grace sobbing, bent double over Judy's body.

Grace did not understand what was happening. She could not see the tiny multiplying parasites that had entered Judy's brain. Gradually, the seizures became more intense and frequent. Grace sobbed as she held Judy tight and pleaded with her to stop. Deep down, she knew Judy had no control over what was happening to her, but the panic that rose within Grace held all of her good sense and reason at bay. She told herself that if Judy could just make it through until morning, things would get better.

From the onset of the first seizure, Judy's condition declined rapidly. She was no longer able to respond to any of Grace's words. Not even a nod or a shake of her head could be expressed as evidence of comprehension. Her eyes began to roll back into her head, and her neck flopped loosely over Grace's arm in between seizures. Grace's little daughter simply could not cope with the overload of parasites in her body, and the effect of the seizures seemed to damage and contort her delicate features.

Suddenly, there came the moment when it felt to Grace as if her own heart had stopped beating. Judy opened her eyes. In the dim light, Grace could see that her stare was blank. It was like she was trying to focus but could not see. An expression of pain crossed her face, and her breathing shallowed and faltered a few times. Grace held her own breath as tears rolled down her cheeks. Every muscle in her own body was tense and rigid while Judy's was becoming more and more lifeless. Then Judy let out one last breath.

Grace waited.

She did not take another.

Grace panicked and shook her gently, "Judy, breathe … breathe!" she ordered, but Judy lay motionless and still and strangely peaceful.

"No, no, no!" Grace wailed as her heart shattered into pieces and clattered to the floor of her chest. She could not believe what was happening. Her beautiful, precious little daughter, who just that morning had been well enough to help her peel the potatoes, had now left her. Forever! It was beyond her ability to comprehend.

Nothing made sense, and nothing seemed real.

Where was Sante? Grace felt a deep need to have her son close to her now as he was the only person she loved and could trust. What was more, he loved his younger sister and needed to know what had happened.

Manwena slept through the events of the night without waking. He did not see Grace pick up Judy's small limp body and carry it outside. He did not hear her cries of anguish. Grace sat on her knees in the moonlight caressing Judy's body and sobbing quietly, her fists clenched in a silent rage as she dared the sky to cave in on her. There was nowhere to go, and no one to turn to. Grace had never felt so insignificant, lost or alone.

It was Sarah who woke and heard the strange noises outside in the darkness. She immediately thought of Judy and hurriedly came out of her hut to see what had happened. She found Grace clutching her daughter, her face pressed into her chest as tears soaked the child's dirty clothes.

"Grace, I'm so sorry," she whispered, placing her arms around them both. "I'm so sorry. I'm so sorry." Tears filled her own eyes.

"Where is God?" Grace whispered accusingly. "Did He not hear us pray?"

"He is here, Grace," Sarah replied in a reassuring voice. "He loves you and He loves Judy. He carries Judy now."

Grace felt the lump in her throat tighten and could not verbalise her protest, but her mind reeled. If God were out there somewhere, why would He let any of this happen? If He could sit back and watch while Judy died, Grace reasoned that she did not want to know Him, even if He was real.

At that moment, a shadowy figured approached and both women froze in fear.

"Mama?" Sante's frightened voice whispered in the darkness. "What is it? What has happened?"

At the sound of his voice, Grace felt a heavy burden of worry fall away. He was still alive, and she wept in grateful thanks. Clutching Judy's body, Grace tried to stand, but her knees buckled underneath her, and she slumped back onto the dirt. Sante had stopped a few meters away and was beginning to realise what had happened despite his mother's incoherence.

"Oh no, no, no," he cried as he came close and stroked Judy's cold forehead. "Oh Mama, no ..."

Grace could not speak. Seeing her son's own pain further broke her up on the inside, and she could only groan as her sorrow drove knives into her heart. It was as if her grief held her locked in a prison. She wanted to scream but was terrified that if she did, she would never again be able to stop. Guilt and pain overflowed from a deep well in the core of her being, and it felt like they were seeping out through every pore of her skin. Nothing seemed to make sense. Sante felt the pain that reached out of her chest and twisted its hands around his own heart. They were united in a silent aching sorrow that blocked out all other sounds and all other forms of life.

Grace and Sante were unaware that Sarah had placed a blanket around them. They sat together, covering Judy's body with their own and wept. They wept until the sun appeared in the east and edged its way up over some distant horizon.

CHAPTER ELEVEN

REFINED BY FIRE

Simplicity -
Light -
A heart without doubt.
Surrendered
To the joy within
And released
From everything.
Needing nothing
Of this world
For it's your love
That sets
Us free.

May this life be a gift of thanks
For all that You have done for me.

Silvia's thoughts turned constantly to her family in those first few days after the horror of her abduction. She ached and grieved over the loss of them. It was an agony unlike anything she had ever known. And the disappearance of Raymond, which was without explanation, was cause for both concern and a cautious thread of hope. At least his death was not a certainty. However, her mother, father and baby Kalunga. She just knew. She had not directly seen them die. She had not been able to look. But she had heard and had felt it in her soul. They no longer breathed in the air she breathed or walked upon the same rough ground.

In her mind, however, they seemed still very much alive. Hundreds of times each day, she found herself compulsively recalling their faces. She heard their voices echoing in her mind. Some of the things they used to say replayed in her head over and over again.

Of her mother, she kept hearing one particular phrase, which now disturbed her. When she would tuck Silvia and Raymond into their bed for the night, she used to often whisper quietly to them. "I don't know much, but I know this much is true. God will never let you down."

She had always said it with such conviction that in Silvia's heart there was absolutely no room for any doubt. Up until the point of her abduction, she had happily and almost absentmindedly adopted her parents' faith as her own. She had always felt that it was their strong faith and belief in God that made them so stable. She admitted to herself now that she had also believed that their trust in God kept them safe. As if it was some secret formula that inoculated them against the horrors of war.

Other people had respected her parent's faith as well. She knew that because of the way people often came to them for help or advice. Even in the midst of turmoil, they had a steadiness and an assurance about them that had always made her feel safe.

But now? What doubts and fears hounded her? This

foundation that had always seemed so solid had turned into quicksand. For the first time in her life, Silvia began to doubt what she had been told because the belief ceased to align itself with her reality. Even though the war had raged around them, while her own family had stayed intact, she had felt protected. But here in the filth, shame and shock of this line of little children, with her family destroyed, and feeling like she was only holding on by a thread, it certainly felt like God had let her down.

Silvia desperately wanted to cling on to her mother's promise. She needed to believe it like she needed a lifeline to hold onto in a turbulent ocean, but the questions kept knocking her down. Why had God allowed this to happen? Why had He let her parents and baby brother be killed when He could have stopped it? Why was she allowed to live when they could not? Why wasn't God rescuing her?

There were no answers, but the questions left her with a feeling of terrible loneliness, desolation and a deep sickening fear.

On the fourth night after her abduction, as she tried to sleep in the welcome coolness and cover of darkness, still roped to the children beside her, Silvia had a dream. It was such a vivid dream that for a time afterwards she lay still, completely disorientated, unaware of her present surroundings and still caught up within the pictures in her mind.

In the dream, she saw her mother, father and baby Kalunga standing together on a grassy hill waving to her. She tried to run over to greet them, but her feet wouldn't move. She wanted to reach them as they all looked so happy and content. Then suddenly her mother was by her side. She was dying. Silvia was panicked, shaking her mother, and begging her desperately not to die. However, she then remembered that she had already died, that this was her mother's way of returning to give her a message. At the same moment of realisation, her mother's eyes opened, and she spoke to her.

"Be careful." Her words came soft.

"Careful of what?" Silvia had asked.

"Of life. Live well."

Silvia had woken with a fright and now sat in the darkness, silently repeating the words her mother had said to her in the dream. "Be careful of life. Live well. Live well. Live well."

A conviction and motivation she could not explain quietly began to grip her. Silvia knew that she had a choice to make, and only one option was the right one. She had to choose to live the way her parents had taught her and to hold onto her faith despite the questions and impossibility of her circumstances.

Silvia intrinsically felt that only by doing this would she have any chance of survival. For if she let go of all that she knew to be good and right and true, she would have no alternative but to open herself up to the opposite. To the evil that crowded the spaces around her, pressing in and sucking the life out of anything alive.

Right there in the darkness, in her misery, anguish and sorrow, Silvia bowed her head and began to pray.

"Help me Lord, for however long I live, to *live well*. Help me, for I cannot do it alone. Help me, for I need You. I choose to still believe that You *are* God. I don't understand why You have allowed this, but my mother taught me of Your goodness. I *want* to believe her. *Help me!* Help me to be brave as Amos is brave. Help me to care for others as Amos does. Help me not to be so afraid. Help me *please*, to live well."

CHAPTER TWELVE

A LOST CAUSE

Our dying world's suicide note:

Think I know what it would say...

"I'm sorry for leaving,

but can no longer bear

the pain you inject into me every day.

The rape, the killing,

The blood on my skin.

I'm stained crimson red

And it seeps deep within.

I've begged you for years

To end my pain,

But you blatantly disregard me

And look on with distain.

Your wars, your destruction

Your unquenchable greed,

You think you can own

This body you see.

But I am your earth

I cannot be owned,

I was created for all,

As a temporary loan.

And now slowly dying

I can no longer win,

So rather than endure,

I choose to give in."

A mos sat roped in the line of children, holding Alinta close to his chest. His little sister was badly wounded, and the deep cut was beginning to stink and fester. Alinta's clothes were soaked with a mixture of sweat and blood, and she seemed to be drifting in and out of consciousness. The extent of her blood loss was difficult to gauge, but Amos knew it was significant, and that she was fighting to keep death at bay. His heart ached as he rocked slowly back and forth in an attempt to bring her some kind of comfort and ease his own emotional agony. His heart screamed, "No, God no, please help us. Please, won't somebody help us?" Over and over, he silently begged for mercy.

A thousand questions drummed in his mind in an unstoppable rhythm that left him no time to consider what the answers might be. His head felt clouded and heavy. "Why has this happened?" his mind reeled. "Why God, why now? Why my little sisters? Why this way? Why my mother and father? Is this all my fault for going back home to them?" Amos knew it would perhaps be kinder to just let Alinta die, but he could not, and his tired, dehydrated mind told him that as long as he held her, she would continue to breathe. He could somehow give her his own strength. Tears ran down his cheeks in a silent and uncontrollable flow.

As Amos sat in the camp, he tried to focus solely on Alinta, occasionally readjusting his position to ensure that she was as comfortable as possible in his arms. He did not look up as he was terrified of being recognised by one of the rebels. If they identified him as a traitor, his life was over. Thankfully, he had not yet seen anyone he knew, and he wondered how much things had changed since he had left the rebels three years before. The rebel movement comprised many different groups that were constantly rotating, so he was eventually bound to run into someone who would recognise him. He dreaded to think what might happen if he ever saw his old commander Lwensha again.

Although Amos had been in this situation before, this time it was different. He was still terrified, but he was not the little boy he had been when he was abducted at age ten. He knew now that the rebel's mind games were all based on lies. But he also knew with certainty that his parents were dead, and there was no hope of ever seeing them again. "Oh why, God, why?" he begged to know. Thinking about it made his heart feel like a lump of dying meat inside him. He couldn't believe this had happened. He had seen them struck down with his own eyes and had felt an all-consuming rage boil up within him against the rebels who sunk them to their knees. Amos did not know how to control the horror that boiled within him. He felt like he was being choked and strangled by grief.

If it were not for his sisters, Alinta, Ruth and Juviance,

Amos knew he would not be able to go on. They were all here in this line, his three sisters and Silvia who sat beside him. Every now and then, Silvia groaned and appeared to be trying to say something, but no words ever came, and Amos was thankful. He did not want to have to talk to her. He had too many unresolved emotions when it came to Silvia, and he could not face looking into her eyes. He never thought it would end like this. The fondness he felt for Silvia, which had been harder and harder to suppress, must now be destroyed, for he knew what lay before her, and he could not stomach the thought of it. His sisters were also fated to walk that same road, and Amos could do nothing to stop it. An overwhelming sense of helplessness smothered him.

The day dragged on, and the children remained sitting in the centre of the camp with the hot sun beating mercilessly on their skulls. Amos began to observe himself as if from a distance. There they were – all bound by their hands except him. Amos sat at the end of the line with the rope around his waist. He cradled Alinta like a small baby, his arms numb from holding her limp frame for so many hours. Silvia fell asleep at some point, as did many of the other children. Amos could not. He just sat with his head down, tears falling onto Alinta's already sodden clothes.

He felt destroyed.

It was not meant to be like this.

The afternoon turned to evening as the clouds raced across the darkening sky. Amos was surprised but thankful that the rebels, who had left shortly after depositing the children in camp, had not yet returned. He hoped they had run into an ambush of army soldiers and all been killed. It was brutal, but he did not care. The camp became quiet when the sun finally set, and he listened intently to Alinta's laboured breathing. When the guards on either side of the line had fallen asleep again, he tried to speak softly to Alinta to give her some reassurance.

"Alinta, Alinta, it's going to be ok," he whispered. "I'm here with you, and I'll make sure you're ok." Amos felt like a fraud offering a promise he knew he had no power to keep, but he felt compelled to tell her anyway.

She stirred and opened her eyes for a fleeting moment. "Mama?"

Amos's heart broke. "No, it's me, Amos. Mama is at home, Alinta. It will be alright," he lied.

"Mama is here?"

"Mama is at home," he choked the words out. "We will see her again soon."

"I want Mama," Alinta cried.

"Shhh," he hushed her. "I'm here little sister. I'm here Alinta. You'll be ok."

"It hurts," she cried.

"I know. I know," Amos began crying again too. "It will be ok. Sleep now. I'm here. I won't leave you."

Alinta's eyes opened and closed once more, and then he felt her head relax and her body become limp. For a moment, he panicked and feared the worst, but then he felt her sigh and breathe in shallow short breaths. She was a fighter.

What was he going to do? His mind raced around and around in circles as he looked in hopeless desperation for a way to escape. He felt like he was pacing behind a stone wall, and though the wall never moved, with each step he continued searching for a break that he knew was not there.

Time became blurred and irrelevant as the night dragged on. Despite his physical agony from sitting in the same position for so many hours, and the deep hunger that sucked his belly in on itself, Amos did not wish the darkness away. The morning would only pull the sleeping children's nightmares from the blackness of their dreams back into reality. At some point Amos was jolted from a trance-like state by the sound of a woman's soft wailing. He scanned the darkness and thought he could locate where she sat, about fifty yards away. He could not see anything clearly but her crying continued unabated for hours. It blended into the very night itself, until eventually, Amos was not sure whether he could actually hear anything at all.

Despite his best efforts to stay awake, he eventually fell into a fitful sleep.

A sharp kick to the sole of his foot woke Amos with a fright. Pain shot up his leg into his spine, and he was immediately annoyed with himself for falling asleep. Alinta was lying across him with her head on the ground, and he quickly picked her up again.

The large man standing directly over them growled. "Get up, get up. All of you, up."

The sun was already quite high in the sky, and Amos stood on shaky legs trying hard not to let Alinta go. She remained motionless, and her breaths had become raspy and hollow.

"Remember boy," Manwena snarled angrily at him. "Drop her, and you kill her."

Amos shuddered inside.

"All of you, lie on your stomachs with your heads down," came the next order. The children appeared to hesitate as if not sure they had understood correctly. "Down," Manwena shouted.

Amos placed Alinta on the ground as carefully as he could and then lay next to her with his forehead pressed into the dirt. He tried to look sideways at Silvia and saw that the other children still had their hands tied and had to almost fall forward in order to get into the required position.

Silvia was crying.

"Listen to me carefully," Manwena said in a slow and deliberately evil way. "If you cry, if you scream, or if you make any kind of sound, you will be killed. You are going to be beaten. This is to make you tough and strong and turn you into soldiers. If you cry it means you are too weak to be a soldier. There is no room for weaklings in our army and you *will* die. Do you understand. Any sound – you die."

Half a dozen boys stood around the line of helpless and terrified children. They held whips made from tree vines and on Manwena's command began beating the children on the legs and backs. Amos was enveloped in excruciating pain. He closed his eyes and bit down on his tongue to keep from screaming. When the first sensation of pain hit it was hard not to cry out, but they all knew that Manwena's words were not just hollow threats. It was only little Alinta, woken from her semiconscious state by the beating, who made a sound.

"Mama," she sobbed and tried to struggle away from the shower of blows that were raining down from above.

Amos panicked as she cried louder. "Alinta, hush," he begged. "Please be quiet."

"Mama!" the little girl screamed.

Manwena shouted at the boys to stop. He had found his target, and that was all he needed. Besides, too much beating and the children would not be fit to walk later in the day. The group had plans to move camp and head further north to the LRA strongholds in Southern Sudan.

"You two," Manwena shouted while pointing his finger at Amos and Alinta. "Come here."

Alinta was not able to stand and lay slumped to one side, her raw wound exposed to the light. Amos tried to stand and move, but it was impossible as he was still roped to the other children. He simply stood and looked down at his feet, not daring to say a word.

Manwena looked Alinta over and examined her wound from a safe distance. Then he suddenly turned and looked directly at Amos. The boy's heartbeat quickened, and his breath caught in his throat. Manwena raised his stick and pointed at Amos in an accusing way. "What relation is this girl to you?"

Amos hesitated before replying quietly, "She is my sister."

"Ah yes, your young sister. She is weak and injured, and she did not obey my command. She must be killed. You will kill her."

Amos felt all the blood drain away from his head and heard distant sounds as the other children began to cry.

"If you do not," Manwena continued when he saw Amos recoil, "you, your sister and two other children will also be killed." Amos stood paralysed in dreadful perplexity. He could not raise his hand to Alinta. He could not take her life. He would not do it. She was his baby sister, and he knew he had to protect her. Yet, he also knew that her life was now as good as finished, and if he did not do it, others would also die.

Manwena suddenly became impatient and appeared to lose control. He pushed Amos backwards onto the dirt and started shouting, "Untie them, untie them. I've had enough of these games. Bring them here."

Suddenly, Amos was loose and being pushed towards the

brutal commander. Alinta was dragged by her arms and dumped in a crumpled heap on the ground, sobbing quietly. Amos felt frantic, so sure now that they would both be killed. There was nowhere to run to, and he was completely at their mercy.

"Them too," Manwena shouted, pointing at Silvia and Juviance. The terrified girls were also brought forward. They were whimpering and shaking with fear.

For what seemed like a lifetime but was only a matter of minutes, Manwena walked around the four ill-fated children, muttering under his breath. Some of the rebels jeered and spurred him on. They were fired up for a bloody show. Manwena's muttering could not be deciphered, but the sound of his voice was like a tap of pure, dripping evil.

Amos looked at Silvia and Juviance. Silvia looked right into his eyes, but it was as if she was on the other side of an invisible wall and couldn't get to him. She did not hold his gaze for long. Her eyes were brimming with tears.

Manwena picked up Alinta and threw her down at Amos's feet, handing him a machete. "Kill her," he shouted coldly, "or you all die."

Amos began to shake uncontrollably, and his voice cracked as he answered this horrific demand. "I ... can't. I can't. Please ..."

Many years ago, he had stood on this same cliff and been forced to jump over the edge. He had promised himself that, no matter what the consequences, he would never again kill another human being.

"Kill her or we bring three more children, and there will be seven. You will all die together."

Amos's world stopped rotating on its axis and began to fall through space as the words sunk in.

This couldn't be happening.

He glanced around at the tight circle of rebels, their faces aggressive and as cold as stone, all waiting impatiently for his decision.

The irony of being given the freedom of choice in such a situation was not lost on him.

Amos couldn't think clearly, and his throat felt like it had completely seized up. Then he saw Manwena's face, his eyes boring down on him, his head tilted, indicating that Amos needed to pick up the fallen machete and use it.

Time stood still.

Alinta lay at his feet on her side, and one hand grabbed hold of his ankle. In her own silent way, she too was begging for mercy as Amos was begging the rebels.

Mercy that he was not able to give.

"Please, no," he begged again.

"Bring three more," Manwena shouted pointing at three young girls.

"No, no." Amos said, now acting only on instinct. He picked up the machete in his right hand and noticed that it felt ten times heavier than it should. "I'll do it, if the others all stay alive." He knew it was foolish and useless to make bargains with the rebels, but he had to try.

Manwena did not flinch, and Amos did not trust him, but in that moment, there seemed no other choice. He knew they may decide to kill him as well but had to hold onto the belief that he was saving as many as possible by ending Alinta's life.

Looking down at his little sister, he saw her body heaving with tears as she let go of his ankle and tried to move away. Her eyes were full of such intense pain, Amos could feel it in the spaces between them as if it were a tangible substance. He knew what he had to do and cursed the bitter, cruel twist of fate that had brought him to this point. Alinta's eyes were swollen and blood shot, but pleading, begging, screaming for mercy.

As Amos raised the machete over his head, he shut his eyes and brought it down hard. The rebels cheered and jostled for position while he immediately fell on all fours and vomited, now not caring what they did to him.

Alinta lay still.

Amos prayed she had died instantly.

"Wait," Manwena shouted above their noise. He was looking at Alinta. "She is still breathing," he announced gleefully.

Amos looked at her in shock. He had tried to kill her in one blow, which he felt was the kindest thing he could do for her, but somehow, she had survived. She was dying, but now in the most excruciating of ways. Amos picked up the machete again and was going to end it as quickly as he could, but Manwena stopped him.

"No," he said seething. "You'd like that wouldn't you?"

Manwena pushed Amos down to the ground next to his sister who was now writhing in agony like a fish out of water. "You did this to her. What kind of brother does that?" Blood started running from Alinta's head wound into her mouth and she began to choke. "You will watch every last breath she takes," Manwena gloated. "You did this. This is your fault. You are sick! What kind of person does this? Comfort her! Comfort her!" He grabbed Amos by the back of the neck and pushed his head towards Alinta's mutilated face, now barely recognisable.

Amos wailed and sobbed as he scooped his arms under his little sister and held her tight.

Her face was contorted. One eye was closed and swollen,

but the other still looked at him. Jerks and spasms were soon replaced by a vacant stillness. Her breaths were shallow, and she occasionally coughed up blood. Amos wiped the blood away from her mouth in a vain attempt to help her.

He sat in the dirt, cradling her in his arms, his tears running freely down his face. His little sister, whom he had protected every night when they had walked from the village into the night shelters in Gulu. His little sister, who had loved to run and play freely with her friends, who was so affectionate and kind to everyone she met, who loved babies and had once whispered to him that she wanted to be a mummy herself one day. Amos's heart was shattered into a million pieces. He knew it was only a matter of time.

The gruesome scene was apparently too much for some of the rebels. Or perhaps it was just that the show was over. They began to walk away.

Before long, Amos found himself completely alone with Alinta who was now almost lifeless. The afternoon was suddenly still and quiet, and a sound ebbed its way from Amos's lungs out into the open air.

"I'm sorry. I'm so sorry," he whispered as he rocked her back and forth. "Oh little sister, I'm so sorry. Please, please forgive me. Please, forgive me. I'm so sorry."

When he had no words left in him, he began to hum a song their mother used to sing. His eyes did not leave her, and after a time, he noticed her trying to speak. He bent his head lower so that he could hear her.

Her voice was a broken whisper.

"Mama."

Amos cried again and rocked her gently. In his heart of hearts, he knew he would never forgive himself.

Could never forgive himself.

"I'm sorry. So sorry. So sorry," he repeated.

Little Alinta's eyes closed for the final time.

CHAPTER THIRTEEN

INITIATION

Dig yourself a grave

And dare to jump on in.

Cover yourself with dirt

And wait for the sky to cave in,

For death can't come too soon

In this shallow pit of hell.

Let the victims scream out loud

But it won't break this evil spell.

Sante had seen it all. The way the girl had sobbed in the line of beaten children. The machete held in Amos's hand. His soul-twisting conflict, and Manwena's delight at inflicting such brutal psychological torture. The near deathblow that left the girl mutilated but still breathing.

Sante had also seen the way he held her. The way he had wrapped his arms around her and sobbed silent into her body. The secret whispered words he spoke to her alone.

Sante had watched. He had seen.

While others walked away, disinterested when the bloodshed was over, Sante had not been able to shift his eyes away. He sat at the base of a rock on the outskirts of the camp where no one bothered him. It was a safe distance. And he cried.

Tears were uncommon to Sante for he had learnt at a young age to block any outlet of his emotions. The expression of fear or sadness usually only resulted in more pain. But as he sat and watched Amos, something within him broke. It felt like the dam wall holding back the tide began to crack open. He simply could not hold his tears at bay.

It is possible to cry in complete silence.

Sante sat with tears streaming down his cheeks as he watched Amos cradling Alinta, but he made not a sound. He thought of Judy. He had not been able to comfort her as Amos did. He ached for her loss. A raw pain he had never experienced before. Her death felt so different from the deaths of others he had witnessed. Sante did not know that death could hold such a sting. It was like a black bottomless well filled up with sorrow. Where did it end?

Perhaps watching Amos grieve was somehow giving Sante permission to release the flood of his own emotion. However, it terrified him. He didn't like how unsafe this sorrow made him feel.

Sante felt a sudden urge to escape. To jump to his feet, run into the forest and never look back. He didn't care where he went or what he might find, as surely anything would be better than his present circumstances. Even death itself – the one place where Manwena would never find him.

He looked around to assess whether such an impulsive act may even be plausible. Manwena was standing a few feet away from the hostage children talking with another commander. He suddenly looked squarely in Sante's direction as if he was somehow reading the boy's mind. Sante quickly averted his gaze. He sensed something terrible in the air and shuddered as he realised his father was plotting more malevolence.

Sante tried to look as casual as possible, lifting his eyes to gaze slowly around the camp. He watched as women carried on with their work like nothing was out of the ordinary. One gathered coal for her fire; one sat feeding her baby on a fallen log; and one squat over a cooking pot as the sun cast her elongated shadow across the ground. He could hear the sounds of birds singing in the treetops and, somewhere, the soft resonance of his mother's weeping.

He glanced back at Manwena and was relieved to see he was no longer being watched. Manwena was again talking intently to the man beside him.

Slowly, Sante began to edge his way backwards towards the tree line. He didn't know what he was going to do, but he couldn't just sit in the dirt waiting for the next round of terror like he had nothing better to do. He had to move.

Inside his chest was a rising urgency to flee.

A soul's silent scream.

The act of movement itself had always helped him to dull his pain. Only when he was motionless, did he feel the terror of his mind crowding in on him, pushing him down to the earth that wanted to swallow him whole. The only time he ever felt comfortable in stillness, was when he lay next to his mother as she told him stories. Her presence kept the demons at bay, but Sante knew he would never be allowed anywhere near her again. His only refuge had been taken away.

Before he reached the edge of the small clearing, Manwena's voice reached him loud and shocking. "Boy," he shouted. "Come here."

And that was that.

Sante did not think. His body reacted before his mind had a chance to object. He was up on his feet, running to Manwena's side like he was a fish being reeled in on a line. There was no option but to obey.

He stood in front of Manwena with his head down and his hands clasped tightly in front of him, wondering desperately whether the shea nut oil had given him away. Perhaps, Manwena had not lied when he had said it would be used to track him down. Perhaps, even his thoughts were no longer his own. Did Manwena know that he had been contemplating escape?

"Today, if you do not learn to obey like a real solider," Manwena seethed, "you and your mother will join your sister in the grave. Do you understand?"

Sante nodded, his eyes still downcast. He vaguely wondered if his father ever got tired of threatening people with death as a consequence for disobedience. Probably not.

The other commander disappeared to rouse more rebels while Manwena held Sante's shoulders squarely from behind.

"Do you see these children? *You* are going to help turn them into fighters."

"Me?" Sante asked, horrified.

"That is what I said, boy. You will learn to be a real soldier, or I will kill you myself and finally be done with your aggravation."

In the next moment, Manwena was ordering all of the children up on their feet. He separated the boys from the girls and stood Sante in front of the group of terrified hostage boys. Amos was among them.

"Today is your initiation," Manwena announced. "Brace yourselves. Today, if you are lucky, you will become soldiers. If you survive, you will become fighters for the greatest army in the world."

Sante was pushed alongside Amos and the other boys into the forest. He turned briefly and caught a glimpse of Alinta's crumpled body as it lay where Amos had been forced to leave her. Now peaceful in death's embrace.

Manwena and a number of other soldiers shouted, taunted and beat the children randomly with sticks as they walked, keeping them in a tight huddle. When they stopped, Manwena silently bade Sante not to move another step by tightly placing his big hand around the boy's thin neck. His grip was like iron. Sante looked into the terrified eyes of the boys as they stood whimpering, still roped together. Evans moved forward and began untying the rope, while the other rebels encircled the group to ensure that none of the children tried to escape.

A moment later, the hostage girls arrived on the scene. They were crying and begging for mercy. Sante's heart sank even lower. Manwena released his grip and received a pot of water from one of the younger rebel boys. As the men and boys stood watching, Manwena began the initiation ritual that each girl had to endure.

"This is a water ritual," he said in a voice that was soft but menacing and made the girls whimper. "You must not make a sound. You are going to be initiated into our resistance movement. Your old life is gone. You will be honoured if you join the militia as a wife of a rebel commander. If you cry out, your lips and your nose will be cut off, and we will cast you out to die slowly all by yourself. This is your first test. You do not want to fail."

Manwena then pushed Sante forward and told him to strip the girls' clothing until they were bare from the waist up. There was no room for hesitation now, as the evil lurking in the air seemed to be suffocating every living thing. Sante moved to obey. He pulled the girls' clothing from them, exposing their immature breasts and dark velvety skin. He did not look into their faces anymore, and his actions were methodical and robotic until all stood shivering in a silent huddle, staring at the ground. Evans moved forward and roughly pulled the girls into a straight line facing Manwena.

Sante backed away with his head down until he stood with the other rebels. He did not want to see this initiation. His head was noisy and chaotic despite the strange silence that lingered in the air. Images of Judy flashed into his mind, and he wondered where his mother was. What would happen to Grace now that Judy was gone, and he was as good as dead?

Manwena began chanting and moving along the line of girls, flicking water on each bare chest as he went. Although the water did not hurt as it landed, the girls winced as though they were being stung with acid that burned their skin. The droplets glistened in the sunlight and slid over the curves of their bodies.

Sante sensed a growing excitement among the rebels as they stood silently watching. Just as they had been instructed, the girls did not move or cry out. They remained focused on the ground, their expressions vacant and hollow. Following the water, Manwena produced a small whip. He did not stop chanting and the noise penetrated Sante's head like a hammer. The whip struck each girl's chest and shoulders several times as he moved along the line. Over and over, he walked up and down, pushing them to breaking point. Sante wondered if his sole aim was to make one of them cry just so that he could relish another killing, but the girls somehow remained strong.

Following the water ritual, the abducted children were

grouped together again. This time, they were ordered to stand in a circle. Manwena stood in the centre with the rebels fringing the edge so that none could escape. "From now on you will call me Teacher," Manwena stated. Then with shocking frankness he added, "You are too many here. Some of you will be killed." Sante froze and the children looked horror-struck. "The weakest and youngest must die. The rest will do the killing. You will learn what it is to take life. You will learn to be soldiers for our resistance movement. We will find out who among you should be killed and who should live."

Sante looked to the sky and silently begged it for mercy. He did not know what else to do. His knees trembled as he anticipated Manwena forcing him to put an axe through a child's skull as he had just witnessed. Would he do it or would he resist and let himself be killed? His mind was turbulent as the horror of having to make such a decision sank into his bones. He looked at the innocent faces of the children before him. They did not deserve any of this.

He wished he had the power to stop it.

"Here is the boar," Evans broke into the circle.

Before the children stood a runty looking pig that squealed and twisted its head from side to side, trying to break free from Evan's grip. The boy held it firm with a rope around its neck, and a moment later, upended the animal so that its feet skidded out from under it, and it lay on its back looking upwards. It immediately began to squirm hard, trying to force itself upright again, but Evans sat squarely on top of the terrified animal's belly and pinned its skinny legs to the ground. The squealing intensified.

"Each of you is to spit into the mouth of this boar," Manwena shouted above the noise. "It will absorb all of the evil that is within you and take it into its own belly. This will cleanse you from your evil spirits. You must be cleansed before you can join our resistance movement."

One of the girls was pushed forward from behind. She hesitated and then walked slowly forward to where the pig lay, its mouth now held open and helpless by another rebel boy as Evans held it down. Sante could see her attempting to gather enough saliva from her dry mouth to spit as she bent over the animal's jaws before backing away again.

"Hurry up," Manwena said as if they were under some intense time pressure. "Everyone must spit. Hurry up."

Quickly, the children moved forward and, one at a time, they spat into the pig's mouth. When they were finished Manwena turned to Sante. "And you," he pointed his long, bony finger into Sante's face. "You must be cleansed in order to move forward and become a real soldier. You spit too."

Sante moved quickly to do as he was told. As he looked down into the pig's mouth, he could see the animal's filthy teeth, and its tongue waving about in frenzy. He quickly spat and saw the glob of saliva land squarely on the pig's tongue. Disgust filled him as he backed away.

"Now." Manwena's voice stopped him. Sante looked around and saw his father holding a machete out to him. "Kill it. This pig is now unclean." He looked up as he spoke. "It is full of all the demons from your bodies. It needs to be killed so you can be free. Sante will slaughter it for us."

Sante looked back at the pig that now lay motionless under Evan's weight as if it was trying to avoid drawing attention to itself. Evans ran his hand across the animal's throat, indicating how Sante should carry out the grizzly task.

He took the machete from his father's hand, crouched next to the animal and placed the end of the sharp blade on the bore's throat. As he slid the machete back towards himself, he pressed down hard and felt the pig thrash in sudden pain as the blade cut through its skin. Blood began to pour forth from the wound as Sante finished the task. He stood up when the blade had made a full incision into the pig's throat.

Death came surprisingly quickly.

Evans pulled the dead animal up by its front legs to the fire that had been set hours earlier and was now burning hot over red coals.

"This is the final part of this important ritual to purify you from evil spirits," Manwena said as Evans hauled the carcass onto the coals. They all stood in silence and watched it burn. Sante looked up at Manwena and noticed how the scar on his face seemed to come alive in the light of the fire. The red glow danced across his face and held him in its hot embrace. The smell of burning hair and flesh made Sante's stomach turn with hunger. The children were not permitted to turn their eyes away from the flames as the pig's flesh roasted.

Another senior commander appeared and began randomly pushing and shoving the children. He held a jar in one hand, and Sante watched as the rebels began chanting and singing. Manwena took the jar and began spreading Shea nut oil over the children's small bodies while the other commander continued pushing the children hard. The oil was placed in the sign of a cross, and the white sticky residue remained like glue on their skin.

One of the girls began to whimper. This was the weakness they had been searching for. Manwena pulled her to the side. The girl collapsed onto the ground and began to cry.

"This is a useless girl. This girl is not strong. She is weak and pointless. Sante, you will have first honour of beating her."

Sante knew there was nothing he could do. He willed the girl to stop crying as he took a large stick from his father's hands.

One.

Two.

Three.

Four.

He counted. He did not look at her.

He swung slow.

Five.

Six.

The girl stopped crying.

Seven.

"Stop," Manwena shouted. "Now you." He pointed to another captive child. A girl walked forward and took the stick from Sante. She began beating. Sante lost count.

"Stop," Manwena yelled again. "You."

One by one, the children were instructed to beat the girl. She no longer made any sound. Sante wondered if she was already dead. The rebels did not seem to think this was relevant as the beating continued until all of the children had swung fair and square at the girl.

Finally, it was over.

Looking among the children, Sante noticed they had already begun to adopt the expressionless vacant faces of rebel soldiers.

"Now that you are cleansed, you may eat," said Manwena. "But from now on, you may never eat unless given permission. If you prove yourself worthy, you will be taught how to become a soldier. Some of you will not be good soldiers and will have to be killed. If you try to escape, we will hunt you down. When we find you, we will kill you, together with any person who may be with you. You cannot hide. The Shea nut oil on your bodies will help us to track you. You cannot keep secrets from our movement. So, if any of you are thinking about escaping, be warned. You will be killed, and you will be an example to all the others. No one escapes from the LRA.

A morsel of food and water was brought to each of them as Manwena spoke. The children received nothing but sour berries and bananas while the soldiers tore strips off the pig and feasted on the roasted flesh.

"Girls," Manwena spoke again, "You will now be given to one commander. You must do whatever you are told and never leave your commander's side unless instructed. There is no other life for you now. If you live, you live only for your new militia family. You must not think of your past. You must only think how you can serve the resistance movement. It is all you will ever know."

Manwena's voice drowned on, lecturing the children on aspects of their new life. As he ate his fill and ranted on and on, Sante noticed his eyes inspecting the young girls. He had first pick and was clearly deciding which would be the best one.

Sante shuddered and looked at the sky. It seemed empty and formless, a lot like the inside of his own dying heart.

CHAPTER FOURTEEN

MORE THAN SURRENDER

Women bleed
like the earth that grieves
for her children.
Crimson blood
drips slowly down the wall.
You watch it;
wait for the drip to fall.

One drop
Sacred
A sacrifice that no one knows about;
A love that no one sees.
A woman's blood
shed for freedom,
in a world that fails
to deliver her
from every man's greed.

Her beauty is tamed,
her will surrendered,
but her soul flies free.

Blood
one drop
falls off the wall
and into the deeper spaces
that only a woman
can see.

Grace sat in the darkness of the hut clutching her daughter's small body. Time passed in a meaningless blur. She was lost in the chaos and confusion of her thoughts, as streams of tears ran down her cheeks. Heaving sobs that came in waves. They would settle for a time, only to return again with full force. Chaos reigned.

The only thing she trusted was her own breath that rose and fell in a steady rhythm. She whispered softly into the silky nape of Judy's neck, letting her lips press against her daughter's cold skin. Eyes closed and head bent, she wept.

Had she looked up, the light in the cracks above would have told her it was already afternoon, but she did not notice. She did not see anything but Judy. She did not hear anything but the sound of her own crying. She could not release her daughter from her grasp and crouched in the corner with Judy in her lap.

In life, Judy had come into her arms and sat on her lap so many times. She had been secure there, and Grace wondered if she still needed to feel that safety. Was her spirit lingering, clinging to her side, or was she flying free over the land? Grace's mind could not grasp death's finality or suddenness in one whom she had held so close and loved so much.

The same old questions nagged at her mind. If God was real, and as compassionate as Sarah had described, why would such pain exist? Wouldn't an all-powerful, all-loving God put an end to this misery? Still some flicker of hope burned within her. Perhaps, it was hope for Judy. Hope that she was not really lost forever. Hope that she would see her again, one day soon.

In the outpouring of her grief, Grace found herself whispering her prayers aloud. They came in snatches between her tears. They came spontaneously and offered an unexpected if fleeting peace.

"Oh God, my heart is breaking. I am lost and ripped apart."

Raw tears ran like open wounds down her cheeks and onto Judy's skin.

"I am at the brink of death myself from the pain in my soul. My life is worthless and nothing."

Pulling Judy in close she hugged her tight.

Time. Meaningless.

The waves of sorrow crashed higher over her head, threatening to drown her with each tumbling rush of emotion. Then with the lull between the waves came an unnerving calm. Its stillness frightened her, but she somehow used the calm to continue whispering prayer. Her hopes and fears were offered into the silence around her as she willed God to hear. Desperately hoping that this greater power might somehow help her find a way out of the torrent she was drowning in. She struggled to breathe.

"God, if You care …" she cried. "If You dare to care for one as worthless as me, then carry my silent ache on the wind. Carry it over the land and over the sea to mothers who live in a different world. Let them see my pain. Let them know that she was their child too. My Judy, the daughter I love to the depths of my soul, was daughter of all. She was innocence in the midst of war. She was laughter that sprang out of this river of tears. She was the heartbeat of this land whose body lies ripped to shreds. She was the sweet morning dew that settles on both the living and the dead. My gift. My daughter. The one who captivated all of my heart." Her voice broke with each utterance, but the outpour continued.

"Her smile and the sparkle in her eyes were never extinguished by the horrors of this life. Oh God, carry her soul on the wind. Let it settle on the treetops of another place where she can see how life should have been. Where she can watch children playing without fear, and she can silently sing with them their childhood songs. Let her know that she deserved a life that was beautiful. Let her run through fields of flowers, laughing until she can run no more. Let her lie down in the sun and look up into the deep blue above and know that she is loved. She is loved more than she will ever know. Let that warm sun stroke her skin and soothe the rawness of her lost life. Let it soothe my loss. Oh God, I cannot bear this pain. Take my life too, and I will only thank You. I will know You are real if You let me escape from this endless suffering. I cannot live with this pain."

Grace's prayer was interrupted when the door swung open, and Manwena barged into the hut. She watched him trying to readjust his eyes to the dim light as he looked around for her. When he saw her huddled in the corner with Judy, a look of disgust and rage ripped across his face. It twisted his features in a grotesque way that made Grace shiver.

"What are you doing? Get out. Get out of here. You have done nothing all day. I need some food."

Grace could not stop weeping and her body refused to move. "If he kills me now," she thought, "at least the torture is over. I can be with Judy."

"Stupid woman," Manwena stormed over to her and grabbed one arm, dragging her to the door. Judy's body fell to the floor in a crumpled heap.

"No!" Grace heard the scream come out of her mouth, but she felt so far away. "Leave me. Leave me."

Manwena turned and struck her across the jaw. The force of the blow pushed Grace's head backwards. "What is wrong with you?" he asked as if her behaviour was irrational and beyond his ability to comprehend.

Grace turned instinctively towards the doorway as another silhouette darkened the entrance. Sante? No, just one of the hostage girls who stood with her head down and her hands grasped tightly together. Grace immediately sensed that she was trying desperately not to cry. Manwena let Grace go and grabbed the girl's small shoulder.

"This is my new wife," he snapped. The young girl stiffened, and Grace noticed a small trickle of urine running down her right leg. She was terrified. Forgetting her own grief for a moment, Grace's heart went out to her. She wanted to hold the girl tightly in her arms and give her the strength she would need to survive the brutality of Manwena. She wanted to grab her hand and run with her into the bush not stopping to look back. She wanted to scream out this injustice into the sky, but instead she simply averted her eyes.

"Prepare me some food woman," Manwena commanded. "If you have not prepared some food for me soon, then that is the end, and you will be killed. I will kill you myself. I am sick and tired of you."

Grace knew this was no idle threat, and in the next few

seconds, her mind swam with the choice that lay before her. She had been given a way out of this suffering. While Manwena had threatened to kill her before, she had never considered it an option – always doing everything in her power to appease his anger. For the first time, she realised that she could let him kill her and finally be free from his abuse. She recognised that she was not afraid of death, even though she did not understand it. There was even a part of her that was curious to know what it would be like. But then her thoughts turned to Sante, and in her heart, she knew that now was not the time to leave him. She looked up again at the hostage girl and saw the terror in her eyes.

Suddenly, Grace knew that this decision was not hers to make and in that moment something unexpected happened within her soul. As her fear of death evaporated, she found a newfound courage, and a sense of freedom welling up within her. There was anger too, for the stolen years and for the enormity of her loss. For the first time in her life, she looked Manwena directly in the eyes and held his gaze.

"I will prepare your food," she said coldly before pushing past him through the hut door without a backward glance at the terrified girl. As she gathered her grains and vegetables, she heard Manwena pulling the girl further into the hut, but Grace did not turn around. She did not want to see the child again until she knew she was a survivor. Her grief over Judy was too raw, and she knew she could not cope with any more.

Sarah appeared at Grace's side the moment Manwena and the girl disappeared.

"Let me help you," she offered, taking some of the green vegetables from Grace's hands. "I have some matoke if you need it."

"Keep it for your children. They need it more than that man does. He will eat what I prepare, and if he is still hungry, I will deal with the consequences. I will not take food from your children."

"But my children are fed."

Grace looked at her friend, and her eyes held a mixture of thankfulness and deep sorrow. "Then they will eat it tomorrow. But if you want to help me, can you fill this pot with water from the stream?"

"Yes," Sarah replied before taking the pot from her hands and hurrying away.

Once again, Grace was left to her own thoughts. She suddenly wished Sarah had stayed. She would have distracted Grace from her angst and grief. Judy was everywhere she turned. Just a few days ago, she had been the one to help her with the food. She would sit by her side quietly watching and learning from her mother. Sometimes, she sang softly in a voice so sweet it melted Grace's heart. Her tears flowed and blurred her vision as she tore up the leaves and prepared a few green bananas for the pot. The fire was out and so she stood on shaky legs and walked around behind the hut to search for more firewood. She needed small kindling and then some bigger sticks to keep it going. Where was Sante when she needed him?

As she rounded the hut, she stopped short and listened to the sound of laboured breathing coming from inside. She thought she could also hear soft crying and knew only too well what Manwena was putting his new wife through. The hostage girl had looked so fragile and young.

Grace tried to push the noise away.

She busied herself with collecting sticks before returning to her cooking pot. Her hands worked quickly and skilfully, using flint to light the fire. Its flames were dancing in no time. The warmth of it soothed the chill in her bones but was not enough to distract her from the commotion inside the hut. Her mind would not stop imagining what Manwena might be doing to the girl.

There had been a few previous occasions when Manwena had taken a new wife, but those young girls had not survived one night with him. Even though trying to stay detached, Grace could not help from hoping that this young girl was a fighter. She did not think her heart could deal with any more loss on this particular day.

Sarah returned from the stream with a pot full of water. She did not say a word, but Grace saw a hesitation in her eyes when she heard the noises coming from inside the hut. Grace merely shook her head in silent acknowledgment. Sarah placed the pot near Grace's feet and handed her some cooked beans she had collected from her own hut on the way through. Grace could not muster the energy to protest.

"Eat these yourself, Grace. You need food as much as he does. You need to regain your strength."

"But I …"

"Please."

Grace did as she was told, eating the beans slowly as she prepared Manwena's food. Sarah sat beside her in silence, and her presence somehow gave Grace comfort. To be in the presence of a person who did not seek her harm was sweet relief. The afternoon sun was beginning to creep low in the trees, turning their leaves golden and hinting that the day was almost over. For Grace, the night could not come soon enough. Manwena would sleep, and she would be left in peace with her thoughts. Her beloved Judy again stole into her mind and lingered there, waiting for Grace to finish her chores.

"There is talk that we will move again," Sarah whispered, interrupting her thoughts. Grace looked up as Sarah continued, "I overheard some of the men talking about it this afternoon. They fear another attack by the army after the last raid. Our camp may have been detected. They were talking about moving north again, closer to Sudan or maybe even into Sudan."

"Who did you hear this from?"

"Aaron and Lewis." Aaron was Sarah's husband, and like Manwena, a commander of considerable power within the ranks of the LRA.

"Are you sure you heard correctly?"

"Yes, positive. I was in the hut and heard them through the door. They didn't know I was there."

"It's just that we've been here for some time now," Grace objected.

"I know. I was beginning to become comfortable too. Just be prepared for a sudden move. And who knows, maybe the food supply will be better further north." Sarah was ever the optimist.

"I can't go," Grace stated.

"What do you mean?"

"I can't leave this place. I can't leave Judy."

"Grace," Sarah whispered in a shocked tone. "They will kill you if you refuse. Judy's body needs to be buried. She is not here any longer. She is free."

"I'm not so sure," replied Grace looking around as she started to cry. "I feel her everywhere. I feel her presence so strongly that I wonder whether she has really died at all. Then I see her body, and I know it's true, but I still feel that she lingers here. I can't leave her."

Sarah's eyes looked deeply into her friend's, and a tear ran down her cheek. "She was beautiful Grace. She was such a beautiful girl. But she would not want you to stay and be killed. She will go with you inside your heart wherever you go."

Grace broke down and again wept in heaving sobs as Sarah tried in vain to comfort her. Her crying was beginning to attract unwanted attention from some of the younger rebels, and it made Sarah nervous.

"Hush Grace, please be calm. Save your tears. Please, please be calm. You will cause us both trouble."

Grace struggled to regain control and straightened her back. She cocked her head sideways, noticing that the noise inside the hut had ceased. If Manwena came out and discovered her talking to Sarah, he might unleash his fury on both of them.

"Go, go. I will be fine. Let me finish preparing this food before Manwena comes," Grace whispered.

Sarah must have sensed his looming presence too for she did not argue and immediately stood to leave. Not moments later, Manwena emerged from the hut. His clothes were strewn sideways as if he had put them on in a great hurry. The army greens that he normally took such care to tuck into place looked shabby and dirty in the fading light. He stood, blocking the doorway with his muscular frame, his square jaw set in an expressionless manner.

"Where is it?" he questioned, not even bothering to look at Grace. She hurriedly put the prepared food into his bowl and bent low on one knee, holding the food above her head with her eyes fixed on the ground. She waited for the blow, but instead felt him lift the food and walk away. Daring to look up, Grace watched as he sauntered over to a group of men that were sitting conversing under a tree. Aaron was among them, and she concluded that with

Manwena's presence, they would probably make decisions about when and where to go next. Manwena sat with his back to her, so Grace quickly moved inside the hut to see if the young girl was still alive.

She entered the room with hesitation, allowing her eyes to adjust to the darkness. Judy's body was still slumped in the corner where she had left her, but now another body also lay on the floor. The girl was badly bruised, beaten and hurting, but she was breathing.

She was alive.

Her face was buried in her hands, and she trembled violently, trying to draw her legs into her chest as Grace approached.

"Hush child," Grace whispered as she gently stroked her forehead. She noticed blood on the girl's torn skirt. "Hush, hush. You will be ok. Everything will be ok." Her words sounded hollow and empty, but Grace did not know what else to say. She knew the terror the girl was feeling and felt compelled to somehow reassure her. "Let me get some water for you to wash," she suggested beginning to rise.

"Please," came a tiny cry. "Please don't leave me. He might come back and kill me, like he killed the other girl."

Grace looked at Judy's body and sighed deeply when she realised the incorrect assumption the girl was making. She never thought she would have to defend Manwena's innocence, but now, for the girl's sake, she had to. "No, he did not kill her," she whispered reassuringly. "Judy was my daughter. She died from malaria." Grace wanted to cry but tried desperately to remain composed. "What is your name?"

"Silvia," came her raspy reply. She had not moved from her crumpled position on the floor.

"Silvia, my name is Grace. I was abducted many years ago, and I know your pain. I know your fear. Just be as strong as you can be. You must be strong. Only the strong survive in this place."

Silvia began to weep again, and Grace slipped her hand over her back and tried to offer her comfort. They sat for a very long time together in the hut as the evening closed in around them. Manwena did not return, and after a time, Silvia drifted into a fitful sleep. Grace returned to Judy's body. She too fell asleep as she lovingly stroked her daughter's cold, clammy hair.

CHAPTER FIFTEEN

WE GO ON

Beauty and freedom

We are taught to adore,

But when ripped away

What is left at the core?

What lies beneath

This empty shell?

Now broken and crumpled;

A new living hell.

Is there any foundation

Holding us strong;

That despite the chaos

Life can go on?

Or do we crumple as well

Into shame and despair,

Seeking deadly revenge

That reaps more disrepair?

Surely there is an answer

And an end to this pain;

Surely someone, somewhere

Can somehow explain.

Amos had watched with a heavy heart as the rebels divided the girls among themselves and took them away. Silvia and his sisters were gone now, and Amos was struggling to believe that any of this was real. He felt like he was living in a thick fog of consuming emptiness and could not see anything clearly. His heart physically ached inside his chest as he sat rocking back and forth in the dirt. Eyes downcast. Tears threatening to fall.

In his imagination he saw himself grabbing hold of a gun and killing as many rebels as he could before they mowed him down. He wished he had found a way to escape while they were all still roped together in the line. Now that the children had been separated, there was no real hope of reprieve.

Although the initiation ceremony was over, Amos knew that it would be at least a month before they were considered soldiers. They would remain on the outskirts of the group until all their training and grooming was complete. Those who survived the coming weeks would finally be issued with their army commando clothes that were usually acquired from dead UPDF soldiers. These clothes became like a second skin to every rebel soldier. They rarely came off. Most appeared to wear them with a sense of pride, but Amos had no desire to put those clothes back on his body again. He equated them with violence and bloodshed and knew he was capable of the unspeakable when he wore the mask of a soldier.

The afternoon sun was beginning to dip low in the sky as another day drew to a close. The sun's intensity ebbed away, making space for the cool night air, as its colour turned deep orange and cast rich golden shadows through the trees. Amos sat facing the sun, watching it sink lower and lower until only its afterglow remained. He wondered how such beauty could exist amid such grief.

This was his land, full of glorious sunsets, tangled forests and open grassy plains. These were his people, set with dark eyes, velvet skin and strong, stocky limbs that made them masters of their dwelling places. As Amos watched the people of the camp move silently about, he felt more and more like an alien. He looked like they did, but everything within him wanted to rebel against the war that held them all hostage. He felt like he was somehow out of place. He was not meant to be here. He was not meant to live this life. He was not meant to endure such grief and mental anguish. He was never meant to see his parents killed or to have held his baby sister in his arms while she struggled to take her last breath. He was never meant to be a killer or to be sitting here in this place at the mercy of men he did not understand.

The only thing he did understand was fear. It lurked in every crevice and occupied every vacant space. Not even sleep was free from it as it arrogantly pushed its way into his dreams. Everyone here was driven by fear. People lost their lives because of it, and fear pushed others to commit horrible atrocities that would haunt them for the rest of their days. Fear was like a tidal wave that dragged them all along in the force of its undertow. There was no escape.

Drifting in and out of a semi-conscious cloud that filled the spaces of his mind, Amos sat in the dirt with his knees bunched up at his chest. He rocked backwards and forwards in a monotonous motion, his small buttocks creating a groove in the soft brown soil. He sat by the smouldering remains of the fire that had been lit earlier that day to roast the sacrificial pig. Its contents had since been devoured but not by Amos. His hungry belly groaned, and he became a bound-up ball of misery. Fear and guilt attacked him from every angle seeking to take him captive, and Amos fought to hold onto his sanity and keep the evil forces at bay.

"You killed your sister!" his guilt screamed at him in an ear-piercing voice that made Amos shudder. *"You lifted your hand and smashed her skull. You are evil. You are sick. How could you kill her? How will you ever live with yourself? What would you see now in your mother's eyes, if you had to tell her what you did? She would never accept you now!"*

"You will be killed yourself," seethed the fear that crept under his skin. *"They will string you up and torture you as soon as they realise that you were one of them. You know what happens to people who try to escape. You have seen it with your own eyes. They will cut you open and let you try to stuff your own insides back into your body as they watch you die."*

Amos sobbed as he rocked back and forth in the dirt, his mind in agony. He tried in vain to battle his demons. "I didn't want to kill her," he reasoned pathetically. "I had no choice. They would have killed more of us if I hadn't."

"Fool!" screamed his guilty conscience. *"What a fool you are. They were just bluffing, playing their evil games with you. They wouldn't have killed others because the girls are valuable wives, and the others can become soldiers. Why would they bother to capture so many if they were just going to kill them all?"*

"No," he objected weakly. "No, it's not true."

"You know you are one of them. You have always been one of them. The only way you can escape me is to join them," the fear whispered. *"You could be a great commander and have many wives if you played this game the right way. It is only a game after all. And out here, evil always wins."*

"Our lives are not games." Amos could feel a righteous anger welling up within him. He tried to block out the sound of the voices and focus on something else. "I won't give in. I didn't give in last time, and I won't give in this time."

"But you already have given in," laughed his guilt. *"You have already done what you swore you would never do again. You killed the one you loved the most. Think what else you are capable of. You are one of them already. Just accept the fact that this is where you are meant to be."*

"No, no, no," but as Amos tossed and turned in inner turmoil, he knew he had nothing to argue. None of his justifications withstood the battle. He had crossed the line and could not go back. A deep depression descended upon his whole being. There was no changing what he had done. Should he just accept the fact that he was one of them or should he continue trying to hide the truth from himself?

As he sat in the middle of this mental battle, the night sky turned from deep blue to an inky blackness that mirrored the loneliness and despair in his soul. The moon rose beautiful and clear above the canopy of trees, and the cool night air held a peace that Amos could not grasp hold of. Everything was quiet, and the stillness seemed to beckon him to rest, but he could not. He continued to rock silently back and forth as the hours dragged on and on.

By the time the sun had begun to rise in the sky, Amos was already awake. He had eventually fallen into a fitful sleep sometime after midnight but had constantly been woken by the horror of his nightmares. In the end, he had decided that it was safer to remain awake and avoid the blackness of his dreams, so he had fought sleep by poking the dying embers in the fire, keeping it alive by offering all the small twigs he could find to feed its unquenchable appetite.

His eyes were heavy, and every cell in his body ached from exhaustion. Every time he closed his eyes, he looked straight into the face of little Alinta as she lay dying. It was as if she now occupied the space behind his eyelids.

As soon as people began stirring, Amos sat himself upright. He immediately noticed that a rope had been tied around his ankle and then looped around a nearby tree, but he could not remember when this had happened. One by one, the other hostage children were brought out of different huts and tied into the same rope.

His sisters came first.

They looked shell-shocked and weary, as if they too had not slept. Both Ruth and Juviance were given to an older commander who was of high rank in this particular rebel militia division. Amos was relieved to see that they were both still alive. They stared at him with desperate eyes, as if silently begging him to do something, but Amos looked away in helpless depression. He could not be the hero they needed.

Silvia was brought out next. Manwena held her by the hair and pushed her along in front of him. He shook her head roughly as they walked, and Amos knew she was battling tears. Manwena roped her into the line behind Juviance and walked away without a word.

The remaining girls and boys were brought out one by one, and Amos counted eleven children in all. He suddenly realised that he alone had been left by the fire all night. A horrible sense of foreboding crept up his spine. Had someone recognised him? Were they going to make an example of him to the others of what happens to traitors? He sensed that something was happening. Everywhere he looked people were moving in silence. They were packing up their few possessions and destroying the fireplaces so that they were hardly recognisable. A woman approached them with some cooking pots and pointed to Silvia.

"You will carry these," she ordered. "Do not lose or break them. If you do ..." She slid her finger across her throat without saying another word.

Silvia picked up the items and held them close to her chest as if protecting them with her life.

"We must be moving," Amos said aloud to no one in particular as the woman walked away.

"Where?" Ruth asked turning her head towards him in the hope that he might know the answer.

"Who knows," he replied. "The rebel militia is often on the move."

No more words were spoken as the children silently watched the rebels slowly remove all trace of their presence from the camp. Amos knew that such care was only taken when the commanders suspected their camp had been found. Were the army close by and tracking them down? Amos shuddered to think that they might be heading up to Sudan. The closer they came to the border, the more likely they were to meet other rebel movement factions, making the risk of his detection increasingly certain. He tried to tell himself that it didn't matter. That he would be better off dead anyway, but still some faint insistent drum beat out a rhythm of survival within him. He did not know where it came from or why it came, but it seemed that nothing could drive it away.

Another woman approached carrying some potatoes wrapped in a thin blanket. She noted that Amos was probably the most able bodied and thrust them towards him without a word.

"Please," he heard himself saying before she retreated. "We have hardly eaten or had anything to drink for days. Please help us. If we are walking today and have to carry things, we at least need some water."

The woman looked as though she was about to ignore him completely, but she hesitated at the last moment. She turned her head and held his stare for a few seconds before nodding as she walked away. A flicker of hope rose within Amos. His mouth was so dry that his tongue felt like it was starting to crack open, and he could smell the dew that had settled on the ground overnight. In a futile effort, he tried to inhale its wetness through deep breaths, but he gave up when he broke into a painful, raspy cough that made his chest and throat ache. He felt little Ruth's delicate hand come to rest between his shoulder blades in silent compassion. It was something his mother might have done had she been there. Her touch sent Amos's fragile emotions spiralling downhill once again. He tried desperately to drag himself away from the mental images of his mother and away from the canyon of blackness that was seeking to envelop him.

"Did you eat last night, Ruth?" he whispered when he had regained his composure.

"No," came her quiet reply. Amos looked at her face as she turned it away, trying to hide her silent tears. His heart was laden with heaviness for her pain.

After a time, the woman returned to the group of stranded children. They looked as if they were standing on a tiny island that was about to be completely consumed with water. Backs to each other, up against the lone tree, they stood. Defences ready, expecting the worst. When the woman held out a tin full of water, initially no one moved.

"Come on," she waved it impatiently. "Drink."

Amos took the rusty tin and bowed his head in thanks. He pressed the edge of it to Ruth's lips and let her have a few sips before offering it to Juviance and then Silvia. One by one, the children drank until the tin returned to Amos, and he inhaled the remaining dregs. The water was gritty and tasted like the ground, but Amos was thankful all the same. He looked closely at the woman's face as he handed it back to her empty. She was small and wiry, her face expressionless. He wanted to press her for food but felt his courage waver. She must have seen the unspoken question in his eyes.

"I know you are hungry," she said. "Everyone is hungry. You must be patient. Do not anger the commanders by asking for food."

He heeded her warning but felt his heart slump. This painful emptiness in his stomach was something that he did not want to get used to all over again. The woman walked away, and he watched as she returned and continued to sort her few possessions carefully, placing them one by one into sackcloth. When everything was assembled to her satisfaction, she lifted it onto her head and walked over to where a group of women were standing. They were silent.

It was not long before the children were once again being forced to step timidly off their precarious island and into the unforeseeable dangers of the forest's ocean. They were pulled by one of the rebels who held the rope tightly in his hand and strode off at an alarming rate. Amos immediately tripped and fell over Ruth who had failed to gain enough speed. Both ended up on the ground, and the rebel at the lead was yanked to a halt.

"Get up, get up," he shouted raising his machete towards them. Both began scrambling madly, and Amos, who was on his feet first, lifted Ruth off the ground with one hand, his other still clutching the parcel of raw sweet potatoes. The rebel glared at him without saying another word.

As they moved forward again, Amos felt a growing trepidation. He guessed that they were heading north and knew that the further they went, the deeper they would get into rebel territory. Time became a slow painful blur as they walked. There was no rest. No food. No water.

The forest began to subtly change in texture until the tall trees were all but gone, replaced by grasslands and wide-open places. The harsh sun beat down, hitting the tops of their heads as if attempting to reduce them all to midgets. It sapped them of their energy and will.

Amos wanted to cry. He wanted to scream and wave his arms at the sky and beat the earth until his hands bled. He wanted to shout that this was not fair. He wished for a miracle. A sign that all would be well, and that the rebel movement would get what was due them in retribution. He hated the evil that lurked in the air and wished he could sob like a baby clinging to its mother's dried up breast.

But he could not. It wasn't even an option. All he could do was place one foot forward and hope that the other foot would follow. And so on. And so on. And so on. One foot in front of the other without ceasing, until the day was done.

CHAPTER SIXTEEN

NEW DAWN

There is a dark web forming,

A black cloud brewing,

That hangs heavy and low against my skin.

There is a terror rising

Full of anger and sorrow,

And it creeps up silently to seep within.

We are the children of war;

We are the soldiers of night;

We are the frontline mowed down

In the battle we fight.

We are young, but so old,

For we've seen it all,

And while the world turns away

We will die where we fall.

There is a terrible ache,

A dense fog building

That grows thick and moist as the night closes in.

I dream of my mother

And her eyes that have loved me.

Will I ever be forgiven for this terrible sin?

We are forced to plunder,

To fight and to kill.

We are forced to look on

As we watch the blood spill.

But this war is not ours,

It is not of our making.

We are the children of shadows;

Can't you see my heart breaking?

There is a price to be paid

When the innocent suffer.

There is a cost we must bear

For the blood on our skin.

We are ALL responsible

For the ones who lie dying.

We will ALL be accountable

For the mess we're now in.

In the cold grey light of an overcast morning, the end of the second night that they had been on the move, Sante opened his eyes in sudden fright. He was not sure what had woken him and looking around, noticed that all of the other rebels were still fast asleep. Even Evans, who was meant to be keeping watch, was slumped over his rifle in a deep slumber.

Sante's heart was beating a thousand miles a minute, and he held his breath, listening intently to the noises of the morning. Something seemed out of place, but he wasn't sure what. Perhaps, he was imagining things. It was sometimes hard to tell dream from reality for a time after he woke. His dreams and nightmares often lingered, as if trying to drag themselves into the daylight, and he would have to beat them back into the recesses of his mind before he could distinguish what was real from what was not. He lay on his side, still as a stone, but his eyes scanned as far as they could reach back and forth across his narrow field of view.

There it was.

A whisper.

A voice slid through the undergrowth as if escaping its captor's grip like a snake that slithered into Sante's open ears.

A twig snapped as if under someone's foot.

Silence returned, and Sante lay frozen in a mixture of terror and adrenalin. It shot through his veins like hot lava burning him from the inside out. He could feel every muscle tensed and ready to burst forth into wild action, but he knew he had to be calm.

He had to be patient.

He had to be certain.

He reached slowly for his machete, moving his arm along the ground as if it were a worm seeking an underground sanctuary. With his hand now resting on the shaft of his weapon, he froze again listening, willing his heart to stop its incessant beating. Silence echoed around them for one long drawn-out minute.

Then another whisper.

The dream was over. Sante suddenly knew that this was more real than any nightmare. They were being surrounded. They had been hunted down.

He glanced over to where his father lay about two meters away from him. Manwena's hat was pulled squarely over his eyes, and his arms crossed over his chest in a vain attempt to ward off the cold. Sante began silently edging his way towards him with his stomach scraping along the stony ground. There was no time to lose.

Hesitantly, Sante pushed his hand into the side of Manwena's shoulder and applied a little pressure while whispering in his ear. "Don't move. Don't move." He did not want his father to jump in fright and give the whole game away.

Manwena's muscles stiffened, and he tilted his head towards his son, his eyes peering beneath the brim of the hat.

"We are being surrounded. Listen." Sante whispered.

Manwena was at once fully alert and ready for action, and Sante almost sighed in relief. Much as he detested the man, he knew his father was a capable fighter and would know what to do. But who was hunting them, and how many were there? The dense thicket in which they had sought refuge for the night was not giving up its secrets just yet.

"Wake everyone, quietly." Manwena whispered as he began crawling towards the other commanders and grabbing his rifle as he did so.

Sante looked around, and his gaze immediately fell on his mother. Grace was sleeping on the outer edge of the group, and if they were ambushed, she would be the first to fall victim to whatever or whoever was out there. He woke other rebels and commanders as he made his way towards her, silently indicating to them using small hand gestures. When he finally reached Grace, he whispered in her ear.

"Wake up Mama, but don't move. We are being ambushed."

Too late. Their movements had been detected and the unseen enemy was giving them no more time to prepare. The sound of gunfire exploded through the trees. Sante grabbed his mother's arm and dragged her behind a large boulder where she sat shaking and breathing heavily, her eyes still gritty with sleep. Everyone was scrambling, and Sante watched as the commanders and rebels formed a tight circle around the rest of the group. They crouched low and fired randomly into the bush. Nearby, someone screamed, and he saw a young rebel fall clutching his leg in agony. The hostage children were still roped together and lying flat on the ground. The girls sobbed loudly and held their hands over their ears, their heads pushed onto the dirt. A number of the boys were trying to shield the younger children with their own bodies. Sante did not have time to contemplate the sacrificial bravery they were displaying.

"Get up," Manwena shouted at him. "Get over here." A rifle was thrust into his hands. Sante stood alongside his father, united in a single will to survive. He had never aimed a gun at anyone before. Adrenaline pumped through his body. He moved without conscious thought. His arms raised, his finger pulled the trigger over and over again. He fired randomly at any slight movement through the trees. His heart thumped. His ears throbbed with the blasts that rang through the air. Sante was unaware of everything except his father standing beside him. Manwena's presence was calm and solid in the midst of the storm. For the first time, Sante felt comforted by his power. This was the first time he had ever felt like they were on the same side of the line.

After what seemed like forever, Manwena shouted at the rebels to hold fire. Sante had not even noticed that the gunfire from the opposite direction had ceased. They all squatted and waited for a very long time, peering silently at one another. Some looked terrified while others smiled in triumph as if they could not think of a better way to start the day. The strangeness of the moment was too much for Sante. His dark eyes searched for some reason or justification for the battle but found none. Instead, his gaze fell on two of the rebels that had been hit and were writhing in silent agony. A third lay still on the ground, eyes open but vacant in a haunting death stare, while his hand still gripped his rifle. In the silence of those crowded moments, Sante could not tear his eyes away from the dead boy's face. It seemed that, no matter how common an occurrence, death never became any easier to confront. How could someone be there one second and simply gone forever in the next?

"You," Manwena indicated to two of the young rebels. "Get up and go see if they are all dead. Circle around us in the bush to make sure. Kill any who remain alive." The two boys glanced nervously at one another but did not say a word. They stood and slowly moved away from the safety of the group, creeping towards the tree line and then disappearing behind it. Sante could hear their rustling footsteps as they stopped and started again. He imagined them stumbling upon bodies. Suddenly, they reappeared, dragging an injured man. They dropped him at the edge of the group, and every eye riveted to his face as he groaned in protest.

"I told you to kill any survivors," Manwena shouted at them in frustration, raising his own gun and pointing it at the man's head, ready to finish the job. One of the hostage girls began to sob.

"No wait," Lewis interjected. "First, let's question him, and then we can kill him."

Manwena hesitated then nodded, using his gun to wave the boys off to continue their scouting exercise. When they returned, they reported that all were either dead or gone. They had found five bodies. All wore army greens.

"Did some run away?" Manwena demanded of the injured man.

"No boss, no. You shot us. No one ran away." His voice was cracked and broken.

"You are lying," Manwena sneered at him, grabbing him by the collar and pulling him forcibly up off the ground. He tilted the man's head back with the butt of his gun and stared him down. "Do not lie to me."

"No boss. Please. I'm not lying. I swear, no one ran. We are trained never to run away."

This answer seemed to satisfy Manwena somewhat, and he threw the man back onto the dirt with a thud. "Strip him and string him up," he ordered.

The rebels moved in to take the man's clothing, leaving him completely exposed and helpless. His hard muscular body somehow looked feeble and weak as he cowered and attempted to cover himself. His hands and feet were tied to two trees so that he stood between them with arms and legs splayed – in a completely exposed position and unable to move.

Manwena walked around him in a circle while the other rebels watched. "Did you know," he began, "that it was my son who alerted me to your presence?" No reply. The man hung his head low, his body quaking. "Imagine that! My son, who I had almost given up hope on, today stood beside me and proved that he has what it takes to be a fighter." Sante sat in shocked silence watching his father's display of pride. A sick feeling skulked around him and sank into his stomach as he wondered whether he was being set up for a fall. "My son," Manwena continued, "will make me proud of him again. My son will take your blood like water from a well and pour it out on the ground. He will slice you in two and watch as your insides fall out. He will become a resistance fighter today, and you can count yourself honoured to be his first kill. He will always remember you." Manwena glared at the soldier while Sante sat behind shaking in terror. He wanted to evaporate like smoke. The other commanders jeered and encouraged Manwena to continue his rampage of verbal violence. They all knew how much he enjoyed a captive audience, especially one that feared him and hung on his every word. The power he wheeled was electric. Sante could feel the charged energy in the air around him.

Suddenly, Manwena changed tack. "How did you find us?" he demanded.

The soldier knew he had no option but to answer. "We were on our way back to our base and found you all sleeping in the early hours of the morning."

"So, it was just luck then? You had not been tracking us?"

"Yes, luck. No, we had not been tracking you." His voice was little more than a whisper.

Manwena laughed aloud and slapped the bound man on the back as if they were a couple of old friends. The gesture seemed so out of place that it shocked even the other commanders into silence.

As suddenly as the smile had crossed his face it was gone, and Manwena returned to his scowl. Oddly, Sante found his angry persona easier to tolerate than the strangeness of his laughter. "Boy," he shouted. "Come here." Sante shot to his feet.

Manwena placed his knife in Sante's hand. "Make me proud of you again." He spoke the words in a seductive, soothing way.

Did he have a choice? Sante knew that Manewna would not allow dissention at this level. His life could be over if he disobeyed, but everything within him wanted to scream out in protest. He looked around at his mother seeking guidance, but her head was down on her knees. Manwena saw the questions in Sante's eyes.

"Everyone, look up here," he commanded. "Watch as the boy becomes a man. If anyone turns away, they will be killed."

Sante did not dare look back at Grace again. Instead, he stared at the quaking hand that held the knife and at the feet of his victim. "Cut him, cut him, cut him." From the back of the group, the chant began in a low tone. It grew louder and louder until all of the rebels were united in one voice.

Sante felt like he had the weight of a thousand sacks of grain pushing down on him, pressuring him, forcing his hands to move against his will. As if he was watching himself from a distance, he saw his hand and the knife move towards the chest of the soldier. He saw it pierce his velvety skin. The wound let the blood inside come seeping out in a snakelike stream that coiled down and around his torso. The soldier screamed in agony.

Sante watched the knife sink deeper and deeper as his hand forced it downward towards the man's groin. He felt the resistance of skin and muscle give way beneath the pressure of the knife's sharp blade. He heard the man's scream turn into a laboured groan as he struggled to breathe his final breaths. Sante watched as blood poured onto the ground from the deep wound he had carved into the man's chest – just as Manwena had predicted.

The new fighter stood shaking as the commander applauded him. He wanted to vomit away the foul-smelling stench that engulfed his nostrils. His victim hung limp and sagging on the ropes that still fastened his arms and legs to the tree, and although Sante did not want to look, he could not seem to tear his eyes away from the dead man's face. Again, the face of death dragged questions out of his soul. How did life suddenly vanish like this? What did it all mean? Painful guilt swept over him in a cloud as he looked upon the devastation his own hands had caused.

Two boys untied the ropes the soldier had been bound with and let his body slump to the ground in a tangled mass of limbs that suddenly appeared oddly disjointed. The ropes were carefully folded away and slowly the group began moving again. Their rest was over.

Sante kept his eyes low. He knew things were forever different now. He was no longer a child. He would no longer be treated like a child. He would now have to stand in line with the other rebels as they fought, raided, raped and stole.

It was the only life he had known, and now he was convinced that it was the only life he would ever know. He was not worthy of living any other kind of life. He was just like his father, perhaps even worse, and he was appalled at the thought that he would grow up to become a blood-thirsty animal that killed on a whim.

Silence engulfed them now as they began to move through the scrubby bush land. Sante could not look at Grace or any of the hostage children. His mind became a black, hollow hole of hunger and pain as they walked. They had not eaten for at least two days, but now that didn't seem to matter. He followed blindly, not caring where they were going or even whether they would ever get there. What was the point? All he wanted was the sun to set on this day and bring it to an end.

CHAPTER SEVENTEEN

JUST BREATHE

Out here

Where earth and sky collide

There is no keeping score.

Out here

Nature breathes in a rhythmic voice

And foundations are stripped to their core.

Out here

In the silence of a new dawn

Our souls just slip far away.

Out here

Life pulses to a different beat.

Till there is nothing left to say.

The pain in Silvia's wrists seemed to consume all of her focus and energy. As they walked, she could not take her eyes from the blood dripping down the rope that bound her hands together. The wounds on her wrists were raw welts of broken flesh and every pain receptor in her body seemed to converge at the place where rope and meat thrashed against one another. Her feet staggered and tripped over roots and stones. They too were cut and bloody, exposed to the angry ground beneath. It was as if her insides were silently protesting against this abuse, the blood bursting forth through her skin to escape the aching agony that consumed her entire body. And as she watched the blood fall, she found a strange type of comfort in knowing that each drop drew her closer to the end. Each drop was another tiny part of her finding freedom as death drew closer.

They had been walking for days. She had lost count of how many. The blur became a surreal nightmare that was both terrifying and exhausting. No rest, no food, and water scooped out of the footprints of animals after it rained or sucked off leaves at the break of day. But the worst part about this ordeal by far, was not the hunger that was slowly driving her insane, or the thirst that felt like it was melting her insides. It was not the fatigue from total exhaustion in an on-going push to reach their destination. It was not even Manwena, whom she had quickly learnt to loathe in a way she would not have previously thought possible.

No, the worst part for Silvia was the utter hopelessness that she tasted in the air on every breath sucked into her lungs. She was finding it harder and harder to even think about God, let alone pray. If she could have stolen a knife and pierced her heart, she would have done so rejoicing. The agony of having to live in hopeless depression seemed like a cruel and twisted form of torture that was attempting to slowly draw her life out from the soles of her feet and the tips of her fingers.

Bound together with the hopelessness was a canyon of sadness. Terrifying images of her parents' murders flashed intermittently before her eyes, and she was subconsciously drawn back to the place where she stood watching them being dragged away. Images of their rotting bodies lying somewhere on the forest floor, her dead baby brother still clinging to his mother's breasts, drove her to despair. Silvia tried desperately to escape these images, but instead, they seemed to be pushing her closer and closer to the brink of insanity.

She had nothing left. Nothing left to fight with.

Raymond was probably also dead, and in a way, she hoped he was. Better death than this insane torture of living.

The only thing that kept her head up was the thought of what her mother had said, "Live well. Live well." These words did something to revive her soul, but often her body protested, and her mind reasoned that to live at all would just be ongoing agony. She felt increasingly trapped.

As they marched, Silvia began to notice that even the rebels were looking tired and depressed. They no longer seemed to care if the hostage children stumbled. They no longer shouted for silence if one of the children cried. They just stumbled along with their heads down, and their machetes dragging. Very few words were spoken.

As usual, when the sun was at its peak in the sky above, they stopped for a rest. It was a precious time to find some renewed strength for, once they began walking again, they would not stop until very late into the night.

Everyone collapsed in a heap under the shade of a giant

African flame tree. Silvia lay on her back and stared up into the branches cloaked in a display of brilliant red. The large flowers hung together in crowded circular clusters surrounded by sprays of tiny green leaves. Her mother had loved the flame trees, which had been so prolific around their village. Sometimes, she would collect the flowers and leaves and turn them into beautiful dyes of golden yellow, crimson and dark brown. Silvia remembered hours spent climbing around the branches with little Raymond following her every move. They used to pick the unopened buds and squeeze them until the water burst out from inside, sometimes trying to wet one another in a childish game of tag. Raymond would squeal with delight when Silvia burst the pods over his head and water dripped down his face. She took a deep, slow breath and relished the relief of a pleasant memory.

From behind her, Silvia heard one of the commanders addressing several women. "We need to eat. Go and find some food," he instructed as if the task should be a simple one.

"Yes, boss." Silvia turned her head just far enough to watch the women as they scurried away. She wished she had been granted the freedom of such a task.

Turning her head towards Amos, who sat slumped beside her, she whispered, "Amos." He did not respond. "Amos!" It took a jab from her elbow to rouse him from his rest.

"Huh?" he grunted, barely glancing up.

"Look at the tree, Amos. It's a flame tree. Do you think we would be allowed to get some water from the pods?"

Amos did not reply for some time. He glanced slowly around at the rebels as they sat or lay sprawled across the ground in the shade of the tree. "I don't know," he finally stammered.

"Should I ask?"

"I don't know."

Silvia grew frustrated with his lethargy, although she completely understood it. He did not appear to care about anything. Not even the possibility of getting water. She was surprised by her own will to do something purposeful. "What can they do to me for just asking?" she reasoned, trying to muster up some courage.

"I don't know," he sighed.

Silvia gave up, turning her attention to the rebels who lay around her. She noticed Sante not too far away. He did not look as threatening as some of the others did, although she had seen what he was capable of just days before when he sliced the soldier virtually in two. She shuddered at the gruesome memory and tried to push it away. "Sir," she whispered. He did not respond. "Excuse me, Sir?"

Sante glanced over at the girl who was speaking before he realised she was speaking to him. No one had ever called him sir before, and he was aware of how ridiculous the title sounded draped across his scrawny shoulders. He glanced nervously at Manwena to make sure he was not paying attention before responding.

"Yes?"

"Sorry," Silvia began nervously, "but we are all so thirsty, and I don't think anyone has noticed yet, but there is water in the seedpods of this tree. If we can climb up and pick some, we can all have a little bit of water to drink."

Sante looked up into the branches above him as if noticing it for the first time, and Silvia wondered if it were possible that he might not know the information she had just shared with him.

Silvia looked to the ground and pointed to a fallen seedpod

that still appeared fresh. It was out of her reach, but Sante shuffled over to it and picked it up. "If you hold it to your mouth and squeeze it, you will get some water out," she instructed.

"Yes, I know," Sante replied. He took the small brown moon-shaped seed and squeezed the soft flesh until it burst between his lips, swallowing a mouthful of musty water. Silvia watched as he immediately began looking around for another pod. Although he did not say anything else, she was sure she noticed his eyes brighten a little.

It did not take long for the other younger rebels to join in with Sante's activity, and Silvia watched in dejected silence as they gulped the water without offering any to her and the other hostage children. Soon the ground was picked bare, and they began reaching up into the branches of the tree.

"Bring us some," Manwena ordered. So, the boys began stockpiling the seedpods at the feet of the commanders. Silvia's heart sunk further. Why had she bothered saying anything at all?

Amos, sensing her gloom, mustered the energy to speak. "What did you expect?" he asked quietly. He had not intended to insult her, but Silvia became angry at his lack of sympathy.

"You know what I expected," she snapped, attempting to turn her back on him despite the rope that bound them together.

"Silvia," he protested in a frustrated whisper. "After everything that we have been through how can you still be so naive? I don't understand it. How can you think that they would give us anything at all? We are worthless in their eyes. They would kill us without even blinking."

Deep angry sobs rose from the pit of her gut, and Silvia began to cry. It wasn't fair. Nothing was fair. This wasn't meant to be happening to her. Feelings of pain, disbelief and shock washed over her. All she had wanted was a little bit of water to wash the dust out of her mouth and the ache out of her stomach. Why was that too much to ask? Was her life really so worthless? The rebels were up the tree now collecting handfuls of pods and having their fill.

"I'm sorry," Amos tried to soothe her and quiet her tears. "Please don't be upset Silvia. You will only make things worse for yourself. Please, stop crying. I should have told you not to bother asking them. It's my fault, Silvia. I'm sorry. Please stop crying."

Silvia tried in vain to stifle her sobs. She had endured so much, and something inside her snapped. She could not seem to control the tears that made her body ache in even greater discomfort.

In the midst of his frantic picking, Sante noticed Silvia crying and stopped in his tracks. He looked at Silvia and the line of hostage children sitting in their own pathetic misery and suddenly felt selfish.

His heart sank.

What was he becoming? A beast, like his father, who thought only of himself?

Gathering as many as he could in his faded t-shirt, he slipped quietly over to where Silvia sat and piled the seedpods up at her feet.

She looked up in shock and could not speak.

"Share them with the others," Sante said before walking away to gather more for the children.

Silvia could not help grinning now and turning to Amos, she handed him a pile to pass down the line. No words were spoken, but they both acknowledged the moment of hope that Sante's act of kindness had brought.

It was several hours before the women arrived back with handfuls of sweet potatoes and cassava. They told the story of how they had stumbled upon an abandoned village where the vegetables were growing wild. They had gathered as much as they could and now suggested taking everyone back with them before nightfall in order to find more. Manwena objected. He began to question them about the village.

"Are you sure it was abandoned?"

"Yes, yes," replied one of the women. "We sat in the bush and watched for a long time before we went out to gather the food. We wanted to make sure it was not a trap. We heard no sounds and saw no evidence that anyone had recently been there. There were no fresh fire remains, and the ground was overgrown."

"Even where we dug for the sweet potato and cassava, we could see there had not been any recent harvesting or cultivating," the other woman chimed in.

"And there was much more food?" Manwena asked.

"Oh yes. The field was large. There was enough food for all of us for at least a week. Maybe more."

Their answers seemed to satisfy Manwena's suspicions, but only to an extent. He turned and spoke quietly to the other commanders before speaking to the entire group, who were hanging off every word. "We will go back to the village late tonight. But we need to be certain that this is not an ambush, so we will not enter the village until we are sure that no army are present. Or until we have killed them," he laughed at his own attempt at a joke.

While they waited for the sun to sink, the women prepared small fires and roasted the root vegetables until they were softened enough to consume. Silvia's mouth watered, but she did not dare allow herself to assume that she would get to taste the smoky sweetness of the potatoes. The thought of Amos calling her naïve again was almost as bad as going hungry for yet another night.

For the second time that day, it was Sante who came to her rescue. Silvia watched as he approached Manwena cautiously and spoke quietly to him. The commander looked over at the hostage children and slowly nodded his head. Sante then spoke to the women, who in turn, handed the children some food.

As Silvia held on to her precious chunk of warm sweet potato, her mouth watered, and her stomach screamed for instantaneous gratification. It took all her restraint to resist swallowing it whole and instead savour every mouthful. Silvia noticed that Amos did not exercise the same restraint and was finished his small meal in a matter of seconds. She did not look at his empty hands. She did not want to have to fight the urge to share, pretending instead to be oblivious to him.

The sun sank low and turned the soft light a brilliant shade of golden orange. For the first time in days, Silvia allowed her body and mind to relax, slipping into an almost trance-like state. She felt like she was spinning around and down into a deep dark hole of nothingness behind her eyelids, but the sensation did not scare her. It was somehow warm and inviting, and she wanted to go deeper and further away from her current reality. Perhaps this was what death was like. Peaceful nothingness. A gentle breeze caressed her face and for a moment nothing else mattered. She did not notice the pain in her wrists and feet, or her aching body. She was not aware of the children tied to the rope around her. She did not even care if Manwena was watching her with lust in his eyes that ripped her heart apart. She was far away in the blackness of her mind where fear could not exist.

CHAPTER EIGHTEEN

DARING TO DREAM

I walked upon the earth

And touched the blueness of the sky.

Said a prayer for you;

Said a prayer for life.

For it seems that we are dying

Where we stand and where we sleep.

We fear to reach for freedom,

And the life we could not keep.

I stood and watched the clouds

Rise up to glory,

Crash like dreams.

Without purpose or a destination

Their power is not all that it seems.

Is this why we die

Where we stand and where we sleep?

When we fail to move with courage

Is it merely death we reap?

Grace was silent for a long time after Sarah's approach. Her friend had again waited until the men were asleep, and then joined her on the outskirts of the fire. It was late, and the moon was already halfway across the sky. Its light cascaded across the darkness like a beacon of hope from the heavens above.

Every night since they had taken up camp in the abandoned village, Sarah had come to seek Grace out. After the death of Judy, Sarah had initially been worried that Grace would do something stupid and get herself killed. Now, she worried that in seeking Grace out, she might be the one to get them both killed. Still, she was drawn to the spark of courage that she saw in Grace's eyes. It was as if losing her daughter had made her more resilient. She had faced her worst fear, but instead of being destroyed by it, day by day, she seemed to be getting stronger.

Perhaps, the truth was that she had nothing left to lose, and so nothing really mattered. Either way, Sarah wanted to draw that courage out of Grace and keep some for herself. She struggled with her own constant fears that flew in the face of her faith.

As a young girl, Sarah had been educated at the best girl's boarding school in Northern Uganda. The nuns there had taught her about God's love and unconditional grace. She had memorised verses of Scripture and believed that this ever-loving God they taught her about, was her Father. Sarah's faith never wavered and kept her strong throughout the trials she had faced, however no amount of praying and pleading had yet delivered her from the rebels or from the fear that pervaded her waking hours.

The two women had begun speaking in coded fashion about the possibility of escape. It was something Grace had never allowed herself the luxury of thinking about before, but now she felt that she had nothing left to lose, and Sarah was the only person she felt she could trust implicitly. Grace knew she couldn't stay with the rebels as Manwena's intolerance of her seemed to be growing by the day. She had to find out if fate would allow her to forge a life away from the rebels. The only thing that held her back was Sante. She could not leave without him, but she could not get close enough to him to talk about her plans.

There was also something else holding her back. Something that she had not allowed herself to dwell on, but that subconsciously played with her mind and emotions.

Sante was quickly becoming a rebel, trailing along behind Manwena like a young prodigy. She watched intently as their relationship seemed to change by the day. Manwena no longer looked at Sante with hatred, but rather with a growing appreciation and respect. It was not something she ever thought she would witness, but it left her perplexed. If she did talk to her son about her desire for escape, could she trust that her words would be kept secret or had his loyalties already changed? It was something she would inevitably have to find out, as Grace knew his fate was sealed if he stayed here. He had never known any other kind of life, and if she were gone, there would be no one left to tell him that there was another way. She had already lost one child, and she knew she could not face losing another. She must at least try.

"What are you thinking?" Sarah finally asked, breaking the silence.

Grace paused before answering. "My thoughts are constantly on *food*."

Sarah looked thoughtfully at the stars above. The word *food* had become their code word for *escape*. With their bellies often empty, it would not be considered suspicious for the two women to be talking about food, should anyone overhear.

Sarah nodded in agreement. "My dilemma is my children," Sarah replied. "I cannot leave them *hungry*."

"I know. I cannot leave Sante *hungry* either," Grace replied. But still, I can't stop thinking about the possibility of *food*." Her voice was little more than a whisper. "The best time to find it would be late, after everyone is asleep. Then we would have time to get lots of food before they wake. It would be a nice surprise for everyone that they won't discover until hours later."

"But it wouldn't be a surprise for the guards on watch. How would we keep it a surprise for them?"

"Perhaps one day, Sante will be trusted to stand guard. Then he could help us find food," Grace suggested hopefully.

"We could be waiting a very long time for that."

"Yes. Realistically, it could be months. My stomach cannot wait that long. I need *food* now. I'm so hungry for it, I could cry."

"There is really no other option," Sarah whispered. "We either find it under cover of darkness, or we don't find it at all. But, even if we had the opportunity, we wouldn't know where to go to find it."

"I guess that's where luck comes in," said Grace flippantly.

"Or prayer," Sarah immediately shot back. "I will be doing a lot of praying."

Grace nodded her head in the darkness knowing that Sarah could not see her clearly. Part of her wished she would stop talking about her God. "Surely, if God was going to help us, He would have done so already," she responded. Grace had never revealed these thoughts to Sarah, though, of late, she often cried out to God.

"God works in ways we cannot always understand."

"That's for sure," Grace replied with a hint of sarcasm in her voice. For once, she agreed with Sarah on the subject. "If this God is real, I don't understand Him at all." She hesitated before speaking again. "I have been thinking a lot about this God of yours. I have decided that, even if He does exist, I don't want to know a God that allows such suffering. You speak of this God's love, but I see no love around me – only hatred. It is hatred that always wins in the end. It is hatred that takes people's lives. It is hatred that has led to so much suffering. Does your God want to wipe out the Acholi people completely so that there is nothing left of us?" Grace allowed her pain to surface.

"Why do you blame God for the mess we are in?" Sarah shot back. "It is not God's fault that the human race has chosen to walk the road of war and destruction. I am sure it breaks His heart."

"Then why doesn't *He* stop it? Is He not an all-powerful God?"

"All powerful yes, but not all-controlling. If you truly love someone, you grant them the freedom to choose their own way. I believe God wants us to turn to Him – not because we are forced to, but because we want to. Because we understand that He is the only way. When we look in other places for answers to life's problems, we always come up empty. Only God can give us what we need. God does the exact opposite of the resistance movement. Can't you see that, Grace? The rebel militia conjures hatred, and out of that hatred comes control, manipulation, greed and every other evil. God, however, loves, and out of that love comes freedom for us to choose which path we travel on."

Something in Grace wanted to believe Sarah's words in spite of her doubts. "If what you say is true, and all God wants is for us to turn to Him, well how do we do that? What do you really mean?"

Sarah's heart leapt as she recognised that Grace had just given her an opportunity to explain her faith fully. She looked around to make sure no one was listening before she spoke again. "When I was a little girl in boarding school, this is the way the sisters explained God's love to me. God loves us so much, that He sent His little Son into the world to show us that love."

Sarah saw Grace's perplexed look and so took a different tack in an attempt to explain her faith. "Imagine if you felt such love for Joseph Kony that you wanted to help him. But he wouldn't listen or turn away from his evil ways, so you sent Sante into his camp to show him how much you loved him. But Kony rejected Sante, and instead, he killed him." Grace shivered at the thought. "That is what God did. He saw that our hearts were all corrupted and turned away from Him, so He sent His Son to show us the way to find true peace. Then He allowed us to sacrifice His Son, and His death bridged the gap between us. His Son Jesus was the perfect acceptable sacrifice. He gave His life for us to say sorry to God on our behalf. All we have to do is accept Jesus as God's Son, and we can go to God. When we accept Him, He wipes out our sins and promises us a life with Him."

Grace had never heard anything quite so mind-boggling. "Can anyone accept Jesus?"

"Absolutely."

"What about Kony? What about the other leaders of the resistance movement who have spent so many years brutalising children and killing innocent people? Can even they be forgiven? Why would God want to forgive them?"

Grace sensed Sarah's hesitation before answering. "That is hard for us to understand, but yes, I believe it's true. If Kony truly turned from his ways and asked God to forgive him, God would do so immediately. We can all be forgiven, but we also have to forgive everyone who has harmed us."

"Oh, so that's the catch," Grace felt herself becoming agitated at the thought that she would have to forgive Manwena and the other men who had raped and beaten her. "Why should I forgive?"

"Because God forgives you," was Sarah's simple reply. "No one is perfect. Everyone has done wrong in some way, but if God forgives you and sets you free, He wants you to do the same for others."

"I can't do that."

"But you must."

"The things I may have done wrong are not as bad as the crimes that others have done to me. It doesn't seem fair or reasonable."

Sarah was quiet before responding. "Grace, you have seen that even your own son is capable of terrible things. Yet, you still love him. Do you think God should not forgive him? Do you think the man he killed, or the man's family should not forgive him?"

"But he was forced to do that," Grace began to cry silent tears at the trauma of remembering the grotesque killing her beloved son had carried out. It was something she had believed he would never be capable of.

"I'm sorry Grace, I am. You are right, it doesn't seem fair. All I know is that God wants us to forgive others. Perhaps, we do it more for ourselves than for them anyway. I know that when I forgave Aaron, I felt free. I no longer felt burdened by anger and hate. Instead, I can look at him and feel pity and sorrow for I know God still loves him and longs for him to be free as well."

"But how can you forgive him for the things he has done to you? I've seen it. Everyone has seen it. We all know he is a man with no mercy. He even takes your daughter as if she were his wife!"

Sarah began crying now. "God never promised that it would be easy, but I must. If I don't forgive him, God can't forgive me."

Grace's tears also began to fall over her cheeks, and her chest heaved with indescribable pain. All the sorrow she had carried and buried deep for so long seemed to be coming to the surface of her conscious mind, and she did not have the strength to push it back down. Sarah placed her arms around her shoulders, and the two women found unity and strength in their shared burdens and trusted friendship. For a very long time, neither spoke, but Sarah prayed with a heart full of hope for Grace.

"God loves you," she whispered.

Since arriving in the village, the rebels had been feasting. The overgrown vegetable fields had been picked clean, and the food prepared, boiled, fried and consumed with gusto. Not even the hostage children were left hungry. They had been divided up again among the commanders and were slowly being woven into the fabric of the group. Manwena continued to leave Grace on the outer as he enjoyed the delights of his new young wife. Every so often, he would summon her to cook or fetch water, but she was not allowed to enter the hut that Manwena had claimed as his own.

Grace had never felt so vulnerable. She had witnessed Manwena push other wives away in the past, usually right before they mysteriously disappeared. Although she was thankful that she did not have to endure his presence, she sensed that one way or another, she was running out of time. Her only aim was to somehow take control of her departure. If Manwena beat her to it, she knew she was headed for the grave. Despite all that she had endured, every day, Grace felt a stronger desire to live. She had not lived through so many years of slavery just to die now. There had to be more.

As she sat stirring a pot of porsho, she surveyed her surroundings. The village consisted of six small mud huts and one cooking shelter. Several tracks marked places of exit into the dense bush around the village. Grace had no idea which direction to head in when she did run, and so, she had begun praying more fervently to Sarah's God. Her prayers were simple but held her deepest fears. She had decided that she really did not want to die yet.

Out of the corner of her eye, she watched as Sante rose from where he had been sleeping under a tree and sat with his knees bent and his arms wrapped loosely around them. He looked over at his mother and their eyes locked. Grace held his stare, trying to communicate with her eyes that she needed to talk with him. Sante looked away, and her heart sank, but then he looked back again. They had not been allowed near each other since Judy's death, so Grace did not want to lose this fleeting opportunity. She tilted her head and shifted her gaze towards the back of the village, attempting to indicate where she wanted to meet him. Again, Sante looked away, and she watched as he casually assessed the current state of play. She knew he was looking for Manwena who was again in the hut with Silvia. He had been there for at least five minutes, and Grace's heart thumped as she realised this may be a chance to connect with her son.

Rising from where she sat, she wandered past the last hut and out onto the track that led to the vegetable field. There was no food left in the ground, but she hoped that because it had been such a well-worn track over the last several days, she would not attract suspicion. She did not look back. The field was only some fifty yards from the village, and once there, Grace bent down and acted as if she was hunting for more sweet potato. To her delight, she actually found one that had been overlooked, and she pulled it out with glee. Standing straight, she looked around. She was alone but felt as if she was being watched, and her eyes scanned the bushes as her heart beat loudly.

Suddenly, Sante appeared at the edge of the clearing and motioned to her. In her haste, Grace dropped the potato and anxiously hurried to his side. They stood in the shadow of a huge flame tree and spoke in whispers.

"Sante, I have to leave," Grace blurted the words out.

"Yes," he replied as if not at all surprised.

Grace wondered if she had made a mistake. Could she even trust him with this information or was he already too far submerged into the identity of becoming a rebel? Would he just run straight back to Manwena and inform him? "Manwena will kill me if I stay."

"I know. I see that. You have to go, but where will you go?"

"I don't know. Will you come with me? We can do it together."
He did not answer her question immediately.

"If we are caught, we will be killed."

Grace heard the fear in his voice. She put her arms around him and hugged him tight. "Perhaps, it is a risk we have to take. Do you want to live like this?"

"No. No, but I'm afraid we will never find our way out. The rebels will hunt us down. They will track us because of the Shea nut oil. They will hunt for us forever, until they find us, and then they will torture us."

"Sante, if we make it far enough away, they will forget about us. We have to try."

He was silent for a long time, his eyes scanning the treetops in the distance. Finally, he nodded, and Grace's heart leapt, but she knew they were running out of time to formulate a plan. "We will have to go at night. I will wait for the opportunity, so you must keep a watch for me from wherever you lie down to sleep. Do you understand?"

"Yes. I will follow you when I see you going."

Grace felt that their time was up, and she gave him one final hug before turning to leave. Before she disappeared onto the track back towards the village and her cooking pot, she turned to him and smiled. "It will be ok," she whispered. "I know it will be ok."

CHAPTER NINETEEN

BITTER SWEET

Tell me now

Before you lay me down,

What all our wars

Have been fought for.

For I am faced

With the hatred in your eyes,

But don't understand

Why it's me that you despise.

Tell me now

Why you use your gun,

To rape our mothers

And kill our sons;

While our rulers sit

And play their games,

With the lives of Acholi,

Who will never ever be the same.

Tell me now

Before you lay me down,

What all our wars

Have been fought for.

And if you cannot answer

This simple question,

Tell me brother,

Why do you kill me at all?

"Quiet," Manwena whispered hoarsely from the front of a shadowy line of figures that crept through the trees. It was pitch black, and they had to feel their way by sense and instinct. Around them, the trees loomed like giants that stood unshaken, their twisted branches creating a canopy above that blocked out the stars. The forest floor was cool and cluttered with rotting leaves and branches that were continuously discarded from above. They all froze, hunched over, as if standing upright was more likely to give them away. After a short time, with their ears all strained to the silence, Manwena began to move again, his black silhouette revealing that he held his rifle on his shoulder pointed up to the sky. He slunk through the undergrowth like he was becoming a part of it. Moving over the ground as a lion stalks its prey, he was so totally transfixed on what lay before him that he could almost taste the blood in his mouth.

Amos could feel tiny beads of sweat roll out of his pours and cling to his body, prickling his skin in the cool night air. He followed the boy in front of him, clutching his machete in fear. It had been a few weeks since the hostage children had gone through their initiation rituals, and although very little training had taken place, they were considered ready to become rebel soldiers. Amos wondered if this was going to be his inevitable end – used as a human shield to protect a resistance movement commander. He may have been given a machete and had the word 'soldier' attached to him, but Amos knew it was mere facade. He was disposable, valueless and would be easily forgotten. On top of that, he lived with the constant dread of being exposed as a defector. Surely, it was only a matter of time.

Sante trod the ground behind Amos, trying to sense where the boy had placed his feet and imitate his moves. It was partly a distraction from his own thumping heart and partly an attempt to protect his feet from injury. This was his first raid, and he wrestled with the significance of it. Did this mean he was now just like the man he had spent so much of his life hating? Why was he so terrified? He thought about his mother's anxious plea to escape with her, and it made his blood run cold. If they were caught, as he imagined they would be, he knew only too well what would follow. But if he didn't go with her, he sensed that she would not have it in her to leave, and everyone was aware of how she had fallen out of favour in Manwena's eyes. The thought of her being killed was too much to bear. As they walked, Sante's mind fought both sides of the tug-of-war.

They came to a small village, and Manwena silently gestured for them to halt. On a scouting exercise earlier in the day, several boys had reported seeing a family living in this village. It was like laying a roast chicken in front of the man. There was just no way Manwena could not take a bite.

They stood in silence and looked out on the scene. Only two small huts, and one cooking shelter made up the village. There was no light and no noise, just an eerie silence. Slowly, the group began creeping towards the huts, their weapons branded high and ready to fight, as if they expected the enemy to be savage.

Once they were blocking all exits so that there was no conceivable way the occupants could elude them, Manwena waved several men into each thatched roof structure. The doors were flimsy creations made from bamboo and did not need much force. A simple push would have sufficed, but the kicking and shouting stirred up their excitement as the men ran inside. Amos and Sante stood side by side, adrenaline running through their veins.

"Nothing," the men shouted as they reappeared.

"What?" Manwena seethed in fury.

"There is no one here, boss," said one of the boys. "They must hide out in the bush at night."

"Find them," Manwena ordered, "but stay in groups."

They split up and began combing the trees surrounding the village. Amos and Sante walked together, each sensing the other's half-heartedness in the hunt. Amos was aware that Sante was fairly new to this game and so felt safer with him than any of the other rebels. Amos had watched Sante's kindness towards the other hostage children and secretly admired him. They had never spoken directly.

Circling the eastern side of the village, they could hear the other rebels rummaging through the undergrowth in frantic fury. Occasionally, there was a shout, and they wondered if someone had been found. It was an impossible search because the night was so incredibly dark, and even Manwena had to acknowledge that the village people could be miles away. Despite the distance, it was possible that they had even walked into one of the towns during the night.

Suddenly, the boys stopped short. A strange sound hit their ears, and they both looked quickly at one another and instinctively stopped to listen. Then it came again, louder this time – the unmistakable noise of a baby crying. Looking upwards in the direction of the cry, the boys saw a terrified woman in the tree above. She was clutching her tiny infant in one hand, desperately trying to put the baby onto her breast to silence its protests, while holding onto the branches with the other. On the branch next to her was a little girl of about five years old. She whimpered as she watched the boys below, and her body shook with an uncontrollable fear. Sante and Amos looked at each other again, this time with questioning eyes. They looked back at the woman. She remained silent, but even through the darkness, they could see the whites of her eyes that begged them for mercy.

They both quickly realised that they were alone in this section of the forest. Amos spoke in a whisper, not knowing if he could trust Sante but wanting desperately to avoid violence. "We can just leave them," he suggested as if trying to give Sante a way out.

Sante did not have to think twice. "Quickly," he said, not looking up again. They walked back out into the clearing where some of the other rebels were gathering. Manwena was waiting, silent and sullen. He hated failure.

The walk away from the village that night was a strange one for Sante. He had never been on such a high. Knowing that he had just saved the life of the woman and her two children left him with an electrifying buzz that he never could have anticipated. His short existence had been so full of pain and misery that suffering was his everyday expectation. But the joy that he felt in knowing that hope had been granted, and life had been spared, filled him to overflowing. It countered everything his reality told him was true. Added to that was the connection he and Amos now shared. In that moment of decision, when they had dared to reveal their true feelings, not knowing if they could trust one other, they had each found a comrade. Sante felt sure that he could now trust Amos with his life.

Manwena was in a fury. He had been looking forward to some action after days of mundane walking and rest. Since his group's departure from the other rebel faction some months ago, he had only managed one raid and a handful of bedraggled hostage children. He needed more than that before returning to Kony's camp in Southern Sudan. He was getting desperate and needed to come up with a plan.

As he walked, he contemplated this issue. It had been easier in the old days before most of the Acholi people who populated the area moved into refugee camps. Back then, many locals had assumed that the resistance movement was a myth, and by the time they realised the truth, it was too late. The rebels had been able to virtually walk into any village and take their pick of the adults and children, usually slaughtering or maiming all who remained. He thought about the possibility of attacking the outskirts of a camp. This had been accomplished by other rebel factions, but reports always filtered back about how heavily guarded the camps were.

Above all else, Manwena did not want to risk his own reputation by being involved in a losing battle. His reputation as a feared commander within the ranks of the rebel militia was his ticket to control and power – something he never wanted to lose. However, if he failed to achieve his objective of adding soldiers and wives to the rebel militia's ranks, his reputation was as good as dead anyway.

He cursed as he walked at the head of the line. There had to be someone to blame for this outrageous waste of time. He decided he would punish the boys who had reported the village. They should have stayed and monitored the people's movements after dark. They should have known better than to assume the villagers would sleep in their huts. *He* should have known better, but he quickly dismissed that thought.

Sante walked a few paces behind Manwena. He stood upright, now, and a smile danced over his lips. As the rebel leader stomped along in front of him, he relished the idea that he held a secret from Manwena.

Suddenly Manwena stopped, and Sante almost ran in to the back of him. Roughly pushing the boy away, Manwena waited until the whole group was quiet before he began to speak.

"Aaron, Lewis," he summoned the two other commanders. All the rebels watched as the three shadowy figures moved some distance away into the trees. They could hear hushed whispers, but try as they might to hear, it was as if the words themselves somehow got lost in the trees. After a time, the men returned.

Manwena indicated that Aaron should speak. "We are going to raid a refugee camp on the outskirts of Lira." Silence hung in the air. "It is not far from here. You must all be ready to fight, although we want to be in and out and not attract too much attention from the army. We will just hit the outskirts of the camp. Take children, but not too young, as we must have no one with us who will slow us down."

"We don't want to attract *any* attention," Manwena corrected him.

Sante felt his heart drop to the bottom of his chest. He was so tired that his whole body ached. All he wanted to do was lie down and sleep, but now sleep would probably not come this night. As they set off, altering their course slightly south, he could have cried, letting his emotions run away from him and howling like an infant. Instead, he gulped the silent scream back into his chest and did not utter a sound.

On they marched. Manwena moved with purpose now. He was determined to make himself known as a great leader in the resistance movement. He wanted what no other man had received. He wanted Kony's respect, and in his mind, there was no other way to get it than with more abductions than any other commander. As the trees thickened, he held his hands in front of him and pushed his way through the undergrowth. He was in a hurry and just hoped that they would all keep up. Several other commanders staked out the back of the line to ensure that no one tried to run. Even though these boys were now all considered soldiers, Manwena had been around long enough to realise that he couldn't trust them. No matter how fervent they behaved, there were always those who tried to escape.

After a number of hours walking in the same direction, the group sensed that they were nearing the camp. It was still quiet in the bush, but Manwena had slowed his pace, and every so often, he would instruct them to stop and listen. Every man and boy instinctively followed their leader and did not dare contemplate otherwise.

As they came out into a clearing, Sante stopped short in shocked surprise. The moon appeared from behind the clouds and illuminated a landscape littered with rows of tents as far as the eye could see. They were squashed together in a writhing mass of humanity. A stench that seemed to encompass decay, sweat and human excrement ascended from the earth and filled their nostrils. Dogs barked, and strange noises reached their ears, but considering the vastness of this place, it was relatively quiet. It was like a beating heart that had a life force far beyond the components of its individual parts. Sante had never seen anything like it. He wondered if anyone who had escaped the resistance movement had made it here, and at once recognised that if they had, their circumstances were not necessarily better than his own. It was a depressing end to the illusion he had long held about the sanctuary that the refugee camps would hold.

Manwena began speaking, loud enough for them all to hear but still in a hushed whisper, "We will fan out. Go in pairs and take your hostages, but do not cause a scene. Be as quiet as you can be. Take children who are sleeping or those who are alone. We will meet back here in a few minutes. Everyone must have a hostage, or there will be consequences." He began moving forward and the group followed.

Sante and Amos fell into step beside one another and headed to the left of the group.

"It would be so easy to escape now," Amos whispered when they were far enough away that no one could hear. He believed that he could trust Sante. "We could just get lost in the camp. They would never be able to find us."

"We can't," Sante was terrified by the suggestion. "You heard what he said, 'There will be consequences.'"

"What can they do to us?"

"They will kill my mother. And, if I return without you, they will kill me! Please, please don't think about escaping tonight."

"Look," Amos reasoned, "I can't remain living like this. I would rather be dead."

"No, no." Sante felt the desperation in his chest rise. "I promise you, we will escape, but not now and not like this. My mother came to me, and she wants to leave. She wants me to go with her. When we go, you can come with us."

"But it will never be easier than it is now. If we have to escape from the group while we're somewhere out there in the bush, the chances of being caught are great. Here it would be easy."

"I can't make you return tonight, but you must know that if you don't come back I will most likely be killed." Sante was now playing on the newfound faith he had in Amos's good nature. "Besides, if you go in there looking like a rebel soldier, the people in that place might kill you themselves."

Amos was silent for a long time. They walked on and neared the edge of the camp, crouching low and surveying the mud-hut city from the safe distance of fifty metres. Finally, he spoke. "Ok. I will not go tonight. But you must give me your word that when you escape you will take me with you. I am usually roped to a tree at night. Even though they made me a soldier, by night I am still stuck on a tree. So, you must untie me, and we will go together."

"You have my word." Sante agreed. But he could not shake the sense of foreboding from the pit of his stomach. "So, how are we going to do this?" he asked, seeking to change the subject and focus on the task at hand.

Amos turned away from him and looked at the camp. "We will have to go in and find some children."

"I can't." Sante was afraid like he had never been before.

"We don't have a choice."

Just then, a small boy emerged from one of the outer huts and began walking to a clearing. He squatted in the dirt as if to relieve himself, and before Sante knew what was happening, Amos was up on his feet and running silently over the ground towards the boy. He pounced on him, and, holding his hand over the boys' mouth so that he could not scream, he physically carried the boy's small frame back to where Sante still lay, paralysed by fear. They both collapsed onto the dirt beside Sante, Amos breathing hard, and the boy writhing in panic.

"Listen, listen to me," Amos whispered in the boy's ear. "If you make a sound we will go and murder your parents or your sisters and brothers. Whoever we find who belongs to you, we will kill if you do not keep quiet and still."

Sante was horrified and wanted to protest, but he could see the logic in Amos's threat. All he could say was, "We need another one."

They crouched again on the cold earth and waited. A few minutes passed, and a young woman emerged from the same hut that the boy had wandered out of. She had a pained look of worry etched on her face, as if she already knew. "Jacob? Jacob?" she called in a loud whisper.

The little boy squirmed when he heard his name, but Sante held him down, and once again, Amos leapt to his feet. This time, he did not have the same element of surprise. The woman saw him coming and started to run, but Amos was fast. He leapt at her like a lion grabbing the hind shank of an antelope and tackled her to the ground. Pinning her there, he spoke directly into one ear. "We have your boy. Don't make a sound if you ever want to see him alive. I have a knife, and I will use it. Stand up and start walking."

With that, Amos stood up and pulled the frightened and dazed woman to her feet. "This way," he indicated, pushing her quickly towards the edge of the camp and out into the blackness of the night. Whimpering quietly, she walked in front of him with faltering steps.

When they reached the spot where Sante and Jacob sat watching in terrified silence, the small boy reached up and threw his arms around her neck sobbing. She held him close, and Amos and Sante lost control of the situation for a moment as the two embraced. Amos felt like his heart was breaking. This had been him and his own mother just a few years before. How could he be doing this? How could he be perpetrating a crime that he hated his captors for? How could he be passing up this opportunity for escape?

"Sante," he said in desperation as he held the knife to the woman to ensure that she did not move. "Listen to me. Once Grace realises that you have not returned, she will run. She will get as far away as she can as fast as she can. She will come to find you. We can't do this. I am sorry, but I can't do this."

Sante thought of his mother and was plagued by guilt. How could he even think about the possibility of escaping without her? "Won't the people in the camp kill us as soon as they realise who we are?"

"We will explain that we were abducted, and that we had no choice, but that we want to be free."

"No," responded Sante sadly. "I was not abducted. I was born in the resistance movement. I am one of them. I can't leave. Not like this anyway." He felt the weight of the world resting on his small shoulders, stuck in the middle of an impossible decision.

Finally, he spoke again, "You go. Go and don't look back, but I can't. I don't belong out there, and even if I wanted to go, I can't leave my mother."

Amos was so frustrated he could have screamed, but there seemed no reasoning with this boy. He groaned in internal agony as he wrestled with his demons. The woman and child clung to each other listening to the boy's debate back and forth. "You promised me that you would leave, and now you say you can't!"

"I did promise, and if you come back with us now, then I still promise. I will do it for you and for my mother."

Amos sighed and shrugged his shoulders in surrender. "Up on your feet," he ordered his captives, trying to repress his own feelings of guilt. "We go."

Sante knew that Amos was angry and wanted to make it up to him as they headed back to Manwena, but no words would come.

Nothing Sante said would have appeased Amos in that moment. He had just let freedom slip through his fingers, and still couldn't believe that he now willingly walked back into the lions' den. He suddenly felt terribly cold and shivered as a rash of goose bumps spread up his arms.

CHAPTER TWENTY

GROWING THICK SKIN

One step beyond your limits

Is where you need to go

To find out what true courage is.

Over the edge

Of what you believed was possible,

You'll find yourself in a place

Where the future and past don't matter anymore.

All that is important

Is each present moment.

Each breath, and your commitment to persevere.

Failure is not an option

When you live in the hope

That is born out of courage.

Hope that tells you that you can

Fight another day.

Hope that is unyielding faith,

Even in the face of contradictory evidence.

Hope that does not listen

To all the reasons why not,

And focuses on the one that tells you why.

Why press on?

Why not just give up?

Give in?

Lie in the dust and let defeat swallow you.

Why put yourself through the pain?

Why?

Because you can

With courage that only comes from within,

And sets you apart from the multitude

Who choose instead to give in.

Silvia woke and hesitantly looked around the empty hut, letting out a sigh of relief when she realised she was alone. She allowed herself to lie in the coolness of the dawn without rushing to rise. Many of the men and boys had left the night before on a raid and had still not returned. She could not help hoping that the army had captured them. Maybe Manwena had even been killed. She dared herself to wish it, as if her thoughts would somehow predict the outcome. She was alone in the hut that she normally shared with Manwena. A night of reprieve from his abuse, and her body was already starting to feel better. Normally when she woke, she could feel new bruises and taste his sweat in her mouth. This morning, she relished the feeling of being free from his bad stench.

Light fell through the open doorway and onto her outstretched hand. She cocked her head sideways and looked at it for a long time, resting there on her palm. She cupped her hand and held it as if she were holding a bottle of precious oil. Perhaps, she would be free soon. Perhaps, she would be able to return to her village and find some of her old friends there. Perhaps, one day life really would return to some semblance of normality. Silvia let her imagination run away with itself to a place of safety and freedom. She craved it from the core of her soul. From places within that she did not even know were there.

A figure appeared at the doorway blocking the light, and Silvia jumped in fright.

"It's ok, Silvia," Grace's soft voice soothed her. "It's only me. The men are still away."

Silvia sighed in relief. "I thought you were …"

"I know. Sorry for frightening you. I have cooked some sweet potato and thought you might like some." Grace held out the chunk of vegetable. She had not dared to enter the hut for fear of being watched.

"Thank you," Silvia took the food gratefully. She did not want to lose the comfort of Grace's presence, so she tried to keep her talking. "When do you think they will return?"

"I don't know," Grace looked over her shoulder suspiciously.

"Are they normally gone overnight?"

"It all depends on where they go, and what they encounter. Sometimes, not all of them return." Silvia sensed Grace's anxiety and suddenly remembered that Sante was with them.

"Your son will come back," she whispered.

"I hope so." Grace was silent now and turned to leave.

"Grace, wait." She turned back to the frail girl lying on the dirty floor and noticed how weak she looked as she struggled to sit up. Silvia was trying to think of something to say to keep Grace nearby. She found the older woman's presence comforting. "Well, I was um, just wondering," she looked down at her hands and picked at the side of the potato as she spoke. "What do you think will happen to us?" She didn't really want to know. She didn't really want Grace to answer, but she could think of no better question.

Grace sighed again and slumped to the dirt with her back up against the open doorframe. "Sometimes, I wish I knew," she paused. "And sometimes, I am so thankful that I don't."

"Will life ever be normal again?"

Grace did not want to squash the young girl's hopes with her own doubts, so she tried to be positive. "I hope so. I dream that it will be, and I guess, I believe it will be. If I didn't believe it, I think I would have died of a broken heart before now."

"How long have you been here?"

"Too long to think about, I'm afraid. Since I was a young girl, like you." She noticed a panicked look on Silvia's face as she averted her eyes. "Oh, but don't worry. Things are changing. I'm sure life will get back to normal soon. You won't be here that long."

"I can't imagine that. I can't see how life will ever be normal for me. Even if I did escape, I will never be able to live a normal life. I will never be able to get married and have children. No man will want me after *he* has finished with me." Silvia could not even bring herself to say Manwena's name.

Grace did not know how to respond as she knew Silvia was probably right and to deny it would just be an obvious lie. She was silent again, thinking back over her own history. After some moments she spoke, "Silvia, I don't know what will happen or where we will go from here, but you must never give up. If one day you find freedom, grab it with both hands. Don't look back. Allow yourself to embrace all the good things in life again. When you think of this time, remember it just as you would a nightmare. Once life starts again, none of this will seem real. It will all just be like a bad dream."

"How do you know it won't seem real?"

"I hope it won't. I pray it won't. I have been praying to Sarah's God lately, and the one thing I ask for, beyond anything else, is freedom. Not just freedom in my body. I want freedom for my mind as well. I want to be free from the spirits that torment me with terror when I lie down at night. I want to be free from fear. Do you know what I mean?"

Silvia nodded. She understood completely. "He does such bad things to me," she whispered as tears started to fall. "I know what you mean, but I would be happy if all I ever find is freedom for my body."

Grace was overcome with compassion for her and entered the hut, hugging her close. "Sweet girl, hush now. It will be ok. He is an evil man, I know," she whispered. "I have been through what you are enduring now. Listen to me, I am going to leave here as soon as I get the chance. If I can take you too, I promise I will."

Silvia looked up and saw the ray of hope being offered to her. "Really?"

"I promise. If it is at all possible."

To Silvia's dismay, the rebels returned later that day with more hostages in tow. She watched them intently from the doorway of her hut as they were dragged into camp. There were fourteen in all, mostly children and two young women. All looked exhausted and terrified, and she knew exactly how they were feeling. She wondered if any of their family members were still alive.

Manwena suddenly left the other rebels to sort out the hostages and headed straight for the hut. If Silvia had been prepared, she would have run outside to hide, but it was too late now. He would see her if she ran, so she cowered in one corner of the hut as he approached. It was a vain and useless attempt to hide. Without a word, he grabbed her roughly as if the sight of her small body disgusted him. He pinned her up against the wall and parted her legs, the force of his body lifting her off the ground. Pain shot straight up through Silvia's spine, and she almost fainted. His violence and volatility were more than she could cope with, the smell of his rancid flesh again reaching up through her nostrils. He puffed and panted, and then dropped her to the floor as suddenly as he had begun. For a second or two, the pain in Silvia's pelvis seemed to increase before it slowly began to ebb away. She felt broken and did not dare look up as he tucked his shirt into his trousers and walked out of the hut.

Silence fell. She sobbed uncontrollably and clawed at the dirt, not caring now who might hear her. The soil etched its way under her fingernails like the anger that entered her soul. He was an animal. A beast who used sex as a powerful weapon against her. Silvia suddenly found herself silently raging against the world. She was angry with her parents for somehow letting this happen to her. She was angry with Amos for his ridiculous aloofness, and what felt like his abandonment of her. He would barely even look at her these days, as if he were ashamed. As if this abuse was somehow her fault. She hated him for it. She was angry with Grace for stepping aside so quickly and allowing Manwena to replace her. She was angry with a whole world that didn't care enough to help. She was angry with God for allowing such things to happen. Why would God even make a world like this one? Inside, she was screaming, concluding that God must be an ugly beast with green eyes and a whipping tongue, who somehow enjoyed watching her torture. Silvia lay huddled on the floor and cried.

It was not long before the group was once again on the move. The commanders had decided that it was too risky to stay in the village, as word of their latest raid would soon send the army after them. So, once night fell, the group began walking. Silvia was no longer roped into a line of children as the only rope they possessed was being used to bind up the new hostages, so she found herself suddenly free. It was as if they had now graduated beyond hostage status. She walked next to Grace in the middle of the group. No one dared speak, but she did not want to lose sight of Grace, silently willing her to remember her promise.

It was a long and exhausting few hours of walking. Silvia was so tired that she felt like the trees above were closing in on her. She slipped in and out of a strange dream-like state and sometimes found it difficult to distinguish between reality and illusion. Every so often, they would hear gunshots in the distance that always made her jump. She longed to stop, but when they eventually did, it was not in the way she had anticipated.

They came upon a river that seemed to stretch as far as her

eyes could see under the light of the moon. Standing on the edge of the water with the other rebels, Silvia wondered how they could possibly get across. Perhaps, the commanders knew where some canoes were hidden in the bushes. Grassy clumps and ant-hill islands dotted the shadowy edges. The moon sparkled on the water, turning its black depths a silvery colour as if trying to see its own reflection. A soft wind stirred up the water's surface and carried ripples of colour towards their toes that dipped in the coolness.

"Where are they?" Manwena hissed turning his face towards Aaron.

Both men looked around as if puzzled by their isolation, and Silvia wondered who they were talking about. "Could we be in the wrong place?" Aaron asked, avoiding an obvious answer to the loaded question.

"No," he shot back. "This is it."

"What shall we do if they do not come?"

Manwena did not answer. Instead, he looked nervously back over his shoulder into the forest as if waiting for someone or something to leap from the trees. "Sit down," he ordered everyone.

Silvia felt her buttocks slide into the mud as she manoeuvred herself into position amongst the other children and rebels. There was a certain sense of security being this close to people who were not presently abusing her, but her heart raced a thousand miles a minute, as if it could feel the lurking danger. They waited, silent, watching the water intently and not wanting to look backwards into the darkness of the trees. Even Manwena sat silent, but his presence still loomed like a threatening menace over Silvia. She contemplated inching further away from him but was too scared to move. And in any case, she was hemmed in by other children so to move would cause obvious confusion. After some time, she felt Manwena's growing agitation. His tongue clicked in a strange rhythm, and his right foot flexed back and forth as if trying to escape from itself.

"They are not coming!" she heard him angrily declare to no one in particular.

Just at that moment, they heard a crack in the bush behind them. A twig had snapped, and Manwena instinctively dropped into a crouching position, half facing the trees, one hand on the ground, the other on his rifle. He was ready to pounce, his eyes darting back and forth, scanning the thick backdrop behind them. Manwena's anxiety oozed out of him like an infection that strangled the entire group in a death grip. Silvia felt like she was suffocating.

Aaron waved his hand and indicated that they should move north along the bank. They crawled in the mud on hands and knees, dragging their few possessions behind them. Silvia managed to grab hold of Grace's skirt and did not let go. She did not care that her tugging made the effort more difficult for Grace, or indeed herself, as she had to crawl on only one hand. She needed the illusion of security that Grace somehow gave.

Another noise in the bush sent them all reeling. Were they being hunted? No one knew for sure whether the noises were animals or humans, and Manwena did not want to risk finding out. He ordered everyone into the water.

"But we can't swim," Evans protested.

"The crocodiles," whispered another terrified rebel. "They will eat us alive."

"Quiet," Manwena whispered, waiting until he held their full attention. "If the army is tracking us, then we are cornered on this riverbank, and they will pick us off like bugs. This is our only chance. You must lie in the water. Lie as still as you can with only your nose and mouth above the water. Do not move until I give the word."

No one dared argue. They spread out along the edge, and Silvia followed Grace as she waded into the cold dark water. Mud squelched around her toes, and a sick feeling of panic began to rise in her stomach. She wanted to cry but forced herself to just keep walking. The water was freezing and came up to her chest before she lowered her body down and tipped her head backwards. Its coolness swirled around her head and made her loose clothing float away from her in a mysterious dance.

Someone grabbed hold of her hand, and turning slightly, she found herself looking into Amos' eyes. He was there by her side, and when he squeezed her hand tighter and gave her a reassuring look, she felt all of her anger towards him melt away. She longed to embrace her friend for she suddenly realised that he had not abandoned her. He was not ashamed of her. He was not disgusted by her filth. What she saw in his eyes was his love and concern. Her old friend was still there, and in the darkness of the night, he no longer had to hide behind his cold stony mask. She squeezed his hand in return and smiled, letting him know that she understood.

They tilted their faces up towards the stars. "Just breathe," he whispered.

Time passed in a blur of eerie silence as the water filled their ears. Silvia was so exhausted that she kept dropping off to sleep, but as soon as her nose sank beneath the water, she woke in a terrified splutter. This attracted Manwena's attention more than once. In an effort to keep her eyes open and her mind active, she began counting stars, but her exhaustion would inevitably cause the stars to blur in brilliant colour right before her eyes closed again. The blackness of sleep seemed to be calling to her from beneath the water's surface. In the end, it was Amos who managed to distract her enough to keep her awake. He began to draw symbols on the palm of her hand, and Silvia had to concentrate to figure out what each one was. When she figured it out, she would squeeze his hand, and he would draw another one.

What seemed like hours dragged by, and Silvia's body began to shake as the cold penetrated through to her bones. She wondered how long Manwena would make them wait in the water. Surely, if the army had been tracking them, they would have either found them or been long gone by now. Perhaps, this was simply all for Manwena's evil enjoyment. She would not have been surprised if he was laughing at them as they struggled to survive his latest manner of torture.

Suddenly, Amos gripped her hand so hard she almost cried out. She instinctively glanced towards the water's edge and saw a line of men creeping along the shore. Under the moonlit sky, their black silhouettes were so obvious that she wondered why they bothered to bend double or walk quietly at all. They wore baggy full-length pants, long sleeve shirts and hats. In their hands, they each carried a rifle. Army! There was no doubt that these were the men Manwena had suspected were tracking them. They had not realised that the entire rebel group was submerged in the water, and Silvia held her breath, desperate not to give the game away. She closed her eyes and began to pray.

One by one, the army crept on, never realising that their prey was lying helpless just meters from the bank. She did not need any more encouragement to stay awake. As the army disappeared into the distance, and for the rest of the night, she lay still and alert, listening intently for any unusual sounds.

When the sun finally rose, and Manwena allowed them back on shore, it was with very desperate faces that they emerged. They lay for a long time, resting in the cool mud and basking in the warmth of the early morning sun. Silvia shivered helplessly. No one spoke, and no one moved. During the night, a strange and unseen force had united them, and Silvia felt oddly connected to this band of weary souls. They had all individually, and yet somehow jointly, begged the sky for mercy and found a shoestring of strength to cling on to. They had survived.

CHAPTER TWENTY-ONE

NAVIGATING CHOICES

Complicated lines are drawn upon the sand.

Etched into stone,

And cemented in the heart of man.

Rules and regulations that govern life;

Keeping it in order

Without question,

Without strife.

We are placed into a box

And dare not wonder why.

Somehow it is safer

Than the freedom we dream about,

But fail to live by.

Freedom without courage

Is a terrifying thing;

There is no map for a journey

That can only be guided

From within.

Without courage,

Life is predetermined

By lines drawn upon the sand,

And you'll be an old man all too soon,

So rise up now

And make your stand.

Sante knew they would have to escape soon. He could feel that Grace's time was short. Manwena was just tormenting her, like a predator that has his prey cornered. Besides, someone was eventually bound to notice all the not-so-subtle glances she gave him and the longer than appropriate stares. She wanted to go. She was desperate to go. Her life hung in the balance. He was the child, and she was his mother, yet somehow in the last few weeks since he had joined the ranks of soldiers, the authority she once held had begun to diminish. Still, he loved her desperately, even if he could not show it. He would give his life to save her, and indeed, that's what it felt like he was doing. He was convinced that the foreboding he felt was a warning of some sort. He reasoned that they were bound to be caught, but if he used himself as a decoy, perhaps, she would make it out alive and return to the life she once loved. His own life felt worthless because he had never known anything other than this war. He wanted to know, certainly. His soul gulped at the thought of freedom like a throat that had never tasted clean water. But it was useless to hope in what he was sure would never happen. Why set yourself up for such a massive fall? Besides, he had now seen the reality of the refugee camps and smelt the despondency that hung in the air above them. What was the point? The only point he could find in any of it was his mother's heart. He wanted her to know how much he loved her. He wanted her to know that he was willing to accept death head on, to chase her quest for freedom. Not because he believed that the freedom would come, but because he believed in her.

Since the night of the river, they had not stopped walking. Sante was exhausted and sick. He walked behind the line of new hostages as they tripped and staggered and fought for each inch of ground covered. It was as if they were the front line in a battle that raged in their heads. The river had been their saving grace and also their curse. Over the next few days and weeks, almost everyone experienced terrible stomach cramps, diarrhea, and vomiting. It left them absolutely depleted. Whenever he needed to dry-retch as they walked, Sante merely hung his tired head to the side and let the bile heave its way up his oesophagus and out of his cracked lips. The effort his body exerted for such a small amount of fluid hardly seemed worth it. There was simply nothing more left inside that could be disposed of. The irony was that even though the water had made them so sick, Sante was so dehydrated that he would have greedily gulped more into his system had he been able. But they had turned from the edge of the river and left it behind them long ago. There would be no going back.

At midday, they sat down in the dust to rest. The forest was sparse and bare around them, and while this gave them a view of the landscape, it also left them all feeling very exposed and vulnerable. Grace, as always, had planted herself on the edge of the group, and today, Sante dared to move towards her. Manwena seemed not to have noticed, so he sat down only a few feet from her side. She did not dare look at him. There was no food and no water to be had, so many of the rebels faded quickly into a delirious sleep.

Grace waited. From the corner of her eye, she had seen Sante approach and knew this might be the opportunity she was searching for to communicate with her son. It would only work if she had patience. She must wait until the time was just right, so she closed her eyes and pretended to sleep.

Sante had picked up a stick and sat, with his head down, drawing lines in the sand. The temptation to sleep was overwhelming, and he had to fight it with every ounce of his strength. He did not look up for a good ten minutes, and then, when he did, it was not at his mother. Turning his head to the left, he assessed the group. It appeared that even Manwena was too sick to care much about anything at present. He sat with his back propped up against a tree, his hands around his stomach and his eyes tightly closed. All but two of the other rebels were already asleep. Aaron was keeping watch, but Sante saw that his attempt was half-hearted as he stared vaguely through the trees at the distant horizon. He knew he had to seize this moment. Edging closer to Grace, he poked her leg with the end of the stick, and she opened her eyes. Holding her gaze, he nodded his head slowly and deliberately. Grace at once realised that he was saying, "Soon," and she could not keep from smiling.

Sante knew that he had to somehow convey to his mother the importance of the promise he had made to Amos. He drew two lines in the sand standing next to each other, then he drew a third line and, from it, an arrow that pointed to where Amos was presently lying. At the same time, he looked over at him, trying to indicate to Grace that a third person had to be included in their plan. Grace seemed to understand what he was saying. She then used her finger to draw a fourth line in the sand. Sante immediately wanted to protest. Four people would be pushing their luck far beyond reason. Grace sensed his disapproval but knew she needed his agreement. She would decide what to do about Silvia when the time came. Grace reminded herself that the promise she had made to the girl had not been absolute. Sante was her first priority, and she did not want him to back out, so she looked at him directly and nodded her head, hoping that he understood.

Grace's boldness was making Sante nervous, and again, he glanced around to make sure they were not being watched. His heart skipped a beat when his eyes fell on Manwena who was staring directly at them with bemused curiosity. He looked like a lion that had just come upon his favourite meal and was watching it naively frolic – unaware that it was about to meet its maker.

Grace noticed Manwena at the same moment. She watched him rise and come towards them through the pile of sleeping rebels. "*This is it,*" she thought as terror rose up her spine. She was sure Manwena knew exactly what was going on. Sometimes, he had a sixth sense about him, as if he could read her thoughts.

"Get up," he commanded her as he stood over them both looking down like black thunder.

She stood shaking. Without a word he grabbed her arm and began pulling her into the bush.

"Wait," Sante protested in a panic, "where are you taking her?"

Manwena stopped for a moment, then turned and smiled patronisingly at the boy. "I am doing what I should have done weeks ago. You will understand one day," he said in a sickly-sweet voice that quickly turned to venom. "Now sit down and be quiet or I will silence you for good."

Sante sat but hated himself for the cowardice that encircled him like a coiling snake. His chest was painfully tight making his breaths come in shallow gulps that left him feeling faint. How could he just sit and watch as the beast dragged his mother away? He wanted to run after them and smash his machete into Manwena's spine, but he couldn't move. He had lived his entire life in such fear of Manwena's wrath that his body obeyed his commands from sheer instinct while his mind was held captive. Sante sat hugging his knees into his chest, feeling like he was five years old again. He watched them walk away until they were out of sight, terrified that he would never see his mother again.

It was late in the afternoon when Manwena returned. Grace was not with him and Sante began to panic. He felt solely responsible for what had happened to her because of his delay in agreeing to escape. He had known her life was on the line. She had known it too, and yet, she had waited for him. She had never faltered in her faithfulness, and now it had possibly cost her life. Sante's heart was breaking. He felt now as if he had nothing left to live for. Why should he endure any more suffering?

Manwena was so smug that it made Sante want to tear him apart. He looked at his father smiling back at him, his evil eyes dancing above the jagged scar that cut his face into two mismatched pieces. "You won't have to worry about her bothering you anymore. I should have done that long ago." He held out a bloody cloth, and Sante glanced down to see three of his mother's fingers nestled into the fabric.

Sante turned his head and began heaving and dry retching uncontrollably as Manwena threw his head back and laughed.

Manwena swaggered away, drunk with bloody victory, to see if he would get another reaction from his fellow commanders. His need for respect was like a drug, and violence was the only way he knew how to get it. The atrocities he committed drove fear into the eyes of his companions and captives alike and fed his hunger for power. It angered him that his own son was not more like him. He began to wish he had actually killed Grace in front of the others, as then he would have received the respect due to him.

Sante watched him walk away. Turning to Amos he whispered in his ear. "Tonight, we go. It's now or never. I have to find my mother."

"But she's dead," Amos hissed, and Sante noted the lack of sympathy in his voice. It surprised him, and he instinctively backed off, not sure what to do. Amos immediately began backpedalling. "Sorry, Sante. I'm sorry for you. It's just that … Well I don't really think that now is a good time."

"It has to be now. If I don't go now, I know I will never have the courage to go. We must look for an opportunity."

"Ok, but I am not going to do anything stupid. We need to be wise."

"Of course, we do. I'm not about to jump up and start running into the bush," he replied sarcastically. This time it was Amos who did not respond. The tension between the two boys and the hopelessness of their situation was causing them to both feel enormously frustrated. Sante gulped his tears down into his stomach. Grace had been his strength, and now that she was gone, he felt so hollow and empty, like all of his insides had been removed, and he was caving in on himself. The grief he felt was unbearable. It was a knife whose jagged edges ripped through his heart, tearing the meaty flesh to ribbons. Amos did not say a word, his thoughts turning to his own mother. Though sitting side by side, both boys felt desperately alone.

CHAPTER TWENTY-TWO

SURVIVAL INSTINCT

Who would I be

If everything in my world disappeared?

What would I be?

A shadow trapped inside an empty space?

A captured animal, that no longer knows

How to be free?

Lying alone,

Naked and exposed.

Would I feel shame or exhilaration?

Would I wish for my world to return?

Or revel in the discovery of my own being?

Questions of purpose may arise.

The meaning of life,

The need for a guiding light.

Who would I be

If it was only you that disappeared?

What would I be?

A bird free at last to soar unrestricted,

Or one lost in the emptiness of space

And searching for a home?

Simply alone

With no other,

Would I seek to find another you?

Or learn to appreciate the simplicity of flight?

She slowly opened her eyes and looked out at the light that flickered around her. It was like looking through a crystal. Everything was sparkling in odd shapes. Nothing was recognisable. Hues of pink and blue danced across her field of vision as though the light bent down to touch her then flitted away again. She closed her eyes, her mind muddled and confused. Her head was aching, totally disorientated in time and place. Where was she? How did she get here? The light seemed to be trying to penetrate through her closed eyelids in a vivid red, and she raised her hand to shield her face from the sun.

As she touched her forehead, she felt a moist stickiness on her skin that caused her to jump in alarm. Looking at her hand, she saw crimson liquid staring back at her. She touched her cheek and felt raw exposed flesh. The contact sent shock waves of pain rippling through her nerves. She tried to sit up but shook uncontrollably and collapsed back onto her side, becoming suddenly aware of the gaping wounds on her left hand. Three of her fingers were missing. Panic welled up inside her as she stared at the bloody cavities left by the absence of her index, middle and ring fingers. All that remained were her thumb and smallest finger, sticking up oddly as if surprised at their abrupt aloneness. Using her teeth, she instinctively ripped some material from her skirt and wrapped it around her hand. It was partly to stop the blood flow and partly to hide the grotesque mutilation from her own eyes.

Oddly, Grace felt no real pain in her hand. She knew she needed to inspect the rest of her body but was too weak to move. How long had she been here? How much blood had she lost? The ground around her was caked hard with it. The repulsive smell reaching into her nostrils, and through to the back of her throat. Lying in her own bodily fluids that continued to seep from her skin, she again closed her eyes on the sun. Her mind quickly slipped away into semi-consciousness as her body heaved against the earth. Perhaps, it would open up and let her in this time. Perhaps, swallow her whole or break her apart bit by bit and devour her. She didn't care. Nothing mattered anymore. She was ready for death to come.

When Grace awoke again, the afternoon was drawing to a close. She struggled to open her eyes in response to the pain shooting through her body. It felt like something was tugging at her skin, trying to rip it from her bones.

In the treetops above, white-backed vultures had been gathering all day. They could smell death in the air and fought for position on the branches, waiting impatiently for the rot to set in. Once the victim below was confirmed dead, they would fight over the flesh, ripping it to pieces with their sharp talons, their bald heads plunging into the carcass, ingesting anything they could rip out and swallow. Their beady yellow eyes stared down in hungry anticipation as the bravest among them jumped over to the near-dead thing and began poking at the meat.

Grace finally managed to open her eyes that were now encrusted with dried blood, and her heart leapt in horror as she realised what the tugging sensation actually was. She screamed in panic, kicking wildly at the huge ugly bird that stood over her. A foot connected with its belly as it opened its wings and hopped a few feet away in fright, but it did not retreat far enough to ease Grace's mind. She turned her eyes skyward and caught her breath as she saw the hordes of vultures lining the branches above her. She knew that if she allowed herself to sleep again, the black devils would tear her limb from limb.

Forcing herself to rise to a sitting position by pushing her right arm up behind her, she began shouting as she waved her bloody stump of a hand in the air. The effort caused such immense pain that she almost fainted, but she caught her head in her hands, somehow managing to force the dizziness away. She had to get up. She knew she had to walk. She made a quick inspection of her legs and feet, relieved to see that they were still intact. Grabbing a nearby tree, she put her arms around the trunk and used it to offset her own weight, pushing her legs underneath her until she was vertical. The vulture had backed further away, somewhat surprised and disappointed that its victim was alive again, and a good five feet taller than before. Still, the smell of fresh blood and the perceived weakness of this staggering human told the bird to remain close.

Grace knew her legs would not hold her if she let go of the

tree. Flashbacks of Manwena uncontrollably entered her mind, and she wept without tears as she clung to the thick trunk for support. She remembered now how he had dragged her here. He had raped her, and then beaten her until she was no longer conscious. She could not recall how or when her fingers were removed. Perhaps, he would keep them as a trophy. She guessed Manwena had presumed she was dead before he walked away and would not have wanted to waste a precious bullet on her. Hatred rose up within her for the evil of her captor, and an intense pain gouged out the hollows of her insides. If she died now, she reasoned, Manwena had won. That single thought filled her with a strange determination. The vultures that looked on made her want to scream in rage. How dare these disgusting birds come so close to making her their victim too? She wanted desperately to reach out and attack them, torturing them as she had been tortured. She was insanely angry and desperate for some kind of brutal revenge of her own, but her arms could not leave the safety of the tree trunk.

There seemed no way forward, and Grace's howling became more hysterical as panic and anger melded together. She could not think straight and did not know what to do. The vulture waited patiently, its eyes fixated upon her as if expecting her to drop and surrender at any moment. She had to think, but a thick fog wove its way through her mind, filling up the empty spaces with heaviness and confusion. The air hung like webs around her as the clouds above built their towers of furious grey mass to block out the sun. Like the vultures, they were just waiting for the opportune time to unleash a torrent.

Grace lost track of time as she clung to the tree. She grew weaker and weaker, but on the inside, she was screaming at death, trying to defy its threats. Eventually, it became clear to her that if she did not move, she might as well just give up. She had to at least try. Looking around, she noticed a large stick that could be used to prop herself up as she walked. A few tentative steps forward, and she grabbed it with her good hand, while she held her injured hand up between her breasts, elevated in an attempt to slow the flow of blood.

Now with her good hand on the stick, Grace felt a sudden surge of victory. One small triumph was hers. She hissed at the birds, willing them back into the darkness from which they had come. On wobbly legs, she looked around, not sure which way to go. There were no tracks. No indicators of where Manwena had gone. Just endless forest that seemed to hem her in. In an effort to save itself, her mind went into an automatic state of motion, creating small and achievable goals for her to achieve. Just one step forward, then another; just get past that tree; now that fallen log; and on and on and on.

Progress was slow, but as she staggered through the bush, something amazing and startling occurred to Grace. She stopped short and held her breath as if trying not to let the thought go. Could it really be? Was it real? Could she dare to let herself even think that she might be *free*? Suddenly, and surprisingly, and terrifyingly, free! There was no one telling her what to do or where to go. There was no immediate threat from the men who had held her captive for so long. There was also no group in which to hide. The prospect momentarily halted her. Where would she go? What would she do? What would happen if she was caught? Would she ever see her treasured son again? It was not meant to be like this!

Freedom had been something she had dreamed of finding on her own terms, not in this unpredictable way. And yet, she recognised a light within her that anxiously wanted to grab the possibility of freedom with both hands. It was a tug of war – one part of her mind paralysed by fear of the unknown and aching over her lost son, while the other dared to feel joy at the prospect of liberation. She sat down on a log, resting her tired legs. She listened to the bush around her. It was all so familiar, and yet she had never sat alone for so long or felt so vulnerable. Like a little child, lost without its mother, Grace was terrified looking around with suspicious eyes and a thumping heart. She simply did not know what to do.

After a time, Grace noticed the vulture again. She had been dropping a trail of blood behind her that the bird could not resist, although, the numbers of onlookers in the trees above had significantly dwindled. This time, she noted in surprise that she was actually thankful for its presence. Despite its evil intentions, the closeness of another living creature made her feel strangely reassured.

"What shall I do?" she said aloud looking at the yellow eyes as if expecting an articulate answer. There was nothing. "Shall I go this way?" she pointed her stick to the right. "Or this way?" Still no response from the creature that looked almost as perplexed as she felt.

Grace gave up, turning her head away from the bird in feigned disgust that he did not measure up to her expectations. "I know you could show me how to get out of this place," she said with her head still turned away. The vulture cocked its head to one side but did not move. Grace sighed, rose from her log, and turned her head to face him again. "I'm moving this way," she pointed into the trees. "If this is the wrong way, you better stop me." She staggered off into the bush leaving the confused bird to contemplate whether this meal was a waste of effort. After some minutes, the large vulture flew up into the trees and watched her from a safer distance as she gradually disappeared. He would turn his prospects elsewhere. Grace put one foot in front of the other and did not look back.

Softly and silently, raindrops began to fall.

CHAPTER TWENTY-THREE

SUICIDE MISSION

Like the fly that just keeps coming

In its crazy kind of way.

Like the water that drips incessantly

Without break or delay.

Like the sun that keeps on rising

At the dawn of every day.

So, I obsess about you

In my own determined way.

I can taste you on my lips,

And feel you in the air.

I could reach out to gently touch you

If only you were there.

I imagine what it's like

To feel you all around.

And I hold on to the hope

That one day, you'll be found.

Freedom!

Being one of the few not still suffering the effects of the night in the river, Amos had been left on watch. It was all the luck he needed to cling to. As the night wore on, he followed the moon's journey across the sky, waiting for it to edge a little higher before he put his plan into action. It was only a half moon that occasionally dipped behind clouds, which was another piece of luck. It seemed like the perfect night. The perfect opportunity to begin his bid for freedom. But there was a strong tugging at his heart that he found hard to ignore. It was making him question everything.

His plan to escape with Sante did not include Silvia and his sisters. He had been able to push all thoughts of taking them aside until now, partly because their plans had never felt truly real, and partly because it was easier to dream about escape without the weight of responsibility their presence entailed. But now that the fantasy was pushing its way into reality, he could no longer ignore the feelings of loss and heartbreak that were beginning to blur his vision. How could he leave them here and run away to freedom with Sante, knowing full well that they were likely the only remaining connections to his past life? How could he betray them? How could he just turn his back, knowing that they trusted him so much? How could he leave them all at the hands of such merciless blood-thirsty men? At one level, the idea was inconceivable, and yet, there it stood before him like a wall he could not climb over or see around. There were no easy answers. In fact, there were no answers at all. Just a sickening sense of his own cowardice that sought self-preservation over the protection of those he loved most. He hung his head in despair.

Sante was dozing in and out of a fitful sleep on the rough ground, not too far from where Amos sat. Or perhaps, he was just pretending to sleep. Amos could not be entirely sure, but either way, it would not take much to wake him when the time was right. They had signalled to each other earlier that evening, and both knew that if the opportunity arose, this was the night.

All three girls were huddled together in the middle of the group. To wake them when they knew nothing of the plan to escape was so risky that Amos began again justifying to himself that he could leave them. In leaving them, he would be saving them from the certain death that would come if they were caught. Perhaps, they would have a chance to escape later on – in a few days' time or even in the coming weeks. Perhaps, his departure would serve as a motivation for them. And yet, how could he go without them? His mind was in turmoil as he weighed up the decision. He had not even discussed the option of bringing the girls with Sante. Despite their alliance, each boy still held the other cautiously at arm's length, constantly testing the boundaries of trust.

As the moon drifted across the sky, the shadows on the ground contorted into different shapes that Amos found disorientating. He tried not to look at the lopsided dark shadows. They somehow made his sense of perspective blur. After some time, he realised that all of the rebels were finally asleep and that if he was to move, he had to move now. He had still not made a final decision about the girls as he inched closer to Sante and poked his leg with a stick. Sante, who was lying on his side facing Amos, opened his eyes. He cautiously sat up and inspected the scene of sleeping rebels that lay before him. All was quiet, except for the drum of their thumping hearts. Manwena was snoring with his head propped up against a tree root. The sickness and subsequent lethargy that lingered among the group was going to aid their bid for freedom.

The boys rose to their feet, and Sante was the first to begin walking softly away. Behind him, he sensed Amos hesitating and glanced quickly over his shoulder. Amos had not moved but was instead looking at the place where his sisters and Silvia lay sleeping. Sante's heart skipped a beat as he consciously recognised for the first time the sacrifice Amos was making to leave his sisters behind. Would he try to do something foolish? Would he jeopardise their plan by attempting to bring them along? Amos looked like he was caught in a spider's web, and Sante could do nothing other than silently beckon him forward.

Amos knew the situation was useless, but he could not seem to move his feet. This was the moment he dreaded, and his anxiety was paralysing. He didn't want to risk the lives of the girls. He didn't want to break his word to Sante. He desperately didn't want to get caught. But he didn't want to leave them either, knowing that he may never see them again.

Sante began waving his right arm in a motion that indicated that they should move. Amos looked at his friend and could see the fear etched in the stark whiteness of his eyes. It was enough to propel him into action. Without further contemplation, he realised there was really no decision to make at all. He couldn't risk the consequences of being caught. The girls would surely wake in fear and make a racket. It was impossible to even comprehend a successful escape with them. An intrusive image of their slaughter entered his mind, and it was all Amos needed to turn his back. With a heavy heart, he began to creep away.

Would he ever see them again? Who would look out for them if he wasn't here? His heart told him that he was a traitor as well as a coward for he knew that if he were truly brave, he would never leave his sisters behind. There was no justification he could find for the action he was taking. He didn't even want to think about how his sisters might feel when they realised he was gone.

The boys were extremely careful about where they placed their feet. They couldn't afford a twig to snap under their weight as anything out of the ordinary might rouse the rebels from sleep. It was only after several hundred meters that they both felt they could even breathe normally again. As the space between them and the rebels grew, they both became less anxious and finally felt it was safe enough to talk in hushed tones.

"Should we stop?" Sante whispered.

"Stop?" Amos was bewildered by the question.

"Yes, stop and hide somewhere."

"We need to get as far away as we can. We need to keep going."

"But we don't know where we're going in the dark, and if we go too far, I will never be able to find my mother," Sante replied.

Amos was agitated. He had just left his sisters, and all Sante could think about was his mother, who was probably long dead by now anyway. "We can't just stop here," he hissed. "The group isn't that far away yet, and what if we fall asleep and they find us? It's not worth the risk, Sante. We will find your mother, but not right now and not in the dark. You need to be patient and, for now, just think of safety. Once we're free, then it will be time to worry about other things."

Sante was silent before slowly nodding his head. He knew Amos was being sensible.

There was a rustling in a bush to their left and both boys jumped. Sante let out an involuntary yelp and backed away. Amos began running, and Sante followed close on his heels. They ran in panic, tripping over branches and groping wildly with arms outstretched, trying to avoid hitting anything in the darkness. On and on without stopping for what seemed like hours. The darkness played tricks on their eyes. Trees took on the forms of dark figures that made the boys jump before they turned back into trees again. The branches scraping their arms and legs felt oddly like hands trying to grab at them. Was that a large animal up ahead, or just a fallen log? They ran on and on until sheer exhaustion forced them to stop, panting and bent double with their hands on their knees.

"What was that?" Sante asked, his mind still sure that they were being followed by some lurking evil. Vomit rose from his gut and burned the lining of his throat as he desperately tried to swallow it back down. He had never been away from the rebels before. He had never known any other life. Perhaps it wasn't too late to go back and just pretend that he had never left. He had been initiated after all, smeared with the Shea nut oil they would use to track him down. How would they kill him when he was found? His breathing became faster and more frantic. His vision blurred as tears fogged his eyes.

"Not sure," Amos puffed in quiet reply. He felt incredibly vulnerable and frightened but did not want to let on. "Think we lost it. Let's hide under here."

It wasn't a suggestion but an order, as he bent and crawled on all fours under the canopy of a small circular bush. The night air was cool and crisp, and an eerie silence hung like a fog the air.

Amos' mind whirled with a thousand different thoughts at once. Ideas about what they should do, how far they might be from any of the refugee camps, how close they were to the rebels. He was only certain of one thing. They were well and truly lost. They were two young children, alone in the middle of the bush, far from anything familiar or safe. But Amos was the eldest, and although he wanted to shun the responsibility, he could not escape the feeling that he was now in charge and had to maintain control of his own frazzled emotions. He sensed the panic and fear that consumed Sante, but he tried not to pay too much attention to it. It would only distract him from the task at hand. He had to get them to safety. In the morning they would keep going; striking one foot in front of the other. It was their only chance.

"We should take turns keeping watch," Amos directed. "Try to get some sleep. I will go first."

Sante tried to find a comfortable position and ended up half sitting with his back propped up against the tree's thin trunk, and his legs curled up awkwardly underneath. He looked at Amos before closing his eyes. Amos had his knees pulled up to his chest, and his arms wrapped around them. His face was hidden in the darkness, but Sante was aware of the eerie silence in the air around them as if it was laden thick with unspoken and unanswered questions. Would they make it? Had they been followed? What would they yet have to face? Hunger and thirst gnawed at him as he fell into a fitful sleep.

When dawn broke, Sante was the first to open his eyes. He looked around to find Amos asleep under the branches of their little nest. Realising that Amos must have fallen asleep without waking him to take over the watch, he sighed in relief that nothing bad had befallen them as they innocently slept. All was quiet outside, so he decided not to wake Amos for a moment, but instead, slipped out to relieve himself. The air was already beginning to warm.

Standing straight, Sante could not resist the urge to stretch his arms above his head. He looked around and saw a rocky outcrop that they must have run past the night before. It was only about twenty meters from their hiding place and rose like a small hill from the otherwise flat ground. A few trees and shrubs sporadically covered the rocks as if protesting against their intrusion in the landscape by somehow planting their roots deep within the cracks to seek out the soil beneath. There was no evidence of any human presence, but Sante did not want to take any chances. He retreated to their hiding place, which felt deceptively secure.

"Where did you go?" asked Amos, who was now awake and sitting quietly.

"Just outside to pee. I saw a rock wall. It could be used as a hiding place, but I didn't see anyone there."

"Before we move again, we should have a plan," Amos whispered.

"Yes," Sante agreed. Although he couldn't think what it should be. Beyond walking and hiding, their options were few.

"They will have probably discovered we are missing by now. Are they likely to come looking for us straight away?" Amos asked. He had not experienced how their particular commanders responded to escapees.

Sante thought for a moment, remembering times when children had attempted to escape in the past. "Yes," he sighed. "As soon as they realise, they will probably send groups out in all directions to search. Manwena knows that it will fall on his head if we are not found, so he will be more determined than anyone." Sante's skin began to crawl as he thought of the prospect of being caught.

"We should keep moving," Amos said, but then hesitated.

"Or perhaps we should continue to hide. If they discovered that we were missing some time last night, they will already be on our trail."

"Then what are we waiting for?" Sante's voice began to quiver. "We can't just sit and wait for them to track us down. It's the Shea nut oil. They will find us. I have seen them use it to find others."

"Ok, let's keep moving then, even though it's daylight," Amos replied. "But we need to be so careful." He was stating the obvious, but Sante listened intently anyway.

"You lead the way, and I will walk at the back," Sante suggested. "And if either of us hear anything, we hiss and get down."

With that, Amos looked his companion in the eyes and nodded his head. There was an acknowledgment of the danger, and yet, it felt like there was no real choice to be made. To simply sit still and hide somehow, felt like they were giving over the little control they had to the rebels; waiting for an inevitable showdown that they were not equipped to fight. At least if they walked, they could determine their direction and speed and, with any luck, find a camp or even a town where they could safely blend in with the crowd.

Sante followed Amos out of their hiding place and fell into position behind him. Amos headed in the direction of the rising sun and made sure they stayed away from the rocky outcrop as they skirted around it. Such places were good hiding spots for humans and animals alike, and he did not want to draw the attention of either. There remained a peculiar quietness in the air, as if even the birds had not yet woken to the new dawn. It made every footstep and every breath seem impossibly loud, and Amos was perturbed by the noise they were making. He had a strange sense of foreboding and, in his anxiety, started walking faster and with more urgency. There was no time to lose.

Branches and light green leaves brushed fresh dew onto their skins as they walked. Their swollen feet felt the coolness of the forest floor, but it did not numb the pain they felt with every step. Sante's feet were particularly cracked and sore, and a large boil had erupted on the base of his right heel causing him to limp. It throbbed with a pain so intense that it shot up his leg with needle-like fingers that pulled at raw nerve endings. He tried hard not to focus on the pain as he did not want Amos to see him struggle, but as the morning wore on, it became ever more difficult to hide. He gritted his teeth and did not utter a word.

The sun rose with a sharp intensity that drove them to pant with thirst after just a few hours. It was imperative that they find water if they were to have the endurance needed to go on. Amos kept his eyes peeled, but the hotter the sun became, the drier the ground began to look.

Suddenly, Amos heard Sante hiss and instinctively stopped in his tracks, crouching low. He looked back at Sante expecting to see a look of fear in his eyes but was surprised by the boy's expression. Sante was smiling, pointing away to his left. Amos turned to see what Sante was looking at and grinned in excitement at the sight of a huge mango tree. Its branches bowed low under the weight of its succulent ripe fruit.

The boys could hardly restrain themselves. Amos knew that even though it wasn't water, there was probably enough liquid in the fruit to keep them going for a time, and they could stockpile as many as they could carry.

"Someone needs to keep watch," Amos suggested, not

volunteering himself this time.

"Ok, I will," Sante said, indicating that Amos should move. He was relieved to remain sitting and gripped the top of his ankle tightly to try and ease the mounting pain. Amos did not hesitate. As Sante looked all around, scanning the bush for any movement, Amos crawled low towards the tree. He quickly began to gather fruit from the lowest branches. He peeled back the soft skin of a particularly large orange mango and closed his eyes as its flavour and softness hit his taste buds. Juice streamed down his chin and he sighed in ecstasy. For the first time since their escape the night before, he allowed himself a moment to truly relax.

Amos realised that he could not carry enough mangoes on his own and beckoned Sante to join him. He watched, concerned, as Sante hobbled over.

"Your ankle?"

"It's nothing," Sante responded, shooting Amos a hostile look that told him to ask no more.

Amos hesitated. "Let's climb up into the tree. It's quite thick up there and will be a good place to hide while we eat. We should also use this as a time to rest before we move again. Eat as much as you can, and then we will carry as many as we are able."

The next hour was spent in pure bliss. The inviting leaves of the mango tree enfolded them into its curtained sanctuary, and they lost themselves in the delicious flavour of the mangos and ate until their stomachs bulged and groaned. For a brief moment, they let go of all thoughts of the past or the future and simply enjoyed the present.

CHAPTER TWENTY-FOUR

RESURRECTED

Ready or not

Here I come

With snarling teeth

And a loaded gun.

Ready or not

I'll watch you run.

You're a pitiful sight

My little son.

anwena was in a blinding rage. Never before, in his time as commander, had anyone successfully escaped, and the fear of his own demise now drove him on. The torture he would inflict on the boys once they were found somehow seemed a hollow satisfaction. He was furious that his own son had disrespected him in this way. It cast shame on his reputation and brought his authority into disrepute. He looked like a fool. They would question how a man who was unable to control his own son could lead a division of the resistance movement. When Kony heard of this, he would probably never let him lead again. He may even cast him out – or worse.

Manwena had believed he had dealt with the possibility of dissention by disposing of Grace. He now realised that she had obviously had more power over Sante than he was aware. Manwena reasoned that the boy was deluding himself if he really thought he'd be able to escape, but it was the very fact that he had tried that so infuriated him.

The unit split up and went out to search in different directions with specific instructions to report back before sundown. The escapees were to be kept alive. Manwena was anxious that he should be the one to savour victory. Not only did he want to kill them, but he wanted to be the one who tracked them down. It would be a good example to the others of the power of the Shea nut oil, the force of his command, and the might of the resistance movement. Once he had proven himself, the dark forces and spirits that Kony often spoke of would also be credited to him.

While most formed groups of four or five to search for the abductees, Manwena had gone out alone. Although he did not like being alone in the bush without backup, he reasoned that he could move faster without anyone to hold him back. His mind was a black fog of turmoil as he thrashed his way through the undergrowth, and he became increasingly careless about the noise he was making that might draw unwanted attention. Rage clouded his judgment and made it almost impossible for him to discern a straight line. His vision was blurred and fuzzy. The tree branches seemed to be clawing at his face like they were trying to rip it apart. The touch of their jagged edges on his skin infuriated him further, and he waved his arms wildly as if trying to warn them to move aside at his presence. They did not; standing instead to rigid attention as he rushed past. He stopped only occasionally to look for tracks or clues that might lead him to the boys.

Earlier that morning, Aaron's repeated shouts of "They are gone. They are gone," had roused him.

"What? Who are gone?" Manwena's mind was initially confused, even though he immediately looked for Sante. Gut instinct had told him that it was his son who was absent.

"Sante and Amos. They must have left in the night."

As the group was organised into search parties, Manwena's rage had darkened. Everyone was staying well out of his way, and unbeknownst to him, even Aaron was relieved when he had decided to hunt alone. They all knew that if the boys were not found, others would be punished in their place. There was always someone to blame.

Suddenly, Manwena stopped dead in his tracks. He felt an ominous presence, as if a looming creature was reaching down to him from the trees prompting him to slow down. He was not afraid, although the tiny hairs on the backs of his arms and neck stood up to attention like those on the neck of a dog that had been threatened. He looked around but, at first, saw nothing except the typical shrubs, long grasses, rocks and trees. Then his eyes landed on a rock to his left, and his gaze was halted. There. A distinct bright red spot of blood marked its surface. He bent to touch it and rubbed the drying stickiness between his thumb and index finger. It was fresh and tantalising. He immediately began looking for another drop of blood, and then another and another. The trail was so obvious, he laughed aloud. An evil intent crept deeper under his skin. The hunt was on.

CHAPTER TWENTY-FIVE

HOPE

I stand on the edge of a sheer cliff

As the wind rushes up the gully

And caresses my face in its grasp.

There is a silence and a peace filling me

As the forest breathes in deeply,

And the air whispers secrets long past.

I might hear them, if I ever stop long enough to listen.

And so, I do.

This time – no pushing forward to reach my intended destination.

I linger in the silence of nature,

And hear God calling my name;

Like a mother seeking her lost child.

I am here.

Right here!

But am I ready to follow Your lead

And give up on my own agendas?

That burning question surfaces again

And this time cannot be suppressed.

What is it that You really want of me?

What is it that You have laid out before me

Down there in the valley that I cannot see?

Will I choose to seek it?

And can I really trust,

That in stepping out over the edge

You will hold me up

And teach me to fly?

G race had lost track of time, as if she had been locked up in a quiet, dark room. Sometimes, she walked with her mutilated hand elevated between her breasts and her other hand gripping the stick that had become like a life support. Sometimes, she let her body simply crumple onto the hard ground, and as if it cradled her, she slept. Had it been days, weeks, or maybe just hours since she had been dragged away from the group? Had she been alone the whole time? Oddly, she did not feel alone, but although she kept looking around, she could not see anyone walking with her. She was confused and sure of nothing save her desire to keep moving.

In reality, it had only been two days since Manwena had forcibly taken her away from the group and from Sante. Since picking up her stick and her determination the day before, Grace had managed to drag her aching body over several miles of rocky terrain. She would sleep sporadically whenever the effort to move became too overwhelming, but the pain in her hand would wake her after no longer than an hour, and she would stand to her feet and set off again. Even though she was lost and disorientated, she had the good sense to know that there was no point hanging around in one spot for too long. She was afraid that if she did stop unnecessarily, she might get comfortable and not want to move again. Then death would come and crowd down upon her, pinning her to the spot and digging a shallow open-cut grave for her to rest in. She could not allow that to happen.

Sometime on that second day, Grace began to suffer the effects of severe dehydration. Although her mind attempted to hold her physical being upright in an iron grip of fortitude, she knew it was losing the battle. She was fighting dizziness and a blinding headache, and step by slow step, she could feel herself unravelling. But she had to move and resist the urge to cave in. She would pick a tree in the distance and aim for it, watching it intently through squinted eyes as it inched closer and closer. Then when she reached it, she would stop and rest her back against its solid trunk and say a little prayer of thanks before picking another tree in the distance to focus on. It was a cycle she continually repeated in an effort to remain vertical and conscious. She began to long for a distinctive hill, rock or ant mound to climb. Anything that would give her some sense of perspective on this flat landscape, and perhaps, even allow her a glimpse of something to aim for. A road or a village would have appeared like a mirage in the desert.

As she walked, Grace's mind wandered back over her past, and the ache of frustration and bitterness marred her face and tightened her chest. She hated Manwena with a deep writhing contempt. She hated what he had done to her. She hated what he had done to her children. In her mind, he was the personification of pure evil, even more so than Kony – the very thought of whom made her shudder with fear.

She had met Kony on several occasions. She had heard his ravings about what would happen to Uganda when the resistance movement won the war. He spoke about how Uganda would become a theocracy and be governed by the principles of the Biblical Ten Commandments. But Grace was no fool. Although terrified by the man who would cut off the lips and noses of people who bothered him – forcing them to eat their own flesh, she had never believed his preaching. In talks with Sarah, she had learned that the very first of the Ten Commandments stated that people should not kill one another. Therefore, in her mind, Kony was quite simply mad. He was justifying killing in order to get to a place where he no longer had to kill. There seemed no rationale for his ravings. There was only evil intent, blinding fear, enforced submission, and greed for absolute power. It made her sick to the pit of her stomach. There was a voice inside her that screamed so loudly, "Why isn't this mad man being stopped? Why isn't he being hunted down? How on earth has he been able to get away with such blatant murder, torture and rape for so many years? Was life just one big sick joke?" Perhaps, God really did hate her and the rest of the Acholi people. Perhaps, this war was somehow punishment for their existence.

Grace remembered the days when she had discovered for the first time that she was pregnant. The little swollen belly of her young body had been an added burden during the difficult time of her early captivity. It had been an older woman in the group who had first alerted her to the idea that she might be pregnant, and she had been shocked and absolutely terrified. She was only a child herself and so far from home. So far from all that was safe and secure. She had panicked about how she was going to cope with a baby. As her time for delivery had drawn near, she had been sent away to a women's camp where other young abducted girls were also waiting for their babies to arrive. Older women in the camp helped her with the delivery and moments after he had been born, she was handed her tiny dark and sticky bundle. Grace remembered the shock of holding the delicate new life for the first time. She was terrified, but in her fear, she also felt an unexpected and incredible awe as she gazed at her baby. Little Sante's screwed-up face was so perfect, and instead of being her undoing, his complete dependence upon her had given her a new purpose and reason to live. In a way, she now realised, he had saved her life.

"Oh God," she whispered aloud as her body once again crumpled to the ground. She caught herself on her knees and, leaning on her stick, turned her eyes up towards the blue skies above. "Oh God, please … please, protect him. Please, keep him safe." Her tears flowed.

Grace bowed her head and sobbed into her good hand. Tears ran in dirty streaks down her blood-stained face. Her eyes were so red and swollen she could hardly see. It didn't matter. In her grief and sorrow, nothing seemed to matter. Where was God? Why didn't He answer? There was too much pain to bear now. How could she go on? It was as if her heart was being twisted around and around by a huge unseen hand.

Grace remained on her knees sobbing for a long time. The temptation to give up slowly began to consume her and corrode her determination. It would be so easy to finally have an end to all her suffering. She could just lie down and not wake up again. She knew death would come quickly. It was calling her into its embrace with such a soft and alluring voice. The other voice in her head, the voice of life – commanding her to get up again and keep going – while still angry and harsh, was growing weaker. This time, she knew she could ignore it. She could just listen to death's welcome and follow its lead. She didn't need to know where she was going, for it would show her the way.

In that moment of heartache, Grace found herself making the choice. No more, she heard herself saying. It's enough. It's over. I'm done. She lay down on the dirt, as if on a bed of pillows, and she waited.

Time seemed to stop. She listened to the sound of her breathing. She felt the mosquitos pierce her skin and didn't bother to brush them away. She was sinking deeper into an endless void, her limbs heavy, yet weightless, as they prepared to atrophy. She was returning to the dust; the voice of life only a whimper now as she lay dying.

"Mama, Mama." Sante was there in her dreams. She couldn't see him, but she could hear his voice so clearly. Had he been killed? Was he coming to her from death itself? Would they all be together again soon; Judy, Sante and herself?

Sante's voice grew louder and louder, until it seemed to be right outside her head. Was it real? But how could it be? How could he be here with her? She told herself that she must be dreaming, but as she opened her eyes, she felt his hands upon her shoulders.

"Mama. Mama," he kept repeating in desperation. She looked up into his dark eyes and was aware that they seemed to take a physical hold of her whole being. His deep eyes were pulling her out of the one-way tunnel she had been heading down. Without another word spoken, they held each other in a locked stare. Sante was not going to let her go, and Grace knew it, but it was with some initial reluctance that she let go of the hand of death and felt herself spin back towards reality.

"Get me a mango," Grace suddenly heard Sante say. It seemed like an odd request at a time like this, and she was not sure whom he was asking. She tried to speak, but only a raspy incoherent sound escaped her lips. Moments later, she tasted the sweet juice of an overripe mango as it was squeezed between her swollen lips. Heaven! She gulped it down, desperately hoping for more. For several minutes, Sante supported her head and fed her mango, like she was a little baby eating food for the first time. The sugary juice and pulp were enough to revive Grace slightly, and she hugged her son and cried into his shoulder, finally convinced that he was real. It seemed impossible, and yet somehow, he was alive and here with her now when she needed him most.

"How did you ..." she began to ask. A dozen questions buzzed through her mind, but another voice from behind her interrupted.

"Sante, we need to move. We are too exposed here. At least, let us find a place to hide while Grace gathers her strength."

Grace turned slightly towards the sound of the voice and saw Amos. He smiled shyly as their eyes met, and then, quickly came to her aid.

With Sante on one side and Amos on the other, Grace slowly rose to her feet. They began moving forward, one foot slowly placed in front of the other. With her arms draped over their shoulders the boys carried much of her weight, making walking much easier for Grace.

"What happened to you, Mama?" Sante asked as they walked.

Grace hesitated before answering. She knew the details were not necessary and would only upset and anger him. "Manwena thought he had killed me," she replied.

"I know," Sante interrupted. "He told me you were dead."

"I must have been knocked unconscious. When I woke, he was gone. I was alone so I got up and started walking. I didn't know where I was going. How did you find me? How did you get here? Where are the others?" Questions began to tumble out of Grace's mouth in a raspy voice.

"We escaped last night. We were hoping to find you, but really, it's a miracle. Although we may have placed you in more danger, now that we are together," Amos blurted out.

"Or the opposite," Grace admitted sadly, as she suddenly realised that her injuries would significantly slow the boys down and make their capture more likely.

"All that matters is that we are together again," said Sante in a voice that silenced Amos from further comment. "I never thought I would see you again, Mama."

"Yes," she quietly agreed as tears ran like silent rivers down her cheeks. She wondered if perhaps God did care for her after all.

CHAPTER TWENTY-SIX

COLLISION

So close,

You are my father,

And yet our worlds

Will not collide.

A political fence divides us

Built with calculated lies.

I am saddened, that in this life

I will never call you friend;

For we are too afraid to question

The lies devised to bring our end.

So close,

You are my father,

But I don't know

Your real name,

For you were taken while still young

And trapped within this violent game.

You will never learn to question

The path that you now tread,

For to do so would bring shame,

And dishonour on your head.

So close,

You are my father,

But our backs are up against

An invisible wall.

We stand on different sides,

And divided, we shall fall.

I had hoped to one-day see

A lasting peace settle here,

But first we had to bravely question

Our own preconditioned fear.

It was unbelievable. Sante kept staring at his mother, as if he was afraid that she would disappear if he took his eyes off her. She was so thin and frail. He could feel the bones in her back that protruded through her tattered shirt. Her skin had an almost grey tinge to it, and her hair was covered in dirt and dried blood. How was it possible that her appearance had changed so much in just a few short days? How was it possible that her weight had dropped so drastically? She had not had much weight to lose in the first place, but now she looked almost skeletal. Sante could not hide his shock.

Grace looked at him and smiled. He wondered if she could somehow read his thoughts.

"Amos," he said, attempting to regain his focus. "Let's head for that anthill and stop for a rest." It had been several hours since they had begun walking.

Amos nodded. He was still clutching a dozen small mangos bundled up in his shirt.

As they arrived at the base of the tall anthill, Grace let go of Amos and Sante and collapsed on the ground with a sigh. Looking down at her again, Sante could see that she was absolutely exhausted. She closed her eyes and let her head fall to rest on a tree stump. He felt very tired himself but was too anxious to relax. Amos handed him a mango, and without thinking, he gave it to Grace.

"You have mine as well," he ordered. He wanted to wake her from her slumber, as he was afraid that she would just lie down and die in front of them. He had never seen her in such bad condition. "I'm going to climb up here and see what I can see."

Grace had no time to protest as Sante turned and began to pull his lithe body up the anthill using the small trees that clung onto its steep sides and sucked their nutrients from its core. Once he reached the tree-covered summit, he crouched low and tried to peer through the foliage. It was difficult to see clearly, but he gradually became more confident, until he was standing vertical and was able to gently move the branches aside to get a better view.

On the horizon, dark storm clouds were forming. The sun behind them cast an iridescent light over the luminous green of the trees that covered every inch of terrain. The sense of perspective he gained from the slight elevation was a liberating feeling that took Sante's breath away. He could not help but smile as he marvelled at the beauty before him and the peace he felt in those few moments. It was such irony. He felt like he was caught in the middle of two worlds. On the one hand, he knew he was running for his life from those who would slaughter him in ways too grotesque to imagine. On the other, he was looking out towards the potential of a very different life. A life that still only existed in the realms of his imagination, but which he desperately wanted to make real. And here he was, with feet on both sides of the precipice, not yet certain which way he would fall. But as he looked over the miles of relatively flat landscape, Sante began to feel confident of escape. And then in the distance, he saw what he was sure must be a road. He wanted to shout for joy. A road! It was a long way away, but it was a symbol. A beacon of light to head towards and follow to hope's end. Perhaps, they would be able to make it to a town or a camp. While the thought was terrifying for the boy who had never lived anywhere but the bush, he knew it was their only chance.

Sante was about to call the good news down to the others when his heart involuntarily skipped a beat, and then began pounding in his chest as if trying to leap out and search for safety. His peace was shattered as he held his breath and looked in horror at a dark figure moving between the trees, not one hundred yards from where the fugitives hid. Manwena! He was tracking them. His machete was slung casually over his shoulder, and he moved like a lion stalking its prey. Slowly from tree to tree, listening, watching, waiting to catch a glimpse of his conquest. He looked like he might even play with them for a while. Watch them from a distance and plot evil tortures until he became frantic for blood and ready to pounce.

Sante crouched low, paralysed with fear. He did not know what to do or which way to turn. Should they make a run for it or attempt to hide and let him pass? Seconds seemed to drag like hours as he watched his father moving closer and closer to his still unseen target. He looked down at his mother and knew she had no chance. She could not run and there was no way she could climb the anthill to hide. She was like a wounded deer caught in the sights of a hunter. There was no escape.

Suddenly, Sante knew what he had to do. He bolted down the side of the anthill and almost landed on Amos who looked up at him in alarm.

"What are you doing?" Amos snapped. Then he saw the frantic look in his eyes and caught his breath.

"It's Manwena. He's tracking us. He's not far away. You two, stay here," he ordered. "Get up the anthill if you can. Be quiet and stay together. I will try to distract him. If I make it, I will meet you here. If I'm not back by nightfall, keep moving. There is a road to the south about a mile away." He lied about the distance to boost their spirits and give them hope. "Go to the road."

With that, Sante ran quickly away from them. He did not look back, but if he had, he would have seen two stunned and terrified faces staring after him. Amos then leapt into motion and began giving directions to Grace on how to get up the anthill. Sante ran on. He moved silently away from his mother and arched his way around the area where he had seen Manwena, hoping to sneak up behind him. As he sensed he was drawing closer, he slowed down and listened. Manwena was a skilled tracker, and Sante knew he had to be careful. His eyes darted frantically around, and his skin itched oddly as if he was the one being stalked. He had to find Manwena. He had to draw him away from the others.

There! Finally, Sante caught a glimpse of Manwena's army shirt as it flashed through the undergrowth and out of sight.

"Hey! Hey, old man. You're a crazy old fool!" He heard the words shooting out of his mouth like rapid gunfire before he had time to think rationally about what he was saying. He felt light-headed as the words tumbled forth.

There was a second of silence, like the calm in the eye of a storm, before Sante fled from Manwena, leading him away from the anthill. He ran as hard as his legs would carry him, crashing and pushing his way through the trees in the direction of the road. "Just reach the road," he told himself irrationally, as if the road somehow offered security. He could hear Manwena hot on his tail. The pain from the boil on his foot exploded like gunpowder.

Although Sante was fast, his youth was no match for Manwena's years of training and experience. His father's body was a powerful machine that was well adapted to the chase. And, while Sante was driven by terror, Manwena was driven by rage. A rage so deep it leapt from him like a physical force and propelled him forward.

Sante felt him closing in behind. There was no time to think or formulate any kind of plan. His body reacted by pure instinct in a desperate bid to survive. He launched himself behind a tree and stood rigid as Manwena accelerated. Had he seen him? Sante could not tell. He held his breath and listened to his enemy loom ever closer. His sweaty hands held his machete shakily above his head. Beads of sweat began dripping down his arms and forehead. The crashing was getting closer. His heart beat louder. Then suddenly, the noise stopped. There was silence. A deep echoing canyon of silence that reverberated off the forest walls. Manwena had realised his son was no longer running and had stopped to listen.

"Where are you boy?" Manwena demanded, as if he expected an answer. He was only a few feet away. Sante's heart thumped loudly, and he shook with terror. What had he done? This was not a fair fight. He was a child and his father a strong fighter. Why would he feel victorious if he killed him? It would be like an elephant squashing a rodent. Where was the thrill in that?

Nervous energy got the better of Sante, and all of a sudden, he could not contain it any longer. He took off again at a sprint, away from his father who was on his heels in an instant. Sante could barely see where he was going. He ran frantically, but his legs felt like they were stuck in quicksand. He could not move fast enough. Branches clutched at his heels as if trying to trip him over. His leathery bare feet felt every stone and stick that tried to pierce the hardness of his skin and expose the soft raw flesh beneath. The infection on his foot throbbed in rhythm as if keeping time with the blood coursing through his veins. Reality began to cloud over for Sante, as he felt freedom being sucked away from him.

Then the momentum stopped. Sante was knocked from behind and tackled to the ground. There was a shocking thud as his head hit the ground with force, tearing the skin away from his cheekbone. Manwena rolled the young boy over and pinned him down by sitting heavily on his chest, his machete held over Sante's throat. Sante tried kicking his legs to get his father off, but it was completely useless. Manwena drew one arm back and smashed his fist into his son's face. The force of the blow was so hard that Sante was momentarily knocked unconscious and lay motionless and limp.

This was the moment Manwena had salivated over. He had total control and power over the boy who had insulted him. He could do anything to him and no one and nothing would stop him. He could not hold back the malevolent grin that crossed his face as he looked down at his son. Bringing his own face within inches of Sante's, he shook him until his eyes opened in groggy recognition. Then he whispered in a hushed and wicked tone, "I've got you now boy. You are mine! Do you hear me? You know what happens to those who try to escape! I will put a stake up inside you until your intestines are pushed out your mouth."

Sante began sobbing uncontrollably. In his terror, he lost control of his bladder and began urinating. When Manwena realised that he was getting wet, he reacted with fury. "Ahhh!" he shouted, grabbing Sante by his neck, lifting him off the ground and pushing him up against a tree. From his belt he took a sharp knife.

"Wait," Sante said with great difficulty. Gasping for breath, he screeched, "The others!"

"Others?" Manwena hesitated, his arm back ready to thrust the knife into Sante's ribs. "You mean the other boy? I could not care less about him!"

"Not just him," Sante yelped, "Mama!"
Manwena loosened his grip a little and whispered, "The hag is dead, you fool." But now, he doubted himself.
With a little more room to breathe, Sante clarified, "We found her alive. If you kill me, you will never find her." Desperately trying to buy himself time, Sante mumbled, "I know where they are."

"How do I know you're not lying?" Manwena hissed.

Sante was stumped. He simply didn't know what to say, but before he could go on, Manwena spoke as if his question had somehow been answered. "Ok," he smiled, as he drove his arm forward and let the knife blade sink deep into the flesh below Sante's ribs. Sante screamed in pain and tried to retract but Manwena held his neck in an iron grip. "Feel that?" he stated. "If you are lying to me, I will take great delight in finishing what I've started. He pulled Sante away from the tree and let go, watching him double over in pain and stagger forward on wobbly legs. "Move boy." He gestured to Sante to lead the way. "Show me where she is."

Sante breathlessly held both hands tight against his side and attempted to prevent blood pouring out of the deep wound. He didn't know what to do. He had just tried to buy some time, but now, he feared he had done more damage. He knew he couldn't take Manwena to his mother and Amos, so he started walking in the opposite direction, hoping that Manwena would not be suspicious.

"How far?" Manwena growled after just a few short minutes.

"Not too far."

The two walked in silence for some time. Manwena kept his machete pressed into Sante's back. He knew the boy could not run with his wound but wanted him to feel the blade against his skin as a torment; a reminder of things to come. Sante could feel his father's impatience mounting. His mind was so disorientated by fear that he could not think properly. His breathing was erratic and shallow as his already depleted body now struggled to conserve strength to deal with the crisis of blood loss.

Manwena was conscious that it was getting late in the day, and he needed to bring his hostages back to the group. In his mind, he was formulating a new plan. If they reached the other fugitives, then he would take them all back to the group together. The slaughter would take place there where everyone could see.

He would make Sante kill Amos first, then he would be forced to rape and kill his own mother. He would then do the honours and kill Sante. It had to be that way. He would show the group that he was in charge. They would report back to Kony, and his status would be elevated. He was getting tired of leading small factions through the bush in Uganda, carrying out raids and taking hostages. In Manwena's mind, it was time he took it easy for a while. He hoped to stay over the Sudan border, acquire a few more young wives, and live like a king. He wanted what Kony had. He prodded his machete sharply into Sante's back and grinned as the boy squirmed in pain.

Sante's eyes were fixed vaguely on the trees in front of him. He didn't know where he was going or what he was going to do. The little hope he had clung to, began to seep through his toes as he realised he was as good as dead. He would never see his mother again.

Suddenly, Sante felt the blade lightly slice his back as Manwena's machete fell to the ground with force. Sensing the scene before he actually saw it, Sante turned to see Manwena lying on the ground with blood streaming from his exposed skull. From nowhere, Amos came into view plunging the heavy jagged rock towards Manwena's head for a second blow followed by another and another until Manwena's head had completely collapsed like a crushed soda-can. With eyes on fire, Amos, now splattered with blood, looked up at Sante. The two boys just stared at each other in silence, barely believing what had just transpired.

Sante fell to his knees in absolute astonishment. Like the blowing out of a candle, in a single moment every ounce of energy left his body. It was over. The transition from terror to relief was quickly followed by uncertainty. Sante's eyes tightly embraced his father's death, not sure whether to celebrate or cry. There was his father, suddenly dead and somehow no longer evil. Manwena's body lay prone, looking oddly vulnerable, like that of a little boy. Perhaps, like the boy Manwena was when he had been abducted by the rebels all those years ago. Paralysed and petrified, Sante lifted his gaze from his fallen father to Amos. In his shock, he was unable to register what happened. He could not speak. He could not move. He gripped a fist-full of dirt for support as his body was starting to tremble violently.

"Come on," Amos gently encouraged, "Grace will be worried."

Amos slowly approached Sante and helped him to his feet. The battered and bloody boys stumbled away from the dead body, back in the direction from which they had come. Before reaching Grace, Sante stopped to look at Amos. As he tried to speak, tears welled in his eyes. Wiping the wetness away as if to bring an abrupt halt to the emotion, Sante managed to find the courage to speak the words he had been fighting.

"Thank you," he whispered.

Amos only nodded.

CHAPTER TWENTY-SEVEN

ALL ALONE

The birds welcome the day once more

Here in this desolation.

Abandoned to the forest, rocks and dirt

I can hear the earth whisper to me.

In what thoughtless haste did they go?

In what careless abandon leave me here?

I sit on ruined knees

And press my face into their callousness.

Where is the hope that warms me?

Where is anything but fear?

Will anyone ever save me,

And take me far away from here?

I am the girl, the forgotten refugee.

Silvia wondered whether there was anything as lonely as being forgotten by the only person alive who she had mistakenly believed cared for her. She wondered how Amos could have left her. It was astonishing that he would leave his sisters and friend and run away with one of the rebels. She wondered if they had perhaps been murdered, and the story of their escape used as a cover. But that didn't seem logical either. In these killing fields, murders were never hidden. They were conducted in the open and then bragged about. Used to deter others from dissention that might threaten the group's enforced cohesion. Now, as she tramped half-heartedly through the bush looking for the boys with a small search party, she could still hardly believe that they were gone. It just didn't seem real. She was hollow and empty and so very lonely.

At the end of the long and fruitless day, her party returned to the group. She was exhausted but anxious to know whether the boys had been found. Even though she wanted to see Amos again, she hoped for his sake that he had remained at large. It was far better that his disappearance remained a mystery, than that he be slaughtered before her eyes.

It was dusk when they made it back to the meeting spot. Everyone appeared to be on the point of collapse. Silvia sat heavily on the dirt and listened as her group leader explained that they hadn't found any trace of the boys.

"Everyone is back now," Aaron declared. "We just wait for Manwena. He may have found the escapees."

"That would be the worst," Silvia muttered under her breath. The acid rose from the pit of her stomach at the very mention of his name.

They sat in silence for a long time before Aaron spoke up

again. By now it was pitch black. Not even the stars twinkled above them, as dark clouds shut out the lights in the night sky.

"We start our watch," he instructed. Silvia could hear the nervousness in his voice. "Tonight, there will be three keeping watch at all times."

She lay down where she had been sitting and tried to get comfortable enough to sleep. If she hadn't been so exhausted, it would have been a difficult task. The rocky ground seemed to push the cold night air right through her skin into the bones that protruded at sharp angles from under her skin. She shivered. She was so hungry that she considered licking the dirt she lay on, but the effort seemed too much. Even a small sliver of food would have felt like a feast. How she longed for some of her Mama's cooking. As she drifted into an exhausted sleep, her mind swam with images of cassava and maize, dripping in rich pink groundnut sauce. It helped her feel a little less alone.

Over the next week, the loneliness Silvia experienced at Amos's disappearance was replaced first by a feeling of numbness, and then one of nagging fear. On that first morning, as she had opened her eyes to the new day, she was confronted by a frustrated and anxious Aaron barking conflicting orders at the group. She had to listen for a moment to understand what he was saying, and even then, questioned whether she might still be dreaming. It appeared that Manwena had not returned the night before, and now they faced a dilemma. Should they stay and wait for their commander, or should they pack up and move as fast as they could? Aaron was obviously in conflict, but Silvia could tell that his babbling was not so much to seek advice, as it was to voice the concerns in his mind.

"We should move," he said hesitantly, and then immediately second-guessed himself. "But what if Manwena is alive and cannot find us?" The question was left hanging like a cobweb in the air because, if that were the case, they all knew there would be hell to pay. They could not abandon their commander. If Manwena returned, and they were gone, there was no doubt that someone would be held to blame. "But if we stay, we may be in danger," Aaron continued debating. "If Manwena has been captured by the army ..." He did not finish his sentence, but Silvia knew he was alluding to their betrayal. The big question was whether Manwena would bargain with the army to save his own skin. If they stayed where they were, they could find themselves surrounded and fighting for their lives before the sun had risen far into the sky.

Silvia did not know whether to rise or just stay lying on the dirt where she had spent the night. In the end, she sat up – just to show that she was alert and ready. Although she barely dared hope for it, inside she found herself praying that Manwena would not return. If she never had to see his face sneering at her again, she would be happy. She even prayed that it would be like some kind of sign that she was not forgotten. That she would get out of this mess alive.

Hope rose as the day continued. Together with Lewis, Aaron decided that they would hide in the bush and wait for Manwena until the sun was setting, then they would have to move. It was justified as too risky to stay longer than that. They would head for the border and should be able to cross into Sudan within a day or two. From there, they would travel to Kony's base camp, deliver the latest abductees and report on all that had happened to their group. Although Silvia desperately didn't want to be taken out of Uganda, as the sun rose higher and higher, there was an increasing likelihood that Manwena would not return. For this, she was thankful.

It was almost dusk when Aaron ordered everyone onto their feet. They were walking once again, and within minutes, Silvia's legs were aching. She had little reserve left, but there was simply no choice. She plodded behind a young boy, her head down, eyes staring deliberately at his swollen feet scraping over stones and gravel. One foot, then another, and another, and another, in ongoing desperation mingled with an intense numbness. If the consequences had not been so severe, she might have simply dropped to the ground and refused to move. But there was no room for such luxuries. The day dragged on in a nauseating kind of way.

Most of the time, Silvia's mind was void of thought. It seemed to get lost within itself, perhaps as a form of self-protection, only to occasionally peek into her consciousness. She had no idea where they were going or what would happen to her if they finally did enter Kony's camp. Even though she was glad not to have Manwena by her side, she was beginning to realise that his absence left her in a precarious situation. Without him, she was no man's property and fair game for all. While he was around, she had not feared the other men so much. No one would have been bold enough to raise a hand against her. She had been Manwena's property, and he alone could decide her fate. Now, she was beginning to feel vulnerable and more alone than ever. The unknown tormented her in those coherent moments before her mind seemed to fall back in on itself again. The vastness of the uncertainty was too much to bear.

The hours passed slowly, but without calamity. At midnight, they dropped like dying flies on a dry patch of the forest floor. Silvia reasoned that she was safe for the moment as everyone was too exhausted to do anything but sleep. Once again, Aaron gave the orders.

"We will rest for a short time, and then we move again. We are nearing the border, and there will be more soldiers during the day. So, from now on, we move only at night. If we cover enough ground, we may even cross the border before dawn." Silvia could not help but wonder how he knew all of this. To her, each mile of bush looked the same. They could have been walking in circles for all she knew.

"Will there be soldiers at the border?" one of the rebel boys asked.

"I just told you that there would be," Aaron snapped back. "Listen!"

"Yes, Sir. Sorry."

"We will be about ten miles from Moyo when we cross the border. We will not go near the town as it is too risky. We cross at night and then, if all is well, head straight to Kony's base."

It was more information than Silvia had been given in a long time, and she was both surprised and thankful. Aaron did not continue, and no one probed him, so she tried to be satisfied with that, but her mind was in a spin. She wondered if she would actually see Kony himself. Stories about the man held a mystical element to them that made him sound not quite real. What would he be like in the flesh? Would he even let her live, once he found out she had been the wife of Manwena who was now feared dead or imprisoned? Perhaps, she would be held to blame for his disappearance. Perhaps, they would say it was witchcraft, and that she had somehow willed it to happen.

With her thoughts still spinning and crashing over each other, Silvia put her head on the cold ground and tried to go to sleep. It seemed fruitless at first, but she eventually relaxed enough to let the waves of exhaustion wash over her and carry her out into an ocean of stormy dreams.

CHAPTER TWENTY-EIGHT

ROAD TO FREEDOM

Lead me gently all the way,

And step by step, day by day,

I will follow.

I know not your plans for me,

For the night is dark.

I cannot see.

And like a weary traveller

With the world to roam,

I only long for one place.

Home.

So lead me gently all the way,

And step by step, day by day,

I will follow.

A weary band of refugees, strangers in their own land and to their own people, walked slowly down the road. They had been following the dirt track for several days now, hoping it would lead them to a camp or town. Anywhere away from the bush. Every now and then a car would fly past, bumping over the potholes at lightning speed. Grace and the boys were too afraid of rebels to flag down any of the vehicles. They walked along the very edge of the road and scrambled into the bushes to hide every time a car was heard in the distance. At one time, they passed a group of villagers too, but were not game to ask where they were going. They just kept their eyes low to the ground and hoped they did not look suspicious. The villagers looked at them strangely, but perhaps it was fear that also made them hurry past. They moved slowly because of their multiple wounds. Grace was staggering, and the ache in her hand grew ever greater. Sante's stab wound was in danger of becoming infected. Only Amos was able to cover the terrain with any kind of ease, but even he was beginning to struggle. Despite the rain two nights previously, when they had managed to drink from small puddles on the ground, dehydration was beginning to take a heavy toll. There was an unspoken acknowledgment that their situation was getting beyond despair.

A strange silence surrounded them. It was as if all life held its breath while they made their bid for freedom. Little was spoken, as they were absorbed in the quietness of their own thoughts. Each wondered where they would end up, and each tried to block out images from the past that compulsively intruded into their minds. Grace and Sante stayed close to one another and used each other for support, while Amos led the way. His presence offered them a sense of security that they did not fully understand. Perhaps, it was because he was from this "civilised" world to which they were heading. Grace and Sante felt so alien that they may as well have been returning from the moon.

They stopped to rest in the early afternoon of the third day. The sun beat mercilessly down on their heads. Attempting to squash into the shade of a tree on the side of the road, they sat in the dust. Not a word was spoken for a long time. Amos attempted to eat the leaves of a nearby bush, but the others did not even have the energy to try. Sante looked at the dust covering his black skin. Was it the dust that made it look like it was turning grey, or was he dying? He could not tell, and the answer seemed oddly insignificant anyway.

After some time, there was the noise of another car in the distance. Sante looked up and motioned that they should move further away from the road.

"Wait," Amos ordered. "I think we should stop this car. Let's ask for help."

"What if they're soldiers?" Grace asked with a distant concern.

"I say we take the risk," Amos replied. "We're not going to make it much further on our own, and we could still have days or weeks of walking in front of us before we reach a town."

Without waiting for further response, he stood to his feet as the vehicle fast approached. Arms high in the air, waving frantically, Amos swallowed the nerves that were rising from his stomach. Both Sante and Grace sat petrified, unable to protest or move. Grace reasoned that, if things turned ugly, at least they were partially hidden and could perhaps remain so, if Amos kept his mouth shut. They just stared in utter bewilderment at what looked to them like sheer madness.

The vehicle was a large truck carrying a horde of people and goods on its open back. It did not slow down as it approached, and as it sped past, Amos hung his arms in dismay. However, to his surprise, a hundred yards beyond where he stood the truck suddenly skidded to a stop and began reversing. He instinctively began to back away and would have probably run into the bush had it not been for his concern over Grace and Sante. When the truck reached him, the driver cautiously stuck his head out of the window.

"Where are you going?" he asked. He was an elderly man with smooth skin stretched tightly across his bony face. His eyes were kind and not in any way hostile, but he tried to hide his obvious trepidation. This was not a stretch of road he had ever stopped on before to pick up passengers. It was in a notorious danger zone, known to be rebel territory, close to the border of Sudan and far from any towns. So, the faster it was crossed the better. However, as he'd been driving past, he had glanced over and caught something in the way Amos looked that made him slow down and stop. As his truck reversed, his head told him he was crazy, and he could feel the tension from his passengers beside him in the cabin. It was not a well-thought-out decision, but an impulsive reaction to something that he could not explain. He now found himself staring at this forlorn creature, malnourished, eyes sunken into his skull, battered and bruised, and in obvious trouble.

"I need to go to a town," Amos replied trying to sound as casual as possible. "Where are you going?" All of the people in the back of the truck looked down in silence as they made their exchange.

"We are on our way to Gulu," the driver smiled. "You need help?" he asked bluntly.

Amos could not contain his emotion. "Yes," he blurted. "I am with two others who have bad injuries. Please, can you take us to town?" He saw the driver's face turn to immediate suspicion as he scanned the bushes behind him looking for the "others" Amos was referring to. The driver feared that he had just landed himself and his truckload of passengers into an ambush. Amos held his breath. "Sir, please, this is not a trap. We need help." He continued, pleading now as he waved at Grace and Sante to join him. He could see that the driver was getting ready to speed away at the slightest sign of trouble.

Grace and Sante nervously hobbled forward. Their wounds were immediately obvious, and if it were possible, they seemed to appear even more desperate than Amos. "Ok get in," the driver instructed. "Quickly, quickly! I'll take you to hospital straight away." Two men from the back of the truck jumped down to help them on board, while the other people edged over to make room for all three newcomers. There was hardly breathing space on board the overcrowded vehicle, but they managed to sit wedged in among the other passengers, chickens and numerous sacks of maize and rice. There were a few nods, but no words were exchanged as the three escapees were scrutinised by each of the passengers. It was perhaps a little too obvious where they had been. Their clothes were in tatters, they were thin and malnourished, eyes bloodshot and wounds open and weeping. Both Grace and Sante were covered in crusted blood.

As the truck began to move forward, a woman beside Grace offered her a water bottle. "You drink it," she instructed, indicating that Grace should share it among them.

"Thank you," Grace cried, almost tearing the bottle open. She took a few mouthfuls and then handed it straight to Sante who started gulping at the bottle's contents. It took an enormous amount of physical restraint for him not to consume all of the water himself, but he managed to hand it across to Amos.

After they had all had a drink, Grace peeled her eyes away from the bottle and looked at the woman who had given it to her. "Thank you," she said again.

"I have some sweet potato here that you can have. You look hungry and tired." This time Grace was handed a bundle of sweet potato tied up in banana leaves. "My name is Connie," the woman continued. Grace felt Connie's intense gaze as she unfolded the leaves and took out a small chunk of sweet potato before passing the remainder on to the boys. She could feel Connie's unspoken questions as if they floated in the air around her. "Are you a rebel? Have you been with the rebels? What kind of things have you done out there in the bush? Are you a killer? Are you even a human being?"

Grace did not look up. She was suddenly flooded with an overwhelming sense of shame and guilt. Out in the bush, there was no law. No need to account for anything. No moral code. But that was not the way normal people operated, and she knew it. How would she ever be able to explain the terrible things she had seen and done? How could she expect anyone to look at her without seeing her past? How could she justify what most people could not even begin to comprehend? How could she ever be forgiven? She knew what the rebels were responsible for, and she was one of them. She felt like she did not belong in the real world anymore. She had changed and become something that normal people did not recognise. The way Connie looked at her made her want to crawl inside her own skin, and in that instant, Grace began to wish she had stayed in the bush.

Connie sensed her discomfort and said no more, instead changing the subject. "We are about four hours from Gulu."

Grace nodded and closed her eyes like an animal trying to hide its head in the sand. She did not want to be rude, but the sense of her own disgrace was like a brick wall she could not manoeuvre around. She felt so incredibly tired. The little nourishment filled her concave stomach like a warm ember. Despite the hard, corrugated surface of the road sending shock waves up her spine with every bump, she let her head rest on a sack of maize and somehow managed to fall into a fitful sleep.

Despite their exhaustion, Sante and Amos were too nervous to sleep. Amos could hardly allow himself to believe that they were on their way to freedom. He no longer knew what that even meant. With his family gone, where would he go? What would he do? For some reason, the prospect of freedom suddenly seemed almost as frightening as enduring life in the bush with the rebels. It was a great unknown that he could not even begin to get his head around.

Sante's eyes glanced nervously around him the entire time. He held his mother's arms tightly and tried to feel the safety of her presence. He was acutely aware that just days earlier, while he was with the rebel militia, this truck, the gullible driver and the people who sat around him would have probably become his victims. He wanted to stare at them long and hard to see if they had any clue as to who or what he was, but as soon as anyone looked him in the eye, he dropped his gaze. He could not face their unspoken accusations, and yet he was fascinated that these people somehow seemed oblivious to the menace lurking behind the trees. Of course, none were truly that naïve. Logic told him that this Uganda was a different place to the one his mother had been ripped away from as a child. All of these travellers had been affected in some cruel way by the evil tentacles of the resistance movement that had permeated every aspect of life in the north. What Sante could not understand was why they all appeared so calm. Some even smiled and laughed with each other. He had so rarely seen people laughing that, although he tried not to stare, he was quite fascinated by their ease.

After an hour or two, Grace woke with a fright and sat gripping Sante's hand. She was momentarily disorientated. She closed her eyes again and concentrated all of her efforts on breathing, as her mind swam around and finally came to grips with itself. Here she was, after all these years, finally heading down the road to freedom. But she could not allow herself the luxury of hope, for fear of it being smashed to pieces. Her body was weak, but she reserved a final piece of energy to keep her mind alert. Her eyes were shut tight, and she sucked air as deeply into her lungs as possible over and over again. The monotony of this action, and the concentration it required, kept her pain and fear at the outer recesses of her mind.

Time dragged slowly by, and their limbs became numb from the pain of being cramped and jolted about in awkward positions. The driver seemed to think that if he went faster over the bigger potholes, they would make less of an impact. His theory may have been correct for the three people sitting comfortably in the cabin, but for those hanging onto the back who occasionally became airborne it had little merit. Still, the escapees remained thankful that they were covering the miles without their feet touching the earth's hot surface. Anything seemed a blessed relief by comparison.

Eventually, the truck began to slow down. Sante and Amos

both noticed that they were now passing many more vehicles as well as a scattering of little villages on the side of the road. As the sights and smells of town emerged from the dust, Amos felt a rising anticipation leaping from his chest. He could not tell if he was more scared than excited, but at least, they were arriving somewhere and finally leaving the bush behind them.

True to his word, the driver bypassed the centre of town and headed west. He stopped occasionally to drop people off along the way so that, when they arrived at a large rambling assortment of brick buildings and stopped again, the truck was already less crowded. A sign told them they were at St Mary's Hospital, Lacor. Nurses and other medical personnel, patients and visiting relatives all clustered in and around the buildings like bees on a hive.

To Sante the whole concept of a hospital was completely foreign, and Grace had to reassure him that they were going to be alright. Sante was desperately afraid that, once people realised he was a rebel born and bred, he would be tortured and killed. What other option did they have? He was from a different world – from a group who had hated, raped, killed and sometimes eaten the children and relatives of these very people who now surrounded him. He felt incredibly exposed and vulnerable.

As the truck approached the entrance, Grace felt her son tremble. "It's ok, Sante," she whispered, trying to sound genuine despite her own beating heart. "These people will look after us." But her words fell on deaf ears, and she knew that Sante's fears would only truly dissipate once he saw for himself that he was safe.

"Here you are," their driver announced happily as he rounded the back of the truck to help them down. They looked groggy as they followed him over to the main entrance. Bypassing people on the lawn outside, their driver accompanied them all the way to the hospital reception and crowded waiting area, while the truck's remaining occupants looked on.

Beyond the sea of people, there was a large desk with several women in uniform sitting on the opposite side. Sante could barely see over the top of the high timber sides, but he was tall enough to watch their eyebrows rise as the group approached.

"These people need medical attention," the driver said, stating the obvious.

The uniformed women looked over the three exhausted and bedraggled refugees, making them squirm in discomfort at the close scrutiny. They spoke quietly together for a moment, shuffled some papers around, and then, one of the women, who appeared most senior in years, spoke up. "Where have you come from?"

There was a stunned silence, as if the answer to the question was something they had to calculate and surmise before coming to the correct conclusion. Grace looked at Amos. Amos stared blankly back at his companions, not exactly sure what to say. "Are you from the bush?" The same woman asked, breaking the silence. "Are you from the north? Have you escaped from the rebels?" She was blunt and unapologetic.

Grace thought it was a big assumption to make, but then she looked down at her withered body and the rags that clung to her skeletal frame and concluded that perhaps, the leap was not so great. She looked up, met the woman's gaze and silently nodded in shame.

The woman turned her head and spoke to the air above their heads with sudden distain in her voice. "You will be able to stay here until your basic medical needs have been taken care of. Then you will be transferred to the UPDF (Ugandan Peoples Defence Force)."

Had they made the wrong decision? Amos was beginning to wonder whether they should have simply told their driver to take them to a refugee camp and then just disappeared into the sea of people. He felt like the fragment of control they had gained on their escape was again being ripped away from them, but there seemed no option. Before they could object, they were being hustled towards a long corridor with doors on either side. Amos and Sante walked in front of Grace, all three flanked by hospital personnel.

A few doors down the corridor, they were pulled to a halt. "Women's ward here," announced their usher, and Grace was directed towards the door.

"I need to stay with my son," she protested.

"You cannot," was the short, sharp reply. "Women only in the women's ward."

Grace could see she had no choice. She was directed to a small bed next to the window in the large room, crowded with other women. Her bed was fitted with two simple white sheets – one folded precisely over the other. As the boys were shuffled on their way, Grace sat down heavily on the bed. The softness of the mattress felt like it could quite easily envelop her in its comfortable skin, and she was so exhausted that she knew she would not mind. The bliss of a real bed in some way signified to Grace the end of a very long and hard journey, but it was also totally overwhelming. At that moment, she was thankful that Sante and Amos could not see her as tears ran freely down her face.

Grace was so far removed from the young girl she had been. She felt like she had lived many different lifetimes over the past decade and gulped back a canyon of raw pain that suddenly threatened to surface. She was no longer alone, and yet, more alone than ever. She now not only felt lost but was also acutely aware that she did not know who she was. She wanted to shake off her own skin and run screaming from the building. She wanted to hide like a small traumatised animal with its tail tucked between quaking legs. She wanted to stop the flood running down her face. She wanted desperately to have Judy in her arms. She could do none of it. There was nothing to do but sit and cry and try to hold the waves of emotions at bay, but it was like attempting to stop a tsunami with a fishing net. And she did not even have the energy to throw the net out to sea.

CHAPTER TWENTY-NINE

REACHING OUT OF THE PIT

Putting the pieces together that fall down over me.

You lay me down; push me into the dust,

And I see what I shouldn't see.

I am only a child.

One small girl, lost and alone.

And I struggle to make sense of how any life

Can ever survive in the war zone.

It's a pit of desperate despair

And a loneliness

That sucks at my soul.

It's a place where even the youngest of eyes

Are meshed with the very old.

Putting these pieces together

In a strange kind of jumbled up way.

Hoping that there will be some kind of rest,

To keep the madness at bay.

Once over the border and into Sudan, the terrain slowly began to change. The forests that had sheltered them from view in Uganda, gave way to wide open plains, dotted by scrub and anthills as tall as trees. On the distant horizon, mountains came into view. Light shimmered in a heat haze above the highest peaks, as if reaching for the sky. Silvia was intrigued by the sight of the mountains, and although exhausted, the beauty of the view helped to keep her mind focused.

Aaron declared aloud and often that it was the safety of these mountains they were heading towards. That this was where they would find Kony and the core LRA faction. He assured the group that he knew exactly where he was going, however progress felt desperately slow. Silvia wondered whether he was trying to convince himself rather than the group, as it appeared that he didn't have any clue at all. He certainly wasn't the natural leader Manwena had been. In fact, he was turning out to be more of an arrogant fool who had assumed grandiose status among a school of smaller fish. No one bothered to speak up against him. Partly, because they were all too weak and exhausted to care, and partly, because they suspected Kony would deal with him, if they ever did reach the LRA basecamp.

The group had been increasingly ravaged in the aftermath of losing not only Manwena but also Grace and the boys. Although thrust together in unusual circumstances, now the rebels and abductees were forced to rely upon one another for survival. This created an unusual co-dependency between the two groups. Boundaries became confused as they were enmeshed into something that resembled a unified group – whether they liked it or not. With their leader gone, they felt compromised and oddly vulnerable. The irony of this was not lost on Silvia. Manwena was the very person whose presence had made her most afraid, and yet the air of authority he had carried had been reassuring at times – although she barely dared to admit this to herself.

They mainly walked at night under the cover of darkness. It was a strange experience in which time became lost and meaningless in the pain and endurance of mere existence. Food in general was scarcer now. They scavenged for it or killed wild animals if they could, but this was dangerous for they were as likely to be hunted as prey themselves. Sleep was only permitted during the day if they managed to find a place to hide.

Silvia's body ached mercilessly, and a constantly disorientating fog filled her head. How much longer could she keep going? How much suffering could one girl endure? The only thing she knew with any certainty was that the end would come. She would eventually get to the point of no return. The point when she simply could no longer stand upon her weakened legs. Then they would either kill her or just leave her and let the vultures do it for them. In her tired mind, it had become not a matter of *if*, but *when*. How many more steps could she take? How many more shallow breaths could she inhale? Oddly, she did not fear the thought of death. Now, it felt like it would be a welcome relief. Even her ability to feel any kind of fear had ebbed away. All she felt was physical pain, constant thirst and desperate hunger. There was no energy left for any other emotion.

At some point, on the fifth night after they had crossed the border, Silvia became vaguely aware that the group had stopped and hushed into complete silence. They crouched in a clump of trees and waited. It was still early in the evening, but the sun had set, and the moon was full, casting a silvery light upon the earth. Silvia preferred to walk by the light of the moon. The group knew it came with risks, but it was so much easier than stumbling across the landscape in the pitch darkness.

She squatted in the bushes next to the rebels and abducted children and stared absently through the trees. Lately, her reality and dreams had begun to blur, and now Silvia initially wondered whether she was hallucinating. She did not really expect to see anything, however as her vision slowly came into focus, and her mind centred, she became aware of signs of life. They must be nearing a village. Aaron waved his arms to instruct everyone to draw closer, and as they edged in, the grass roofs of a few huts could be glimpsed through the shrubs and trees.

They crept in further. Closer. A silent menace that was getting ready to pounce. Aaron instructed some of the rebels to begin encircling the village. The blades of sharpened machetes glinted like lion's teeth in the moonlight.

Silvia watched, entranced for a few beautiful moments, as the scene unfolded before her. Children played in the light flickering from the evening's fire, and the village women busied themselves with chores. It was almost as if she had gone back in time and was watching a scene from her own past. There was serenity and peace and a mesmerising freedom in the way the children played. They gathered for a song and then scattered laughing as one boy jumped up and entertained them with a funny dance. Silvia thought of Amos and the fun they used to have around the fire at night with his sisters and little Raymond.

Aaron's instructions cut through the air like the sharp end of a knife. The mirage was about to be shattered and permanently altered. As Aaron gave his brief instructions to attack, Silvia wanted to scream out to the villagers. She wanted to tell them to run from the evil bearing down upon them. She wanted them to know that this was it. This was the end of their time. The end of their lives. They had to escape now, or there would be no turning back.

The rebels knew the drill. Silvia trembled as she squatted in the undergrowth and dug her heels into the dirt. Her mouth would not open. No scream of warning would come. She knew then that she was nothing but a coward. She closed her eyes and sucked humid air deeply into her lungs while praying desperately. "God, please help them. Please God, save them."

Moments later, chaos erupted and the sounds of children happily playing were replaced by screams of terror as the villagers panicked and ran in all directions. The ground vibrated under their feet. The rebels had them surrounded. Silvia had not moved from her place in the bush. When the signal was given to strike, she had stayed rooted to the spot and watched the scene unfold as if it was all happening in slow motion. She could not make her eyes look away.

Suddenly, she saw a small girl running towards her. The little girl was crying and had not seen Silvia crouched in the bushes, until she tripped and fell over her. Silvia quickly placed a hand over her mouth before she could scream and told her to be quiet. She tried to reassure the girl that she was not going to hurt her, but the child was terrified. She knew she had to move before they were both caught.

Silvia looked around desperately for a hiding place. Lit up by the moonlight, about fifty yards to her left, she saw a rocky outcrop. Adrenalin pumped through her veins and gave her body an incredible burst of energy as she ran bent double towards the rocks with the little girl gripped under her arms. They jumped down behind some boulders and slid quickly under a bush.

The darkness of the night helped to conceal their hiding place. Silvia felt the little girl shaking beside her, but she had stopped attempting to get away. Silvia hugged her gently and hushed her without words. They could no longer see what was happening, but Silvia's ears were tuned in sharply to the sounds of the attack that was still in full swing.

Suddenly, from the far corner of the village opposite to where Silvia and the girl hid, there came a different noise. The roaring sound of a heavy vehicle ripped through the trees, and many men shouting aggressively in a strange language she did not understand. Silvia heard the truck screech to a halt and the popping sound of gunfire. It was one thing to use the element of surprise when attacking unarmed civilians, but now Silvia was the one shaking. Trying not to move, with her heart pounding in her chest, she gulped for air. It was almost impossible to keep her breathing under control. She knew the rebels were no match for men equipped to fight on their own terms.

After only a few short minutes, it was clear that this was one battle the rebels had lost. Their numbers began to quickly diminish, and the voices of the armed men could now be heard clearly as the gunfire subsided.

For a moment, Silvia found herself contemplating the idea of giving up. All she had to do was rise to her feet and walk back into the village. The men would probably shoot her, and her suffering would finally be over. She could join the fallen that now rested on the ground forever. For a moment, the temptation felt overwhelming. She had had enough of this war. She had had enough of death and pain and hunger. She had had enough of loss and fear. Only her own death would bring her peace, and the suffering could all be over so quickly.

Then she felt the little girl move in to hug her closer. Silvia could feel how terrified she was. Her whole body shook, and she wept silently. Silvia guessed she was about five, a similar age to her little brother Raymond. It had been a long time since Silvia had held a child in her arms like she used to hold Raymond, and she knew she could not walk away. Her arms were around the girl protectively. For the second time this night, she could not move.

Whether from exhaustion or fear or both, Silvia and the little girl fell asleep. It was the first time in months that Silvia had slept in peace. A peace that was unreasonable, considering the circumstances, and yet, there they were under the rock, asleep and sheltered for a time from harm and danger.

CHAPTER THIRTY

ALMOST

Hear me cry,

And don't you dare deny

That this pain is real.

Don't you say that I don't matter.

Don't you turn your eyes away.

Don't go on pretending

That you'll get around to helping

On another given day.

I've nothing left

But my precious pain.

Nothing to hope for,

Nothing to gain.

For I have denied love

And scoffed in its face

So now my hope ebbs

With slow and unrelenting agony,

Into outer space.

Amos felt panicked. After a brief examination by a doctor at the hospital, he had been given the all-clear and released from care. They told him he could not stay in the ward, as there was only space for the very ill. However, he was given permission to wait outside on the hospital lawns for his friends.

Wait outside?

The thought terrified him. At least inside the hospital walls, he felt relatively safe. But there was no choice. Amos shuffled out of the double swinging doors as if he was a baby bird being thrown out of its nest too soon. He felt as if all eyes were upon him, accusing him, seeing through his flimsy mask to the menace that lurked beneath. He wasn't ready to be pushed out.

Sitting down heavily on a cement slab with his back up against one of the hospital walls, he lay his head on his knees and let his arms fall over his feet. He was slightly more comfortable that way, thinking that no one could see him. If he kept his head down and hid his eyes, perhaps he would be left alone.

It was late in the afternoon. He had not been given any food at all in the hospital as that was the job of the relatives who came to look after their own sick and dying family members. As he sat waiting, he could smell the delicious aroma of sweet potato and maize begin to cook over charcoal fires in the smoky evening air. If only he had some relatives left to help him. If only he had his family. Most of all, he wished for his mother. The woman who had been so ready to welcome him back into her embrace after his first escape from the rebel militia. Where was she now? Amos couldn't even bring himself to answer the question, but in his heart, he knew. She was gone, like so many others – lost to the insanity of war.

Surges of helplessness and utter desperation clawed at his mind. "What now? What now?" The unknown was terrifying, and the loneliness of the moment threatened to overwhelm him. Even as he felt this, it struck him that both times after he had escaped from the clutches of the resistance movement, he fell apart when he finally reached safety. He wondered why he was able to suppress his fear in the bush, where death could pounce on him at any moment, but he collapsed internally whenever he was in a relatively safe environment. He felt like a small, helpless child again, trying frantically to build a wall of sand that the winds of fear kept blowing away.

Try as he might, Amos couldn't seem to control the thoughts that now pushed and shoved their way into his mind. He had no choice but to give in to the journey that his mind was taking him on.

He saw the face of his friend Silvia. At one time after his first escape, he had begun to wish he could be more than just 'friend' to her. He had foolishly allowed himself to fantasise about what it would feel like to have her in his arms. Throughout the ordeal, he had desperately tried to squash those feelings, but they never completely vanished. Now however, her big beautiful dark eyes stared at him, accusing him of abandoning her. Her eyes seemed to be silently begging him for answers that he didn't have to give. There was no justification for leaving her. All he could do was berate himself and try to look away from her image, but her eyes followed him. Haunted him. He so desperately wished he could reach out and touch her. Keep her safe. Take her to a place where there was no war. Where he could be forgiven for the terrible and unforgivable things he had done. But what was the point in wishing for something that could never be? A deep dark hollow pit opened up within his soul as he watched her eyes, and he began sinking into utter despair.

Then he saw his sisters, and it was as if his heart stopped beating for the pain. There was little Alinta whom he hadn't been able to save from his own murderous hands. How he ached for her. How he wished he could change things. And his other two sisters, Ruth and Juviance, now lost to the whims of cruel and twisted men who abused their bodies and tortured their minds. He had been helpless to stop it. He had been helpless to do anything but watch on in anguish. And now they too seemed to be asking him why. Why had he left without them? Why had he not cared enough to save them too? What would his mother think if she knew he had run away like a coward and left his little sisters alone in the bush with the rebels? Would she still be so forgiving and so ready to embrace him? He doubted that it was possible and was suddenly somewhat relieved that he would never have to confess his crimes to her. Every time his mind offered a new justification for the things that he had done, he quickly shut it down. There was nothing left. He had nothing left. He *was* nothing. Nothing but a wound-up ball of misery, pain, starvation and complete devastation. He barely even felt human.

Amos lay down on his side, keeping his head tucked deep into his chest. He sobbed quietly to himself and prayed for sleep to come, but it eluded him. Despite his exhaustion, he could find no rest. Around him he heard the muffled voices of women as they sat and gossiped, all the while cooking and looking after their young children who ran around on the green lawn or sat quietly beside them. They seemed happy and carefree and appeared to still live in the illusion of hope. The illusion that everything in life would work out the way it should. Amos almost scoffed aloud as he considered this falsity. *"Why do people cling to hope?"* he wondered. The reality of his own life shouted loudly at him, saying that he may as well give up now. For even though he had escaped the rebels, so much was wrong and out of place and so permanently altered, that things could never be right again. He had no idea what the future held, but he knew that it would not hold any of the people he really needed. They were gone. And it was his own fault.

Almost without thinking, and in an instinctive drive to escape his own emotional anguish, he rose from his spot on the cement and began walking. He walked past the ladies on the grass who were oblivious to his presence. He walked around the side of the whitewashed walls, past the beds of colourful flowers and out of the hospital gates. Being on the move again allowed him to push his thoughts aside, and he was caught up into the sights and smells of a town that was beginning to come alive. As the heat of the day dissipated, and the coolness of evening really set in, children lost their apathy and found a second wind. He walked past groups of boys playing football with balls crafted from tightly wound plastic bags and twine. They shouted loudly to one another and showed off their skills and speed in an impressive display. Something inside Amos wanted to stop and watch them, but instead, he put his head down and kept his feet moving.

He knew Gulu a little, from the days he used to bring his sisters in to sleep at the night shelter. However, they had never ventured past the shelter itself. He had never stopped to really explore the bustling town as he had always been anxious to return home. In the past, the cars and crowds and noises of the streets had always made him nervous, but now he was too tired and depressed to care.

He walked past rows and rows of market stalls, where women

sat behind their piles of maize, pineapples, bananas, beans and many other products that sent Amos's senses reeling and made his stomach churn. He attempted to look casual as he surveyed the scene. There was plenty of food. More than enough to cater for the needs of three hungry refugees, but the problem was not the quantity; it was how to steal some without getting himself beaten by an angry marketer, who no doubt wouldn't take kindly to thieves.

His eyes fell on a young girl weaving her way through the market stalls with a large straw basket balanced on her head. Her hair was braided in long plaits, each beaded at the end and gathered together in a band at the base of her slender neck. She was tall and elegant, and Amos was captivated. He was certain he had never seen such a beautiful girl before. She looked slightly older than him, he guessed about seventeen. She stopped and let her hands fall onto a bunch of plump yellow bananas. After assessing whether they were suitable, her gaze rose to the woman sitting behind the generous display of fruit. Amos could not hear the negotiation, but he watched as they spoke for a few moments. The girl removed a small purse from under the strap at the top of her long skirt, pulled out some money and handed it across to the marketer.

When she moved on, Amos followed her. The noise and the crowds around him seemed to disintegrate into nothingness as he watched the way she walked, and the flow of the colourful material draped around her legs. She continued to stop occasionally and fill up her basket, until it was almost overflowing with produce. Despite the obviously heavy weight on her slender frame, she walked with ease, her back straight and strong. There was a confidence about her that Amos had rarely seen. The girls and women in the bush always walked with their heads downcast, and their eyes averted. Their shoulders were stooped, and their faces blank and expressionless. This girl was so very different. She held her head high and occasionally smiled at the people she passed. She reached down to pat the tops of children's heads. She looked like she was completely comfortable in her own skin. He suddenly realised as he admired the carefree way she moved, that she reminded him of someone. She reminded him of Silvia.

When she began to walk away from the market, Amos came back to his senses. His stomach was telling him that he needed to find food, but he didn't think he had the confidence or energy needed to steal any. If he was seen by anyone, he knew he'd have to run and the thought did not appeal to him at all. Instead, he decided to try a more direct approach.

Looking around, he surveyed the women behind the stalls. Some sat with blank expressions, some looked bored, and others gossiped with their neighbours while waiting for customers. Amos did not think that any of them looked particularly friendly, so he turned his attention to the food. When he had found a stall that sold both bread and bananas, he stopped. As well as getting some fuel into his own churning stomach, he wanted to take a loaf back to Grace and Sante. The woman behind the stall appeared bored as he approached her with his heart thumping. She looked at him suspiciously.

Not knowing quite what to say, Amos stood for a moment in awkward silence before he finally opened his mouth to speak. "Mama, I have sick friends in hospital. Can I please have some bread? I don't have any money, but my friends need help. Please ..."

She scoffed loudly and shook her head. "You need to pay like everyone else. Go and earn it like the other boys do." She waved him away by pointing out onto the street.

Amos turned around, curious to see what she was talking about. Sure enough, out on the street where the cars drove and parked, he saw boys everywhere. They were dressed in rags just like him. His mother had told him before about the street children. They were those without parents or a home who had to somehow survive on their own. The thought that he was now one of them sent a shiver up his spine, and yet, he watched what they were doing with interest. Leaning up against a tree for support and a sense of obscurity, he stood for perhaps half an hour just observing the action.

It seemed to Amos that the way it worked was quite simple. A car would park on the side of the road, and the boys would race to it. The owner of the car would then choose one of the boys to mind his car while he did business in town. The boy would hang around the car, talking to others, sometimes sitting on the curb or the hood of the car, but he would never leave it. Then, when the owner returned, he would place some shillings into the boy's hand and drive away. It seemed like a simple way to make money.

Once again, with his heart beating with unreasonable force, Amos approached the street. Cars passed him, and he kicked the dirt between his toes, wondering how he could get in on the action. A car was slowing down on the other side of the road with a crowd of boys running behind it. *"Now or never,"* he thought as his feet started to run.

He caught up to the crowd as the car pulled to a stop and moved to the back of the pack. A woman opened the door and stood up. Amos could see she was a little nervous and eager to get away from the boys, so he raised his arms in the air like the others and started calling out to her, "Hello, hello." It was not a greeting, but a plea to be picked. As he began yelling like the other boys, his feet shuffled forward, and he was suddenly engulfed by the small group, getting pushed this way and that. The lady pointed to one of the bigger boys at the front, stepped sideways around the car and quickly moved away. Amos stood where he was for a minute and watched her as she glanced back over her shoulder. The group of boys began to disperse and look for the next car – all except for the boy who now slouched over the bonnet of her car as if it were his own.

"Hey, move away," he yelled at Amos angrily.

Surprised by his aggression, Amos walked back to the opposite side of the street and watched as the boys ran after yet another car. After only one failure, he felt disillusioned and was beginning to think that with this constant competition from the others further attempts would be pointless. He did not have the energy for the battle.

Suddenly, an expensive looking car pulled up and parked right beside him. Other boys saw it and were running towards him, but Amos was the first to be seen by the driver as he scooted around the side of the car and stood waiting for the door to open. A few seconds later, he found himself in a small crowd of boys, once again all pushing and jostling for position with their hands in the air, waiting to be chosen.

The driver slowly opened his door and stood to his feet. "You," he pointed to Amos.

It was a stroke of incredible luck, and as the driver locked his car and walked away, Amos couldn't wipe the silly grin off his face. He was thinking about the money which would soon be placed into his hands and the bread he would be able to buy for

Grace and Sante. Real bread! It would be such a special treat, and he couldn't wait to watch their faces light up when they saw it. However, Amos quickly came to his senses when he realised that the boys didn't move away as he was expecting them to. They stood back from him but hung around and began asking him questions.

"Who are you?" asked one of the biggest boys in the group. He was tall and thin with a ripped unbuttoned green shirt draped over his shoulders. He was one of the few boys who actually wore a shirt.

"Um … Amos," he replied cautiously, leaning forward slightly onto the car.

"Who told you that you could come onto our street?" The same boy continued.

"What do you mean?" Amos was confused.

"You can't just come onto anyone's street and start working. This is *our* street."

Amos could feel himself getting angry now. There was no way he was going to let these boys push him away from the car when luck had just turned in his favour. "It's just a street," he said boldly. "It doesn't belong to anyone. I can come here if I like, and I can do whatever I like." He could feel the pressure in his neck rising and knew that perhaps it wasn't the smartest thing he could have said. The boys collectively began to edge a little closer.

"That's not how it works around here," shouted the boy in the green shirt. Before Amos realised what was happening, one of the boys picked up a big rock and threw it hard onto the bonnet of the car. The rock landed with a thud and bounced off the surface leaving a messy dent in the shiny white paint.

Amos gasped in horror and looked around. He wanted to run

now, but just then, the boys surrounded him and pushed him onto the ground near the car door. His feet and arms were restrained under the weight of at least eight boys.

"Get off, get off, let me go," he shouted as he struggled with all of his might, but it was useless. He was so weak with hunger. He now found himself well and truly pinned.

"Bring him," he heard the boy in the green shirt command. Before he knew what was happening, he was being dragged away from the car and off the main street. It was all happening so fast that his mind couldn't keep up. He was helpless to free himself, which made the panic rise. Struggle as he might, Amos was no match for the strength of the boys who held him. Following their leader, they quickly moved into a tiny alley between two shops. Amos scanned his surroundings, desperate for escape.

The boys dragged him to the end of the alley and threw him against the wall. He stumbled and fell onto the ground, but quickly staggered to his feet. Eight boys surrounded him. He had nowhere to go. Looking from one boy to the other, he waited, petrified – like a baby animal might feel having been separated from its mother and cornered by a pack of ferocious wild dogs. He tried to talk, but no words came. His throat was dry, and his mind in a whirl.

The first blow came to the side of his head. It stunned him, and he fell to the ground, instinctively covering his head with his arms and tucking his feet up into his chest. Feet began kicking into his sides, on top of his head and into his back. The pain was excruciating. He shut his eyes tightly and cried, desperately hoping that the end would come quickly.

The boys were shouting, cursing him with vile names and willing hell itself to break loose upon him. It was as if he was the release for their pent-up anger, hostility and frustration at a world that had dished them up nothing but rubbish. Someone needed to pay and, on this day, that someone was Amos. On and on and on, until eventually he slipped into unconsciousness.

CHAPTER THIRTY-ONE

DIVERSION

Just when you think you can't go on

The audacity of hope steps in.

When everything in you wants to give up,

Hope won't let death win.

It gives you a tangible lifeline.

A small craft in raging seas.

And there is nothing else that can be done,

But to hold onto hope's possibilities.

"Samera … Samera," came a gentle voice. Silvia woke with a fright and instantly tried to jump away as she looked up to see a large man bending over her, and the little girl she cradled. Her mind reeled as it was pulled from sleep, and she remembered the events of the night before.

"Hush," the man spoke to her, before continuing to say something in a language she could not understand. Silvia wanted to back further away, but the boulders blocked her in from behind, while the man's large body almost entirely covered the entrance to the hiding place. He continued speaking for a moment and then paused. He spoke again, and when she did not respond he switched suddenly into her native language.

"You are Acholi?"

Silvia wasn't sure if he was asking or making an observation, but either way, she did not want to answer. To be Acholi was to be labelled as the bait used by the rebels in their war. Silvia had no idea who this man was or what his affiliations might be. All she could sense was his confidence. He was not afraid.

Just then, the little girl stirred and opened her eyes. She looked up and immediately smiled, lifting her arms up to the man so he could collect her into his own. Silvia saw the familiarity between them. Clearly, she had been held in this man's arms every day of her short life.

"Papa," she cried before she too spoke in the unfamiliar tongue. She wrapped her arms around his neck and buried her face in his shoulder. The man said a few comforting words to the girl before looking back at Silvia. He still blocked the entrance so she could not get away.

"You don't need to be afraid," he told Silvia in a firm but gentle tone. "I am thankful to you. You have saved my daughter's life. I thought she was dead, killed last night in the raid. But when I couldn't find her among the slain, I knew there was a chance she had made it."

Silvia's mouth was completely dry. She could not speak or think of anything to say.

"What is your name?" the man continued.

Her big eyes looked back in terrified silence, and a word formed in the back of her throat but would not come out.

"My name is Nswana," he continued undeterred. "Please

come. My wife has made some food, and you look like you need to eat. Please come. We can talk later."

The man began backing out of the small cave with the little girl still clinging to him like a baby monkey. Her whole body was now wrapped around his torso. Silvia had no choice but to follow.

"Come, come," he said gently in Acholi. All the way down the boulder and back towards the camp, he repeated the words. "Come. It's ok. You are safe."

Silvia didn't quite believe him, but she was willing to risk everything on the promise of food and water. Her body told her that without it she would probably not survive the day anyway. She could not look at the man's face and followed a short distance behind as he continued to beckon to her. Silvia watched his bare feet walk over the ground, and she sensed his strength. He was not just tall in stature, but he was muscled and his legs and back straight like the trunk of a tall tree. She knew she should probably run, but where to? There was nowhere she could go to hide, and she could not run fast enough to get away from this man. He would catch her within five paces, even with the little girl clinging to his neck.

"Come, come," he continued gently.

As they neared the village, her focus changed. The early morning light streamed through the trees like funnels that cast a golden glow over the carnage. Suddenly, she began to see what she had only been able to hear the night before. Men were dragging bodies to one corner of the village. She recognised some of the dead. She watched in shock as two men picked up Aaron's feet and dragged his lifeless body to where others already lay. Sarah also lay there, along with some of the rebels. Several grass huts had been burnt to the ground, and there was a quietness in the village that unnerved her. It was as if so much death hung in the air that it somehow extinguished the oxygen. Silvia walked slowly, her breathing rapid and shallow. She felt panicked but could not stop her eyes from surveying the horrifying scene.

Then she saw a small group of children sitting under a tree on the right of the village. They were clearly terrified and exhausted. A man with a rifle stood guard over them. There was Ruth, one of Amos's little sisters. She cried out when she saw Silvia and tried to run to her, but the man caught her swiftly with one arm and made her sit down. There were no rebels among the children. There were no commanders. Just six of the youngest who had been in the group. Sarah's children were there. Silvia looked for Juvience but could not see her.

Silvia expected to be taken to the children and made to sit with them. In the eyes of the villagers, they were all part of the attack. Age was irrelevant in this moment. These were the children who had been a part of the destruction of the village. Silvia knew that there was every chance they would have to pay.

Nswana read her thoughts again. "Come, come," he said and directed her to a small fire near one of the huts that was still standing. "Sit here."

Silvia did as she was told, but she moved as carefully as she could and watched the children from the corner of her eye. They watched her too. She felt all of their eyes glued to her, as if they sensed that their fate lay in her hands.

A woman ran from inside the hut and let out a scream of joy, grabbing the girl from Nswana's arms. She hugged her fiercely and cried as she swayed back and forth, one hand protectively resting on the girl's head. Nswana spoke to the woman, and she looked over at Silvia and smiled. Moments later she and the girl disappeared into the hut.

Nswana turned to Silvia and handed her a pitcher of water. She received it gratefully and drank deeply, relishing the sensation of the cool water washing the dust out of her dry throat. It was almost euphoric.

"Can you speak now?" Nswana asked. "I need you to talk."

Silvia nodded slowly. What choice did she have?

"What is your name?" he asked.

"Silvia."

"And where are you from?"

"From a village near the town of Gulu in Northern Uganda."

"Why are you here?" Nswana was brief and matter of fact, but Silvia sensed that he was not unkind. She decided to speak honestly.

"I was taken from my village by the rebels. I don't know when it was. Maybe some months ago, but it feels like longer. They killed my parents, but I think there is a chance that my brother survived. Other children were taken at the same time. Some of those over there are also from my village." Silvia pointed to the children under the tree.

Nswana nodded as if the story was one that he had heard before. "But why are you here now," he questioned. "Why did you come into this part of Southern Sudan?"

"Recently some children escaped, and our commander never returned when he went in search of them. Another commander brought us here. One of those dead men," Silvia motioned with her head to the pile of bodies. "He told us that we had to come here. He was trying to find the LRA basecamp. We had walked for many nights, and then last night, we found this village. That commander was the one who told us to attack." Silvia looked down at the dirt, not quite knowing what else to say.

"My daughter," Nswana broke the silence. "What happened?"

"I was hiding in the bush," Silvia began. "I couldn't get up, so I just hid. I should have warned the people, but I was too afraid." There, she had said it. The truth of her cowardice was revealed.

Nswana didn't seem to notice her confession. "What happened next?" he asked.

"The little girl, your daughter, was running away. She was trying to run out of the village, and she tripped over me. She didn't see me hiding in the bush. I knew they would either kill or abduct her too, so I ran with her to that hiding place. It just happened so fast. We heard the truck and a lot of noise, but we were already hiding. Then we must have fallen asleep until you found us."

Nswana sighed deeply as he sat reflecting on her words. His silence made Silvia uncomfortable, yet she could do nothing but wait for him to speak. She sat staring at her cracked and broken feet. Finally, he spoke into the air, his words hanging heavy in the morning light.

"Your commander was foolish," he stated. "Most LRA know not to come to this region of Southern Sudan. Here, we have an army stronghold. That is the only reason this village has remained. They have lived under the protection of the army. I am guessing your commander got confused about where he was, as most LRA do not want to fight armed men. The LRA are cowards," he spat. "They take only those who cannot defend themselves. Anyone who is a threat, they try to kill, but they are fools. Brainwashed and arrogant, crazy people." Silvia could hear a rising anger in his voice as he continued. "They killed some of our women and children last night. We lost a few of our people, but they lost everyone. Only those children and you remain here. I can see you are not one of the rebels. I believe your story, and you saved my daughter. For that, I am very grateful. I will therefore help you and these children to get back to your home."

Silvia could not believe her ears. A bubbling excitement began to rise within her as she dared to believe his words. She looked over at the children and couldn't help but smile. That old smile that used to be a permanent feature of her face was still there. It had just been hiding. Silvia caught Ruth's eye. She wanted to run over and hug Amos's little sister, but she stayed sitting and attempted restraint.

The woman appeared once again from inside the hut. She carried a plate of steaming food that she handed to Silvia with a smile. "Eat," she said. "You need to eat."

Silvia looked down at the plate in astonishment. There was so much food! Matoke and sweet potato covered in a pink peanut sauce, the shade of the sky at sunset.

"Eat now," the woman repeated.

Silvia couldn't restrain herself any further and began gobbling the food in large mouthfuls. Although it was more food than she had eaten in months, she initially felt that it didn't even scrape the sides of her empty stomach. The woman refilled the pitcher with water, and Silvia washed mouthfuls of the savory peanut sauce and matoke down with little sips of the sweet liquid. She could feel strength returning to her bones with every bite.

After a while, she became aware that the group of children were all watching her wide eyed. Feeling guilty and incredibly selfish, Silvia stopped eating. She finally found the courage to speak again.

"Thank you," she whispered. "Thank you. Those other children over there are like me. They are not soldiers. They are just children. Can you please give them some food too? We have not eaten for many days, and they are starving."

Nswana looked over at the children. Silvia watched his eyes carefully, but she found no malice in them. Finally, he replied, "Yes, we will feed them too."

CHAPTER THIRTY-TWO

THREAD

You spin in a whirlwind

That refuses to slow down.

It sucks you into its heart,

And turns your whole world

Upside down.

All fantasy and illusion

Is stripped down from your side,

And you spin in a cycle

That will never let you win.

When the torrent of air

Finally calms

And spits you from its core,

You'll be in another world,

And nothing will be as before.

Life's certainties forgotten,

Life's foundations fading fast,

But whether you sink or choose to swim

Is not dependent on your past.

The lessons that life offers

Are found in the hardships that you bear.

Don't fail to examine truth;

Never pretend that you don't care.

For one day you may be granted

The chance to make amends,

And if you fail

To move with courage,

You will stand alone and lonely

In the end.

S ante wasn't at all surprised that Amos had gone. That's what people did. They disappeared. Amos had finally found the freedom he had been searching for, so why would he give a second thought to Sante and his mother? No, Sante wasn't surprised at all. But what did surprise, and perhaps even shock him a little, was the disappointment he felt at Amos's absence. It was a feeling he didn't understand or trust. It made him feel incredibly vulnerable. And it seemed that no matter how he tried to rationalise it away, that annoying and hollow feeling remained. Had he honestly believed that Amos was his friend? He had to admit to himself that foolishly he had. He had felt such a bond with Amos. He was the first boy Sante had ever let close enough to peer under his mask. And he had let himself believe that Amos would be there waiting for him when he and Grace were released from hospital. But now, as they were about to be set free, he listened as hospital staff enquired of the other patients and relatives if any had seen a young boy fitting Amos's description. None had.

Why had he trusted him? Why had he called him friend? He had allowed him to lead them out of the bush and away from the only life he had ever known. He had allowed him to take them into this strange and ridiculous world of white walls and social rules. A world that Sante did not pretend to understand. He had allowed Amos to do all of that because he had simply trusted him. All his life, he had listened to Grace talk longingly about this world, and then, when Amos joined her chorus, it had been as enticing as the promise of wild honey for Sante. He had been willing to die trying to find this 'better life', but everything he had found so far was strange and hollow and frightening. And now he felt let down. Amos was nowhere to be found, and he and Grace were about to be moved from the hospital to a 'rehabilitation centre'. He felt alone and angry and yet, sadly, not surprised.

They stood like lost souls on the steps of the main entrance where they had been told to wait. Grace mostly kept her head down and did not say much. She had not said much since they had arrived at the hospital. Sante was concerned about her state of mind. He watched out of the corner of his eye as her fingers worked frantically backwards and forwards along the outer edges of her skirt. Every now and then, her eyes would dart up and look around nervously, then back down to what she was doing, but he knew she wasn't really seeing. Her mind was elsewhere.

Earlier in the day, while they were undergoing the process of discharge from the hospital, Sante had tried to speak to her. He had hoped she would be able to give him some reassurance and comfort about where they were being moved to, but none was forthcoming. Instead, he was met with a quiet strangeness that was not like Grace at all.

"Don't worry too much," the doctor had tried to soothe him when he had seen the worried look on the boy's face. "It is not uncommon for people who come out of the bush after a long time to go into a kind of shock. We see it quite often – in different forms, of course. This is why the rehabilitation centre we are sending you to will be good for you. It will help your mother to adjust." He paused then, looking Sante over as if trying to ascertain how much 'rebel' was in him. Sante squirmed under his gaze. "It will help you too," he had stated, before turning on his heels and leaving the room.

As he thought back over the conversation now, he wasn't sure how much of it he understood. What on earth was a rehabilitation centre? It sounded complicated and frightening, and he wondered whether it would be like a prison – a place where they might lock up former rebel soldiers who couldn't be trusted to live within the confines of society.

At that moment a white van pulled up beside them. A man jumped out of the driver's door and virtually leapt over the bonnet of the vehicle to greet them, both hands extended. Sante slowly extended his right hand and looked up into the smiling face of the man who was busily shaking his whole arm and introducing himself as Benjamin. He was talking fast, but the words he said scrambled inside Sante's brain. He couldn't get over the man's big grin. His white teeth gleamed, and his mouth was so large that Sante guessed he could probably count all of his teeth if he kept his head still long enough.

Benjamin suddenly rushed back to the van and yanked open

the heavy sliding door. He grabbed something from inside and carried it back towards them. Sante saw that it was a colourful piece of material. Benjamin wrapped it around Grace's shoulders and gently led her towards the open door.

Sante had not moved or spoken since Benjamin had appeared like a whirlwind in front of them, but now he too was being summoned.

"Come, Sante," Benjamin waved him over. "Sit here next to your mother."

Sante vaguely wondered how this stranger knew his name. His stomach was a knot of anticipation and anxiety. Was this safe? Where were they going? He felt so out of control and at the mercy of the strange people that milled around him. At least in the bush, he had learnt that if he kept quiet and followed orders, he could stay out of too much trouble. Here, the rules seemed more complicated, and he felt like the ground was sliding out from beneath his feet.

"Come, Sante," Benjamin repeated as he leapt back to his side. He placed one hand on Sante's back while the other directed him to the van, but when Benjamin felt the muscles in Sante's back tense, he began speaking again. "Are you nervous?" he asked, but he did not wait for an answer before continuing. "Sorry, sorry, of course you are." He now spoke in a quiet and deliberate way. "You can trust me, Sante. I know how you feel. I have also lived with the rebels in the bush. I understand what it is like to return to town. It is hard. Very hard at first. You feel like everyone is looking at you. Judging you. You don't feel safe, and you are completely out of your comfort zone." Sante gasped as Benjamin described his emotions perfectly. "But trust me," he continued, "it gets better. Sante, look at me. You *are* safe here. I am taking you to a centre where you will be safe. You will stay for a while, until you are ready to leave."

Sante took a deep breath, and then, a few words escaped before he could trap them. "I have always lived in the bush." It was a statement. A confession. A declaration. He wanted this man to know that he *didn't* know how he was feeling. How could anyone know what he was feeling when he hardly knew himself? It frightened him at some level that Benjamin seemed to be correctly assuming how he felt. Was this witchcraft? Was it a trap?

"Oh, I see. Well then, it will no doubt be extra hard for you, and you will need to be more courageous than most boys your age are able to be." It was a dare. "Do you think that you're brave enough to come with me?"

Sante looked at his mother sitting helpless in the van staring at her fingers, which still worked their way along the hem of her skirt. He knew that he had no choice. He couldn't leave her, and they had nowhere else to go. Shrugging his shoulders as if he didn't care, he walked towards the van, climbed in next to Grace, and let Benjamin slam the door shut from the outside.

Inside, the van looked old and rusty. It had a faded green carpet on the floor and the vinyl on the seats was cracked and breaking. The windows had once been tinted, but now, something resembling a patchwork quilt of dark textures ran across each glass panel. The air was stifling.

"Feel free to open the windows," Benjamin called over his shoulder from the front seat. "The trip to base is about half an hour."

The rest of the journey was taken in silence. Benjamin concentrated on avoiding the many potholes in the road, and also narrowly missing the other cars in the process. Despite the terrible conditions of the road surface, the van moved with a frightening speed. Sante watched as the town flashed past him in a blur. It was all so new to him. The sounds, sights and smells appeared as a confusing, chaotic jumble that had no natural rhythm. He was especially surprised by the endlessness of the noise – from car horns to people shouting, dogs barking and children running around playing beside the road. It all seemed to blend into one big noisy mass of dirty mayhem.

After a time, the intensity of the town waned, and they turned onto a road that was mud and gravel. The potholes were worse here, so Benjamin had to slow the van down considerably. Out of the window, Sante saw small villages. They looked odd next to the stone houses, but nonetheless there were little clusters of mud huts with thatched roofs and vegetable gardens planted right up to the very edge of the road. Sante wasn't sure whether the village had invaded the town, or the town had invaded the village, but the two seemed to coexist at numerous sites along the road.

Eventually, the van pulled into a driveway. On one side of the high fence was a looming gate, while on the other was another random clump of huts. A few children from the village ran over and peered into the windows of the van. They did not stay long, once they saw that it was only Sante and his mother inside. Sante wondered whom they had been hoping to see.

A guard sat at the gate with a rifle slung over one arm. Benjamin tooted the horn at him, and he lazily stood to his feet and swung the gate aside, barely glancing up from under his peaked cap. The van swung into a sprawling garden with manicured grass and numerous flowerbeds. It was a large compound with two long buildings on either side and a smaller one in the centre. Children were everywhere – playing all over the grass. The sight of their fun made Sante instantly nervous. He had no idea what this place was or why they were really there. The questions started churning over again in his mind, but he could not voice them aloud.

Benjamin parked near a small house which sat between two much larger buildings. He swung himself around the outside of the van once again and opened the door.

"Welcome to the HOPE rehabilitation centre," he said. "Please follow me."

Sante helped Grace down from the van and firmly held her hand. He could feel that it wanted to return to the folds of her skirt, but he shook her arm and when she looked at him, he shook his head. He was suddenly determined not to have people think badly of his mother. She needed to snap out of her strangeness and return to normal. He led her to the door Benjamin was directing them to, and they followed him in.

Inside the room were a couple of long pews. The floor was smooth grey cement and faded posters hung on the walls.

"Please, take a seat here," Benjamin instructed. "I will just go and fetch Maggie our house manager. She will come and talk with you and show you around."

Once again, Sante was left waiting on the whim of others, which made him feel nervous, but as soon as Benjamin stepped out of the room, he took the opportunity to talk with Grace.

"Mother," he said firmly, still holding her hand. Then more gently, "Mama."

She looked at him with a puzzled expression on her face. Did she even know where they were?

"Mama, do you remember when I was little, and you used to tell me stories about the life you had outside the bush?" She nodded in vague recognition. "Well Mama, we are here now. We are out of the bush. We are where you have always wanted to be. I know this is not easy, but I need you to help me. I don't know anything. I don't even know how to speak properly to these people. You understand about town and life here. I need you, Mama. Please help me. I can't do this alone." Sante reasoned that, if he appealed to his mother's strong nature to protect him at all costs, she might snap back to her present reality.

"Where are we?" Grace asked in a confused tone.

Elated to finally have some words that made sense coming from her mouth, Sante gave her a hug. "Oh Mama, we are in something called a rehab—, rehabil—. Oh, I can't remember the name of it now. Some place they put people like us."

The confused expression on Grace's face was replaced by one of sorrow. "Oh no," she said, "Oh no, oh no."

"What is it, Mama?"

"Oh no, oh no."

Sante was incredibly frustrated. He had no clue what was wrong with her or how to make her think straight.

Just then, Benjamin re-entered the room followed by a young woman. Like Benjamin, she too had a very welcoming and open smile. She extended her hand, first to Grace and then to Sante.

"Hello and welcome," she said. "My name is Maggie. You must be Grace and …"

"Sante."

"Oh yes, Sante. But now the hospital told us that there was another boy also with you?"

Sante hesitated, but there was no reason he could see not to tell the truth. "Yes, Amos. He came with us out of the bush. He has gone. While we were in hospital for several days, he left. We have not seen him."

"Oh, that's a shame," Maggie said. "Perhaps he will find his way here after a while. I will tell Benjamin to leave a message for him, if he returns to the hospital to look for you."

Sante was silent. He knew there was no point but saw no value in trying to argue with this friendly lady.

"Now," Maggie began. "Let me explain what we do here at HOPE."

As she started speaking, Sante tried to focus on her words and understand what she was saying, but a lot of it was just too foreign for him to comprehend. She said words like 'community', 'therapy', and again the word 'rehabilitation'. It may as well have been a different language. He could not be sure whether Grace was able to comprehend any better, but he watched her worried expression gradually soften and her posture relax. This was of some comfort and reassurance to him.

They spent the afternoon touring around the large compound. Sante was given a bed in a room that he would share with five other boys, while Grace was housed in the women's quarter where Sante was not permitted. His bed was below that of another boy, and both were covered entirely by a green mosquito net that hung from the ceiling.

At the end of the day, as he lay on his bed and pulled the sheet up around his chin, he was thankful for the net. Even though it was transparent, the net served liked a curtain that gave him the illusion of privacy and solitude. He tried to wrap his head around the last week. So much had changed, and he felt so uncertain about all that was to come. Maggie had spoken kindly to him and promised him that he would be happy in this temporary home, but he was very apprehensive. It was just all so new and unfamiliar. Even sleeping indoors away from the night-time sounds of the forest was strange. After the other boys had dropped off to sleep, the space around him seemed unnaturally quiet. In the bush, this kind of stillness had often come right before a battle. Or right before they all jumped out of their hiding places and ambushed helpless victims. This kind of quiet came right before the screams and terror.

As he lay there, his mind began flashing back to images of fights and war and machetes hacking into limbs. He saw Manwena's eyes as they stared up into the sky. Vacant in death and yet somehow still frightening. He saw the man he had sliced into pieces. As if watching from a distance, he saw himself raise his arm high and bring it down upon that man. He saw again the look in his mother's eyes after he returned to her side. It was a look he had never seen before, and a look he couldn't read. Even now, he still wondered about it. Did she hate him for what he had done? Did she feel sad? Or was she somehow proud that he had not backed down from his father's challenge? He had not dared to ask her.

He saw Judy, his baby sister. He ached for her and wished he had died in her place. Perhaps then, Grace would not be struggling like she was at present. If she still had Judy, perhaps she would still have a reason to live. But it felt like she had given up. She had finally set herself free from the resistance movement, but she was falling apart. This too scared Sante.

He tossed and turned for what felt like hours that night. There was so much going around and around in his mind, and such a heavy ache in his chest that it was hard to breathe – as though the air itself was trying to suffocate him. He began to wonder what it really *meant* to be free. He had listened to his mother's stories and dared to hope for another life, but freedom felt strange. He didn't feel 'free' at all – as he had imagined he would. Instead, he felt like he was in yet another prison, only this one threatened to swallow him whole.

CHAPTER THIRTY-THREE

NEW HORIZON

Destiny is revealed quietly,

In the most unlikely kind of way.

It is when I least expect it

That I hear a quiet whisper say,

"You're standing at the crossroads

With the devil on your back.

You can walk ahead to safety

If you dare to cross the gap."

It's a risk to live with courage,

But behind you it's clear to see,

The devil's lurking in your past

Waiting to drag you down eternally.

Stand up, move on, and don't look back."

I hear this soft voice say,

"Trust in me, my precious child

And I will light your way.

Give me your hands to hold

And let me be your feet.

I will carry you to safety

And the devil you'll not meet."

No longer standing at the crossroads,

I'm running down the road.

Soaring like an eagle

Into destiny's abode.

Several weeks had passed in a peaceful haze. One quiet afternoon in the village, Silvia sat in the flickering light and listened to the birds singing in the trees above her. Their songs were so beautiful and melodic that they almost seemed rehearsed, but Silvia knew that wild things had a natural flow. It was as if the rhythm itself was the very thing that helped them find their place in the world. Their songs were both a part of who they were and a calling out of praise, as if they were declaring their thanksgiving from the treetops.

She listened, holding her breath in an attempt to hear with greater clarity. She thought of her mother, who had always loved the birds, who had been the one to teach her to sit and listen to nature and had constantly pointed out the wonder of the natural world. Silvia realised for the first time that she had begun to do what her mother had once done for her. She had begun to see. She had begun to actually open her eyes to the world and look at it carefully in a way that allowed her to appreciate even the smallest of creatures. For everything, from the grand to the most insignificant, appears miraculous, if you watch it for long enough.

The last several weeks had been the first time since her abduction that Silvia had been able to stop and think without fear lurking over her head. And, while she was so grateful for the reprieve and change in her circumstances, there were challenges that came hand-in-hand with the extra time and space. Challenges that she had not foreseen. She finally had time to think about her loss, and fear was replaced by a deeper grief than she had previously known. It crept in slowly. Like the rainy season in Uganda, once her grief had appeared on the horizon, it just kept on coming. An unrelenting sadness that welled up from the bottom of her soul and felt like it may never end.

Every night, Silvia and the children from her LRA faction who had survived, slept together on the floor in a room in Nswana's family hut. In some way, it reminded Silvia of the warehouse floor where she used to sleep Raymond. It wasn't comfortable, but it was safer than being out in the forest, and she was so thankful that the endless night-time walks were a thing of the past.

Only after all of the other children were asleep, and the village itself was silent, would Silvia allow herself to cry. As memory flooded her, silent tears would stream down her cheeks. Every night since they had found refuge in the village, Silvia had cried herself to sleep.

She cried for her parents whom she would never see again. She cried when she recalled their final moments and the horror she had experienced as they were dragged away. The feeling of complete devastation and despair was just as real now as it had been on the night when she lost them. She cried because picturing their faces was becoming more difficult, as if they were fading even further from her own memory.

She cried for Raymond, and the great feeling of emptiness she felt whenever she remembered his smile. She cried because she desperately hoped that he might still be alive, but she was afraid of having her hopes smashed.

She cried because she didn't want to be faced with yet another brutal loss, and yet, hope would not allow her to let go of the possibility of Raymond being alive. She cried when she imagined what it would be like to see him again.

She cried for little Alinta, and also for Juviance who had died in the night of the raid. She cried for the absence of her friend Amos. He had now lost two of his sisters. He didn't know that Juvience had also died, and Silvia couldn't tell him. She knew it wasn't very likely that she would ever be able to tell him. She cried over the pain of being left behind by Amos and how utterly useless his abandonment made her feel — as if she were a piece of rubbish he had simply cast aside. Silvia knew this wasn't necessarily a fair assumption and that there might be another explanation that took the control out of his hands. However, she couldn't get over how his leaving made her feel, and she struggled not to resent him for it. The battle with her own emotions in regard to Amos also made her cry.

She cried as traumatic memories and images reappeared in her mind. They came intrusively, bullying their way into her awareness without an invitation. Silvia found such memories distressing and difficult to get rid of. She tried to distract herself, which sometimes worked, but the images inevitably returned.

She cried over who she had been, and all that had been stolen from her. She cried because of the terrible knowing that, even if she did return home, everything had changed. Indeed, there was no longer such a place, called home.

Silvia did not like to let others see her cry. So during the day, she hid her sadness and focused on those before her. She was the oldest among the children from her former faction who had survived, so the other children clung to her like she was their mother. Only a few of them remained. There was Amos's sister Ruth, Sarah's two children, and another two young children Silvia had not previously had much to do with. One was a young boy recently abducted in a raid, and the other the child of another woman who was killed.

Although Nswana's village had lost some of its own people on the night of the raid, after all of the bodies had been buried and funerals held for those the villagers had loved, their life quickly resumed normal routines. It was a matter of survival. Life had to move on. For Silvia, it was comforting and reassuring to be within a village community once again. In spite of her grief, as the days went by, she felt herself relaxing for the first time in months. She was becoming increasingly attached to Nswana, his wife Charity, and little Samera who rarely left Silvia's side.

Now, as she sat in the light, watching the birds in the treetops, she was flooded not with sadness, but with peace. In this moment, all of her past and every emotion the grief conjured up seemed to fade into the glow of the afternoon. It occurred to her how strange the human race could be. Watching the birds and listening to their songs, she could not imagine one bird deciding on an action that would deliberately destroy all of the others. She could not imagine any of the animals she had ever observed in nature attacking their own kind with the intent only to destroy. If the birds or other beasts did behave in such a way, how strange it would seem. How illogical. The animals she had watched in the wild seemed to understand that they needed one another. If they did kill, it was usually for food, not for a thrill or for a deluded sense of power or control. She wished the human race was more like those she now watched singing joyfully from the treetops.

Silvia shook her head at the thought. All of her loss came down to something so illogical she knew she would probably never be able to make sense of it. There was no understanding to be gained because the war she lived in was nothing short of crazy. One group of people seeking to destroy another. The hate-filled proclamations of one man pushing others to achieve his evil agenda. One group of birds attacking, brutalising, raping and destroying another. In her young mind, it made absolutely no sense.

Samera appeared at first light in the doorway of the room where Silvia lay sleeping. She was ready to play, but Silva's stomach churned, and she struggled to sit up. Despite sleeping a full night, she woke up exhausted once again.

"Come and play with me Silvia," Samera tugged at her sleeve. "I've been waiting forever." Silvia couldn't help but smile at the little girl's exaggeration. She felt a genuine fondness for little Samera. They had a bond that had first been forged under the rock on the night they had hidden from danger, but the more she got to know Samera, the more Silvia loved her. Samera was slightly older than Raymond would have been. She had a sweet disposition but was also cheeky and always ready for a joke or a little mischief. Silvia adored this personality trait, perhaps because it reminded her of herself in happier days.

"Silvia, what's wrong with you?" Samera exclaimed impatiently.

It was a good question. Silvia wished she knew the answer. Mornings had suddenly become difficult in so many ways.

"I guess I'm just tired," Silvia replied feebly. "You go out and wait for me Samera. I'm coming. Go and help your mother."

Samera sighed and shrugged her shoulders, letting her disappointment be known, but she did as she was told. Silvia observed that the other children were also awake, and that she alone remained in the hut. She tried to sit up but felt sick to her stomach. Movement seemed to produce bile that wanted to be vomited out, so she groaned and curled up on her side, allowing herself a few more minutes of rest. She was just so tired and, moments later, she slipped back into sleep.

Later that same afternoon, Silvia sat with Charity, preparing food for the village.

Charity asked in broken Acholi, "Silvia, how old you?"

The question caught Silvia by surprise. Charity didn't speak to her often because Acholi wasn't her first language, and she lacked the confidence needed to break out of her mother tongue. "Um, I am twelve I think," Silvia hesitated. "Or maybe thirteen. I don't really know as I lost track of time in the bush."

"Ok, I see." Charity replied, stringing the words together in a stilted manner.

"Why do you ask?" Silvia was curious to know.

Charity stopped what she was doing and looked at her in a way that made Silvia uncomfortable, "I am worried you," she said, pointing at Silvia as she said the words.

This made Silvia even more curious. "Why?" she asked

perplexed.

"Have you, feeling sick?" As she asked, Charity held her stomach and pretended to vomit to show Silvia what she meant. "You ... sick."

Silvia wasn't sure if she should admit the full extent of her sickness. She didn't want to be seen as a liability and knew that the extension of grace this community was giving her could be jeopardised if she was perceived as weak and needy. They didn't need another mouth to feed from someone who was unable to work or be of assistance in the daily chores. She looked down at her feet, but she felt Charity's eyes looking at her.

"Silvia," Charity continued in a gentle voice, "how you feeling?"

"I'm fine really," Silvia reassured her.

"Silvia, I watch ... ing you. You not so fine."

"Most of the time I'm ok. I just feel sick in the mornings. Sometimes, I vomit, and then I feel better. Perhaps it's because my body isn't used to having so much food. Or perhaps I'm just exhausted because of everything that's happened. I don't understand it myself. I was fine out in the bush. The sickness began shortly after coming here. But I can still work hard and help you with the cooking and other chores. I'm a hard worker!"

"How long you with rebels?" Charity asked, ignoring her justifications.

"I don't know exactly. Some months I guess, but I'm really not sure."

Charity sighed, and Silvia saw that it was compassion rather than judgment or frustration in her eyes.

"Do you know why I'm sick?" she asked without thinking.

Charity hesitated and then nodded. "Yes."

"Oh, ok," Silvia could not hide her surprise. "Well, what is it then? And how do I fix it? Can you make me better? I want to be a good help to you here in the village. I feel bad that I'm sick."

"Silvia, you going to be ok. I will help you. Or we go take you back Gulu. We help you. You save Samera. I not forget that."

Silvia could feel herself getting nervous as the anticipation of bad news drew closer to her. She could not speak so Charity continued.

"Silvia, I have seen of your sickness …" she hesitated again.

"What is it?" Silvia couldn't restrain herself.

"You be with baby." Charity's hands drew an imaginary curve in the air over her stomach to indicate a large belly. Her message was unmistakable.

Silvia was speechless, her heart racing, and the blood pounding in her ears. Charity kept speaking, but Silvia didn't hear her. Instead, her mind was grappling with Charity's last statement, trying to make sense of what it might mean. How could it be possible? She was just a girl. She was too young. But as she thought of her sickness, she suddenly remembered her mother Jossy. She had watched Jossy struggle with sickness in the early stages of her last pregnancy. The vomiting and exhaustion had meant that Silvia had to step up and do more of the chores around the village, so her mother could rest.

"Silvia, it's ok," Charity said softly. "I help you."

Tears slid down Silvia's cheeks, more from the shock of this news than anything else. She simply had no other way of expressing the turmoil that raced around her mind and the fear that gripped her heart.

The older woman put her arms around Silvia's shoulders and held her close, like a mother protecting her from harm. But it was too late. The damage had already been done. For the first time since arriving, Silvia allowed herself to cry in the presence of another.

CHAPTER THIRTY-FOUR

QUESTIONS

Gentle hands touch

In a way I do not understand.

It brings me to tears.

Feels like it was always meant to be this way

But I just can't seem to let it be.

To just BE

Is such a complicated task.

There are too many unwritten lines

Too many unanswered questions.

To many unspoken words ...

And I cannot trust

Even the safest melody.

Can you hear me?" the voice was muffled.

Amos tried to rouse himself. He tried to search for the voice, but it was as if he was at the bottom of a long black pit. He was trying to reach up to the light, but he kept slipping back engulfed by inky blackness all around him. There was peace in the darkness. It was so pleasant to rest. There was no pain. Still, the voice was insistent. It nagged at him to come, as if staying in his slumber was not allowed. He wanted to shout and tell the voice to go away, but no sound came. He had no voice. He could not even open his eyes. He was just so tired. The blackness sucked him backwards. Again, his resolve crumbled, and he sank back into the silence of his semiconscious mind.

"Well, it's about time." Someone near him spoke aloud.

Where was he? Amos struggled to open his eyes, but they were barely cooperating. He managed to peer out of two tiny puffed-up slits in his head. Everything looked fuzzy. His hand reached up and touched the place where his eyes should be. He felt nothing but swollen mounds of painful flesh, and the slight touch of his fingers made him wince in pain. Someone placed a hand on his forehead and spoke with their face close to his ear. He wondered if his ears were also in a state of disrepair.

"You're ok now," the voice said. "You're going to be ok. You're in a safe place."

Amos was totally confused. "You were found in an alley," the voice continued. "No one knows how long you were there, and no one saw what happened to you, but you're safe now. We will look after you. No one will hurt you here." A pause followed, then a question, "Do you remember what happened to you?"

An involuntary sound came from the back of his throat as the question triggered his memory. Yes, he remembered. He tried to nod. He remembered the boys and the bashing. What he was confused about was how he had come from the street to his current location. Of this transition, he had no recollection.

"It's ok," the voice said again, perhaps sensing his disorientation. "You don't have to answer. Just rest and recover. We will look after you. There is a toilet outside that I will show you when you're a little stronger. I will go and fetch some food and water. You need to get some nourishment into you. It will help you regain some of your strength." The voice got up and walked away from him. Amos sensed that he was alone and groaned aloud. The pounding pain in his head was unbearable. It felt like someone was hammering hard upon his brain.

He tried to look around through the slits of his swollen eyelids. He was lying on a bed with his head on a flat pillow. Although his entire body was aching, it felt good to be on a soft mattress. The room was nondescript. Just a bed and a little table next to it. A book sat on top of the table, but he didn't look at it. There was nothing else in the room. The walls were a faded shade of blue, as if they had been painted a long time ago. Near the bed, which was pushed up against the wall, was a window. It had four large panes of glass and was encased by a row of metal bars on the outside. Amos wasn't sure if the bars were to keep people out or him in. As he strained his head to look at the bars, a feeling of dread began to creep over him. What if he was in danger? What if he had been taken to some kind of prison? What if the street boys had accused him of denting the car he was meant to be guarding, and now he was being locked up where no one would ever find him?

Just then, someone walked into the room. It was a woman. She spoke with the voice he recognised from a few moments earlier.

"Here you are dear, some food and water for you." And she placed a bowl of steaming delicious sweet potato and rice, with a pink ground nut paste spread generously over the top, on the table next to him.

Amos's doubts and fears vanished as he stared at the food. Just the smell alone was completely overwhelming. The last time he had eaten food like this was with his mother. Trying to sit up, he felt the woman place her hands on his shoulders and gently lift him forward. Her hands were soft. She then moved the pillow back up against the wall, so that he could slouch against it.

Amos was aware that his stomach was beginning to grumble in desperate protest against any further delay, and he was suddenly acutely in tune with just how hungry he was. Reaching over with his right arm, he tried to take a spoonful of potato and sauce without spilling it, but the movement was awkward.

"Here, let me help you," the woman offered. He did not argue as she produced another pillow, placed it on his lap and balanced the bowl on top. It was now much easier to reach.

Concentrating on the food before him, Amos avoided eye contact with the woman who now seemed to be hovering. He took the first bite of food and let it slide down his throat. As soon as the food hit his stomach, Amos was overcome. He started shovelling food into his mouth as quickly as he could with a desperation that shocked even him.

"Slow down a bit," the lady urged. "You'll make yourself sick."

Amos looked up into her eyes. She was around the same

age as his mother would have been. She had a kind face that was smiling at him despite her instruction, and she was dressed in traditional Ugandan attire – a long wrap-around skirt and elaborate top with material that stuck out well beyond the ends of her shoulders. Both top and skirt were of matching material, printed in colours of the earth: reds, browns and yellows. And she smelt good. She smelt clean.

"It's good," he heard himself say in a raspy voice that sounded nothing like his own.

"Well, you can take your time. There is no rush. You will be able to have three meals a day here."

Amos almost choked on his next mouthful. "Three meals a day?"

"Yes. The meals are generally served in the main hall, but until you are stronger, I can bring them to you."

All he heard was "Yes." Three meals a day! The thought was incomprehensible, and it piqued his curiosity once again. "Where am I? Why are you looking after me?"

"You're at the Ark Project," she replied. "We care for vulnerable children and young people who have no home. Do you have a family? What is your name?"

Amos shook his head and stopped eating. Something in the woman's gentleness told him it was safe to talk. He spoke in short, delayed sentences as his mind cautiously released the information. "My name is Amos Mbwenda. I don't know if I have family alive. I don't think so. But I have two friends. They were in the hospital. I went to look for food to bring back to them when I was … attacked," he paused as his mind flashed back to the boys on the street and anger welled up inside him.

"Might your friends still be in the hospital?"

"I guess so. How long have I been here?"

"You were brought in three days ago."

"Three days ago," Amos repeated her words in shock. "Have I been in this bed for three days?"

"Yes. You were in a very bad way," she continued. "We weren't sure that you were going to make it."

"Have you been looking after me all that time?"

"Yes."

"Why would you do that?"

"What do you mean?"

"I mean," Amos hesitated, trying not to sound ignorant but still curious to know the answer. "Why would you take care of me? You don't even know me. Why would you do that?"

"Because that's what we do here. We care for people. We believe everyone is important, no matter how great or small. Everyone is special and significant."

"Well ... I mean ... Why?" Amos didn't understand what she was saying. Her statements raised more questions in his mind than they answered.

"Why?" She paused as if surprised by his confusion. "Why is everyone important?" He nodded because he could think of nothing to say. She continued. "Is that hard for you to understand?"

"I ... I guess so."

"Well, I look at it this way, Amos. I believe God handcrafted each and every one of us and loves all of us equally as His special creation. You know, just like a mother loves all of her children equally. Even if you were more difficult or troublesome than the others, your mama would have still loved you because you are and always will be a part of her. So, in the same way, as far as God is concerned, we are all important and very special to Him. If you are important to God, then you are important to me." Amos just stared at her and then blinked and turned his gaze back to the food. She persisted, "I know that it can be very hard to understand the greatness of love. Especially, when we see so much horror in this war – so many children who have lived through such atrocity; so many people forced to do the unspeakable and to witness the unimaginable." Amos wondered if she somehow knew about his past. "Human nature usually wants someone to blame. We think we need someone to blame and exact revenge upon. We need to fight for our idea of justice in an attempt to make it all ok. But no amount of payback will ever make it ok. Our pain remains. Retaliation only leads to more suffering, pain and war for future generations. Without love, all we have is the lust for revenge … Without love, the cycle of war is endless."

"Yes. It is endless," Amos agreed.

"But Amos, there is a way out."

"What do you mean?"

"There is a way to put an end to the war. But it is hard for people to accept, for it is God's way and not man's way. Somehow, it seems easier for a man to kill the brother who offended him than to forgive him, but God outlines a pathway to peace. Not just peace in the world, but peace in our hearts."

Amos had heard similar things before from his mother, and he had always struggled to believe in this concept of reconciliation, but he decided to play along and ask the obvious question, despite the fact that it may give him away. "What about Kony and his rebel commanders? Does God love them? Does God love them, even though they have abused, raped, killed, mutilated and terrorised tens of thousands of innocent people? Does God want me to love the men who killed my family?'"

As he spoke, Amos could feel the pressure building in his head. He hated the rebel militia commanders and their cult leader with every fibre of his being. Not just for his own suffering, but also for the pain he had watched countless others endure and, most especially, for the painful memory of little Alinta. The grief that lay upon his heart was like a blanket of rotting leaves, covering every corner so that there was no escape. Kony was responsible, and in Amos's mind, he and his commanders were the ones who had to pay. To suggest that God loved these evil men and wanted reconciliation for the sake of peace was simply outrageous.

"Amos," the lady quietly whispered. "I believe that God's love is far beyond what our human minds can ever comprehend. God sees and knows our suffering, and He also knows exactly who is responsible for it. Yet, I also believe that God's love is so great that if anyone of us, including Kony and his commanders, truly humble ourselves before God and turn from our wicked ways, God would give us a second chance to live – whether in this life or the next. That's not to say there are no consequences for a person's actions. Young man, you just need to understand the difference between forgiveness and justice. God is bigger than one man's actions. God is God. Man is just man. Man's justice has an important place, but the ultimate judgment belongs to God, not to man. God's idea of justice is not always the same as ours. His ways are different to our ways, and His thoughts are much higher than ours. He often has a different perspective on things than what we imagine."

Amos just shook his head sadly. He felt sorry for this lady. She seemed like a genuinely kind soul, and yet, he could not fathom the depth of the delusion she was afflicted by. He concluded that she must have been brainwashed. Or perhaps, she was on Kony's side after all. He was confused and overwhelmed and just hung his head and stared at his almost empty bowl of food.

"Do you know what has really happened in Uganda?" she suddenly asked.

"What do you mean?"

"Well ... I mean why there? Why has this terrible war happened there? Why not in some other part of the world? Why was it our people who had to suffer?"

It was a good question, but not one he had an answer to. He just shrugged and waited for her to continue, half of him interested in what she had to say, and the other half defensive and wanting to shut her down.

"Most blame Kony. Blame his evilness. I think it's more than that."

"What do you mean?" he asked again.

"Well, people are people wherever you go. Most people exist behind the thin veneer of culture, traditions and rules about what is right and wrong. These things give life a certain balance and predictability. They let people feel safe. But if you peel back what's on the surface, you discover a raw evil lurking beneath that becomes uncovered in times of war. In fact, war often becomes the justification, rather than the reason, for evil to prevail. Evil is like a spirit that entices and then entraps people into it's sticky web. If you're not careful, the temptation into evil can consume you. It all starts in the mind, then becomes a part of our reality, until it ends in death. Unless of course, we turn back to God, repent and are forgiven."

Amos put his head in his hands and thought of his beautiful sister Alinta who had died in his arms. It had been his doing. His own hands had killed her and then comforted her as she cried for her mother. Did he too get caught in the sticky web of evil the woman spoke about? Was he aligned with Kony himself? The pain beneath his skull intensified, and the woman's words left him feeling hollow. She must have felt his anguish as she suddenly became apologetic.

Her next words hit him like a train. It was as if she had just read his mind. "Amos, I know you can't understand how to forgive yourself for the loss of those you were responsible for. I used to feel the same way you do. I lost my four daughters to this war. I understand what grief and pain and anger is. I have lived through it, and I have felt an all-consuming hatred towards those who took away my children. That hatred was both my strength at one time, but also my undoing as I started hating myself for not being able to protect them properly. If only I had … well, let's just say that my anger towards the rebel movement, together with my own self-loathing, only kept me trapped and unable to live. I understand loss and pain, but it wasn't until I understood what God had done for me that I found an escape from my deep hurt and hatred. You see, I stumbled upon a revelation that completely set me free. I'm talking about 'real' freedom. It's not the type of freedom that comes through apology, justice or even revenge. It's the type of freedom that delivered me from the hurt and hate that fuelled my longing for retribution in the first place. Amos, you too can experience that kind of freedom … if you want to."

Amos was silent, letting her words spin around in his brain. He wanted the freedom she spoke of, but still couldn't truly grasp what she was saying. He just felt condemned and sorry for himself. He could not speak and hoped she would leave him to sleep.

"Amos, I'm sorry, this is all very heavy. Let me be quiet now.

If you want, let's talk about this later. We have plenty of time. For now, you get some rest. Oh, and my name is Wendy, by the way. I don't think I actually introduced myself properly."

Amos nodded in acknowledgement of her belated introduction.

"Tell me the name of your friends in hospital, and I will see if I can track them down."

"They are Grace and Sante," Amos replied.

"Their last names?"

"I don't know, but they are mother and son."

"Ok. Let me see what I can do."

"Thank you," Amos mumbled cautiously, still confused about where he was and somewhat uncertain as to why this lady was so willing to help him. Chances are, he thought, she wouldn't find them anyway.

"I'll come back and check on you in a little while. If you feel up to it, I can show you around later. Now get some rest."

"Ok," he managed to agree, happy to finally be left alone.

The food in his belly warmed his bones, but Amos tossed and turned and could find no more rest. All he could see and think about was Alinta, his other sisters and Silvia, whom he had abandoned. He couldn't help but feel responsible for all of their deaths, not just Alinta. He felt the finger of accusation pointing at him as if it were a dark shadow that followed him around laughing at his sorrow. The weight of his guilt hung like a thick, suffocating layer of smoke and in the silence that gave him time to think, depression settled in his heart in a way he had never felt before.

CHAPTER THIRTY-FIVE

A THIN LINE

Into the fray.

Into the light.

Into the raging storm.

You don't need to see the end of the road,

For it's in the journey you are reborn.

Into the wild.

Into the night.

Into the deepest blue.

You just need to take the next tiny step

And trust that the lights will guide you.

Silvia had not said much for days. She sat, worked and slept alongside the other children, but she was quiet. Occasionally, Ruth would come and sit beside her or ask her a random question in the hope of getting her to speak again, but, while she was physically present, Silvia's mind seemed to be in another place. Ruth was becoming increasingly concerned about her. At nine years old, she had known Silvia her whole life, and knew her well enough to realise that, for Silvia, silence meant something was wrong.

Ruth had her own battles. On the night of the raid, a number of weeks earlier, she had lost her little sister Juviance. She and Juviance had been together at the back of the group when Aaron gave the order to attack. Holding Juviance's hand, the girls had run when they were told to, but they had no idea what they were doing. In the chaos that quickly erupted, Ruth had looked around for somewhere to shelter and pulled Juviance inside one of the huts. They had been crouching behind the wooden door when the truck rolled into the village.

The shouting and the gunfire had been frightening, but it was only noise, until suddenly, Juviance crumpled in a heap on the floor beside her. A bullet had pierced the thin crack between the wall and the door and hit Juviance directly in the forehead. She died instantly. Even as Ruth had bent to gather her sister in her arms, she could feel how lifeless she was. From one moment to the next, Juviance has was simply gone.

Ruth had lost all sense of reason and screamed violently at the shock of her sister's sudden death. She screamed for several minutes, staring in horror at Juviance's body, before curling up on the straw mattress in the opposite corner. She had huddled into a ball, making herself as small as possible. She had closed her eyes on the horror of the moment, placed her hands over her ears, and sobbed. Ruth was terrified someone would find her, but there was nowhere to run. Outside the hut, the screaming and gunfire had continued for some time. She could not move. Paralysing fear held her tightly bound up in a perfectly isolated prison.

As Ruth now sat beside Silvia in the corner of the hut where they slept, she remembered that night. A heavy lump gathered in her throat and she tried not to weep. It was very difficult to process the gravity of such a deep loss. In many ways, Ruth was having trouble even thinking about it. She spent her days pretending that Juviance was just around the corner or doing an errand that she would return from soon. She found this helped ease the pain of having to face the loss every moment of the day. But there was no hiding from the reality of it for long. Even though Silvia wasn't technically her sister, Ruth now felt like Silvia was all the family she had left in the world. She wanted to tell Silvia that she needed her, but simply didn't have the words.

In the silence, Ruth picked up Silvia's hand and held it close to her heart as if she were cuddling a doll. The two girls sat together for a long time, both lost in their thoughts.

Outside a rooster crowed, greeting the day. Almost simultaneously, Silvia bent to one side and began heaving, pulling her hand away from Ruth. Ruth watched horrified as Silvia crawled on hands and knees towards the open door so that she did not vomit inside the confines of the hut. It was the first time Ruth had really noticed that Silvia was sick. Suddenly, her silence seemed a little easier to understand. Ruth followed her outside.

Silvia sat up after vomiting the contents of her stomach into the dirt beside the hut. She had wanted to escape further away where her shame was more hidden, but the speed of the nausea's onset had taken her by surprise. She felt weak but a little less sick now that the vomiting was done.

Ruth was standing nearby staring at her strangely. "Are you ok?"

Silvia shook her head.

"What's the matter."

Silvia did not reply. She let out a heavy sigh and looked away.

"Are you very sick?" Ruth continued undeterred.

"I'm ok."

"Um," Ruth hesitated, not understanding Silvia's reluctance to answer her. "You don't look ok. You look sick. What's wrong?"

"It's nothing Ruth, I'm fine. Please leave me alone."

A little hurt by Silvia's abruptness, Ruth turned to go and then turned back. "Silvia, you're lying. You're not ok. I don't know why you're lying, but you are now my only sister. I don't want anything to happen to you."

"Nothing will happen to me Ruth. I'm fine. You're too young to understand. Please leave me alone." Silvia let the irritation she felt register in her voice. It was too early in the morning for an interrogation.

Ruth turned on her heels and ran back into the hut, salty tears running down her cheeks. She had only meant to help, and Silvia had sent her away. She was hurt and scared of losing Silvia too. She sat with her back up against the wall and cried. Outside, Silvia could feel her anger stirring as she listened to Ruth sob. The girl's tears would have Charity and Nswana asking what her problem was. Silvia was trying desperately to hide her sickness from everyone, including Charity, and now Ruth was going to highlight it. Silvia wanted to yell at her to be quiet. Instead, she walked in the opposite direction and began organising a small bucket of water to wash in. She would talk to Ruth later, when she felt calmer.

It had been a week since Charity had approached Silvia and talked to her about the possibility that she might be pregnant. In Silvia's mind, it was a horrifying thought. Pregnant at her age and with a baby that belonged to the most frightening evil man she had ever known. This was not an idea she could contemplate. She told herself that it was just an idea but not the truth. She was just sick and would soon get better. After all, she had seen everyone get sick after the night they had spent in the river. She was just taking a long time to recover. This logic seemed a lot more likely to Silvia than the crazy idea that she was pregnant. At least, that's what she was desperately trying to tell herself.

Silvia was thankful that Charity had not mentioned it again. In fact, Silvia wondered whether she had forgotten as she treated Silvia just like all of the others. She didn't act like there was a major problem, which in Silvia's mind there would have been if she had been pregnant with a rebel's baby. Charity continued to be kind to Silvia and allowed Samera to play with her. Silvia took this as evidence that she couldn't be pregnant. Her logic wasn't necessarily watertight, but in Silvia's mind, if she were pregnant surely Charity and Nswana would have been looking for a way to get rid of her quickly.

Despite her attempts to dismiss the pregnancy idea, the worry that plagued her would not go away. It was as if the idea was a small seed that had taken root. Try as she might to get rid of it, the thought seemed to consistently come back. Sometimes, Silvia felt like she must be going crazy. All she could do was attempt to distract herself and keep busy. She helped Charity with the cooking and other chores that needed doing, and tried to be a surrogate mother to the children who needed her.

Now, as she prepared her bucket of water to wash in, Silvia went to her usual place up behind the rocks, where she had hidden with Samera on her first night in the village. It was a beautiful morning. The elevation of the rocky outcrop allowed her a sense of perspective that was simply not possible when standing among the trees on the forest floor. From here, she could see for miles over the landscape. The sun was edging its way higher, breaking free from the horizon's grasp. Colours of deep red and orange were splashed across the distant sky, taking Silvia's breath away. She still felt unwell, but, as if to defy the sickness that was seeking to draw her into the earth, stooped and weak, Silvia stood tall and reached her hands up to the sky. She looked up at her fingertips as they stretched upward, framed behind the painted colours of the sunrise, her hands reaching up into the light.

In the glow of the sun, Silvia noticed that her hands looked old. They were heavily creased like the hands of an old woman who had spent many years working in the fields. She brought her hands down and inspected them closely, turning them over in the light.

"Old hands," she whispered.

Silvia looked up again, away from the village and out towards the horizon. Tall trees and swaying grasses punctuated the land. She felt the hot wind blow against her skin. From this vantage point, she could almost believe that the land she stood above was not one of war. It looked so peaceful and serene. She could not tell where Southern Sudan ended, and Northern Uganda began. Indeed, she could not even tell whether she could see her homeland at all. It was all just one land, marked only by creation and not by the lines man invented to divide it.

Silvia bent over and began to wash her face in the bucket. The water was cool and refreshing. She moved on to her neck and then her arms. Hot wind dried the water that glistened on her skin almost as soon as she was finished. As she stood again, Silvia felt something stir within her. That question returned.

"What if you are pregnant? What if Charity is right?"

She shook her head, as if trying to shake the thought off her.

It kept coming.

"What if you are having a baby? The baby will be a rebel. It will be the son of the man who raped you. The man who was responsible for killing your parents. You will never escape Manwena if you have his child."

Silvia sank backwards onto the earth, wrapping her arms around her legs and hiding her head in her knees as fears bore down on her.

"You will never be able to be a normal person again. You will be branded as a rebel. You will never be able to return to Uganda. Who will accept a girl with a baby from a rebel?"

Silvia began to weep. She had no answers and no defence.

"You may as well kill yourself. Your life will be over anyway if you are pregnant. Go ahead and kill yourself because the shame will be too much for you. No one will miss you. No one will even notice."

Silvia could feel the tears running down her face and onto her knees. She was simply terrified.

"Silvia?" she stiffened at the sound of another voice. Slowly, Silvia raised her head to see Nswana standing before her. His tall frame was silhouetted in the sunrise. "I came to find you. Charity said you had not returned. What is the matter?"

She couldn't reply. This man had shown her a kindness like that of her own father. Silvia trusted him, but she still remained on guard. People in general were not to be trusted anymore. Even her best friend Amos had let her down.

"Are you worried about the pregnancy?" Silvia was shocked by Nswana's bluntness and his apparent acceptance that Charity's assumption was true.

"Yes," she nodded, feeling cornered. "Charity told you?"

"Of course. She is worried about you. She knows you are young and have already been through much trouble. Now you listen to me Silvia, because I have something important to tell you. Do you know why I speak Acholi?"

"No," she replied, curious and hoping he would tell her.

"My mother was Acholi," Nswana continued. "She was like you. At the beginning of the war, twenty years ago, she was taken from Northern Uganda. She became pregnant and had me when she was still very young. We lived with the rebels until I was five, and then she escaped. We found this safe village and lived here until now. I was young when I came here. My mother was young too. She would still be alive today, but she died from malaria several years ago. I was her only child." Silvia watched Nswana intently. She could see he was speaking from his heart.

"I loved my mother very much," Nswana continued. "She was a strong woman. She told me that she had made a choice early in her life that she would be a good mother. That she would give her child all the love she had, and that she would teach me a new way. She was determined that I would not grow up to become a rebel. That is why we escaped. She risked her life to show me a different way of life."

"But your father was a rebel?" Silvia asked.

"Yes. My Father is related to Kony. That is all I know, and all my mother would ever tell me. She would not reveal his identity as she thought it might endanger me. Remember, it was a long time ago when the war was quite new, and Kony himself was a young man."

"But, how … I mean …" Silvia felt lost for words. So many questions swam around in a confusing jumble in her mind that she didn't quite know where to start. Nswana spoke for her.

"Silvia, if you are pregnant as it appears you might be, there are choices to make. You must decide how you want to live. But you must not blame your baby for what has happened to you. The baby is innocent and has no choice in the matter, but you do have a choice. You can choose to be its mother, or you can choose to walk away. I know this is a hard decision. Many babies are abandoned because the mothers cannot face the burden. If you decide not to be a mother, you must tell Charity, so that we can arrange to care for the baby. I will not see you throw away a child when I was in that child's position once. I understand how fragile life can be. To live is a gift."

"I would never throw away a baby," sobbed Silvia. A sudden protective instinct hit her at the very thought.

"Good."

"But … if I am … then this is the child of a … a … a very evil man. What if …"

"Silvia, the father may have been evil, but the child is innocent. The baby is not evil, even when conceived in violence. The baby has no choice. You have to decide what you will do. But, if you want to be a mother and keep the baby, you should love your baby. If you think you can't, I will understand. The circumstances are difficult. But, if you can't, please let us take care of it."

Silvia didn't know what else to say, so she simply nodded.

"If you need to talk about it, I am here and Charity also."

"Ok."

With that Nswana turned and began walking back towards the village. Silvia watched him go, the morning light reflecting off the sleek dark skin and muscles in his back. She knew he was a good man. His very presence was both powerful and reassuring. She wondered why Charity and Nswana seemed so sure that she was pregnant when she had spent the week trying hard to convince herself otherwise.

She looked down at her stomach. It had not changed shape, and if it wasn't for the sickness, she knew Charity would never have suspected she was pregnant. There was still a possibility that this was all a mistake. Silvia sighed deeply. She still felt very conflicted and upset at the thought, but somehow Nswana's story had given her a bit of comfort. If the kindest man she knew was the son of a rebel, perhaps there was hope. Perhaps, *who* a person became had more to do with what they were taught, than who their parents had been.

Then, as if carried by the wind straight down from heaven itself, the voice of her mother floated softly back into her mind. The voice she had once heard in a vivid dream.

Silvia took a deep breath and let the words escape her lips.

"Live well", she whispered under her breath. "Live well," she paused and thought hard for a time before the next question quietly escaped her lips.

"What does 'living well' look like in this impossible situation, Mama?" she whispered into the air. She felt like she walked upon a thin wire, and the only real option open to her was to take another step forward and keep going. If she deviated, she risked falling over the edge.

In the silence of the morning, as a soft wind caressed her face, Silvia found something begin to stir within her. A flame began to flicker. The longer she sat and thought, the more it grew until she could no longer resist its truth. And there, on the rock, Silvia began to make her first real decisions as a free person. They were simple but courageous, for they required her to live without the consequences of the past imprisoning her. They required her to step forward into the future with courage and determination despite the chasm of uncertainty that lay ahead.

As she sat in the morning light and let her eyes scan the horizon, Silvia made a vow that she knew she would keep for the rest of her days. It almost felt as if her life depended on it, and she silently acknowledged that perhaps, it did.

Silvia promised herself that rather than continuing to live in fear, as if she were still being hunted, she would not allow fear to hold her down or dominate her thoughts. Instead, she would become a survivor. If she were pregnant, she would be the best mother she could be. She would love her baby because her baby would be a part of herself and also a part of her own family. Nswana was right. The baby would be the innocent one in the fallout of her past, and Silvia had seen enough innocent people suffer. She did not want to add to the carnage of innocence lost. So, she simply decided to love, rather than to hate. She decided to protect rather than to disregard.

The second promise Silvia made to herself was that she would search for and never give up on finding her little brother. She would always leave room in her heart for the possibility that he too had survived. Unless his death was proven, she would let hope live and give it a space to breathe in her soul.

"Live well. Live well." Silvia knew the words were easy to say, but it would take all the courage she possessed to put into practice each day. The weight of her position lay heavy on her like a great responsibility. She had been given a gift that was denied to many, and she needed to honour the children who had never received the chance to live again. She would live well for Alinta, Juvience and the thousands of children just like them, who had lost the opportunity to live at all. The ones who lay buried alongside their unfulfilled hopes, dreams and potential. Those who had been left alone and lost in shallow graves. The ones whose stories would never be told. Silvia felt as if she carried within her own soul, a piece of each of their stories, but hers was still unfinished. For them, she knew she had to do her best.

There was a journey ahead of her with many pages left to write upon. Regardless of the potential dangers, Silvia was finally free to choose for herself – to *live*.

CHAPTER THIRTY-SIX

A FRIEND

Let us extend grace

Rather than justice

Let us speak truth

Not political lies

Let us stop judging

And start forgiving

Let us not deny

The tears we all cry

Let us fear hatred

And get on with loving

Let us be friends

Not just passers-by

Let us give respect

Instead of indifference

Let us live life

And not fear to die.

Grace was struggling to focus. Her missing fingers bothered her. It was as if there was a deep, throbbing pain inside them, even though they weren't there. It didn't make any sense, but she couldn't take her mind away from the ache. Added to that, every time she looked down and saw her grotesque hand, she thought of Manwena. She wondered if he'd put some kind of curse on her just to add to her misery. Perhaps, a curse that would slowly corrode her mind and finally leave it in a similar condition to her mutilated hand.

Grace desperately wanted to be happy that she and Sante were safe. She wanted to feel the exhilaration she had imagined she would at finally being free after so many years of captivity. Instead, she felt overwhelmed and fearful at the strange unfamiliar sights and sounds that had eluded her senses for so long. The anxiety she was experiencing was on par with what she would have felt had members of the resistance movement followed her out of the bush and stood all around, taunting her and poking her with sticks. Of course, her rational mind told her that they weren't, but fear overwhelmed her. She jumped at every little sound and caught herself behaving in ways that she knew must look strange.

She had begun muttering under her breath, and she couldn't seem to leave the hem of her skirt alone. Her fingers raced over it again and again as though they were searching for something. Somehow, these odd tendencies temporarily calmed her nerves. She felt worthless and disgusting, and she saw the way Sante looked at her as if he was embarrassed. She knew she wasn't mad, but she could tell that people were beginning to wonder. She even admitted to herself that the attraction of *assumed* madness was starting to appeal to her because nothing about reality seemed to be making much sense. Why couldn't she just embrace this new life? Why was she so afraid when, now more than ever, she should be feeling safe?

Grace and Sante had been at the HOPE Centre for over a week. Sante seemed to have adjusted and settled in quite well. Grace sat in the setting sun every afternoon and watched him as he played football like a star. She was happy that he was finally able to run and play and shout without fear. He even laughed occasionally as he played. She had never seen him spontaneously laugh before. She should have been in rapture. What more could a mother ask or hope for? What more could she ever want?

She did miss Judy. She thought about her often and was deeply saddened that her little daughter was not there running free with Sante. But not even the absence of Judy could completely explain the hollowness and anxiety that coursed in her veins.

One afternoon as she sat watching the boys, her eyes fell on a woman to her left who was washing clothes in a bucket of water. A little girl hovered around her ankles while she worked. The woman was small but strong. What shocked Grace and made her stare, however, was that the woman's facial features were missing. Instead of a nose and lips, she had ugly crevasses left where they had once been. Grace tried not to stare, but she couldn't seem to help continually looking towards the woman.

She knew what had happened to the women, even without having been told. She didn't even have to ask. She had witnessed many women mutilated by the rebels. It was a cruel form of torture for victims the commanders decided not to kill in a twisted display of 'mercy'. Instead of death, they were left lying in puddles of their own blood and hysterical tears.

Grace however, had never before seen a woman whose wounds had healed. She had never seen what a face looked like when the blood had been wiped away, and scar tissue had formed over open wounds. A knot sat at the top of her throat as she watched the little girl play around her mother. Raw hard bitter tears began to fall off her chin.

Grace was suddenly and unexpectedly overcome by grief. Not just her own, but the painful and brutal suffering that so many people carried. She wondered about this woman. There must have been a point, after her mutilation, when she decided that she still had life left within her – because surely, it would have been easier to just sit down and die. She tried to imagine the woman picking herself up in her own bloody mess and walking until she found help. Holding her head in her own mutilated hand, Grace let the tears run freely. She was grateful that all she had lost was fingers.

Tears were second nature. They were as familiar to her as breathing, and sometimes, they were unstoppable in the same way. Her tears had to flow like her breath had to be let out, over and over and over again. There never seemed an end to them. Head in her knees, Grace sobbed.

Suddenly, she felt a hand on her shoulder, and she turned sharply in fright. Looking up, she found herself staring straight into the woman's disfigured face. Up close, she could see the marks where the razor had sliced the deepest. The deeper the cut, the more profound the scar. The woman's face was a patchwork of messy skin that looked like it had all been stretched in the wrong way, but through her own tears, Grace could see that she was attempting to smile.

"What is it my sister?" the woman asked Grace, her eyes full of mercy.

Grace could not speak. There were no words. She was choked and drowning in her own tears as this beautiful soul wrapped her arms around her and held her close. Grace felt incredible warmth that she did not understand. She could not pull away. Instead, she leant deep into the arms of mercy.

Grace and Hanna became firm friends in the days that followed. Every afternoon, they would sit on the step at the edge of one of the buildings and watch the young boys play football. Hanna was a survivor, just like her. They were both strong and resilient, but also both broken in their own way. Their lives had been shattered by the horrors of war, and yet, somehow, through it all, they had managed to hang onto the thread of life that kept moving them forward.

Grace had not felt it right to ask Hanna about her past, but her friend had offered to tell her anyway. It was like a gift that Grace held gently. She admired her friend's courage that allowed her to actually voice her greatest and most difficult trial. She told the story simply, without too much detail, but it was enough.

"I had been planting maize when the rebels came into my village. My husband and two young children were there as well." As if she was diving into a pool of water, she took a deep breath before continuing. "The rebels took my husband, and they killed him in front of us. Then they took my youngest child and ... He was too young to serve them. He was no use to them, so they just ..." Hanna wept at the memory but kept on. "The other boy was already seven. They bound him and took him away. I was expendable. They would have killed me except I was visibly pregnant at the time. I heard one of the rebels say it was a bad omen to kill a pregnant woman, so they mutilated me instead."

"Oh Hanna, I am so sorry." It was all Grace could offer.

"It was terrible pain. I can't describe the pain. Not just the physical pain, but also that of losing all those I loved in an instant. It was too much for me. I wanted to die then, but I couldn't. After the rebels left me, I waited for death and it would not come. I waited for days, and it never came. Before I could die someone came and found me. It was a family who were moving to the refugee camp. They took me with them and looked after me."

"How did you end up here?" Grace had asked.

Hanna hesitated. "The people in the camps were very cruel to me. Even after my wounds got a bit better, I guess the smell and the sight of my face was too much for people. I knew I would never be acceptable to them. I was taunted and some of the children would throw stones at me saying a witch had cursed me. When my daughter was born, I began to feel very unsafe. I feared for my baby's life, so I spoke to a nurse who sometimes came to attend to the people in the camps, and I told her my concerns. She could see I was in danger, so she brought me here together with Rose." She smiled then. "I called my baby Rose because that was the name of the nurse. She was very kind to me. She is a 'Masungu' from England, and she still comes to visit me here sometimes. Maybe you will meet her one day."

Grace smiled at her friend as she watched Hanna cradle her little daughter. Without knowing it, Rose had saved Hanna's life, and in turn, she became her reason to live.

"How long will you stay here?" Grace asked.

Again, she smiled. "The HOPE centre staff have allowed me to stay on as a cleaner, for now."

Grace shook her head sadly as she thought of Hanna's past. Like all of the victims of this war, their pasts now seemed inescapable, reaching into and shaping their futures. It wasn't fair or right or just, and yet her friend had an unmistakable joy about her. She did not seem to feel sorry for herself. Instead, she was able to appreciate all that she felt she had gained. She was inspirational.

Then, Hanna let Grace in on another secret. She leaned over and quietly whispered in Grace's ear. "Shall I tell you something amazing?"

Grace was intrigued. She just nodded.

Hanna creased her scars into a smile. "Well," she paused, "I've been told there are doctors who can help women just like me."

"What do you mean?" Grace asked confused.

"They are special doctors that can work on faces that have been damaged." She looked over at her daughter playing in the dirt a few metres away and smiled. "Maybe one day ..."

CHAPTER THIRTY-SEVEN

EXPOSING THE DARKNESS

Freedom

Yours and mine,

The ability to simply BE,

But are we ever truly free?

Can't you see the irony

That creates for men such misery?

Freedom as we know it

Carries a cost,

Requires responsibility.

Brave men have fought and died

For the belief in liberty.

Sacrificed their lives

So that others could be free.

But is it real?

Are we free?

Or will we require more martyred men

Believing ... hoping ...

That another war will deliver liberty?

Freedom won't be found

In the blood of battlefields.

If it's our intrinsic right

Then it's our minds that have to yield.

No amount of bloodshed

Will change the mind of a man

Who is set against his neighbour,

Unwilling to understand.

Freedom

Yours and mine,

The ability to simply Be.

If you live a life that honours ALL men

Perhaps, you'll find

True liberty.

The moment Wendy showed him the small red book, the same one his mother had wanted him to read, Amos felt that the closing of a circle was upon him. As if God Himself was leading him back to the same place and making the same request. When Wendy asked him to participate in a rehabilitation course that was starting the following day, Amos felt compelled to agree despite his reservations. As a way of honouring his mother who had wanted him to read the same book, he had to take this opportunity to find out what it was she had so desperately wanted to share with him.

Amos had been at the Ark Project for almost a month now. Long enough for his physical wounds to heal and his fears to subside. He saw that the people who ran the project were genuine and caring, and he began to trust that they did not want to harm him. In some ways, Wendy had become like a second mother. She spent time with him, just talking through his different trials, thoughts and feelings. Of course, he had not revealed to her any of his darkest moments. The crimes he'd committed were things he tried hard not to think about. He never wanted to confess to anyone, what he had done. He knew the state of his own heart, but he did not want anyone else to judge or condemn him, as living with the burden was already difficult enough. So, despite a growing ease with his current environment, a deep self-loathing silently gnawed away at him.

On the first morning of the group, Amos entered the room quietly and joined the circle of participants sitting on the ground. He felt awkward and terribly uncomfortable.

"Welcome Amos," said Wendy who sat opposite with a red workbook upon her lap. "We are so happy to have you join us."

He nodded, trying hard to look relaxed, while his heart raced away with itself.

Looking around, Amos saw the by now familiar faces of some of the other young men and women who lived at the project. He did not know any of them well, as he had attempted to keep very much to himself, but he smiled shyly at the girl on his left and she greeted him with friendly eyes.

Wendy proceeded to introduce the program and explain a little about it. "This red book is the instruction guide for an educational course called EMPOWER," she began. "It has been used here at the Ark Project for a few years now and has also been used by many other organisations in Northern Uganda. The aim of the program is to help all of us who have been affected in some way through this interminable war; to assist us in reconciling our past so that we can get on with our future. There are two main parts to the program. The first teaches us how to take back control. The traumatic events we've experienced can have many effects on us. We are all different so we may react in different ways, but some of the more common things that can happen to people include constant nightmares, flashbacks to the past, uncontrollable thoughts, feelings of fear that come at odd times, not being able to sleep properly and feelings of terrible sadness. This program teaches you ways that you can take back control." Wendy paused before continuing.

"There is also a second part to the program, even more important than the first. We will come to that part if and when you are ready for it. The program is like planting a field for harvest. The first part ploughs and prepares the garden of your mind for planting; the second sows seed and tends carefully to the weeds that can choke your heart. The harvest is up to you. I have personally seen many lives changed through EMPOWER. If you would like to be a part of this group, we will meet every afternoon for the next few weeks. There's no pressure to attend. You can make your mind up after today's class whether you want to be a part of this group or not. However, if you do decide to attend, I want your commitment to be here every day. It is no good just coming a few times. To reap a harvest, you have to put in the work. Everyone clear on that?" Several people nodded.

"Now before we begin, lets introduce ourselves."

Amos sank down into his seat. He didn't want to be put on the spot and have everyone looking at him, but there was nowhere to hide.

When the girl next to him finished introducing herself, she turned to Amos and asked, "What's your name?"

Several days into the group, Amos found himself captivated by what he was learning. The lessons were so simple, yet so practical and liberating. Participating in the group had forced him to get to know some of the other people at the Ark Project. Together, they learned valuable skills that helped them to take control over residual nightmares and pervasive flashbacks. With each day, Amos developed greater emotional security and stability. However, the day arrived, as he had been forewarned, when he was encouraged to talk about some of his personal experiences, the memories of which he buried and guarded with determined desperation.

Some of the group had already shared their experiences with Wendy in private, but Amos did not feel compelled to do the same.

In fact, he dreaded it and considered dropping out of the group before his turn came. Wendy pointed out that all of the thought and feeling control exercises learned to date were preparing him for this moment. While he had come to respect Wendy and wanted to do his best, he couldn't imagine voicing aloud the disturbing secrets he held. The thought of revisiting memories of his past made him want to vomit.

None of it made sense to Amos. How could there be freedom by facing up to the thing he feared the most. Wendy continued, "Think of it like this. The key to your cage has been sitting in the searing sun. To touch it will mean getting your fingers burned. While the pain may last a few minutes, the liberty that comes from unlocking the cage door lasts a lifetime. Amos?"

"I … don't think I can."

He rationalised that if he let Wendy know his disturbing past, he would probably be thrown back onto the street. While other children would likely have been victims themselves and might have also been forced to commit horrendous atrocities, surely none had committed crimes as gruesome as the dark memories he laid claim to. None of the stories he had heard seemed to match the horror of his own. The murder of his little sister; the way he had become one of them and abducted innocent people; the thoughtless, selfish way he had run away, leaving his sisters and Silvia behind …

"Nothing you were forced to experience in your past defines or determines who you are today, Amos – unless you let it," Wendy encouraged. "What defines you, Amos, is the how you freely respond to the choice presented to you now. The choice about who it is you want to become from this point forward. You are defined by who you are and who you belong to, not by what you've done or what was done to you. However, to get on with your future, you must first face, confront and reconcile your past." Wendy paused, allowing her words to hang in awkward silence.

Amos found himself talking. He hadn't meant to. It was the way she looked at him. She didn't need to say much. She quietly coaxed it out of him. Everyone else had gone and in the comfort of relative seclusion, Wendy gently said, "Start at the beginning." And so he did …

Tears poured down his face as he recalled tragic and painful moments. His first abduction felt like nothing in comparison to his second. Like a storm that raged, waves of terror and sadness clashed with strong emotions of anger and rage. Amos exposed the wounds of his heart that had been so unjustly inflicted but also confessed his own betrayal. His own cowardice. His abandonment and disregard for those he loved, so he could save his own skin. He confessed too, that he hated himself for it. He should have stayed. He was in physical agony when he thought of comforting his sister as she died in his arms crying out for their mother. Amos sobbed uncontrollably at the memory, hardly able to explain to Wendy what had happened, but she was able to decipher the general story. Wendy touched his arm and just let him cry.

Sometime later, after all his tears were spent, Amos managed to compose himself. He wiped his face and looked up at Wendy, nervously anticipating her response. She surely must be horrified and ready to see the back of him, but what she said next took him by surprise. There was no judgment or condemnation in her voice, but neither was there any overt sympathy. In a calm, soft, neutral voice, Wendy simply encouraged Amos. "Start from the beginning,

Amos. I want you to tell me your story again."

That was the last thing he felt like doing, but in the seeming comfort of Wendy's neutral response, Amos complied. He went back to the beginning and once again relayed the circumstances around his first abduction – the easiest of his traumatic memories to retell.

As he narrated his experiences for the second time, Wendy began asking a few questions, requiring Amos to fill in the gaps. The personal questions made his recollections more vivid and detailed. His mother's name, the names of his sisters, the feelings he could recall having at various times. Systematically, Amos worked his way up once again to facing some of his more horrific memories. However, it somehow felt a little easier than his first recollection. He was able to voice many of the horrendous details of the abuses he suffered and the atrocities he committed, without becoming completely overtaken by emotions.

"Amos," Wendy whispered when he had finished, and the tears were being wiped away. "You are going to be just fine."

As he let the waves of emotion wash over him, he noted somehow these tears were different. They were tears of relief. The darkness had been penetrated by light.

CHAPTER THIRTY-EIGHT

A FLAME

On the darkest nights, when the stars all shine bright,

There is a girl left alone in the candlelight.

A girl from the forest without a home.

Child of the war

Child lost and alone.

She was sent to us with a story to tell,

A child of the hunted, now escaping from hell.

A child of the forest

A child of the war

This hunted angel has a story to roar.

Though she carries within her the remnants of pain,

It is now her courage that will be fanned into flame.

S ilvia sat in the carriage of an overcrowded bus as it trundled across the arid African landscape. People, livestock, sacks of food and bags of various descriptions were crammed into every available space around her, but she had somehow managed to find a seat beside an open window. Ruth sat close to her side and Nswana on the seat behind. His presence gave her a deep sense of security, and she was able to relax and relish the feeling of warm air blowing on her face, bringing with it an array of familiar smells.

They passed deserted villages where only the remains of broken-down huts and old fire pits indicated that life had once abounded. However, on the outskirts of the towns, when the bus slowed down, groups of laughing children raced alongside them, and women sold roasted maize and cooked cassava through the open windows. Nswana bought some with the little money he had, and handed generous portions to the girls, who savoured every morsel of the delicious food.

Occasionally, in the distance, Silvia spotted a vast sea of grass roofs that indicated a refugee camp. She found herself wondering about her little brother Raymond. Was it possible that by some miracle he had survived, and was existing among the millions of other souls squashed into one those camps? She knew she would probably never know the answer, but it gave her some comfort to think that he might be out there somewhere.

As the hours past, Silvia's mind began to cast backwards. From the beautiful life and family she had once known to the precarious uncertainty of her current situation – she saw it all, as if she was watching it happen to someone else. It was an odd feeling, knowing that it had happened to her but feeling strangely numb and disconnected from the events that had dictated her journey. The last several months spent in Nswana's village had been a wonderful transition. Although a part of her wanted to stay, she had always known that her time there was limited, and she had a deep yearning within her to return home. When Silvia had tentatively expressed this to Nswana a few weeks ago, he had kindly offered to escort Ruth and her back to Gulu.

Silvia looked down and ran her fingers across her swollen belly. There was no denying it now. She smiled as she thought of the new life growing inside her, and then shook her head as she realised how far she had come – from total denial to eventual acceptance and now, even the beginnings of anticipation at meeting her baby. The only fear that lingered was whether the baby would look like her or ... But it wasn't a thought worth considering. Either way, she knew she had an important role to play and had already made up her mind that she would love this baby, no matter what. He belonged to her.

Silvia was suddenly aware of how tired she felt – so desperately tired. Although she was thankful for the chance to return – something she had longed for since being torn away such a long time ago – heading back to her old home evoked a flood of emotions she could not deal with just then. Silvia knew she had to hold every ounce of emotion captive as if that flood had been held back by a dam and would break once the cracks began to appear. She tried hard to keep her mind focused as she sat and let the wind blow across her face. It carried with it memories from a home long gone but not forgotten.

Silvia remembered the love she had known as a child. A love founded upon simple unconditional care. She remembered the way her mother smiled at her, and the way little Raymond used to cuddle up to her at night. She remembered Amos, whom she had thought was her truest friend until the moment he disappeared into the bush with Sante. She wasn't sure how to feel about him any longer, or if she would trust him if she ever saw him again. On the one hand, she understood well the desperate need to escape that had existed within them all. But, on the other, she was still confounded by how he could have left her. She longed to know why he hadn't taken her with him − if indeed there was a reason beyond the seeming lack of care. So much pain might have been avoided, if he had been kind enough to remember her and his sisters as he fled. Silvia found herself wanting to be angry with Amos, although she knew this was misplaced. Still, the confusion she felt over him lingered. Almost everyone else in her life could be slipped neatly into a box of either good or evil. Everyone fitted somewhere, except him.

Silvia sighed deeply and forced her eyes to focus on the horizon. Although she was young, one of the things she had come to accept about life was that it was full of loose ends that could never be tied off. She had never had the chance to say goodbye to her parents. She had never seen her baby sister grow. She had been ripped away from a home that she loved and forced to survive in horrendous circumstances. There had rarely been any warning before one door was slammed shut and another flung wildly open. Somehow, through all the uncertainty and trauma however, there persisted within her a strong desire − a desire to *live*. Where it came from, and why it came, she didn't know. In her most difficult moments, while out in the bush with the rebels, death had seemed like the easier, more comfortable option. It would have been an escape from the pain, uncertainty and trials that often threatened to swallow her whole, but she couldn't deny that the desire to live was still there. Like the sun that was slowly beginning to sink over the horizon and set the night sky on fire to give it a life all of its own, this hope and the need for the life inside her to grow was a flame that could not be extinguished.

As she stared into the setting sun, watching the sky turn the distant clouds a brilliant orange that lingered hot over silhouetted trees and the untamed African landscape, Silvia allowed the peace of her current moment to wash over her. Nswana had warned her that the bus trip would take a few days to reach Gulu, and, while the other passengers often appeared restless and uncomfortable, she didn't care about how much time passed. In fact, she wished for the journey to continue for as long as possible. She felt safe in this cosy corner of the bus with Ruth by her side, dosing in and out of sleep, and her protector so close by. Looking out on life from a somewhat hidden vantage point, where she felt secure and free from trials was a comfortable place to be. She savoured the moments and refused to let her mind think about the journey to come.

As the night wore on, and her eyes became heavy, Silvia stared up at the big yellow moon that had appeared over the horizon and now seemed to be following them across the countryside. She tried to tell herself this wasn't the case but having never travelled in a bus and watched the moon before, she found it difficult to decide which reality was the real one. Indeed, the moon did appear to be following them. Silvia wanted to ask Nswana about it, but felt silly, like she should know the answer but didn't. So, she decided to keep quiet and just watch. Surely, it would grow tired soon enough and give up the chase?

Suddenly, Silvia remembered an evening a long time ago, when she had awakened while in the night shelter with Raymond by her side. That night she had stared up at that moon through a crack in the roof. She remembered a shaft of light streaming in, and the dust dancing like diamonds in the silvery air. She was surprised how vividly the image returned to her now. How safe and cosy she had felt amongst all of the other sleeping children with little Raymond curled up beside her as if he hadn't a care in the world. Even though they had to sleep far from home, she recalled her own naïvety and denial that anything bad would ever happen to her family. She had rebelled, in her own small way, from the very idea of it, never dreaming of what was to come.

It felt like a lifetime ago. She thought of how good it had been to hold little Raymond in her arms, to feel his warmth next to her and to listen to the sound of his breathing. Slowly, as she let her mind remember his sweetness, a crack on the outer shell of her heart began to appear. The dam threatened to burst. No one would have even noticed the silent tear that slid down her cheek, but it was the first tear she had allowed to escape in a very long time. Oh, how she longed to hold Raymond close to her again and tell him that he was safe. That it was all just a bad dream they would wake up from in the morning.

Silvia wrapped her arms around Ruth and let the little girl fall into her side. She was asleep, and for a moment, Silvia found herself pretending that she was Raymond. That her little brother was safe and back in the very place he had loved to be – by her side.

Silvia woke to the sound of people talking and laughing. The bus had stopped moving. She looked out of sleepy eyes and saw through the window that most of the people from the bus were standing outside talking and eating. She saw Nswana and Ruth. He held the little girl's hand and was approaching a small food stand.

Silvia knew this wasn't Gulu, but she didn't have any idea where they were. She slowly sat up and rubbed her eyes; suddenly aware of how urgently she needed to relieve herself. She began to move towards the edge of the seat and stood, picking her way carefully over the bags and various goods stacked up in the aisle that people used as extra seats. Upon reaching the doorway, she stepped gingerly out onto the dusty road, her legs stiff from sitting for such a long time. There were a few small food stalls along the side of the road, as well as a local market where the villagers sold their produce. Behind the market were open fields of long grass and further in the distance she could see a few villages.

"Silvia, finally you woke up," Nswana exclaimed over the general clatter of voices.

"Sorry," Silvia said, immediately assuming her sleeping was an imposition.

"No need to say sorry. It was good that you slept. We didn't want to wake you." Ruth nodded agreement beside him as she munched on a large cob of maize. Its golden kernels were burnt brown from the charcoal it had been roasted on. Nswana handed her an equally large piece.

"Thank you Nswana, but first I need to go."

"Oh, yes," he nodded and pointed across to the field of long grass. As she looked closer, Silvia could see that there were a few other heads sticking up from the grass as people squatted to relieve themselves. She headed out to find her own space and privacy, while Nswana and Ruth waited.

"Where are we?" Silvia asked upon returning, now able to think straight and hold a proper conversation.

"On the outskirts of Kitgum," Nswana replied. "We crossed

the border in the early hours of the morning. So, we should be in Gulu sometime today." He handed the maize back to her, and she began eating hungrily. Ruth had already finished and was eating a piece of sweet bread. A big treat! Silvia noticed with delight that Nswana had bought half a loaf, and there was plenty left over. She couldn't remember the last time she had eaten bread.

"How are you feeling?" he asked as he watched her eat the maize.

"Fine," Silvia replied. She didn't know what else to say. The emotions she felt over returning to Gulu were far too difficult to express.

"You don't feel sick anymore?"

"No." Her sickness had faded away a week or two before.

"That is good Silvia." She could only nod and was thankful that Ruth piped in.

"What will we do when we get there? Where will we go?"

Silvia stopped eating. She had been wondering this too but had not wanted to ask or even admit that they didn't have a home to return to. She assumed Nswana must have known this, but she feared that, if she confirmed it, he might not have agreed to let her return. Nswana looked at the girls thoughtfully before he spoke.

"That is a good question, Ruth. Probably one we should talk about soon. Do you want to go back to your village and see if anyone still lives there? Or is there someone you know in town?"

"I don't know," Ruth responded.

"Silvia?"

She was silent, and he could see that she was thinking. The thoughts came like a flood followed by an unexpected wave of emotion. The dam was cracking, and she could feel the pressure inside her mounting as she tried hard to hold it all in.

"I ... I don't know either," Silvia whispered.

Nswana put his arm around her shoulders protectively. "It's ok. It's ok. We will figure it out." His compassion pushed the wave over the edge of the dam wall, and Silvia felt the tears sliding down her cheeks. She tried to stop them, but they just kept on coming. A cascading stream of water that seemed to have no end. Nswana handed her a cloth to wipe her face, and the three of them sat on the ground in the sun and simply waited. For the moment, there seemed no point in talking anymore. Nswana let Silvia cry and did not try to talk her out of the torrent that stirred and welled from within. He simply sat and held her close, much as she had once held Raymond. He had become like a father or an older brother, and Silvia was thankful. Though she could not tell him, this man had allowed her to see that the heart of a man was not necessarily evil. There were some good men. Nswana was one she believed she could trust completely.

Stepping off the bus into the noise and chaos of Gulu's crowded central station was overwhelming. Silvia felt as if she was stepping into another world. Even though she had been here before, her return felt like the beginning of another life. As if she was experiencing it all for the first time. There were people everywhere, swarming like bees around a hive. Women carried huge baskets on their heads as they navigated their way in and around the buses that groaned under ever increasing weight. Children trailed after them, trying hard not to get lost in the crowds. Men shouted at one another, as bags and packages of every description were thrown in conveyer belt like fashion onto bus rooftops, where they were tied down precariously with bits of rope and cloth slung together. There seemed no order to the scene, and yet, she knew there was. Somehow, everyone would find their way onto the right bus at the right time and make it to their destination. Success would not be measured by achievements of time and efficiency, for no one wore a watch, but rather by safe arrivals. On these rickety old buses, which were packed to the brim like sardines in a can, safe arrival fell into the realm of the miraculous.

Silvia stood still, hugging a small blanket protectively to her chest as she waited for Nswana and Ruth to exit the bus. Exactly where all these buses were going was a mystery to her, but somehow, the people getting on and off them seemed to know. She took a step backwards, as if it would put distance between her and the sea of chaos that threatened to swallow her.

The hand on her shoulder from behind was protective and strong. She did not have to turn around, for she knew it was Nswana.

"This way," he directed as he moved around Silvia. Ruth was in his arms, and she followed close behind.

Nswana moved with purpose through the crowd, and Silvia found herself vaguely wondering if there was anything he was afraid of. Every now and then, he turned to see that she was still following close behind. He did not smile, but his eyes were reassuring, and Silvia found her fears abating.

As they reached the edge of the bus station, he turned his back against the large iron fence and faced her.

"It's getting late. We should find a place to stay for the night."

Silvia nodded. "I know a place." She said it without thinking but regretted it in the same breath. Could she really take them to the warehouse she used to sleep in with Raymond? Could she really lie down once again on that hard concrete floor without him by her side? Nswana was indicating that they needed to move, so she began to walk in the direction she knew would take them there. Her mind protested, but her legs appeared to have a will of their own.

When she saw it come into view some fifteen minutes later, Silvia stopped dead in her tracks. It was just as she remembered. A big wooden building that was set up for a market by day, and a children's sleeping quarter by night. There were many children already beginning to arrive. A lump stuck in her throat, and she found it impossible to speak, but Nswana had seen the direction of her gaze.

"There?" he asked. Silvia nodded. He was right, they did need to find shelter, but why had she led them here?

CHAPTER THIRTY-NINE

REDEMPTION

You penetrate my tears with gentle love.

You reach down to where I am

And wait for me.

No expectations.

No demands.

You wait until I am ready to reach up.

Forgiveness: The opportunity to begin again.

Sante's initial misgivings about the HOPE Centre had vanished in close parallel with his introduction to football. He loved the break in routine every afternoon. It was a time to just be free. To run and play with the other boys in the safety of the walled compound. Football was the only thing on their minds, and they played with an enthusiasm that paid little heed to aching and exhausted legs. They were like lions finally released back into the wild after being caged for too long. A tattered white soccer ball thrown into their midst held the magic required to strip everything away from their complicated lives, except the foundations of childhood. The very thing that was usually the first casualty of war was also the first to return. It was like watching flowers bloom in the desert after the rains. Nothing could stop them from just being kids.

After they were all exhausted and famished, evening supper was served in the big food hall. Sante always sat next to Grace, and they would eat quietly together. For the first week after their arrival, she didn't say much to him at all, and he was silently concerned about her mental state. But as the days passed, he began to see her relax. Slowly, she started to look around, smile occasionally and speak with him. Sante and his mother had a close bond that he knew could not be broken, and the relief he felt as he observed her stress melting away, helped him to have further confidence in their new home. Sante had a general sense that she would be ok. She was a survivor.

Although it was all very new, Sante found himself loving everything about his surroundings. The people were friendly and actually smiled and laughed with one another. He watched the staff and those who had been at the Hope Centre for some time, and he saw genuineness in the connections between them. It was like he was witnessing a new world unfold before him, and he was intrigued by every detail. He wanted so desperately to trust that it was real and not an illusion that would vanish like a dream. He also recognised a new and growing desire to have what they had. He wanted a freedom that would allow him to laugh like the other boys did, as if they had no bad memories or nightmares to drag behind them. But he had no clue how to go about finding such a freedom, or even how to ask for it, so he just watched.

For the first time in his life, he also slowly began to feel truly safe. He did not feel the need to doubt or fear everyone around him. One morning after he woke, he lay on his bed thinking about the life-changing journey he was on. It dawned on him that, for the first time in his life, he could get up without the shadow of worry hanging over him – without that dark and foreboding feeling that this day might be his last. He breathed in as deeply as he could and tried to grab and hold tightly to the safety net he felt he was in. There was so much he had to learn, and so much he didn't understand, but he did know that he never wanted to feel that fear again.

He had waited his whole life for this. Not for a second chance, but a new beginning – the experience of life without fear, the ability to find peace in the air around him. It was as if angels' wings were shielding him from the fear he had known since birth. He was free. He had been pulled from the wreckage, and he was allowing himself to take comfort.

Yet, there was something that still held him captive. It was a deep and all-consuming sadness that he couldn't quite escape. Was it sadness over the death of his little sister? Was it guilt over the atrocities that he had committed? The man he had killed still invaded his dreams. Was it the hollowness he felt when he thought of his father? He had assumed revenge would feel good, but, although he hated Manwena, there was no joy to be found in his death.

One morning after breakfast, while meeting with Maggie and a few boys of his own age, he was confronted, challenged, and then given the key to purging the sadness that cleaved deep within. It came in an extremely unexpected way.

There were about fifteen boys in the group that morning. Many had become familiar faces, but there was one new boy there. He sat in the circle looking nervous and unsure of himself. Sante gasped when he recognised the boy. Evans!

"Before we begin today," Maggie started, "I would like to introduce you to Jacob. He is new here at HOPE, and I would like you all to make him feel very welcome."

Jacob nodded, and Sante looked between Maggie and Evans in shock. Was this a set up? Was Evans there in disguise, pretending to be a refugee when he was really a rebel? Perhaps, he had been sent to track down Sante and Grace, and either bring them back or kill them. Sante wanted to hide, but there was nowhere to go, and his discomfort became very obvious as he looked nervously around.

"Sante?" Maggie asked.

Her question made Evans look in Sante's direction, and Sante saw his own shock mirrored in the boy's face. There was a moment of stillness before chaos erupted. Sante started reacting before he could even think about what he was doing. He jumped to his feet and picked up his chair, holding it out in front of him like a weapon.

"Stay away from me," he shouted at Evans who still sat staring up at him in disbelief.

"Sante! Put that chair down," he heard Maggie exclaim, but he was already lunging forward in Evan's direction.

Evans dived off his chair and hit the floor milliseconds before his face collided with the hard-wooden legs. Then he was up on his feet and defending himself as Sante danced around him and tried to swipe him hard across the head with the chair. In Sante's mind, he was defending them all against this invader, and he didn't understand why no one else was helping. Didn't they know that this boy was a rebel who was capable of anything?

Suddenly, strong arms grabbed Sante from behind, and the chair fell to the floor. He jerked his body trying to get free, but it was no use.

"You shouldn't be here," he heard himself shouting. "You're one of them. You're not Jacob, you're Evans." He looked at Maggie and shouted, "He's a liar. His real name is Evans."

Sante was forcibly dragged out of the room and into Maggie's office where he was placed on a chair. Benjamin sat down beside him. Moments later the door opened, and Maggie entered followed by Evans. Sante sprang to his feet.

"Sit down, sit down," Maggie ushered him in a reassuring way.

Sante sat and remained silent now. He was confused, enraged and afraid.

Maggie spoke firmly. "Sante, I don't know what your history is with Jacob, but I want you to know that we are aware of his past – just as we are also aware of your history with the rebel militia. However, you need to know the war is not just raging out there Sante, but the war ... the war is also raging inside of you. For as long as there is war in the hearts of men, there will be war on this earth. War is not welcome here!"

With that, she got up and left the room. Sante looked at Benjamin and peered at Evans with a poisonous glare.

"Boys," Benjamin said, keeping his eyes on both of them, "today will be a hard lesson for you. But if you want to move forward into a life free from the burning splinters of bitterness, this is a lesson you need to learn. Today, you will begin to understand a mystery. Today, I am going to introduce you to a new kind of violence. A violence that will rage and wrestle on the inside of you until freedom emerges victorious. Today, something will die, and you must kill it dead. Unless a seed falls to the ground and dies, there can be no germination, no growth and no harvest – no new freedom can be born. Unless you learn to let go of and demolish the hurt and pain of the injustice, bitterness will be wedged in your heart like a cleaver that divides and ultimately conquers. Today, your fight with each other ends, and the fight within yourself begins.

Benjamin paused, letting the silence linger between them like thick coiling smoke that refused to dissipate. Quick glances were exchanged between boys – neither one knowing exactly what was about to happen. "Today," Benjamin continued, "you will wage the most difficult war of all. It's a war within yourself, and if you want to survive, it's a battle you have to win. It's a mystery," Benjamin repeated. "This battle is not against flesh, blood and the things you can see. This fight is for your soul. This fight is for your freedom. This is a fight within to be able to surrender."

"To win, you have to lose?" Sante contested – bewildered by the riddle. "I've never heard anything so stupid."

"This may be the most difficult fight you ever engage in," Benjamin continued in a confident, firm voice. "It will seem unfair and unreasonable. That's why it's a mystery. You must do the thing you think you cannot do. This battle is not fought with guns or even physical strength. This battle is fought with the outrageous and scandalous weapon of grace. There is only one way to defeat the enemy. The enemy is defeated when you extend the gift you think you cannot give. You don't win by losing, you win by yielding."

Still confused, Sante looked to Evans who was staring intently at the floor. Benjamin grabbed Sante by the shirtsleeve and pulled him to his feet. "Watch this," Benjamin said. "You are tough, right? Strong? Well, let's put that strength to the test. Let's see how tough you really are?" Benjamin raised his hands with open palms and motioned to Sante to take his position as if ready to fight. "You think you're strong, but you cannot win this battle in your own strength. You are not strong enough. The point is, neither am I, and yet, I will win!"

Incensed by his belligerent confrontation, Sante primed himself to fight. "Let's go!" He challenged.

Benjamin laid out the terms for the contest. "Take your stand, and I will take mine. The first person to move their feet or take a step loses. The person who remains standing unmoved wins." With that, Sante launched at Benjamin with an aggressive thrust against his open palms, endeavouring to push him off balance. Benjamin absorbed Sante's blow by pulling his hands backward and yielding to the forced exerted against him. Sante desperately tried to regain his balance but was helpless against the carry-through momentum that landed him in Benjamin's arms. As the two stood awkwardly embracing, Sante sheepishly composed himself in the face of unexpected defeat.

"How did you do that … how did you beat me?" Sante enquired.

"Many people will cross your path in this life, and many will hurt you in one way or another," replied Benjamin in a matter of fact way. "You can't control what people do, but you can only control the way you respond. You have tried to beat me using force, but I won the battle by choosing to yield to that force. Rather than fighting you, I had to fight myself to win … I had to fight the urge to retaliate with force." Benjamin sat down, leaving Sante bewildered. "Everyone at one time or another will experience injustice," he continued. "Most people will never have to overcome the things you have had to face – that too is a part of the injustice of an imperfect world. It's not fair. Yet, what you *do* with your pain and hurt is totally up to you. It's a choice you must make.

"A choice?" Sante spoke up as if he couldn't stop himself. "No one has ever given me a choice about anything. And now you say I *must* make a choice?"

"Yes," Benjamin continued. "Like it or not, you do have a choice now. The choice is between life and death. In order to save your life, you have to lose it."

"What?" Sante exclaimed. "That's crazy talk. What do you mean? Are you saying in order for us to live we have to die? If anyone is dying today, it's not me!"

"Stop," Benjamin retorted. "Listen to me carefully. The rebels are not just militia intent on destroying the lives of villagers ..." Benjamin stood to his feet and placed his hand cautiously on Sante's chest. "The rebel is in here, and it's destroying you. This is who has to die. The rebel on the inside. The rebel that rages with anger; the rebel that poisons your dreams with venomous terror; the rebel who lusts for revenge and retaliation; the rebel who takes no responsibility, yet blames others and sucks on the blood of bitterness; the rebel who wants those who have hurt you to be hurt themselves in order to feel the pain that you have felt; the rebel who wants to rise up and throw chairs across the room at ..." Benjamin paused and turned to look at Jacob, who appeared captivated by the discussion. "Do you hear what I'm saying, Sante?"

"So ..." Sante nervously shuffled his feet. "So, how do I kill him?"

"You suffocate him. You don't give him air to breath. If you don't let him feed on the memories of injustice, he dies. Sante, when you stop scratching at the scab of hurt, pain and bitterness, you allow your wounds to heal. It feels good to keep scratching the rash of injustice but doing so just makes the rash angrier and the wounds more painful. The only way to kill off the angry rash is to stop scratching it. And that's the battle. That's the battle you have to win. The battle is not against Jacob, or even those who have committed the most heinous of crimes against you, your battle will be within yourself, and there's only one way to win that battle."

Sante grabbed hold of Benjamin's hand and pleaded, "Teach me … Teach me that way. I want to win this battle!"

Jacob quickly stood to his feet, startling both Sante and Benjamin. "Me too, I want to learn this way. What's the way? How do we do this?" With tears welling in his eyes, he whispered, "How do we become free from the pain?"

Benjamin took a few moments to gather his thoughts. The boys' pointed questions seem to linger in the air, desperate for resolve. Benjamin looked at the boys intently, and carefully proceeded. "If it's truly freedom you seek, you have to let go of your pain. If you have resolved that you can no longer stand under the weight of it, then the only way to dissolve your pain is to extend to each other a gift. The most expensive gift imaginable! The gift you think you cannot give. To reconcile your past and get on with your future, you have to extend to each other the gift of forgiveness."

Sante looked suspiciously at Jacob, and Jacob returned his mistrusting stare. For several moments, no one spoke. Without breaking his glare, Sante found his voice and retorted, "So have you ever had to forgive anyone?"

Benjamin accepted Sante's challenge, gently replying, "I understand more of what you've been through than you probably realise. When I was a young boy, I had three brothers. We lived in a village outside Gulu. One night, we were taken – all four of us. We were forced to walk for days carrying weapons for the rebels. We walked over the border into Sudan. I was the second oldest brother. My younger brothers became very weak, and after a time, they couldn't stop falling. They were having trouble to rise." Benjamin hesitated for a moment and looked at each of them before continuing. "What happened to my brothers and me has taken me many years to overcome, and it took me a long time to truly forgive. You see, forgiveness is like lighting a fire for cooking. You cannot just do it once, and then never have to do it again. Every time you come to cook you have to light the fire once again. When you first learn how to light a fire it is difficult, but after a while, it becomes easier and easier, until you do it automatically and hardly even have to think about what you're doing."

Benjamin's analogy was a little lost on Sante and he interrupted, "So, what happened to you and your brothers?"

"Well, after several days, as I said, my younger brothers could not go on. The rebels gave my older brother a choice. He could kill the younger boys, or I could kill him. Either way, they were not letting us move on before someone died. My older brother was in a terrible situation. I was also in a terrible situation. I did not want to kill my older brother, but I did not want him to kill the younger two boys. What could we do?"

"What *did* you do?" asked Evans.

"My brother killed the younger boys to save himself." Benjamin said it in a matter-of-fact way before continuing. "Over the next months, I saw my brother turn into an enemy. He could never forgive himself for what he had done. He never spoke to me again. He became one of them as he felt he had no choice, I guess. I eventually managed to escape, but as far as I know, he still remains with the rebels today."

"And you have forgiven him?" asked Sante. "Even though he killed your brothers and probably would have killed you too. Even though he stopped being your brother."

"Yes," Benjamin replied. "I have forgiven him, and I continue to forgive him. I pray that, one day, I might be able to tell him that, but if not, at least the forgiveness I have for him has set my own heart free. It has allowed me to go from hating my brother to having compassion for him. I honestly feel very heart-broken for him. In spite of all the evil he may have done, I will still call him my brother, if I ever see him again. What he did was not right. What he continues to do is not right, and I will never say that his actions are ok. However, as a young boy, he was faced with a very difficult situation. An impossible choice. No boy should face such a dilemma. I carry a great sadness for what happened – not only to my younger brothers, but also what has happened to him. And in some strange way, I feel thankful that my younger brothers escaped the life he now lives as a rebel. A life of war, brutality and killing will turn any heart into a place of evil – a place where love can no longer reside. That is not life. I have learned through the power of forgiveness that we do not have to end up bitter and twisted. Forgiveness is the only way to move forward in life and to live the best life you can. You do not have to become perpetrators of the next war for the next generation. We all have a choice to make. I have simply chosen to live as a free man. I will not carry on the cycle of someone else's war."

Sante was surprised by Benjamin's past. Evans looked equally shocked. Not because his story was unusual, but because he did not appear to be a man with that kind of past. He did, indeed, appear to be free.

Benjamin continued speaking before they could interject with any more questions. "I have a challenge for you both," he said. "I want to ask you both to share your stories with each other. I want you to be open and honest, because regardless of how you view each other, you are both victims of this war. You may have committed crimes and done terrible things, but those crimes do not define you. Your past does not need to predict your future. One of the best ways to make sure that you can be set free from your past is to speak about it honestly. Pull out all of the dark things that you have buried and speak openly, because secrets lose their power when they are exposed to the light. If you choose freedom, you will be choosing not to condemn each other. Darkness and light cannot coexist in the same place at the same time, and just like night and day, when the sun comes up, the darkness runs away. Are you willing to do this?"

Sante and Evans looked at each other nervously then looked back at Benjamin. Both nodded slowly.

"So, Jacob, let us begin with you."

Sante sat back in his chair nervously. Would Evans really air all his dark secrets out in public like this? The shame would surely be unbearable. He hadn't even told the truth about his name.

Sante was shocked when Evans began to speak. "My name *is* Jacob," he said looking directly at Sante. "Jacob Evans. I was very young when rebel soldiers abducted me. I don't remember exactly how old. I don't remember how long I was with them, and I don't know how old I am now. But I was young when they came into my village. They came at night. I remember being terrified. They made me kill my mother and my father, and then they told me that I was one of them. I had nothing to go back to. I had no one. I was alone apart from the rebels." Jacob tried to stifle sobs as he told his story for the very first time.

"I told them my name was Evans because that was my father's name. I didn't want to forget his name. I never told the rebel militia that my other name was Jacob. They only ever knew me by my last name. Carrying my father's name somehow gave me courage, even though, at times, I was so ashamed to have his name."

"So, how did you get away then?" Sante interrupted, suddenly curious.

"We were ambushed. After you left, Manwena also disappeared quite unexpectedly and abruptly. He went out to hunt you down and never returned. We tried to get to Sudan. On the way, we came upon a village, but while we were taking the hostages, we were attacked out of nowhere. Most were killed, I think. I'm not even sure who attacked us. I managed to escape. I just ran into the bush and kept on running. I didn't look back."

Sante was speechless. His military faction of the resistance movement was no longer. It hit him hard that had he not escaped when he did, he may also have been killed. Something in Jacob's tone told him that the boy spoke the truth. He had never seen this side of him. The Evans he knew was a cold-blooded killer.

"And the years in between your abduction and escape," Benjamin interrupted. "What were those years like for you?"

Jacob looked down at his hands and watched the tears fall into them. His mind was awash with nightmarish memories. "They were survival. They taught me quickly after my abduction how to be a killer. I killed my own parents. Every kill after that seemed like nothing to me. I somehow managed to overlook those people, like they didn't even exist. I guess, I knew it was wrong. I know there's no excuse. But, just like your brother, who is probably still out there in the bush somewhere, I told myself that nothing mattered. Life was like dirt, only good for being stomped on."

"Jacob, you are right, there is no excuse. But I want to tell you something. Sometimes, the hardest act of forgiveness is when we have to forgive ourselves. We can't hide our own past, and the evil of our hearts from ourselves, but we have the same choice to make. As we must choose whether we forgive others, we must choose whether we can forgive ourselves."

"How?" Jacob simply asked. "How do I possibly forgive myself. I killed my own parents. Not even God could forgive me for that!"

"He can, Jacob. And you can learn to. Remember, it is a choice. It is an action like lighting a fire. Choosing to forgive yourself is not a feeling. It is finding a way to untie the cords that bind you up and giving yourself permission to be the person you want to be – the person you were created to be."

Jacob was silent, but Sante could tell he was deep in thought. Then it was his turn. He took a deep breath and launched, figuring that he had nothing to lose. If Benjamin was right, then Sante knew somewhere deep within, that he desperately wanted and needed the same freedom he saw in the older man's eyes.

His memories came out in a jumbled-up way. From accounts of his father's abuse, his mother's pain, the loss of his sister, his own initiation into killing … It was all there. All a part of the pain stored in his tightly compacted soul that slowly leaked its way out into the air.

At the end of many hours talking together, the boys were both exhausted. Benjamin prayed for them as they knelt side by side, suddenly united in brotherhood and asked God Himself to forgive them.

Sante felt a strange indescribable emotion that he could not quite make sense of overcome him like a flash flood would cover parched ground and seep into the cracked earth. His heart felt raw and broken, but somehow freer than it had ever felt before. A heavy burden was literally being lifted off his soul. The burden of sadness and pain he had carried his entire life was disappearing. Ebbing away into the unknown. Would it come back? Was it an illusion? He didn't know the answers to these questions and the thousand others he now wanted to ask Benjamin, but for the moment, it was enough. He had been dying of thirst, and someone had just given him a long cool drink of water. The refreshment felt so good that it brought a rush of unexpected peace and joy to his soul.

Sante looked over at Evans then, wondering about the boy's past. He had only ever known him as a rebel. Someone who was always willing to kill. Was he really once just an innocent child who was taken from his family? Sante had no recollection of Evans ever arriving in a group of abducted children, but then perhaps he had just been too young at the time to notice. He guessed that Evans was a good three or four years older than him.

"Forgiveness is choosing to let go of your anger and bitterness towards the people who have wronged you. It is not saying that what happened is ok. In fact, the people who hurt you, don't even need to be sorry. Forgiveness is the action *you* choose. You choose not to dwell on what others have done to you in the past, and you choose not to take revenge. When you let go of your own hatred, no matter how much you feel that hatred is justified, then you set yourself free to walk into the future without the pain of the past dragging you down. Forgiveness does not mean you must befriend those who have hurt you. And it doesn't mean you put yourself in harm's way if someone continues to try to hurt you. It just means you give yourself permission to let it go."

"If it's not excusing the evil of others, then what is it?" asked Jacob. He was beginning to sound genuinely interested in what Benjamin was saying. "Why do you even call it a choice? It doesn't make any sense to me at all."

CHAPTER FORTY

THE GIFT

One single rose

Tilts towards the sun,

To bask in God's golden glory

Until her time is done.

A kaleidoscope of colour,

That captures the light.

A fragile but courageous beauty;

She cannot be hidden by night.

This single rose

Never questions why.

She is simply strength and dignity

As she continues her quest for the sky.

It had really happened. Grace was still in shock. She sat on the step in her regular position watching the boys play football, but she didn't really see them. Instead, her mind ran back over the events of the past few days. She shook her head in disbelief. She smiled. Somehow in the midst of her friend Hanna's journey, she was beginning to find her own courage again.

"Grace? Grace, where are you?" she had heard Hanna calling.

"I'm here Hanna. What is it?" Grace had been worried until Hanna appeared around the corner, and Grace caught the look in her eyes.

"Oh my … Grace," Hanna rushed over to her friend and held onto her with both hands. "I have just spoken to Maggie. The doctors have had a cancellation, and they can do my operation. And there is an organisation who pay for the doctors, so it's free!" Hanna was practically jumping for joy. "Grace it's free! I'm going tomorrow!"

"Oh Hanna, that's amazing!" Grace struggled to find words. She threw her arms around her friend, and they hugged each other tightly.

"Grace," said Hanna more seriously now. "I want you to come with me."

"What?" Grace was shocked. "What do you mean?"

"Maggie said they were allowing me to take someone along for support. She offered to come. But Grace, I told her it would mean a lot to me if you could be there."

"Really? Me?"

"Yes." Hanna was crying now. "Will you come Grace?"

"Of course, I will," said Grace hugging her again, and desperately praying that she would be the support Hanna needed.

Early the next morning, the two women were driven to the hospital. Grace was relieved that this time they did not have to speak to the ladies at the front desk. Instead, they were met by a team of three doctors who escorted them into a private room with a table and several chairs. They were told to sit down. The doctors were kind and friendly, but both women were nervous. Hanna put her hands around Grace's arm and held onto her much as a small child might. One who was afraid and seeking comfort.

"Hanna," the most senior-looking doctor began speaking. He was a white man with a full head of grey hair. "My name is Dr Michael." He held out his hand for both women to shake, which they did hesitantly.

"I am Dr Abraham," said the next one. He was an African-looking man with a European accent. Grace was intrigued by him, but she tried not to stare. She had never heard an African with a white-man's accent before.

"And, I am Dr Lesley," said the only female doctor in the room. She held out her hand and smiled.

"This is my friend, Grace," Hanna said. "Maggie said she could come with me."

"Yes, she can," replied Dr Lesley. "Grace, you can stay with Hanna until she goes into theatre. After that, you will be driven back to the HOPE Centre. The operation will take several hours, Hanna. You will probably need a few days to recover before you see visitors."

Hanna looked disappointed, but she didn't voice any objections. The doctors went on to explain to the women exactly what they were planning to do. They showed them some photographs of other women they had operated on. The before-and-after pictures made Hanna smile, and she squeezed Grace's hand in excitement.

After an hour or so, when their many questions had been answered, Hanna was taken into a room and prepared for surgery. Dr Michael had already drawn lines on Hanna's face in a black pen. Grace stood beside her friend and smiled, not quite knowing what to say or do. She must have looked concerned, for Hanna reassured her.

"Grace, it's going to be ok. I'm excited. I'm ready for this."

"Yes," Grace agreed, smiling down at her and stroking the top of her forehead with one finger. "Oh Hanna, you are so brave." Hanna just smiled.

Grace held her hand as they wheeled the bed down a long corridor. Finally, Dr Lesley told Grace she needed to stop outside the theatre door. Grace looked down and smiled again at her friend, shocked and inspired by her courage.

As Grace watched Hanna disappear through the doors, she leant her back up against the wall and thought deeply about her friend. It was not just undergoing the surgery that made her so inspirational. It was that Hanna had already been cut up once in her life. Her life had been tragically altered and twisted as a result. But now, here she was, bravely putting her demons to rest as she once again placed herself back into an incredibly vulnerable position under the hand of people who would hold knives to her face. Grace knew that the image of Hanna lying on that bed about to be wheeled away would be permanently etched into her mind's eye. It was an image that perfectly described without words, what true courage was.

Grace hoped and prayed that when she saw her again, she would see a woman whose beauty was as radiant on the outside as it was on the inside.

It was a week before Hanna returned to the HOPE centre. There had been complications. Grace had taken it upon herself to care for Rose, and she tried to love her in the same way that Hanna did. Still, the little girl had cried for her mother.

When they saw her again, Grace was somewhat disappointed that her face was still covered in bandages. She worried that the doctors had made some terrible mistake. Perhaps, they had made things worse for Hanna. But once again, it was Hanna who reassured her.

"The bandages can start coming off next week," she said excitedly as she hugged her friend. "But Grace, put your hand here. Gently, touch it. Can you feel? I have a nose!"

Grace smiled and began to cry. Her beautiful friend was so dignified. "I can't wait to see your face," she whispered. "And, I'm so glad you're back."

CHAPTER FORTY-ONE

HOME

You have travelled further down the path

Than you ever thought you'd go.

You have felt the winds of adversity

Strip edges off your soul.

You have faced into the gale

With broken hands, in head bent low.

You have seen the wicked triumph

As they seek the final deathblow.

You have not known how humanity

Can be called human at all,

And the questions that go around

Leave your mind upon the floor.

You have known the pain of loss

And the grief that batters so,

But it seems that there is something

That will never let you go.

It is hope when all seems lost.

And faith despite despair.

It is love for life and living

Even when all seems unfair.

Hold on and don't let go

As you continue around each bend,

For you cannot see just yet

Where your journey ends.

The night in the shelter had been difficult as Silvia had known it would be. There were too many reminders of all that she had lost, and the memories of Raymond were so vivid and deep, that initially it had been hard to settle down. Comfort was also more of an issue now that her belly was growing, and the concrete floor seemed much harder than she remembered. But with Ruth by her side, chatting as they lay in the dark, and Nswana somewhere on the periphery of the shelter, Silvia finally settled enough to fall into a deep sleep. She was so exhausted that there would be no fighting sleep, even if she did try.

Dreams came loud and dark into her sleeping mind. Dreams that lead her back down trails she did not want to walk. Back into the bush and the nightmare. Back into the hands of men who sought power and were possessed by such greed that anything in their path was destroyed. In the dreams, Silvia tried to get out of their way. She tried to run, but her legs felt like they had lead weights strapped onto them, making it impossible for her to move. She tried to hide, but the trees were too thin. The men gained on her, as if she were the sole object of their lust-fuelled existence.

She tried to scream, but no sound would come, and she knew they would not be swayed from their purpose. The end was inevitable, so she closed her eyes and waited. The inevitable would come.

Several times during the night, Silvia had woken with a start. Her eyes opened in the dark and peered around, as if searching for something to grab hold of – something to reassure her that she was ok. Her breathing remained heavy for several long minutes, until she was finally able to convince herself that it was only a dream. Slowly, she would unwind enough to sleep, but it took some time. In those moments, she had wished that Nswana were closer with a comforting word.

When the dawn finally arrived, Silvia felt exhausted. Sleep had not refreshed her, and she lay still for some time, wishing she didn't have to move. She recalled the mornings she had woken with Raymond by her side and imagined that he was with her now, scrunched into a foetal position with a blanket bunched up at his feet. She sighed deeply. She did not want to open her eyes to life's realities today.

The other children in the night shelter had begun filing towards the door, as silently as they had always done. Silvia remembered when she was a part of this migration. Every night she and Raymond would join hundreds of other children who moved from outlying villages into the centre of Gulu to find a place to sleep. A place they all hoped was out of the reach of LRA fingers greedy for fresh recruits. Silvia had not thought much of it at the time as it was just what they did, but now, as she woke from sleep, she looked on as an outsider. She was present, but she was no longer running home to the comfort of her mother's arms. She felt that she was no longer a part of those whose lives might be saved. As she watched the children with a strange feeling of envy at their innocent and unquestioning movements, she noticed Nswana walking towards her. He looked like he was surging against the tide as he searched for the girls.

"Nswana," Ruth called happily when she saw him. "Nswana, we are here."

Silvia closed her eyes again. She wondered how Ruth could remain so cheerful, but then remembered that she had once been just like Ruth. She recalled how her own easy smile and optimistic disposition had at times irritated Amos. How he had been blunt and cold towards her when she was too eager or happy on the walk home.

Silvia's heart softened towards the younger girl as she felt Nswana's presence. She opened one eye and watched as he sat next to them. For a moment, he didn't speak. The girls waited. Nswana took a deep breath in and let it out slowly. He was watching both girls intently. "How was the night?"

"Fine," Ruth piped up. "We slept well."

Silvia raised one eyebrow, closed her eye and kept her mouth shut. She wondered what the point was. Why had she ever thought a return to Gulu would be a good idea? There was nothing here for her anymore. Her family and friends were gone, and her home probably destroyed.

Nswana's next words made her wonder if he was reading her mind. "Girls, I think there is somewhere we need to go today, even though it will probably be pointless. You said your village was close to Gulu. We need to at least see if there is anything left. Maybe some family or relatives remain."

Silvia sat up slowly. She saw the look of excitement on Ruth's face, and her heart sank. He must have seen the fear in her eyes.

"Silvia, I know this will be very hard. It will be very

confronting and difficult." He turned to Ruth. "Child, it is very unlikely that we will find anyone left. You understand that, don't you?"

"Yes. Of course, I do," Ruth stated in childish defiance. "But then there is also a chance … I mean you just never know."

Nswana sighed again, and Silvia looked away, trying to hide the tears that brimmed under her eyelashes.

"Silvia? You don't have to come, if you don't want to. You could wait here for us to return. However, before we can find some kind of alternative arrangements for you here in Gulu, we do need to just make sure that there are no relatives left. Sometimes, people wait a long time for their loved ones to return. Some never give up hope. But you don't have to come, if you can't face it."

His words stung in a way that felt like a challenge. Although the thought of going back to her village was unbearable, the idea of sitting like a coward in Gulu and waiting for Nswana and Ruth to return was no less torturous. She had to go. She had to see it and know for herself. She had to put a true image to the one that her mind had been conjuring up since she had been dragged away.

Silvia stood up. "If we have to go, then let's go," she said, sounding braver than she felt.

Ruth jumped up beside her and Nswana rose slowly. "Are you sure Silvia? You know you don't have to do this."

"Yes, I do." Silvia looked him squarely in the face. His eyes were kind and full of a deep compassion that tempted her to cry, but she stood resilient. "I do have to go, Nswana. You know that I do. So, let's go."

That was the end of the matter. Silvia led the way out of the shelter and down the path she knew so well. Her feet didn't hesitate and nor did her mind have to think. She knew the way home.

Past the smells of bread in the early morning that she remembered so vividly. Past the market stalls being set up for the day, and the skinny dogs and chickens that loitered beneath the tables waiting for scraps. Past the makeshift homes that were established like a kind of inner-city refugee camp all clumped together. They walked on towards the edge of the town without stopping and without word between them.

Suddenly, the trail lay before her, just as it always had, like a small opening at the end of the road. Just as it had been on the day her feet had last felt the earth beneath them on the journey home. The trail itself seemed to be caught in time. So much had happened, and so much had changed both within her and around her, and yet, it appeared to Silvia that even the blades of grass remained unchanged, like they were trapped in a light that held them eternal as it danced upon their luminous green stems. Was she dreaming?

They passed the trail that led to the hidden mango tree she and Raymond used to sneak away to, whenever Amos wasn't with them. They passed the rocks Raymond used to jump off. And, as the trail slowly began to narrow, she recognised the exact place where her feet used to begin to run as they sensed home. The closeness of it was tantalising. So vivid and real that she almost wanted to believe her mother was there, waiting. Had it all just been a bad dream?

Something ignited within Silvia without warning. It felt like a high prison wall around her heart suddenly came crumbling down, and she found herself falling into a great engulfing chasm of hope. She began to run. Maybe, just maybe, there was a possibility … Her breathing became heavy, and everything but the trail faded from view. She ran by instinct more than by sight, her feet knowing the feel of every stone underfoot as if greeting old friends. All Silvia could see was the trail home and her mother waiting there for her with open arms.

"I'm coming Mama," she whispered as she ran. "I'm coming."

Her mother was there. She was right there in her mind's eye, waiting for her. Silvia burst into the village with hope glistening in her eyes and stopped dead in her tracks.

It was just as she remembered – her family's huts and the cooking shelter all gathered in a small circle. It was just as she remembered – only it wasn't. It was so very different. The small huts had crumbled like her hope suddenly did when confronted with the emptiness of this lost and abandoned life.

Silvia's breath caught in her throat as she looked around. She had thought about this moment for so long, and suddenly it was here, but it was not as she had wanted it to be. All life was gone. Not even an animal remained. Just the broken-down huts that used to be so full of laughter, love and all the people she cared about most in the world.

Silvia fell to the earth in a heap, racked with a pain she had never known. A pain deeper and more piercing than the accumulation of all her fear and sorrow, for now there was no more guessing. No more imagining and certainly no more hoping. Truth and reality had brought her a brand-new dagger that pierced every fibre of her being. Finally, the dam wall broke wide open, and the river of grief began to run.

Nswana bent beside her and put his hand gently upon her head. He did not speak. Silvia closed her eyes tightly, not wanting to look again at the destruction of her home as she cried and cried – unable to stop the flood of tears. Only her mother's face remained. The face that should have been waiting to greet her as she finally arrived home. All hope ebbed away from Silvia's heart.

Ruth was crying too, and she huddled into Silvia's side. After some time, Nswana spoke. He was concerned for the girls and wanted to let them grieve, but the longer they sat, the more nervous he began to feel. "We must go back to Gulu." His words were an instruction rather than a suggestion. "I feel it is perhaps not safe for us to stay here. Let's go." His consolation would have to come later. Nswana lifted and half carried both girls as they turned and began the painful journey away from the home they would never see again.

Silvia did not look back.

CHAPTER FORTY-TWO

SEEK AND FIND

Dawn breaks softly

Upon the broken ground.

There is heartache and there is pain

Everywhere I look around.

But there is something else here too.

Underneath the rotting leaves.

It's nature at its finest

Bringing life from our disease.

For it's not until death occurs

That any seed can grow.

It's not until the heart breaks open

That we see God's work on show.

And we know we'll never be alone

Even in our darkest hour.

For it's in the dark He plants His seed

That will one day be His flower.

She had been right all along, but she never said it. Instead, Wendy let him discover the truth for himself. She let him be real. No need for pretence. She gave him permission to be himself, unapologetically. She loved him unconditionally. And it was through that tender care, that Amos slowly began to shed the outer layers of his emotionally defensive armour, which allowed him to eventually become vulnerable enough to tell his story.

It had been as she said it would be. In voicing what he had hidden, it somehow lost its terrible power over him. The grip of fear was loosened enough for him to walk away, freer than he had been in a very long time. He couldn't really explain how, or exactly when, it had happened. He just knew it had. He had found what he had been looking for. It was freedom. But not just freedom from chains and tyranny and brutal men. It was freedom from the mental demons that plagued him within. Freedom from the sinking fear that he would never be good enough. Freedom from the sickening belief that he was a part of the problem – the belief that, at some level, *he* was evil.

Rather than being part of the problem, Amos learned that the ability to forgive both himself and others would allow him to become part of the solution. In letting go of his hurt, pain and bitterness, he found that his eyes were suddenly opened to a bigger picture of life all around him and the valuable role he could play in it. For the first time, he started thinking about living with purpose, and in that, he found liberation.

"I'm proud of you, Amos," Wendy said with a smile. They sat in her office together and talked over coffee. It was bad coffee, but the company was like a sweet taste and refreshment for his soul. Wendy was his confidant and friend – like a second mother.

"You have come such a long way in only two-and-a-bit

months. Do you remember the scared boy you were when you arrived here?" He nodded. "You even look like a different person now. You're physically stronger and bigger, and you walk differently. You carry your head high."

"I guess I've learnt a lot," he said humbly. "And I have found a faith that I never thought I would."

She smiled. "Faith is like fertile soil, Amos. In faith, anything can grow. Just make sure you always plant what is right. Plant good seeds in your heart and mind because whatever you plant will grow."

"Yes," he agreed thoughtfully.

"Amos, I have to tell you something now that you may not like to hear. You see, here at the Ark Project, people stay until they are ready to leave. We cannot keep people here indefinitely. You have your whole life ahead of you, and I believe that you are now ready to go and live it."

Amos's heart sank. He knew he'd come a long way, but the thought of leaving his sanctuary was terrifying. Outside the walls, the war raged on. He had no family and nowhere to go. Would they really just send him back out onto the street?

"Can't I work here? With you?" he asked trying to hide his desperation.

"No. Not at the moment anyway. But Amos, there is something else I need to tell you. Do you remember when you first arrived and told me you had two friends in the hospital with you?"

"Of course."

"Well, I did some searching, and I found them."

Amos was anticipating bad news. "Where were they? Why didn't you tell me?"

"They had been taken to another rehabilitation centre called

HOPE. I didn't tell you straight away because I was concerned that if I did, you may not stay here, and there was no room for you at HOPE. I spoke to the managers there, and we agreed to keep things as they were and tell you later on, when the time was right for all of you."

"Really?" Mixed emotions rose within him. "But they must have thought I abandoned them."

"You will get a chance to explain very soon. Sante and Grace have also been doing well. The HOPE centre has found a small place for you all to stay, if you want to. It is in their village extension program. Grace will be a housemother to several children. You and Sante can live under her care. Of course, this is completely up to you now. But Amos, I would advise you to do this. You will have everything you need. You will live in a supportive community, and you will be safe. You will have a chance to attend school or vocational training. You are very fortunate to have been offered a place in their care."

Question upon question burned into Amos's mind, but he could only mutter one. "Do Grace and Sante know I'm here?"

"If they don't, they will soon. They're on their way."

"Here?"

"Yes."

Amos shook with anticipation. "How long do I have to decide on this?"

"When they arrive here, shortly, you will be taken to see the village, and after that, you can decide. It's up to you."

Amos took a deep breath and let it out slowly. He fiddled nervously with his fingers, and his mind swam with questions. A few minutes later, a car rolled up the gravel path and stopped outside the room where he and Wendy sat. A man bounced around the rear of the car, slid the back door open, and there inside, sat Sante and Grace.

Amos stood, but for a moment he couldn't move his feet. They looked so different from the dirty, malnourished, bruised and battered refugees he had last seen. There was flesh on their bones, smiles on their faces, and a definite sparkle in their eyes. If he had passed them on the street, he may not have even recognised them.

"Amos," Sante leapt out of the car and came towards him with a huge grin on his face. He held out his hand and exclaimed, "My brother!"

Amos grabbed it and pulled him close into a bear hug. "Sante," he said as excitement filled him. "I never thought I'd see you again. I never meant to leave you."

"I know, I know. They explained what had happened to you. I only found out yesterday. I've been so excited to see you."

Grace emerged from the car and stood behind Sante. Then, as he stepped aside, she too embraced Amos. "My son," she whispered tenderly.

Amos's eyes filled with tears. He knew now that his decision was made. And, for the first time since leaving the bush and the rebels behind him, he knew he had a family once again. Perhaps, found in an unlikely place – in the arms of a former rebel-soldier who was once his enemy, but Amos knew that it was right. It was the way it was meant to be. His old life had died, but out of the deep canyon of death and despair, a new life was beginning to emerge.

Amos smiled, took a deep breath and let it out slowly.

"Ok," he said. "Let's go home."

CHAPTER FORTY-THREE

LIFE

Arise, Oh Daughter

For your time has come.

You're no longer the hunted

With nowhere to run.

Arise Oh Daughter

Shake off the shackles of fear.

For you are beloved

And your freedom is here.

Arise Oh Daughter

Mother Africa's delight.

Live well and live now

With the future in sight.

Arise My Daughter

Let your head be held high.

For the seed of promise within you

Will never die.

ilvia sat in the half-light of the setting sun outside the night shelter. She waited for Ruth and Nswana to appear around the corner of the dusty street. They had gone out earlier in the afternoon in search of food and a familiar face, but in all of Nswana's searching over the last week no one seemed to have ever heard of Silvia or Ruth. Silvia sat in limbo and felt like her strength was fading. Despite the growing child in her belly, she had lost the desire to eat. Since their visit to her village a week ago, a dark cloud of despondency had settled over her mind, and it seemed to suck the energy from her bones. It shot questions and seething statements at her as randomly as lightning bolts.

"How will you ever raise a child? How will you feed a child? You will be homeless. Once Nswana leaves, you will be on your own with a baby and a young girl to care for. No one will help you. No one cares about you. Look at all the lost children around here. People don't care. They turn their heads when they see you on the street. They wish you would go away."

The onslaught was unrelenting, and Silvia had no energy left to fight. She wished she had never been back to see the destruction of her village, and the way the jungle was reclaiming it as its own. She could have still been living in denial with the sweet lie of false hope. It would have been a better place to be. Hope may have proven itself a liar, but at least the lie had given her a lifeline while she drowned. And, although the drowning seemed inevitable, it was somehow easier to tolerate when hope was alive. Without any hope left, she just wanted to curl up and die.

Nswana and Ruth eventually returned. Their silence stated the obvious. Yet again, no one had recognised Ruth or heard of Silvia. No one cared. Nswana tried to push some sweet potato into her hand, but Silvia shook her head.

"You need to eat."

"Later," she tried to reassure him, although they both knew she had no intention of allowing the food to pass her lips.

"Your baby," Nswana pressed.

Silvia just hung her head. She could not even cry. Tears seemed like a waste of energy.

"Silvia, tomorrow we will stop looking." Nswana was trying his best to sound upbeat. "I have searched enough. I have asked most of the children who come to the shelter at night, as well as many people in the town. But today, I spoke to someone who told me some good news. A woman I met on the street told me there is a place for girls who have come out of the bush. That means girls who have escaped the rebels. She told me that this centre could look after you and Ruth, if they have room."

Silvia looked at him absently. She wondered if she should try to muster up an enthusiastic smile just for him. He had already done more for her than anyone would have expected or asked of him.

"He must really care," hope seemed to tease as she considered his face. Silvia decided that, if only to release Nswana from the sense of obligation he felt towards her, she would go along with his plan. She nodded her head.

It was settled then in Nswana's mind. In the morning, he would take the girls to the centre and just pray that they could find a place for them. He would then make the long journey back to his home, his wife and his own little girl who he was missing terribly.

It was almost dawn when Silvia woke in fright as another dream ripped her from sleep. She lay on the concrete, surrounded by all of the other children in the night shelter. Her back ached against the cold floor.

As she lay there, reflecting on the dream that had danced behind her eyelids, Silvia suddenly sat up. She had remembered something. In the dream, she had been running wildly through the bush, but this time she was not being chased. She had been running to find help. Her mother was in labour.

Now wide awake, Silvia knew she had to find Nswana, and she didn't want to wait until the dawn had broken. She needed to find him now. He always slept somewhere on the outer edges of the shelter, away from the children, yet close enough to be there if they needed him. In the grey morning light, Silvia began to carefully pick her way through the twisted limbs of sleeping bodies. She didn't want to disturb any of them, but there was an urgency within her that she hadn't felt for some time.

At times, she used her hands to balance, trying not to topple as she searched for fragments of space in the mass of bodies. Their breathing was gentle and easy, as if they slept on the most comfortable beds in the world. Silvia wondered how human beings were capable of turning such living nightmares into something that felt almost normal. Finally nearing the edge of the bodies, she looked around for Nswana and saw him sleeping, slumped with his back against the outer wooden wall, his arms folded across his chest. She continued to move towards him, her focus now split between the children she walked over, and keeping herself in line with his position.

"Nswana. Nswana," she hissed when she reached him.

He woke with a start, ready to spring into action if she needed him to. "What is it, Silvia? Are you alright? The baby?"

"Yes, yes, I'm fine. It's just that I had another dream, only in this one I remembered something. I remembered … I mean, I hadn't forgotten, but somehow, I had. It was like the dream reminded me of something I didn't think about until now."

"What is it?"

"There is a lady. I met her once when my mother had her baby. She lives in town. Her name is Carol. Perhaps, she will help us or knows some of my relatives. She knew my Aunty, and I don't know, but perhaps, she knew more of my people. I only met her once. She probably won't remember me. Oh Nswana, can we at least try? Before we go to the centre today, can we go to Carol's house? I remember where it is. At least, I think I do."

"Yes," Nswana reassured. "Of course, we will see if we can find her. We have nothing to lose."

Silvia finally relaxed beside him. She sat against the wall and looked over the sea of children before her. Some had begun to stir. She had felt a glimmer of hope returning with the feeling of urgency over finding Carol. Perhaps, it was just another dead-end – another grab at something that would leave her empty-handed. But she knew that Nswana's statement was true – they had nothing to lose.

Nswana sighed as he sat beside her, and then unexpectedly, he began to speak, "You know something Silvia?"

She didn't feel like she knew much and didn't know how to respond to his strange question, so she remained silent.

"This makes me very angry and very sad all at the same time." As he spoke, he swept one arm in an arc as if painting a big brush stroke over the scene that lay before them. "All of these children who must come and sleep in places like this at night, just so they are safe. So, they don't get stolen out of their beds. It's such a crazy thing, and it makes me angry that they have to do this. That, for these thousands, there is no safer place than in the company of strangers. And it makes me so sad, because I picture that this is what you and Ruth used to do every night. I can't help but imagine my own child here too. We live in sad days, Silvia. There is so much pain and suffering that I wonder if it will ever end. Of course, most wars end, eventually, but the toll it has taken and the devastation it's left behind for the Acholi … I do wonder what will become of us."

"I remember coming here at night," Silvia whispered. "It wasn't so bad. The worst thing about it was leaving my parents in the village because I used to worry about them, but Raymond didn't mind coming. He thought it was an adventure." She hesitated before speaking again. "These children are Acholi. They are saving our future. They are a kind of resistance army that is somehow stronger than all of the hatred and killing. If the LRA can't touch them, then maybe, we have a chance."

Nswana was thoughtful for a time before speaking. He glanced sideways at Silvia and wondered at the wisdom of this young girl. From the first time he'd met her, after she had saved his daughter, he had known there was something special about her. Something different that he couldn't quite define or describe. It was as though she possessed something that pulled her ever forward. Something timeless and much bigger than herself. Yet, as he had observed her over the past months, he saw that she was not conscious of this herself. She was just a child after all, and much of her potential still lay untapped. Nswana silently acknowledged that this was perhaps part of the reason he felt such a burden of responsibility to help her.

Silvia shifted uncomfortably as she silently waited for him to speak. "You know, you're right, Silvia. Perhaps, anger and sadness are not the correct emotions to feel about these children. In their own way, they are an army and fighting the war on their own terms. Seeing them should make me proud of our people. Our children are saving themselves, even when there is no one else to save them."

Silvia nodded. "Even when they have to save themselves." As she spoke the words, she saw Raymond's face before her. His big innocent eyes seemed to be peering deeply into her soul. Had he been able to save himself when she hadn't been there to help him? Had he survived? She knew he would have tried. As she sat in the dawn's grey light, his image seemed so real that she almost dared ask him for the truth, but the moment she opened her lips to speak, his face disappeared.

Silvia stood before the large iron fence and hesitated. Nswana and Ruth were right behind her, and her heart thumped so loudly that she was sure they would hear it. Anxiety rose quickly from her stomach into her throat. Then she felt Nswana's hand on her small shoulder, and it gave her the courage she needed. She raised her fist and banged loudly on the metal gate.

The door opened slowly, and a young man stuck his head around it. "Yes?"

Nswana patted Silvia's shoulder and confidently explained Silvia's connection to Carol, making it sound much much stronger than it actually was. Silvia looked at the dirt that clung to her feet and was thankful he was doing the talking for her.

The man nodded his head and disappeared. Moments later, he returned, opening the door that led into the small courtyard.

He left them there and hastily returned to his position behind the locked gate. They stood for a moment waiting.

"Hello?" came a friendly voice around the corner of the house.

Silvia smiled shyly as she saw the familiar face and frame of Carol. She had only met her once before, and yet, she felt immediately at ease as the old woman smiled.

"Hello," Silvia replied. "I am Silvia. You probably don't remember me, but we met once. You helped my mother ..."

"Oh Silvia," Carol interrupted as she threw her arms around her and hugged her affectionately. "Yes, I remember. Come, come, you must come this way. I have something for you."

Silvia glanced up at Nswana and saw the puzzled and surprised look that passed over his face as Carol took her by the hand. She was sure that her own expression held the same surprise. Was she hearing correctly? Within her, the war between despondency and hope raged on, and she didn't quite know whose side she was on. Despondency felt like it had the upper hand, and yet, hope would simply not give up. No matter how many times it got knocked down, it seemed to rise again. A part of her wished it would just give up and accept its fate.

Carol sensed Silvia's hesitation and turned to reassure her. "Silvia?" She looked up into Carol's face.

"Yes?"

"I do remember you. I remember you well. And there is someone else here who remembers you too, and who very much wants to see you. Someone who has been praying for you since you left."

Silvia's heart began thumping so hard within her chest that she thought it might burst right out. Who could Carol be talking about? A big lump wedged itself hard at the top of her throat and prevented her from asking any more questions as Carol lead her around the corner of the main house. Nswana and Ruth followed close behind.

In the large lush garden under the canopy of tall trees, were a number of small huts. It looked like a village had been built right within the confines of Carol's property. Carol led them to the hut closest to the house and called from outside.

"Jossy, Mama Jossy."

Silvia's heart dropped into her feet at the shock of hearing her mother's name. Before she had time to truly process what was happening, the door to the small hut opened and out stepped Jossy. Silvia's mouth dropped open in surprise as all of the air around her seemed to vanish. Her mother also seemed shocked and stood fixed to the spot as seconds slowed to feel like hours. Silvia could almost touch the woman she had dreamed about seeing for so many months – was she real or just another illusion?

Suddenly, the silence broke as Jossy tossed her arms into the air and cried loudly. In a single motion, she was there, sweeping Silvia up into her embrace, whooping, singing and crying – all at the same time. Silvia suddenly woke up as if from a dream to finally realise that this was real. Her mother was here. Her mother was alive and holding her. She burst into tears and held onto her so tightly she didn't know if she could ever let go.

There were no words as pure joy ran in rivers down her cheeks.

"Look. Look ..." Jossy exclaimed.

Through her tears, Silvia shifted her gaze to the door, and there, under the small arch, stood her little brother Raymond, with his big brown eyes and soft cheeks. He stood smiling shyly as if he too wasn't sure whether this was real.

"Oh, oh …" Silvia sobbed. She laughed and cried and tried to catch her breath. She held her arms out for Raymond, and he ran into them, his little face pressing hard into the curve of her belly. Everyone was crying. Silvia looked at Nswana to see that even he had tears streaming freely down his face.

"I prayed you would come back. Every day, I prayed for you," Jossy whispered as she hugged her daughter tightly again. Silvia could still not speak as joy ran together with disbelief. After all the time that had passed, and all those months of desperate agony, she had never really expected to see her mother alive again. Her tears came in gushes that felt uncontrollable, but she knew she had to pull herself together.

"Shhh, you're ok. It's ok. You're home." Jossy looked down at Silvia's pregnant belly, and Silvia stood hesitant. The growing baby made it all too obvious that she wasn't the same child who had disappeared months earlier. As if reading her thoughts, Jossy looked from Silva's belly up into her daughter's tear-stained eyes.

"I see you my girl, I see you. You are my Silvia. Do not be ashamed, my daughter, for you will be a good mother, and I am here to help you. You are safe. You are home. That is all that matters now. You are home."

Tears streamed down Silvia's face as she held tightly to her mother with one arm and to Raymond with the other. Ruth also held her side and Nswana stood weeping, trying unsuccessfully to wipe his tears away.

The girl who was lost was now finally home.

She was home.